PURSUED BY THE PAST

PURSUED BY THE PAST

P.D. WORKMAN

ISBN: 9781989080917 (IS Hardcover)

ISBN: 9781989080900 (IS Paperback)

ISBN: 9781989080894 (KDP Paperback)

ISBN: 9781926500492 (Kindle)

ISBN: 9781926500515 (ePub)

ISBN: 9781926500522 (Google)

pdworkman

Also by P.D. Workman

Reg Rawlins, Psychic Detective

What the Cat Knew

A Psychic with Catitude

A Catastrophic Theft

Night of Nine Tails

Telepathy of Gardens

Delusions of the Past

Fairy Blade Unmade

Web of Nightmares

A Whisker's Breadth

Auntie Clem's Bakery

Gluten-Free Murder

Dairy-Free Death

Allergen-Free Assignation

Witch-Free Halloween (Halloween Short)

Dog-Free Dinner (Christmas Short)

Stirring Up Murder

Brewing Death

Coup de Glace

Sour Cherry Turnover

Apple-achian Treasure

Vegan Baked Alaska

Muffins Masks Murder

Tai Chi and Chai Tea

Santa Shortbread

Cold as Ice Cream (Coming soon)

Changing Fortune Cookies (Coming soon)

Hot on the Trail Mix (Coming soon)

Zachary Goldman Mysteries

She Wore Mourning

His Hands Were Quiet

She Was Dying Anyway

He Was Walking Alone

They Thought He was Safe

He Was Not There

Her Work Was Everything

She Told a Lie (Coming soon)

He Never Forgot (Coming soon)

She Was At Risk (Coming soon)

Kenzie Kirsch Medical Thrillers

Unlawful Harvest

Parks Pat Mysteries

Out with the Sunset (Coming Soon)

Long Climb to the Top (Coming Soon)

Dark Water Under the Bridge (Coming Soon)

High-Tech Crime Solvers Series

Virtually Harmless

AND MORE AT PDWORKMAN.COM

To those seeking the past, and those pursued by it.

Chapter One

ACCESS DENIED.

"Dammit!" Vanna slapped the desk in frustration. She had put her password in twice and she knew that if she got up to three or four, it would lock the email account up. It wasn't like she didn't know her password. The first time, she assumed that she had just slipped and hit an extra key, or typed the password for another account without thinking. The second time, she had typed the password in carefully. But it had been rejected again. There was no point in typing the same password in again. She would just get locked out of the account, and getting a password reset would be a pain in the neck that she didn't need today. The work was piling up and she had planned to get right onto the Munro file so that she could get the work out the door, virtually speaking.

She checked her caps lock key. It wasn't turned on. She opened the word processor window and swiftly typed the password in to make sure that none of the keys were sticking and the keyboard hadn't been changed to Spanish. Or some other oddity that might make the email account reject her password. Her password was displayed on the screen. No problems. So why was the email program rejecting it?

Vanna opened up her internet browser and typed in a search to see if the email server was offline or experiencing some other technical difficulty. But the status line was green. Operating normally. At least, no one else had reported a problem yet.

Vanna returned to her email tab and pecked in the password one character at a time.

ACCESS DENIED.

She swore again. Worse this time. One of those words that she wouldn't have let her mother catch her using. Even damn would have raised Erica White-Austin's carefully penciled eyebrows. Vanna would get one of those trademark Erica White-Austin disapproving looks. Disapproving and disappointed. But her mother wasn't there and Vanna pounded the desk with her fist and cursed the email providers out thoroughly.

She hated to have to waste the time with a password reset, but it was easy enough. Click password reset. Send the reset code to her phone. Type it in. Type the new password. Type it again. In two minutes, she would be back into her email with a new password. It was just annoying when she knew she had entered her password correctly.

Maybe the site had been hacked. Vanna clicked the password reset link. That was probably it. Someone had hacked the email server, so they had automatically reset all passwords and all clients had to pick new passwords. That kind of thing had happened before with other accounts. Vanna fidgeted with her ring while waiting for the unlock code to be sent to her cell phone. The antique gold looked good against her slightly dark skin. Lydia always said she envied Vanna her complexion. She said Vanna always looked like she had just come back from a sunny island or tanning salon. Even when everyone else in the area was pasty white from the one hundred sixty-eight days of rain per year and many more which were overcast. Vanna's skin had always been darker than her mother's and sister's milky, china doll complexions.

Her phone didn't buzz. She looked at it to see if the code had come through without her realizing it. No messages. She looked at the computer screen and clicked on the password reset link again. She would probably mess things up, getting two codes at once and not knowing which one of them to use. But she was impatient to get into her account and access the work that Munro's executive assistant had sent.

"Come on, come on…"

Still nothing. Vanna looked for some other link or button that might help. She looked at the number on the screen showing where the reset code had been sent. All of the middle numbers had been masked by asterisks, with only the area code and the last two digits showing. But it wasn't her cell phone number. The area code was right, but the last two digits, bizarrely, were not the last two digits of her phone number. Vanna stared at them. She looked back at her email address to make sure that she had entered it correctly and wasn't trying to send a password reset to someone else's account. It was her email address. There were no other buttons to press. She would have to talk to a real person.

Vanna groaned and swiped her finger across the screen of the phone to call up the phone app. She had to click a few more links and by-pass the knowledge-base articles on how to reset a password before it would finally give her a phone number to call. Vanna looked at the clock and sighed, waiting for the call to be answered after navigating through the menu system and being placed in the queue. A recorded voice apologized for the longer-than-average wait time. Vanna wondered again if they had been hacked and now half the email provider's users were sitting in the queue ahead of her, waiting for their password resets. She tapped her nail on the desk, waiting for the call to be answered.

The minutes crept by. The recorded voice continued to keep

her updated, advising that the call would be recorded, that she could have them call her back instead of waiting, and apologizing again for the longer than usual wait time.

"This is Chris, thank you for waiting."

Vanna was so surprised she just about dropped the phone when the man's voice overrode the robot.

"Oh. Hi, this is Vanna."

She explained the problem in as much detail as she could and waited for Chris to reset the password.

"What is your PIN number?" Chris questioned.

"My PIN number?" Vanna tried to recall. "I thought you had confirmation questions."

"We also have PIN numbers."

"You have both?"

"Yes, ma'am," he said patiently.

"Oh." She closed her eyes. "Four three two one?"

"Thank you ma'am…" he tapped it into his computer. "No, I'm sorry, that's not it."

"One two three four?"

"You're not allowed to use that."

"I don't know. Can you just ask me the security questions?"

There was silence for a minute, and then he sighed. "Of course, ma'am." Another pause, while he waited for his computer to bring the questions up on the monitor or took a sip of his coffee. "The name of your first pet."

"I… I have never had a pet. That's not one of my security questions."

"I'm sorry, but that's what's showing up on my computer."

"Are you sure you entered my email address correctly?" Vanna asked. She spelled it out for him again.

"Yes, ma'am. That's the account that I have. I'm sorry, but if you can't provide the PIN number, or answer the security questions, there is nothing that I can do to help you."

"Well, all I want is a password reset. If you send a password reset to my phone, I can take it from there. But I didn't get one from the automatic system."

"What is your phone number?"

Vanna recited it for him.

"I'm sorry, that's not the phone number we have on file."

"That's the only phone number I have. Did a couple of digits get reversed? Can you tell if it's close? I'm kind of dyslexic. I do that sometimes."

"No."

"You can't tell me?"

"It isn't close."

"There is something wrong with your system! Am I the first one to complain? This must be happening to other people too."

"There is no known system problem."

Vanna closed her eyes. "Come on, there has to be something that you can do to help me. I need to be able to access my email. I have work to get done."

"Are you sure you didn't change your password? Does anyone else have access to your computer or your passwords?"

"No, of course not."

"Do you use the same password for multiple accounts?" His voice was overly-patient, like she was a child demanding chocolate at bedtime. "Have you had any problems with viruses lately?"

Vanna remembered that she had let her anti-virus subscription run out, but she pushed the thought aside. She still had an anti-virus. It would find any of the big viruses. Surely no one could have hacked her system.

She felt nauseated. "No, no problems."

"And there is no one else who has access to your email account? Or who knows the password that you use on this account? Maybe just because you've used it for something that you share? Maybe a child or a boyfriend…?"

"No, I—" Vanna stopped. Tino, of course. She might not have told him her password, but he'd shoulder-surfed enough times while she was typing it in to have picked it up. He knew her hobbies and tastes and could probably guess at it in a few tries even without seeing her type it in. "No, I've never told it to anyone. But if someone has hacked my account, how can I get access back? What's the phone number that is on file? If I know the number, I'll know who hacked it…"

"I'm sorry, we can't give out confidential information like that—"

"When was the password and phone number and everything changed last? I was just in my email last night. It's not like I forgot them."

There was a pause while the man examined her account. "You accessed it last this morning," Chris corrected, "a couple of hours ago."

"A couple of hours ago I was out at breakfast with my mother." There was a tightening in Vanna's throat. She swallowed and tried to keep her voice steady. "Is that when everything was changed?"

More waiting and tapping. "Yes," Chris agreed. "Your phone number, password, and security questions were all changed at that time."

"You can change them all at the same time? Doesn't that just play right into a hacker's hands?"

Chris sighed. "I am going to escalate your call to a level two. I'll freeze access to your email account at this time. Until you are able to prove your identity and re-secure the account."

"How do I do that?"

"The level two tech will explain the procedure to you. We will require identification and the verification by a third party."

"A third party?" Vanna repeated. What was she supposed to do, have her mother call in for her? It was turning into a nightmare. She had so much work that she needed to do on the Munro file, and on her other files, and the simple task of getting access to her email account had already turned into an hour-long job.

"Such as a police officer, lawyer, or banker," Chris said. "An authority who will examine your ID, compare your face to your picture ID, verify your address, and so on. The level two will explain it all to you."

"What? I don't have time—"

There was a click and Chris was gone. The phone rang a few times and was picked up by another robotic voice apologizing for the delay. Gritting her teeth, Vanna put the phone on speaker and started to compose a text to Mr. Munro's executive assistant to explain that there might be a delay in getting her work in.

———

By the time Vanna got off the phone, she was both furious and drained. She couldn't decide whether she wanted to throw the computer across the room, or lie down on her bed and go to sleep.

But there was too much to be done. Now she had a bunch of running around to do to try to get her email account unlocked again so that she could get to work. The hours were slipping rapidly away from her.

In spite of the fact that she had already been on the phone for an extended amount of time, Vanna dialed the number that she knew from heart. She had already removed him from her favorites list, but she knew it anyway. It wasn't actually the first time she'd removed him from her favorites list. She tapped a fingernail on the desk impatiently, waiting for him to pick up. Vanna noticed that her fingernails were grimy. Again. Her mother always criticized her nails. 'I have no idea how you can get them so dirty so quickly. They always look like an auto-mechanic's. You need a manicure.' Vanna hoped that they hadn't been that bad when she had breakfasted with Erica a few hours ago. But she hadn't really done anything messy since then, so they must have been. Her mother's nails were always perfectly clean and manicured, with flawless French tips. She despaired of a daughter who couldn't even keep her nails clean.

"Vanna!" Tino greeted. She was sure that he was delighted to hear from her. After their last fight, she had vowed never to speak to him again. Now she was stoking his ego, making him think that she couldn't live without him.

"You think that you can hack my email account?" Vanna demanded. "That's the most childish play for attention that I've ever seen! You've messed up my entire work day, thank you very much!"

She was greeted by silence. Apparently, Tino had been shocked into speechlessness by her sally. She felt good about that. Vanna liked the feeling of putting him in his place. Telling him how she really felt.

"What are you talking about?" Tino finally asked.

"Don't play dumb with me. You know exactly what I'm talking about. You hacked my email account, changed all of my security information so that I couldn't get back into it. Really mature, Tino."

"I didn't do that. I'm not a hacker."

"You don't need any technical skills to break into my email. Watching over my shoulder, or guessing what my password is. You really messed up my day. And now I'm going to have to go through all of my other accounts and change all of my passwords."

Vanna bit her lip after saying it, realizing that she had just given him a heads-up that she used the same password on other accounts as well. She was going to have to secure her auction account right away. And her vendor accounts. And of course, the accounts that she used for her Virtual Assistant work and cloud storage. She started to make a list in her head of everything that had to be changed immediately. All of the accounts that Tino would know or guess about. She knew she shouldn't have used the same password on everything. But trying to remember or keep track of a different password on every account was impossible.

"Vanny," Tino reproached, "I wouldn't do that. I wouldn't do anything that would threaten your work. What kind of guy do you think I am?"

"Hmm, maybe the same kind of guy who tows cars that are legally parked so that their owners have to pay their hard-earned money to get them back?" Vanna suggested. "That kind of guy?"

"That's different," Tino snickered. She could picture his dark, square face, just a little too blocky to be considered hand-some. She could picture the way that his eyes would dance, thinking about how he had pulled one over on so many wealthy car owners over the last year or two. It was different. He figured that they owed him a living, just by virtue of the fact that they had so much more money than he did. He knew that Vanna wasn't wealthy in spite of the Austin family wealth. She was trying to support herself without reliance on her family's money. She wanted to be her own person and not owe anyone for her living. "But honey, I promise, I didn't touch your email account. Are you having computer trouble? I could call Jimmy to look at it."

"No, I don't want you to call anyone. I didn't call you because I need help. I called you to tell you that you're not getting away with this. And that I know it was you."

"It wasn't me," he lied. His voice was low and smooth but held a note of amusement that just made Vanna that much more sure that he was guilty. "I wouldn't do that to my girl."

"I'm not your girl. We're finished. So from now on, you just stay out of my business," Vanna snapped. "Got it?"

"Why don't I come over to take a look at it for you?" he suggested. "Maybe there's something I can do. You sound really upset."

"Of course I'm upset! You've ruined my day. Maybe made me lose the Munro file! And all for what? So that you could prove that I need you? That I can't survive without a man in my life? Well, news flash, I can survive just fine. Just stay out of my stuff."

"Call me when you change your mind."

Vanna poked the end button angrily.

———

Lydia called while Vanna was sitting in the guest chairs at the bank wondering how much longer it was going to be before she could get in to see the manager to confirm her identity and get her email account opened up again. Lydia was like a younger version of Erica. Blonder, fewer wrinkles, and nicer. But she had the same knock-out face and figure that set all the men at the country club on fire and made them drool over the Austin women like they were royalty. The Austin women other than Vanna, anyway.

"I know you're working," Lydia started out, "but I wanted to know how breakfast went with Mom…"

"I'm not working," Vanna said. "My email account got hacked and I have to prove my identity to get it unlocked and get access again. I'm sitting around at the bank, waiting for the manager to look at my ID and everything."

"Oh. Well, can't you just do a password reset? You just have them send it to your phone…"

"It's a lot more complicated than that. He changed my mobile number too, so I can't send a reset to my phone. And he changed the security questions."

"St. Valentine?" Lydia questioned.

"Tino. Yeah. Who else would do that to me? It's not just some random stranger."

"I can't believe that he would do that," Lydia said. "That sucks. Did you call the police?"

"No, I figured it was easier to get in at the bank. But with how long I have to wait…"

"Why would you report hacking to a bank? I thought you said it was your email account?"

Vanna's thoughts jumped to her bank account. That was another account that she was going to have to change the password on. If Tino got access to her bank account, he could really mess things up for her. Maybe she could change it while she met with the bank manager.

"No, I just had to come to the bank to verify my identity."

"And you aren't going to report Tino to the police?"

Vanna thought about it. He would be angry if she made police trouble for him. Really angry. A little bit of mischief messing around with her email account was one thing. She didn't need to really upset things by reporting him to the police.

"Umm, no. I'm just going to get it straightened out. I don't think that I need to get the police involved."

"You should! You should have reported him to the police a long time ago. You just give him license to do whatever he wants."

Lydia really didn't know the extent that Tino had hurt Vanna in the past. But Vanna had broken things off with Tino and that wasn't going to happen again.

"I just want him out of my life," Vanna told her big sister. "If I report him to the police, then we're still connected. He'll be trying to talk me out of it and… I just can't have him in my life anymore. In any form."

"Okay," Lydia agreed reluctantly. She trailed off and was quiet for a few seconds. "So… how about Mom? How did breakfast go?"

Vanna tried to readjust her thinking. To put aside the email fiasco and any thoughts of Tino, and to review her meal with Erica.

"It was about how you'd expect," she said. "The same as usual. She thinks I'm wasting my life. Why don't I get a real job? Do something worthwhile. Become a socialite, like her."

"She wouldn't say that," Lydia protested.

"No. Not in so many words. Except for the real job part. But you can see it in her eyes. The way that she asks me what I'm doing. Tries to persuade me to move back home so she can take care of me."

"She just worries about you."

"Because she thinks I'm a failure."

"She doesn't think you're a failure. Just that you're not… grown up yet. You're her baby."

Vanna snorted. Yes, she was the baby and her mother still thought that she was a little girl or a rebellious teen. Not that she was a grown woman who was capable of running her own life the way that she wanted to.

"She's going to have to learn that I am."

"I know. Give her time. She will."

Vanna tried to scrape some of the dirt out from under her nails with her keys. "How long was it before she started treating you like a real person? A grown up?"

"I don't know. I got married and had the kids so quickly, she pretty much had to accept that I had left the nest. You leaving home, but not going to school or getting married… that's harder for her to swallow."

"So I should just settle down with Tino and have a couple of kids and then Mom will leave me alone?"

Lydia giggled. "Don't you dare! I'd kill you. Just don't let Mom get to you. It's okay to just be who you really are. You're a cool person just the way you are."

"You've been watching too much Sesame Street."

"Maybe you should watch it now and then. It's very educational."

A paunchy man in a wrinkled white shirt approached Vanna, his eyebrows raised.

"I have to go," Vanna told Lydia. "Looks like the bank guy is ready for me now."

"Okay. Take care. Hope you get this all straightened out. And think about… talking to the police about Tino."

"I'll think about it."

Vanna hung up and stood, extending her hand to the bank employee, whose name tag said 'Phil.' "Hi, I'm Vanna Austin."

———

It had been a long day. Hours had been wasted in the effort to get access to her email account again. Once Vanna could actually log in, she spent some time looking through her folders, worried about what data she might have lost. She figured she would open up her inbox and it would be filled with hundreds of spam messages. But even though it was pretty full, it was mostly messages from her clients and friends, along with some newsletters and sales letters, and very few messages that were obviously spam.

She couldn't find anything out of place in any of her folders; everything seemed to still be there and in the right place. It was a big relief, but a bit disconcerting. Like coming home to find that your house had been broken into and the thieves gone, but nothing taken or broken. She expected some kind of damage. Some kind of evidence that someone had been going through her stuff.

Vanna had shaken off the eerie feeling the best that she could and jumped into her work. Munro's press release and mailing directly to various editors and news outlets had to get out before the markets closed, so she had to work quickly to disseminate it. There was a bunch of follow-up that still had to be done after the markets closed and she worked long into the evening to get caught back up again.

Eventually, her brain was too exhausted to deal with any more work and Vanna closed her files and shut off the computer. She didn't have a lot of time left before bed, but she could at least spend an hour on her latest creative project. She had found a really cool project online, making old bottles into pendant lights. There were a number of different interpretations that other people had done. Some of them were really stunning. Maybe not the kind of thing that Erica would put in her dining room, but they were going to look great in Vanna's kitchen. And she might make a proposal to some of the nearby diners and bars to see if any of them wanted to contract for a few. They were unique and had a great ambiance. A real conversational piece.

As she carefully cut the bottoms off of the antique wine bottles that Sandal had helped her to find, she thought about other variations on the pendant light theme. Olive oil bottles in an Italian restaurant. Whisky bottles in varying colors. Different sizes and shapes of glasses. There were a lot of different things she could try.

Her eyes were starting to burn by the time that she put her supplies away. She yawned and rubbed them. She would have a lot of work to do in the morning to try to get caught up on the other clients that had been neglected while she dealt with the hacked email account.

Chapter Two

Vanna hadn't checked her physical mailbox for a couple of days and decided that she'd better take a look and make sure that she hadn't missed any bills that needed to be paid. Luckily, she didn't run into the same kind of problems with her snail mail that she had run into with her email. The key turned smoothly in the lock and opened the door. She could tell even before she took the mail out that most of it was junk. A couple of bills mixed in. She sorted through them as she walked up the stairs back to her apartment. One envelope was unusual.

It looked like a personal letter rather than a business letter. Who, aside from socialites like Erica, still sent handwritten personal mail? Maybe to a grandma who didn't have email or any social networks, but certainly not for a twenty-something technology native like Vanna. The address on the outside was handwritten, in small, neat letters. Ivanna Austin. Obviously not someone who really knew her, in spite of the personal touch, or they would know that the only person who still called her Ivanna was her mother. She might have suspected it as being from her mother, except that it wasn't Erica's handwriting. And Erica still wrote out all of her invitations by hand personally.

Vanna let herself back into her apartment and threw the rest of the mail down on the table, opening up the personal letter to satisfy her curiosity. As Vanna read the first couple of lines, she fell with a plop into her chair. She sat and read through the rest in disbelief. And re-read it. And read it one more time before reaching for the phone and dialling Lydia.

There was lots of background noise and Vanna knew that it was a bad time. One or both of the kids were screeching in the background and she could hear a TV show and a noise that might have been a fan as well. Lydia's voice was distracted.

"Van? What's up?"

"Lydia... I got a letter from my mother."

"Really?" There was a clanging noise. Lydia might have been making breakfast. Or something for supper that had to be made ahead of time. "What did Mom write you for? Invitation or apology?"

"No... not Mom. My biological mother."

"Would you guys pipe down?" Lydia shouted. The voices quieted slightly, the fan turned off, and Lydia spoke to Vanna again. "What did you say?"

"My biological mother. My birth mom. She sent me a letter."

There was a crash, but Lydia said nothing about it, ignoring it. "Your birth mom? Really? What did she say? How did she find you?"

Vanna looked down at it again. She hadn't been able to absorb the details yet. Just the fact that the letter had come from her birth mother. The mother that she had never known. Of course, she had wondered. Had made up fantasies in her mind about what kind of person her birth mother was. How she was different from Erica. How she and Vanna would get along just like sisters. But in spite of the rockiness of her relationship with Erica as Vanna navigated the teen years, Vanna had never had any desire to track down her birth mother. She didn't want to meet her or find out anything about her. Vanna had never been one of those adoptees who at eighteen signed up on all of the registries and databases to try to track down her biological relatives. She'd never had any desire to track down her other family.

"Um… I don't know. She said… she just wanted to see how I was… make sure I turned out okay."

"Wow. Are you going to meet her?"

"No," Vanna said immediately. She had no desire for a face-to-face meeting. "No, I have to decide whether to write her back or not… but I'm not meeting her."

"Why not? I think that would be really cool." Lydia sighed. "I always envied you for being adopted."

"You did? Why?" Vanna couldn't fathom this. She'd always envied Lydia for being Erica's biological child. She looked like Erica, moved and talked like her, was able to please her. Vanna would always be too different. Too dark, not interested in Lydia's charities and social scene. She had little in common with her adoptive family. She didn't feel like she'd ever completely belong.

"I would love to have another family," Lydia answered. "I used to fantasize about another mother out there somewhere, and one day I would find out and she would take me off somewhere and… I don't know, buy me a puppy or something," Lydia finished lamely. "Well, I told you it was when I was little, right?"

"I don't think that she wrote to me because she wants to buy me a puppy," Vanna laughed. She dropped her eyes back down at the handwritten note. It all seemed so strange.

"What's her name?"

"Uh—Julia Cortez."

"Huh. That's pretty, right?"

Vanna stared at the name. "It's Hispanic. Latino. Whatever."

"I guess so," Lydia agreed. "Are you surprised?"

"Just a little." Vanna thought about her own dark, straight hair, and her slightly tanned skin. Each of them had wondered aloud at one time or another just what her ethnic heritage was. Where her darker skin came from. Julia's name seemed to answer the question. Vanna was at least part Latino.

"That's really cool," Lydia said. "I wonder where she comes from. Mexico?"

"I don't know."

"I guess you've got plenty of time to figure it out, ask her all of those questions."

"Yeah."

"Oh—shoot!" Lydia's voice rose in pitch and volume. "I've got something burning here. Gotta go. Call me later and we'll talk about the details, okay? And congratulations!"

"Thanks."

"Bye!" Lydia hung up.

Vanna stared down at the letter. *Congratulations?* Like she'd achieved something or won a prize? She didn't feel excited or happy about the disconcerting communication. She wished that she hadn't gone down to get her mail. Or that it hadn't been there.

———

All day, Vanna hadn't been able to get the letter out of her mind while she did her work, putzed around a bit more with the pendant lights, ran errands, and tidied up to keep everything in order. But she couldn't seem to escape it.

One of the problems, besides how to answer the letter, was how to tell Erica about it. It wasn't the kind of thing that you could just keep quiet and not happen to mention. Oh yeah, did I mention to you…? That approach wouldn't work. Especially not with Erica. But Vanna didn't want her mother to think that it was a big deal, or that she had gone out looking for this contact. In the past, a couple of times Erica had made comments about Vanna's birth family, with remarks such as 'If you ever want to look for them, I will understand. I won't be threatened.' And Vanna had always assured her, truthfully, that she had no desire to look for her birth mother or any other member of her birth family.

Vanna fussed and fumed about it all day, running through scripts in her mind. 'Mom, you'll never believe what happened…' But nothing seemed natural. It was all forced, awkward.

It had been easier when her father was alive. He'd kind of been the buffer between them. He'd talk to Vanna about how to approach her mother, or he would prepare the way for her, soften Erica up before the conversation. But with him gone, the conversations between Vanna and Erica could be stilted.

She decided that this was a conversation that needed to happen face-to-face. With reluctance, she climbed into her little Mazda and took the scenic drive to Erica's Estate. She kept the radio on, not really wanting to think about the upcoming discussion. It was afternoon, so if Erica White-Austin were keeping to her usual schedule, she would be in her solarium. Vanna rang the bell and it was answered by Misty, Erica's personal assistant. A ridiculous name for such an efficient, no-nonsense, middle-aged woman. But she refused to go by Miss Chatsam.

"Ivanna. So nice to see you. Is Erica expecting you?"

"You know she's not. Is she in the plant room?"

"Yes. I'm sure she'd be delighted to see you."

"Thank you, Misty."

The older woman nodded her reply. Vanna continued past her and made her way through the great hall toward the back of the house. She didn't know whether she would find her mother pruning flowers or writing letters. In fact, she was doing neither, but sitting in a lounge chair with a book and a glass clouded with condensation. Erica looked up from her book at Vanna's entrance.

"Ivanna! My dear!" she extended her hand. "Why didn't you let me know you were coming? Come have a seat."

Vanna leaned down to kiss her cheek, then sat in the matching chair, but didn't stretch out. "What are you reading?"

Erica displayed the current ladies' book club read before inserting her bookmark and setting the book to the side. "Have you had a nice day, dear? So dreary today."

Vanna looked out the window at the gray overcast sky. But inside Erica's solarium, it was warm, the full-spectrum sun panels bathing the room in bright light and the nearby waterfall keeping the air moist and fresh.

"I don't mind the rain."

"You never have," Erica observed. She took a sip of her drink. "Do you want something? Ring for Misty and she'll bring you tea or fresh juice or whatever you want."

"No, I'm fine." Vanna took a deep breath and couldn't see any way of approaching the subject other than straight on. "I have something to tell you."

Erica set the drink on the table beside her. "Your sister told me about your letter."

That took the wind out of Vanna's sails. "What? She told you?"

Erica merely nodded.

"She should have let me!"

"She wanted to give me a heads-up so I wouldn't be shocked when you got around to telling me."

"Got around to—? I'm telling you right now. I just got it this morning!"

"We didn't know how long it would take. Sometimes you have trouble talking about personal things. And Lydia didn't want me to be upset when I heard. She didn't want me to be surprised and be upset with you and make things tense. Are you going to meet her? You should."

It was too much all at once. Vanna couldn't begin to unwind the questions and to think through what kind of response to give. Her mother's tone was flat and emotionless. She smiled with her mouth, not her eyes. Vanna couldn't get a read on her.

Even though they had talked before about Vanna's birth mother and that it was okay to look for her, Vanna had never been able to figure out how Erica really felt about it. Was she threatened? Jealous?

Vanna reached over and pressed the button to call for Misty. Erica took another sip of her drink. "I told you I don't mind. I knew when I got you that you had another mother and that you might want to meet her someday. I'm okay with that."

Misty strode into the room, her high heels clicking across the tile. She smiled at the two of them, eyebrows raised.

"Misty… could you get me a coffee…?" Vanna asked, rubbing her forehead.

"Of course, Miss Ivanna. Just be a moment."

They waited in silence for her return. Erica looked at her book but didn't pick it up. It was a few minutes before Misty returned with a coffee tray for Vanna and put it on the table next to her. Vanna poured herself a cup and took a sip. It was boiling hot and bitter. But it was fresh and strong and that's what she needed. Vanna added several cubes of sugar.

"I don't want to meet her."

Erica looked at her, one eyebrow raised in surprise. "You don't?"

"I told you that before. I don't want to meet her. I've never wanted to meet her."

"Even now? After she's reached out to you?"

Vanna shook her head. "Even now."

"Well." Erica took another sip of her drink. "That's a surprise."

Vanna had no idea why Erica should be surprised. Vanna had always been happy with her adoptive family, she considered them her only family. The woman who had conceived and given birth to her was just a name on a file somewhere.

———

Vanna agonized over her reply to the letter. She didn't want to be rude and make Julia feel bad. But she also didn't want to encourage any further contact. Julia wanted to know that she had turned out okay. That was fine. Vanna would assure her of the fact. But she didn't want to meet and she didn't want an ongoing relationship. It was difficult finding the right words.

"Do you want me to read your reply?" Lydia asked when Vanna talked to her about it over the phone. Everything was quiet in the background. Apparently the kids were down for a nap or hypnotized by the TV.

"No…" Vanna wrinkled her nose. Now she had to handle Lydia as well. Make sure that she didn't feel too badly about being excluded from reading either Julia's letter or Vanna's reply. This was a part of Vanna's life that she didn't really want to share. Not fully, anyway. She wanted to talk about it, but she didn't want Lydia or her mother involved in it personally. "No, it's okay. It's coming together. I just… I worry that her feelings will be hurt."

"Well, there was never any agreement that she would be able to have contact in the future," Lydia pointed out. "There are all of these open adoptions now where the birth mom is allowed to have future contact, but that was never the case with your adoption, right? Mom and Dad would never have agreed to that."

"I have no idea," Vanna said. "They never said anything to me about it. Mom always said that it was okay if I wanted to search when I got older. You would think that if she had the information or had promised that we could have contact in the future, she would have told me then."

"Yes." Vanna could hear her sister juggling the phone and the beep of the microwave. "I don't think that Mom would ever keep that a secret."

"Is it dinner time?" Vanna questioned.

"No, but the only time I can eat in peace is when the kids are down. So you're going to have to listen to me eating…"

"How are they?" Vanna giggled. Christopher and Paul, Lydia's preschoolers, were always into mischief and Lydia cracked Vanna up when she recounted their latest escapades.

"Same as always," Lydia said. But she was not distracted into talking about them. "So… do you know anything about your birth mom or about Mom and Dad getting you? It seems like nobody ever talked about it. I always forget that you are adopted until someone makes a comment about how different you look."

Vanna pulled on her dark hair in irritation. Always the ugly duckling. "I dunno. I was never really curious like some kids are. I always just wanted to belong in our family."

"Well, you do! Of course you do. Mom and Dad chose to adopt you. You weren't an accident."

"I don't know much about it," Vanna confessed. "Even now… I don't really want to know. Is that weird? I know that I was older. I wasn't a newborn. They don't have pictures of me when I was a baby. You don't remember when I was adopted? You were old enough to remember something, weren't you?"

"Hmm…" Lydia chewed in her ear. "I really don't. I kind of remember being able to remember… but the primary memory is gone. I was four and you were two. Is that right?"

"Sounds right," Vanna agreed. "That must have been weird for you, suddenly having another little girl in the house. Were you jealous?"

"No, I don't think so. As far as I was concerned, you were just a big doll. I could play with you, feed you, dress you. Even in school, I remember being so proud that I had a baby sister that I could dress up when the other girls just had toys. They wanted dolls that cried and everything, but I had a real baby."

"I was four when you started school," Vanna pointed out. "Not a baby anymore."

"You were so small. I know you weren't a baby, but I don't think you were as big as other four-year-olds. And I could still make you do whatever I wanted."

Vanna laughed. "You always could."

"Until you hit that rebellious teenage phase."

"Yeah."

"When are you going to get through that?"

Vanna chuckled again, but when she looked back down at the letter in her hands, she stopped laughing and sighed. "I just don't know what to say to her. Do I thank her for giving me up? Do I tell her that she gave me the best family that I could wish for? I just don't know."

"Write from your heart. What do you want to say? It isn't like one of Mom's 'thank you' letters. There's no prescribed form. You just tell her what you are feeling. She'll respect that."

"Yeah."

"I can look at it if you want," Lydia offered again.

"No. It's fine. I don't need you looking at it. I just wanted some ideas."

"Okay. Well. I hope that helps. Just don't waffle over it. If you don't want her to contact you again, you have to tell her that."

"I don't want to say that. I don't want to say 'don't ever contact me again.' If I just don't offer to meet her or give her any more contact information… she'll get the picture, right?"

"You have to tell people what you really mean. If there's one thing that I've learned from marriage…"

Vanna tuned Lydia out as she went into lecture mode. Vanna didn't need a lecture on proper communication. Open and honest communication had never been the standard growing up in the Austin family. There were always innuendos, undertones, things that you had to figure out. She was still trying to figure out her mother and what she really thought about things. Lydia's breakthroughs on communication were sort of like the preachings of the newly-converted. She and John Paul had gone through marriage counseling and done a bunch of communication and trust-building classes, and it was like she had discovered a whole new religion.

Vanna was still working out whether she was agnostic or an atheist.

———

Saturday arrived and Vanna looked over her task list, trying to figure out which things were most important to accomplish. She had managed to catch up with most of her computer work, so she didn't have to spend her weekend on it. Which meant that she was free to work on her pendant lights and maybe to do some antiquing or a junkyard run. Then she could sleep late on Sunday and curl up with a hot chocolate in front of a good movie or two, getting all rested up for Monday.

She logged into the Birchdale upcycling group site. She'd hardly had a chance to look at it all week and she knew that there were a couple of meet-ups planned for the weekend. It was always fun to get together with a group of the girls to exchange ideas and get together for tea after a tiring day of treasure-hunting.

Looking at her watch, Vanna realized that she was already running late. Sue Anne and Darma had set up a meet at the uptown flea market for nine o'clock. If Vanna was going to be able to make it in time, she was going to have to forgo a shower and hop to it. She could grab a muffin on the way out the door and have something at the market's lunch booths later if she got hungry.

In ten minutes, she was dressed, brushed, made up, and rummaging through her purse to make sure that she had every-thing she might need. Fabric samples and paint chips, a measuring tape, several sturdy nylon bags… She checked her phone as she ran out the door to make sure that no one had texted her about any of their finds yet and hopped into the Mazda.

The flea market was the place to be Saturday mornings, whether you were an upcycler like Vanna and the girls, a low-income dad looking for a new couch, or a high-class socialite on the prowl for antiques. But not Erica, of course. She would never be caught dead at the flea market. While most of her peers saw nothing wrong with grubbing through the junk at the flea market looking for treasures, it wasn't Erica's thing.

The parking lot was already three-quarters full when Vanna got there, even though technically Vanna was still an early bird. The really avid treasure hunters were there in the predawn hours watching the vendors unload their trucks, hoping to catch a bargain before the merchandise even made it to the tables. Vanna scanned for Darma's yellow Rabbit but didn't spot it in the usual area. She looked at her watch. It was nine-oh-five and Darma was compulsive about punctuality. It was unheard of for her to be late.

"Vanna! Vanny, over here!"

Vanna looked around and spotted Sue Anne's blond curly hair and wildly waving hand. They were across the parking lot, almost to the door. Rather than taking their place in the ticket purchase line, Sue Anne and Darma waited for her.

"I didn't see your car," Vanna said, puffing a little bit from hurrying to catch up.

"It's in the shop," Darma explained. "We've got a rental today."

"Oh. What's wrong with it?"

"Transmission, I think," Darma said, wrinkling her nose in disgust. "It's going to cost a fortune. And they'll probably have it for a week. My poor baby!" Her dark eyes looked suspiciously misty.

"Oh, too bad. What are you driving today?"

"White," Sue Anne answered. "A Prius." She motioned down the aisle that Vanna had just jogged down to get to them.

"A Prius?" Vanna repeated. She looked at Darma, who was always going on about yuppies and their cars.

"I know, I know," Darma waved the query aside. "Sue

wanted to try it out. I still say my Rabbit gets just as many miles…"

Vanna nodded. She did not want to get into a discussion of car politics and oil prices. They all got into line.

"You looking for anything today?" Sue Anne asked.

"I'm keeping my eyes out for some more bottles. I think these pendant lights could be really popular at local eateries. And I'm still looking for a coffee table that will work for that display top project. How about you?"

"Something to make into a bookshelf," Sue Anne said, her eyes rolling upward as she thought about it. "I don't know what yet… something unexpected."

"Did you see that one I pinned? With a baby grand?"

"I don't think I'm going to find one of those at the Birchdale flea market."

"You never know! But no, probably not," Vanna admitted. She turned to Darma. "And you…?"

"Just on the prowl for collectors' items," she said with a shrug, "nothing specific today."

"I wonder if Kelly will be in today? He was traveling down south to some new stores. So he might have some new mementos for you to look at."

Darma nodded. "Hope so. How was your week?"

Vanna took a deep, calming breath so that she wouldn't get too piqued when she told them about it. She led in with the news of her email account being hacked and the great lengths that she'd had to go to in order to get it unlocked again, losing most of the day's work.

"With everything in the cloud these days, it's worse than a hard drive crash. At least if my computer craps out, I can head over to an internet cafe or the library and still access my data. But if I can't access what I've stored," she shook her head, feeling that tight, sick feeling in her stomach all over again. "Boy, it's really scary."

"I need to back up my storage," Sue Anne murmured. "The

company tells you that they keep copies of everything and have their secure backups. But that's not going to help if the company goes belly-up or their storage facility burns down, is it? Now I'm scared. I don't want to lose anything."

"Probably nothing will happen," Darma assured her. "But Vanna's right. It would be a disaster to get locked out of all of your accounts."

"And that's not the most interesting thing that happened this week." Vanna proceeded to tell them about the letter. By the time she was finished, they were in the doors, had their tickets and were roaming down the first aisle.

"I can't believe it!" Sue Anne gasped. "Your birth mom! I always forget that you're adopted."

Darma gave Sue Anne an amused look. "Vanna's skin is closer to mine than to yours and Lydia's," she pointed out. "How can you forget?"

Vanna held her arm next to Darma's. She wasn't sure that was quite true. She didn't have milk-white skin like fair-haired Lydia and Sue Anne, but her natural 'tan' wasn't nearly as dark as Darma's Indian complexion. Darma just laughed.

"So what are you going to do?" Sue Anne demanded. "You're going to meet her, right? Do you think she'll be anything like your real mom? I mean, like Erica? I wonder if you have any siblings! Or if she'll tell you about your father."

Vanna studied some books that she had no interest in, trying to slow her thoughts down and keep calm. Brothers and sisters? A father? Having her birth mom reach out to her was hard enough. She didn't want a whole clan. She already had the Austins and that was enough.

"I'm not going to meet her," Vanna said, without looking up from the books.

Sue Anne and Darma were silent. Vanna didn't look at either of them, not wanting to see the expressions on their faces or if they were trying to discuss her behind her back. She moved on to the next stall without looking back at them.

"Vanna!" Kelly greeted in a booming bass. He was a big man, twice as wide as Vanna across the chest and towering somewhere over six feet tall. He didn't even have the grace to have a beer belly, but instead looked like he's stepped out of a lumberjack commercial. "Come and see what I've got for you today! And where's your friends, I haven't seen—" he cut off as Darma and Sue Anne followed Vanna to the stall and laughed. "Ladies, ladies, you have to come see what I have for you today!"

He had bottles for Vanna, beautiful blue and green glass, with no chips. And he had some rare coins to show to Darma.

While Darma looked over the merchandise, Kelly looked expectantly at Sue Anne. "And what can I get you today?"

"Bookshelves," Sue Anne said.

Kelly's black brows knit together and he worried this bit of information. "You can get bookshelves at Wal-Mart. What kind of bookshelves?"

"Something I can make into bookshelves. I don't know what, yet. I'm still looking."

He grunted as he took Vanna's money for the bottles. Then he bartered with Darma on a couple of the coins, the two of them going back and forth in heated tones like the most seasoned street vendors. Vanna exchanged glances with Sue Anne. She could never be comfortable haggling over prices like that. She'd rather get ripped off than to have to negotiate head-to-head. Kelly and Darma finally came to a landing and money and coins were exchanged. Kelly thumped his fist down on the counter, swearing that Darma was a thief to take him at those prices. But a huge grin split his face and Darma carefully tucked away the coins, looking like the cat that swallowed a canary. The girls turned to go on.

"Bookshelves," Kelly said, stopping them.

Sue Anne turned back to face him. "Do you have something?"

"Not me. But there's a young kid down the third aisle. He

sells fancy painted skateboard decks and he gives a discount if you turn in your old deck and swap them out right there. I guess he repaints the old decks, but I don't imagine that all of them are in good enough shape to be reused as skateboards."

Sue Anne frowned.

"You ask him if you can take a look," Kelly advised. "Lots of color, popular icons, distressed… I bet they'd make good bookshelves. Sand down any splinters and anchor them directly to the wall…"

Sue Anne nodded. "I'll take a look."

"See you next week!" he called out, as they moved away from his booth again.

The skateboard decks were a hit, and Sue Anne bought half a dozen of them. Vanna's stomach was rumbling. She looked at the time. "I need a coffee. Are you going to take those out to the car?"

"Yes, I don't want to have to carry them around all day. They're heavy. Meet you in the food court?"

Vanna nodded. "Some of the others might be there now."

Darma and Sue Anne headed back out to the parking lot with the skateboard decks and Vanna took her time wandering to the food court, daydreaming over the displays that she saw along the way. There were so many projects that she would like to start, so many crafts that she would like to try her hand at. But she knew from experience that she had to keep at her current projects until completion or she would just end up with an apartment full of half-done junk. It was too easy to chase the next fad.

In the food court, she found a larger group of the upcyclers and sat down with a cup of coffee and a cheese bun. Those who had been there early showed her their finds. The late arrivals were mostly newbies, the inexperienced who didn't know that you needed to get there early before the merchandise was picked over. There were some upcycling tourists from other parts of the state or even out of state. And one Canadian who was looking a little worn by the crowd and the noise. But a couple of the latecomers were the experienced vultures. They knew that prices would go down in the last hour or two before closing. Vendors didn't want to have to pack and transport everything back home again. A good negotiator could get rock-bottom prices as the day wound up.

Vanna sat back and let the gossip wash over her, considering where to go next.

Chapter Three

There was another letter in the mailbox. Vanna looked at it, her heart pounding. She didn't even want to open it. Why had Julia sent her another one? She had taken such pains to be clear but kind in her return missive. Julia apparently hadn't understood that Vanna wanted her to stay away, to just leave her to live her life the way that she wanted to.

She already had one mother who didn't think that she was mature enough to be on her own. She didn't need another.

Vanna tromped up the stairs slowly, turning the matter over in her mind. She didn't open the envelope. She considered the idea of marking it 'return to sender' and putting it back in the mail, but that seemed cruel. Julia already knew where Vanna was and that she had received the first letter. To return the second would just be mean.

Back in her apartment, Vanna carefully placed her keys in the dish by the door. She laid the envelope down on the table and went back to her computer. She still knew it was there, lying on the table behind her, but she didn't want to think about it. She didn't want to acknowledge it. If she just ignored it, she could go on and do her work. She'd get caught up in things and not have to think about it.

But putting the letter out of her mind wasn't so easy. It seemed to grow bigger and bigger in her mind, darker and darker. Demanding to be dealt with. She worked for a while on the Sandusky wedding mailing list, making sure that everything was properly formatted, looking up zip codes, and checking for duplicates or any other potential issues. But the more she ignored the letter, the more she couldn't help thinking about it.

Since ignoring the letter was going to be impossible, Vanna would just have to bite the bullet and see what Julia had to say. Maybe she had just sent a note to say 'thank you for your letter and, of course, I will abide by your wishes and not contact you again.' Maybe.

Vanna got up and walked back over to the kitchen table. She very deliberately looked through the other mail. A couple of bills. And she read through the flyers page by page, even though normally she just chucked them in the recycling bin. Or made *papier mache* out of them. She knew that she was avoiding dealing with the letter. She knew that she was stalling and that she actually had no interest in what was in the sale flyers this week. She should, because she should be saving every penny she could, but she really didn't care. The only thing that she cared about was the small envelope with the neatly printed address on the front.

Surely Julia had understood and had just written back to acknowledge the communication.

Vanna used her finger to slit the edge of the envelope and pulled out the letter inside. Dismay sank down into her belly and sat there like a rock. It certainly wasn't just a short note acknowledging her communication. It was longer than the first. Three sheets of writing paper, densely written, both sides. Vanna didn't want any contact and Julia had responded with a vomit of words, stirring up all kinds of emotions and questions.

Vanna sat down with a thud on the kitchen chair which hurt her tailbone. She couldn't take her eyes off of the letter. Like a vacuum cleaner, her brain just sucked it all in and she was help-less to stop reading.

Julia had missed her. Had wondered for years how Vanna had turned out. Had spent countless nights lying awake, weeping over the loss of her baby girl. Julia wanted to talk to her. A letter couldn't sufficiently express all of her deep feelings. Words on a page just couldn't convey it all. If Vanna would just talk to her on the phone, she promised that she wouldn't bother her any further.

Vanna felt sick. She went to the bathroom overwhelmed with the swirl of words. But she didn't have to throw up. She took a drink of water and sat on the toilet, eyes closed, trying to ground herself. She knew she was overreacting.

One phone call. Then the woman would leave her alone. Vanna was curious in spite of the dread that pressed on the pit of her stomach. What would Julia's voice sound like? Would it be like hearing herself on the phone? Or would she sound like Erica? Or a complete stranger?

She opened her eyes for long enough to vacate the bath-room and put the letter back on the kitchen table. Then she walked to her bed and pulled a blanket over her head and shut her eyes again. She snuggled down. Shutting everything else out, she tried to go to sleep.

———

She didn't tell anyone about the second letter. Not Lydia. Not Erica. Not any of her friends from the upcycling groups or the people that she did work for. It was as though if nobody else knew about the letter, it didn't really exist. She could continue to talk to everybody about the normal things and they wouldn't ask her about the second letter or about what she was going to do about it.

But the letter continued to sit on her kitchen table, gradu-ally disappearing under a pile of flyers and other junk mail.

And Vanna knew it was there. She looked at the pile every breakfast, lunch, and supper that she ate at the table. Every time she got herself a cup of coffee, she knew it was there, peeking out from under the materials that covered it. She couldn't continue to do her crafts at the kitchen table if she let the papers continue to pile up. There simply wasn't enough room to work around them. They made her anxious, sitting there on the table instead of in the recycling bin where they belonged.

Finally, Vanna pulled the letter out. She smoothed it out on the table and gathered the rest of the papers and threw them in the bin. Just the letter sat there on its own, waiting to be answered. Vanna got herself a cup of coffee and added lots of sugar. Seeing how much sugar she put into it would have made Erica's toes curl. But Vanna needed fortification and she didn't handle alcohol well. Hot, sweet coffee would have to do the trick. She sat down and started the phone app on her smart phone.

Without allowing herself to come up with another excuse not to call, Vanna looked down at the letter and dialed the number that Julia had given her. Probably Julia would be at work. Vanna could listen to her voice on her voicemail message and leave a message letting Julia know that she was well and please not to contact her again.

But on the second ring, a woman's voice answered breathlessly. "Hello?"

"Oh… hi, is this Julia?"

"Vanna?"

Vanna was taken aback. "What—? How did you know it was me?" she demanded. She winced at how rude it sounded. Her birth mother would think that she was a mannerless cow. So much for being well-bred. She could just hear Erica's voice in her ears 'we must always be gracious, Vanna. If we are not gracious, we are not showing ourselves to our best advantage.'

Julia giggled. There was an awkward silence, and then Julia

tried to answer and Vanna tried to apologize at the same time. Vanna fell silent, embarrassed.

"I don't get a lot of calls," Julia said. "Everyone who has this number is in my contact list, so when it was a number that I didn't recognize… I just hoped it was you."

"Oh."

They both said 'sorry' at the same time and were quiet again.

"I'm so glad that you called," Julia ventured finally. "I know that you weren't looking for me, but I'm so happy to have found you… I had to hear your voice."

"Well…" Vanna steeled herself. Best to get this over with as quickly as possible. "I just wanted to let you know that I'm okay, you know. Everything turned out great. I have a really nice, close family and I never lacked for anything. Really. My family has been great for me. They really have."

"That's nice," Julia said. "They seemed like they would be a nice family. I knew that I couldn't keep you, I just didn't have the resources. But I wanted you to have a chance at a good life."

"Well, you did a good thing," Vanna assured her, feeling like the words really weren't conveying all that she wanted them to. "I'm really happy with the life that you gave me."

"Uh-huh…"

"I just wondered—"

"It's so nice to hear your voice. You sound sort of like my mother," Julia said. "I'd love to see you face-to-face—"

"I'm not really ready for that—"

"I know, I know. You said in your letter… but do you think… maybe you could send me a picture? I've never seen you. Since I gave you up, I mean. I'd like to see what you look like now."

Vanna rubbed her forehead and took a big swallow of the syrupy coffee. "I don't know…"

"Oh." The disappointment in Julia's voice was clear.

Vanna felt bad for hurting her. "It's just… well… I'm not really comfortable with this…"

"But you called," Julia pointed out. "That's a really big step for us. I'm so glad that you could call me. Maybe a picture… maybe later…" She trailed off and Vanna looked for a way to fill the silence, without agreeing to do anything else.

"It's really nice to hear your voice too," Vanna offered. "I'm glad that I called you too. But I'm just not ready for anything else."

"Well, maybe… we could just exchange a few more letters…"

"I really…"

"If you don't want to, that's okay," Julia said heavily.

Vanna had been guilted by the best. She knew that she shouldn't react to this ploy. Julia was just trying to manipulate her.

But this was not Erica. Erica had been there for Vanna's whole life. She knew how to manipulate Vanna because she had raised her. Julia was different. She had no idea what Vanna was like or how to persuade her to do something. She had lost her daughter, had been missing her for all of these years and had just finally managed to make contact again. Vanna could only imagine how that must feel. She couldn't just tear all hope away from Julia.

"I don't know. Let me think about it, okay?" Vanna suggested.

"Okay," Julia agreed.

"I don't know… just give me a while to think about it. And I'll get back to you…"

"I'll be waiting."

Vanna put her head back, she rolled her shoulders and shook her head back and forth, trying to relieve the muscles that she was holding tense.

"Okay… bye…"

"Good-bye," Julia breathed. "I love you."

Vanna ended the call and swallowed hard. She rubbed her forehead and temples some more and took several big swallows of the still-hot coffee, trying to calm her nerves.

So much for ending the relationship cleanly.

———

Vanna decided that what she needed was a little retail therapy. She had managed to pick up a few nice bottles and other items at the flea market the previous Saturday. But that meant that she didn't have enough of the light fixtures to complete all of the bottle pendant lights. Unless she was going to do something else with the bottles, and right now, she was focused on the lights. So she packed up her purse and headed out.

There were a few good thrift stores near the harbor and they were bound to have some old light fixtures that she could repurpose. It had been a few weeks since she had done the rounds to see if anyone had anything new in stock. And at thrift stores, the stock could turn over pretty quickly.

She went to New Beginnings first. Maud was always happy to see her and had sometimes put a little something to the side for Vanna if she knew what projects she was working on. It would mean a long chat to catch up on all of the news. But you couldn't beat Maud's knowledge of what was going on in the area, who had acquired what, who was expanding or closing, and where the sales were. You could spend three days searching the internet for local information and not get anywhere close to what you could find in a half-hour chat with Maud.

There were a few vehicles parked in front of the shop, but Vanna didn't recognize any of them. Maud's head went up at the sound of the bell as Vanna entered and immediately she was all smiles.

"Vanna! It's been forever! How have you been?"

"I'm good." Vanna felt immediately buoyed up by Maud's sincere pleasure at seeing her.

"What are you looking for today? Or are you just browsing? Are you still working on those hanging lights?"

"Yes. Have you seen anything that I might want?"

"I've got some good stuff," Maud assured her. She got up off of her stool behind the sales counter and waddled over to the far corner where Vanna knew she usually kept anything requiring electricity. She was a big woman. Come to think of it, she and Kelly would have made a good couple if Kelly wasn't already married and Maud had some interests outside of her shop. Vanna joined her in the corner, where Maud started to pull various fixtures off the shelf, showing them to her quickly. "These lamps are hideous, but they have perfectly good cords and sockets that you could use. And this chandelier, all kinds of little light sockets, if you wanted to do smaller bottles or champagne flutes or something like that. And the fairy lights," she pulled out a tangled webbing of tiny LED lights. "If you wanted to do something different, you could do a mass of small lights in a big bottle or vase on a table…"

Vanna's brain was going a mile a minute as she examined the various offerings. She knew that if she weren't careful, Maud would sell her the entire store. She had a budget to keep to and she couldn't let herself get swept away with a hundred new ideas to improve on what she had come for. But the fairy lights were darling and it would be such an easy project… Vanna took them from Maud.

"Do they work? Did you test them?"

"Of course I tested them. Bring them over here and plug them in, try before you buy."

"Thanks."

Vanna looked at the other light fixtures as she walked over to the power bar extension cord that Maud offered. She couldn't buy everything…

Chapter Four

I vanna," Erica's voice took on a plaintive tone that made Vanna wince. "I am hoping that you will join us for dinner next Sunday. If you could take some time away from your treasure hunting to spend with your family…"

Vanna rolled her eyes, glad that Erica couldn't see her. "I might be able to swing by," she said cautiously. "Is Lydia coming? Is she bringing the kids?"

"Yes, of course, she's bringing the entire brood. And her adoring husband."

"I think I'll be able to make it, I just have to check my calendar. What can I bring? What are you going to have?"

"You don't need to bring anything but yourself. Everything will be provided. It is not a potluck."

"I could bring a bottle of wine?"

"No, dear. Nothing, really."

"Okay…"

"And will you…" Erica hesitated, composing the question carefully. "Will you be bringing your boyfriend along? Just because I need to know numbers for the caterer…"

"No. I told you, I broke up with Tino. He's out of my life for good." Vanna felt unaccountably guilty for the assertion.

She hadn't told Erica about her hacked email account and wondered whether Lydia had passed that information on too. Just because Vanna had broken up with Tino, that didn't necessarily mean that he was out of her life for good. He always had a way of insinuating himself back into it every time she thought she was rid of him.

"Ah." Erica's voice was dry, withholding judgment on the truth of this statement. "I see. Well, don't think that you have to bring a date. We are quite happy to see you all on your own."

"I wasn't planning..." now Vanna wondered whether she should bring someone. But she had no idea who she would bring. She hadn't exactly been dating anyone else. Even between break-ups with Tino, she never saw anyone else. It had just been the two of them for a couple of years. On and off, and back on again.

"If you do plan to bring someone," Erica said smoothly. "Do let me know ahead of time. A couple of days. So I can let the caterer know."

"Sure. Of course. I'm pretty sure it will just be me."

"That will be delightful."

———

Vanna had brought a bottle of wine. She knew that Erica would be disappointed in her if she didn't. They had a nice dinner. The boys had been excused to go veg in front of the television, leaving the adults to their drinks and after-dinner conversation. Lydia pulled a blanket over herself to nurse Mandy, ignoring Erica's look.

"So, Mom..." Vanna started.

Erica turned her eyes toward Vanna, giving her a vague smile. "Yes, dear?"

"I was just wondering... about my adoption."

Lydia had been discussing something with John Paul and

stopped dead. She turned around and looked at Vanna, and then at Erica.

Erica looked at Vanna, eyebrows raised. "What about your adoption, Ivanna?"

"I don't know… how much you know. I was two when you adopted me?"

"Just after your second birthday. I was so glad not to have to go through diapers and potty training again." Erica looked over at Lydia and gave her a dry smile. "Your sister was very… willful about the whole toilet training thing."

Vanna giggled. "And what did they tell you about my birth family and the first two years of my life?"

Erica pursed her crimson lips and shook her head. "We really didn't know very much. It wasn't a private adoption, it was through DSHS, so we assumed that you had probably been removed from your birth family for neglect or abuse. But they said that the circumstances were confidential, they weren't at liberty to release them. So we just…" Erica shrugged. "We just assumed that you had gone through something traumatic and gave you as much love as we could."

Vanna tried to swallow the lump that swelled in her throat. She glanced aside at Lydia, who gave her a warm, sympathetic smile. Vanna rubbed the corners of her eyes. It had been a long day and she was tired. Wine always went straight to her head.

"Thanks, Mom. You guys were pretty great parents. So… you never found anything out? Nobody slipped up and told you something that they shouldn't have? I didn't tell you anything about my previous family?"

Erica frowned. "You didn't speak when they brought you to us. Didn't you know that? You were almost five before you started talking."

Vanna's mouth hung open and she only closed it with an effort. "What? No, I didn't know that!"

"I forgot about that!" Lydia said. "I didn't have any other siblings, so I thought it was just normal. I remember other kids asking me why you didn't talk. But I just said that you were too little…"

"You were very small for your age," Erica agreed, "so people didn't really realize how old you were. And they assumed that you were shy of strangers; they didn't know that you didn't talk at all."

Vanna sat back in her chair, thinking about this. "But you don't know what happened, why I didn't talk?"

"No. Like I said… we assumed that you were abused or neglected or went through some kind of trauma… they said that there was an active case in the court system… that it all had to remain confidential, to protect your identity."

"They never told you how the case was resolved? When it was all over?"

"No. We didn't have any contact with DSHS after the adoption was finalized. When you were three. I don't know what case it was or how it was resolved. Just that eventually, you started talking. And you never told us anything that happened to you in your previous home."

Vanna puzzled this through. The wine was making her light-headed, but she tried to focus. She thought about Lydia's kids. Even when they didn't say anything, you could tell a lot just by looking at them. Lydia could tell the instant she walked into the room if they were hiding some sort of mischief. Most of the time, she knew when she came across a mess who had caused it. And she knew when they were coming down with a bug, or feeling scared or just sad. They didn't have to say a word, she just knew.

"You must have guessed at some things," she said to her mother. "Just by the way that I behaved and reacted to things."

"Of course…" Erica agreed. "You were afraid of everything. Shy of strangers. You had nightmares. Loud noises reduced you to tears. Heights… but specifics… no."

Vanna nodded and dropped her eyes to the table. She could feel her face flushing from the drink. Her eyes were itchy and the room, strictly climate controlled, was suddenly hot.

"I'm sorry," Erica said. "I wish I could tell you more."

———

Vanna rolled over and rubbed her eyes, trying to figure out why she felt so groggy and what had woken her up. She realized that her phone was buzzing and grabbed it off the side table. With fumbling fingers, she attempted to hit the cancel button, but instead answered the call. She swore under her breath and tried to put on a cheerful, awake voice.

"Vanna here."

"Vanna… it's Julia. Your birth mom. I'm sorry, did I wake you up?"

Vanna cleared her throat. She looked at her clock and saw that she had overslept, thought it was still a little early to be making calls if Julia didn't want to chance getting her out of bed.

"I'm up," she said, which was true. She was up now. "What's wrong?"

"Oh, nothing is wrong… really… I was just thinking about you… I had a really hard night."

Vanna sat up, holding the phone to her ear and trying to get her bearings. She squinted at the stream of sunlight coming in through the window. "Oh? What's up?"

"Some nights it's really hard… thinking about you… what you must have gone through all of these years, all alone, wondering…"

Vanna couldn't help but wonder if Julia was drunk. What was she so sad about? Vanna had grown up in a wonderful home, not a cold, dismal nineteenth-century orphanage. She had never been alone. She had never wondered about her birth mother. Never missed her, anyway.

"I'm fine," she insisted. "I grew up in a wonderful family. I wasn't sad and lonely."

Julia made a sniffling, sobbing sound.

"I had great parents and even a big sister to play with and get into scrapes with. I didn't have a sad childhood."

"Really?"

"Yeah. You really don't have to worry about me or feel sad about it. You did a good thing, giving me up."

Vanna's eyebrows bunched up when she thought about what she had learned the previous evening. Julia hadn't given her up in a private adoption. Vanna had been removed from the home after some traumatic incident, maybe abuse. She shifted uneasily. Julia hadn't mentioned anything like that. She had implied in her letters and previous phone call that it had been her decision to place Vanna for adoption. But maybe she had. Surely not all public adoptions were forced? A parent could still recognize that her child needed to go to a better home, even if she wasn't a good parent. Or perhaps there had been an abusive spouse or boyfriend and she realized that the best thing she could do for her daughter was to allow DSHS to take her away.

"Really?" Julia questioned. "Do you think so? It was the right thing?"

"Yes, I do." Vanna didn't know what else to say. She couldn't think of a tactful way of asking about the circumstances. She couldn't just ask Julia if she was abusive or negligent. "Um… are you okay?"

Julia sniffled and breathed some more in Vanna's ear. "You're so kind to be worried about me," she said, a sob still in her voice. "You turned out to be a really nice girl."

"Thank you… I really need to get going here, I have work…"

"What do you do for your work?"

Vanna got up and walked to the kitchen to turn the coffee on. Julia wasn't going to let her off of the phone yet. But Vanna really needed to get moving.

"I'm a virtual assistant."

"What does that mean?"

"I do administrative and secretarial work for people over the internet. When they need help organizing an event, or coordinating a mailing, proofing documents… anything, really, that you need someone else for, but you don't want to have to pay for extra employees or temps or whatever. They don't have to live here in town, they can be from all over the world."

"That sounds really cool," Julia said. And she sounded genuine. Not like Erica, who thought that it was time that Vanna went out and got a *real* job.

"It is. It's fun to work with a lot of different people, on a wide range of jobs. It keeps me from getting bored. And I can set my own hours, so if I want to go out and do something during the day, I just catch up in the evening. Lydia says that I end up working too many hours, but—"

"Who is Lydia?"

"My sister. My older sister."

"Is she nice? Is she adopted too?"

"Yes, she's lovely. She's a really good sister and we get along really well together. We're best friends. She's not adopted. She's Mom and Dad's natural child. They couldn't have any more children after she was born, so they adopted me."

"So you had a sister. That must have been nice."

Vanna had already mentioned more than once that she had a sister, that they got along well together. Julia definitely sounded drunk.

"I really have to go now," Vanna said firmly. "I have to get to work."

She winced at how lame that sounded. Hadn't she just said that she could pick whatever hours she wanted to work? It sounded like she just wanted to get rid of Julia. Which she did. But the truth was, she did work long hours to keep her business going. Choosing which twelve hours a day you wanted to work wasn't quite the same as just working whenever you felt like it.

"Yes, you wouldn't want to get fired," Julia said and hung up abruptly.

Vanna was left holding the phone to her ear, wondering whether Julia had meant to be sarcastic or had not gotten the part about being self-employed. She lowered her phone and launched her email, trying to just put the call out of her mind.

———

"She just keeps calling," Vanna confided to Lydia, stifling a yawn. Julia had called again, not early this time, but late into the night. Vanna had a hard time getting off of the phone with her. "I don't know what to do about it. I can't just say, 'don't call me anymore,' that would be really rude and she *is* my birth mom. I don't want to make her feel bad, but I really… I feel really uncomfortable talking to her. Especially with the stuff that mom said. She never talks about when I was a baby or why I went into the system. She just talks about how guilty she feels about it and she keeps asking if we can meet."

She could hear Lydia filling the sink in the background and the kids playing together. "Why don't you just stop answering her calls?" Lydia asked.

"I know… I should. But she knows that's my number. She'd realize that I was avoiding her…"

"Well, maybe she'd get a clue," Lydia said, her tone annoyed. "She won't respect your wishes when you've told her that you don't want any contact. You need to show her. Quit trying to be nice about it and protect your space. She'll stop calling eventually."

Vanna shrank from the idea. Julia would feel abandoned. She already felt bad enough about Vanna's adoption. Half the time she called, she was crying. Vanna couldn't just ignore her. It would be cruel.

"She's never said anything about why she had to give you up?" Lydia asked.

"No… she doesn't really talk about me… I mean, she says she feels bad, but it's more about her than about me." Vanna hadn't realized it before she put it into words. But it was true. All of Julia's bad feelings were focused on herself and how badly she felt, not on how Vanna felt. It didn't matter that Vanna was happy or that she had a good childhood. She couldn't seem to take that in. She was so focused on her own bad feelings that she didn't really listen to anything Vanna told her. "I wonder if she is drinking or on some kind of drugs," Vanna said. "She just doesn't make sense sometimes. She doesn't seem to hear anything that I tell her."

"You should definitely cut her off," Lydia advised. The dishes that she was washing clinked softly in the background. "You don't need all of this extra stress in your life."

Chapter Five

Vanna was crunching through the budget numbers on the Sandusky wedding and was irritated when her phone started to ring, breaking her concentration. She looked at the display, a tight knot in her stomach telling her it was going to be Julia again. It wasn't, but just as bad; it was Tino. Vanna sighed in exasperation and picked it up. She knew Tino. Ignoring him wasn't an option. He would just keep calling until she picked up. If she refused to answer it, he would be banging on her door. And she preferred not to have Tino banging at her door.

"What is it, Tino?" she demanded, trying to keep the irritation out of her tone.

"Babe, I miss you. Can we talk? Go for a coffee?"

"Oh, Tino…" Vanna shook her head. "I don't need this now, on top of everything else…"

"Everything else?" His voice was concerned. "What else is going on? Is something wrong?"

"No, nothing is wrong. I just have a lot on my plate right now, okay? You need to find somebody else."

"There is no one else. It's always been you. I don't want anyone else, Van."

"Tino. I'm busy. I've got work to do. I don't have time for this. Please."

"What's going on with you? You sound really stressed out. You got a big job to do?"

"I have multiple big jobs to do and having to answer the phone every two minutes isn't helping."

"This is the first time I've called!" He sounded slightly offended. "I'm not calling you every two minutes!"

Vanna realized that she was blaming Tino for Julia's repeated calls and that wasn't fair. Tino had been staying out of her way for the past few weeks. She couldn't be mad at him just because of what was going on with Julia. "No, sorry, it's not you. I've got somebody else who's been calling me and won't leave me alone…"

"Who else is calling you?" he asked suspiciously. "Do you want me to take care of it? If someone is bothering you, I can warn them off."

"No, nothing like that. It's just that I don't really want to talk to her…"

"Her?"

"My birth mom."

"Your birth mom? Why didn't you tell me you had gotten in touch with your birth mom? That's great!"

"Why would I tell you? We're not together anymore. And it's not great, it's irritating. I don't want her in my life."

"You can't push everybody important out of your life, Vanna. This is something important to you."

"No, it's not. My own mother is important to me. Erica. Not my birth mom. She had to give me up when I was little. Having given birth to me doesn't give her the right to take over my life."

"If Erica's important to you, then why do you push her away too?" Tino challenged.

Vanna was taken aback. "I don't push her away! What are you talking about? I'm always over there, visiting her, going for dinner, or going out for breakfast or shopping together."

"Not like when your dad was alive. You go when you have to and then you complain about her and how she judges you. You don't go see her just to visit her."

Vanna bit back an angry reply. Like Tino didn't have any faults of his own? Who was he to criticize her for her personal relationships? He didn't understand the relationship that she had with her mother. And how could he understand how she felt about her birth mother?

"I'm not going out with you," she said, returning to the original subject of the call. "We're done. Okay?"

"No, it's not okay," Tino's voice was that soft, sweet tone he used to cajole her that warmed her right through. "I love you, Van, and there's no one else for me. I know we've had our rough patches, but we can work it out. We always do."

"I know," Vanna said. "And I… have feelings for you, too… but…" she tried to figure out how to make him understand without referencing his temper, his abusive behavior. The sweet Tino always felt so bad for his explosions afterward. He felt so bad that he made her feel guilty for holding it against him. But she'd forgiven him so many times and still he hadn't been able to overcome his fiery nature. "Tino, I just can't do it anymore. We're… not good for each other."

"Why not? Why are we not good for each other? Why can't you work on the relationship? Help to make it work, instead of just pushing me away, taking the easy way out?"

"I have worked on it. You know that. I've tried. But you…"

"I what?" Tino challenged, his voice low and even.

"You…" Vanna gulped. "You have anger problems. I just can't…" she trailed off. "I just can't, Tino. Not anymore."

He was silent. Vanna breathed, holding back tears. She wanted so much to tell him yes. She would get back together. They could go out for a coffee, just as friends. But they had been down that path so many times before. The moment she opened the door a crack, he was fully in her life again. And things would only go well for so long and then something would set him off again.

"You're seeing someone else," Tino accused, his voice taking on a harshness that wasn't there before. "That's what this is all about. There's no birth mom calling you. It's got nothing to do with my temper. I've got *that* under control. That's not it at all. You're seeing someone else. *That's* why you won't let me talk to you."

Vanna laughed. The thought that she could fit a new boyfriend into her crazy life was ridiculous. She wished she *did* have a new boyfriend; it would have made it so much easier to tell Tino no. He'd be able to see that she'd moved on. And she'd have a protector if he got violent. A new boyfriend would be good all around. But she didn't have one and Tino was ridiculous to think that she did. Or that she would hide the fact from him if she did.

"There isn't anyone else. I'm busy and I'm trying to deal with my birth mom, and your… problem… is not under control. I'm not going out with you, Tino. Now, I have a wedding to prepare for, so—"

"What?" he roared in her ear.

Vanna pulled the phone away from her face. She went suddenly cold. She was relieved that he was on the other end of the phone and not in the same room as her. Vanna knew that tone. She knew that had he been in the same room with her, he'd be at her throat now.

"No…" she couldn't even find the words to protest, to explain to him.

"You're planning your wedding? Exactly who are you getting married to, if you don't have a boyfriend? This is a little fast, don't you think? Especially when you just admitted that you still love me!"

"No… no Tino…" she tried to interrupt him, and he kept raving.

"You are not getting married to another man. I won't let you! I'd kill you before I let you marry another man!"

Vanna's mouth was so dry she could hardly speak. There was no moisture in her mouth. Not a drop of spit. She had left her water bottle in the other room and had finished her coffee. She wanted to go get her water bottle, but she was frozen, rooted to her chair. Just as badly as if he was standing there in front of her. Vanna worked her mouth, trying to get the words out. Trying to say something that would stop the flow of rage on the other end of the phone.

"Valentine!" she said, as sharply as she could.

Tino stopped short. She never called him by his given name. She knew how much he hated it. The shock of hearing her use it was apparently enough to stop him, at least briefly, from continuing to spill his vitriol into the phone.

"I'm not getting married."

It was a few seconds before he could gather his wits to speak again. And now he sounded boyish. Chastened. Embarrassed by his outburst.

"But, you said…"

"I have a wedding to prepare for," Vanna repeated, her voice choked. "For a client. I have a client who is getting married and I am helping her coordinate the arrangements."

"Oh. Oh, well when you said you had… I thought… I just jumped to conclusions…"

"It's time to hang up now," Vanna told him.

There was quiet for another moment, his breathing, still labored from his rant, rasping in her ear. Then he ended the call.

———

Vanna looked up from her work with the pendant lights when her phone rang. Julia's number, familiar to her now, flashed across the screen. Vanna relaxed her shoulders and continued to work, letting it ring. She was in charge. She didn't have to answer the phone just because it was ringing. She could decide for herself whether she wanted to talk to Julia or not. After a couple of minutes, it stopped ringing and was silent. Vanna continued to work with the fixtures. The phone started to ring again, making her jump.

"Sheesh." Vanna took a deep breath and tried to force herself to relax. She looked at the phone again, hoping that it would be Lydia this time. Or even Erica. But it was Julia's number again. She was going to pull Tino's trick, calling over and over again until Vanna finally gave in and answered.

Her nerves would be frayed by the end of the evening. Better to just bite the bullet and answer it. She'd make Julia understand that she didn't want to visit and that would settle things. Vanna scooped up the phone.

"What?" she demanded.

There was silence on the other end. Vanna knew that she shouldn't have been so impatient, but she'd had enough of harassing phone calls.

"Julia… I've had a really bad day. I'm sorry. It's just not a good time for me."

"I'm sorry…" Julia sniffled. "I didn't mean to make you mad…"

"No. It's okay. It's not you. Really. I just have had such a crappy day. Could we talk another time?"

She realized that she had just offered to talk again instead of brushing Julia off and smacked her palm to her forehead. Why couldn't she get out of this relationship? How did Julia keep sucking her further in?

"I… I guess. I was just feeling so sad… remembering… before I gave you up…"

Vanna had been reaching for her cup. She froze with her hand out. "What about it…?"

"It was so hard. I didn't want to give you up, Vanna."

"No… I get that. But it all worked out okay."

"Do you remember anything? From when you lived with me, I mean. Anything from before your adoption?"

"No. I was too young. I don't remember anything."

"Nothing? Not even a face? An impression?"

"No."

"You were two," Julia pointed out. "You were old enough that you might remember something."

"No, I wasn't. Maybe if I'd been able to talk to my mom and dad then, they could help me to remember now. But I couldn't talk."

"You couldn't?" Julia sounded surprised.

"Did I talk when I was with you?" Vanna asked, feeling off-balance.

Julia's response was hesitant. "Ummm… a little. I don't remember very well. It was a long time ago."

"My mom thought maybe something traumatic happened. Did… something happen?"

"You were taken away from me. *That* must have been traumatic."

Vanna felt an unexpected wave of disappointment and rebelled, trying to stuff it back away. Did she *really* want to know what had hurt her as a young child? Did she really want to know the trauma that she had gone through and that it had been more than just being taken away from the only home and mother she had ever known? She didn't want Julia to tell her what their circumstances had been like. But she did, too. She was trapped between wanting to know and being afraid to hear about it.

"Yes, I guess that must have been it," she told Julia.

They were both silent for a few minutes. Vanna could have just hung up then, but she didn't. She just waited, knowing that Julia would speak again.

"I'm sorry," Julia said. "I'm sorry for all the things that happened to you."

Julia disconnected. Vanna sat there wondering what she had

meant. Was Julia sorry for the bad day that Vanna had had? Sorry that she had given Vanna up? Sorry for Vanna's less-than-adequate start to life? All of what things? What was it she was sorry for?

———

"Miss Austin, I have been trying to reach you for two hours!"

Vanna glanced at the clock and at the stack of work next to the computer. "Yes, Miss Sandusky. I was working on a project for another client and could not be interrupted. I needed to give it my full attention."

"I was given to understand, when I contracted your services, that you would make yourself available for me! I don't expect to be ignored!"

"I'm available now. What can I do for you?"

There was an audible 'humph' on the other end of the call. Vanna waited, wondering whether she was going to continue her tirade, or decide that she wanted to get the job done instead. But Maria Sandusky apparently decided that she wasn't going to get anywhere in the argument.

"It is a disaster! My fiancee is in town tonight and there are last-minute changes to the guest list. I wanted to be able to go over the finalized list with him. We don't have very long before the invitations need to be sent out. But this current list is a mess! I must have it when I see him tonight! Really, it cannot wait another day. Tonight is the only time he is free to go over it."

Vanna rolled her eyes. Maria couldn't be looking forward to a very intimate marriage if her man was never in town. He wouldn't settle down once he was married, Vanna told herself wisely. Men didn't change just because they got married. He'd be away just as often once they got married. Maybe more so. And then where would Maria be when she wanted to cuddle?

"I can probably squeeze an hour in this afternoon if I put

everything else aside. How many changes do you think you have to the list?"

"There have to be at least a hundred!" Maria's voice rose in pitch. "And they simply must be done tonight."

"Yes, I heard that part. Can you send them straight over to me? I'll get started."

How she could have one hundred changes to a three hundred name guest list, Vanna didn't know. But if she wanted to keep her as a client and to get paid when her contract was due, she was going to have to baby her a little more.

"You'll get it done?" Maria demanded.

"The sooner you can get it to me, the sooner I can take a look and get started. I can't make any promises until I see how involved it is."

"You promised me that you could handle this," the woman accused, in a voice rising to a screech.

Vanna pressed the 'end' button. Blessed silence. In thirty seconds, the phone was ringing again, with Maria Sandusky on the other end, even screechier than before.

"You hung up on me!" she accused.

"I thought you rang off to go send those changes to me," Vanna countered, her face flushing at the lie. "It must have been a dropped call. You'd better go get them on their way."

After an incoherent splutter, Maria hung up. Vanna watched her inbox for the emailed changes to show up.

———

After sending Maria Sandusky her finalized list, Vanna looked at the time and put a call through to Darma and Sue Anne.

"Vanna!" Darma greeted. "We didn't see you anywhere on the weekend. How are you? Not sick…?"

"No, I'm fine. Hey, I was looking for dinner company tonight. I've been so wrapped up in everything lately, I really need to get out. I know you guys don't eat until late, so I was hoping my timing was still okay."

"Sure, we haven't started on anything yet. Why don't you come over here? I'll make some bruschetta; that will go with whatever Sue Anne has planned. You bring something gooey for dessert and we'll make an evening of it."

"That sounds really good. Is Sue Anne there? Are you sure it will be okay with her?"

"Vanna, she'll be delighted. She always loves having company and it's been too long since we had anyone over."

"We could just go to a restaurant so that she doesn't have to cook."

"Nonsense. Home is much cozier. You can even wear your pajamas and we'll call it a slumber party." Darma yawned. "I think we all need a night to just relax."

"Okay. That really would be lovely. So bring dessert; anything else?"

"Just yourself. If you want to work on a project, bring it along. If not, we can put on a movie."

Vanna sighed. It sounded heavenly.

"Thanks, Darma. And if Sue Anne doesn't want to cook, let her know I'll spring for a pizza, okay?"

"No problem. See you soon."

———

Getting out of her car in the parking garage, Vanna felt relaxed and at peace for the first time in a couple of weeks. She had really needed to just connect with friends, to be herself and not have to worry about offending anyone or have to appear interested in something that she was not. It was like she had finally been allowed to lay down a heavy load.

A dark shape loomed up ahead by the elevator and Vanna squinted, trying to get a good look at him to reassure herself that it was just one of the other tenants. But the figure was big and blocky. She was pretty sure that it was not anyone who lived there. She walked closer to be sure. The big man turned around and saw her approaching.

"Where have *you* been?" he demanded.

"Where have I been? What are you doing here, Tino? You don't live here." She navigated around him and pressed the elevator button.

"You tell me how busy you are, that you can't go out with me, and you're out with some guy! You're too busy for coffee with me, but you have time for dinner with him?"

Vanna looked at him, incredulous. "I told you that we can't get along together," she said. "I wasn't too busy for coffee, I didn't *want* to go for coffee."

His face was tight and pink. Vanna knew she was on rocky ground. She couldn't act like a wimp in front of him, but she also couldn't push back too hard. Misjudge it one way or the other and he would explode.

"You could have gone out with me," he said stubbornly. "We could have had a nice dinner. But instead, you take off with this…?"

Vanna cocked her head. "Sue Ann and Darma," she said. "Not that it's any of your business, but I wasn't out with a date. I was just visiting with some friends, watching a movie together. You need to leave me alone. Stay out of it."

The elevator doors opened and Vanna tried to make an exit. Tino's arm shot out, blocking her from entering the elevator.

"You're not just running off on me. You have some explaining to do."

"Let me go home," Vanna said firmly. She glanced around for help. There were security guards, but they had a whole building to watch and only swept the parking area every twenty or thirty minutes. A lot could happen in twenty or thirty minutes. But there had to be other people coming and going. It was a busy part of the evening. There were lots of tenants in the building. Surely someone would come around and Vanna could make an escape once there were witnesses.

Tino saw her look around and smiled grimly. "There's no one here to help you," he sneered. "You have to talk to me."

She had her sneakers on, not heels. She could run if she had to. If she had the opportunity. He was busy preventing her from entering the elevator. It would take a few seconds for him to change direction. But would it be long enough? Tino was tall, practically all legs, she knew he had a huge stride. He always had to slow down if they were walking together. She would need more than a second or two head start to beat him.

"Let me go. This is silly. I told you I was just over with Sue Anne and Darma. If you don't let me by, I'll call the police."

"Will you?" His smile was self-assured. She'd never called the police before. She'd always been too scared, or else the fight was over and there was no point. If she tried to reach her cell phone now, he would just snatch it out of her hand and throw it away. She'd never get the first digit dialed.

"Fine." Vanna changed direction and took a step back toward her car. If she could get to her car, she could drive away. He couldn't fight a ton of metal.

Tino's smile disappeared at her retreat. "Hey!" He stepped after her, arms out. "Hey, where are you going? You can't go anywhere!"

Before Vanna could get another step, he had grabbed her from behind. He flung her in an arc back toward the elevator, propelling her face-first into the wall between the two elevator cars. Vanna put her hands out to protect her face. She turned around, facing Tino, the wall at her back, trying to stand her ground. Tino swore at her, the word hitting her like a slap. She shook her head, tears springing up in her eyes. This was the part she always forgot. The part she always made herself forget. She didn't want to deal with an abusive partner, so she wrote those parts away. Focused on the good times. How much she liked to be with him when he was in a happy, calm mood. How much fun they had together. How great and attentive he was when he was happy.

"Tino, please!"

This time, it *was* a slap, not a curse, that hit her, flung out recklessly, like he didn't care if he made contact or not. Vanna put her hand over her face, crying out.

"Hey! Hey, what's going on over there? What are you doing?"

Tino swore under his breath and ran. A minute later, an older man was in front of Vanna. One of the other tenants. His face was familiar, but she didn't know his name or what apartment he lived in.

"Miss? Are you okay? Did he hurt you?"

Vanna kept her hand over her face. The world spun around her and she was afraid that she was going to faint dead away. She closed her eyes. "I'm fine. I'm not hurt. I just… need a minute."

"He hit you! Who was that? I'm going to call the police."

"No," Vanna stopped him with her other hand, preventing him from reaching for his phone. "No, it was a misunderstanding. I don't want the police involved. It's just… I'm fine. Really."

"Let me walk you back to your apartment." He pressed the elevator button and the doors opened immediately. Vanna staggered inside. Her rescuer also entered the elevator. "What floor?"

"Three."

He pressed the button and was silent. His eyes nearly burned holes in her, but he didn't say anything.

"It's fine," Vanna repeated. "Thank you so much for your help. But I…" She didn't know what to say.

"If he's hurting you, you need to do something about it," he told her. "If I hadn't been down there…"

"He wouldn't have done anything else. He was done. I'll be safe now. Thank you."

He walked her to her door and stood there waiting while

Vanna got out her keys and fumbled with them in the lock. "I'm going to wait until I hear you lock it from the other side."

"Thank you. I'll be fine now."

Vanna went in and shut and locked the door behind her. She looked back out into the hallway through the peephole and saw that the man was still standing there. He waited for a few more seconds and then he went back down the hall.

———

Vanna stood at the door for a long time, just breathing and trying to get her heart rate back down to normal. Eventually, she made her way into the kitchen and started the coffee maker going. She knew that she shouldn't have coffee before bed, or she was going to lie awake. But she needed something to settle her nerves.

While it brewed, she went to the bathroom and looked at herself in the mirror. Thanks to her complexion, there wasn't a mark where Tino had slapped her. If it had been Lydia, she would have been sporting a big bruise, but it took a pretty hard blow for Vanna to show it. Even if she did call the police, it would be her word against Tino's, with no visible injuries on either side. And heaven help her if she ever called the police on Tino. There would be fireworks like no one had seen before.

But it was throbbing. She soaked a clean cloth in cold water and held it to her face to go back to the kitchen. Her evening was ruined, but she would salvage what she could. A bubble bath before bed, fuzzy pajamas, and hopefully the coffee wouldn't keep her up too late.

In spite of the coffee, she was dozing in the bathtub. She was listening to soothing music on her phone, with a few scented candles lit on the bathroom counter. The ringing of her phone was jarring. She startled, splashed, and just about went under the surface of the water. One of the dangers of having a big, antique bathtub. Vanna let it ring, but she knew who it was. He wasn't going to give up until he had a chance to cleanse his soul. Tiredly, she pulled herself out of the bathtub, bending over to pull the plug. By the time she had wrapped herself in a bath sheet, the phone had stopped ringing.

But it wasn't the end of it. She knew it wouldn't be. She dried off while she waited for it to start ringing again. When it did, she picked it up. She didn't even say hello, she just put it to her ear.

Tino was blubbering. "Oh, babe, I'm so sorry. I didn't mean to do that, you know I didn't. It's just that when you start getting on my case about my temper, I just… I just feel like I'm being judged… it's not like you're perfect!"

"I never said I was," Vanna pointed out. She felt queasy with guilt. She knew that she had pushed him too hard. He tried to control his temper, but when she pushed it, he was bound to snap.

"No, you're so much better than I am," Tino sobbed. He must have downed several bottles between running out of the parking garage and calling her. "You're the best. I know you can't ever be with me, because of that. I know, but I'm trying, babe, I really am. You don't know what it's like to be me…"

"I know you'd like to change." But liking to change and committing to change and doing something about it, wasn't quite the same thing. Tino might like to change, but he wasn't ever going to do anything about it.

"I do," Tino's tone was sincere, tortured. "I want to change. I'd do anything for us to be back together again. I can't stand the thought of you with someone else. That's what was driving me crazy, Van. I was going crazy thinking that you were out with some other guy. I got all wound up. I didn't know that you were out with your girlfriends."

"If you want to change, you need to get into an anger management programs. Or Rage Anonymous. Just *wanting* to change doesn't do anything."

"But I'm getting better. I'm working on it. You can tell, right?"

"You have to get into a program," Vanna repeated. "That's the only way you're going to be able to change."

"I can't do that," his voice was lower.

"Why not?"

"Everybody would find out. I could get fired from my job. Do you know how people would look at me?"

"It's *anonymous*. No one else would know unless they had the same problem. And then they couldn't very well judge you, could they?"

"I just can't do that, Vanna. It's too risky."

"Goodbye, Tino. I'm going to bed now."

"Good night, Vanny…"

She pressed 'end' and went to bed.

Chapter Six

Vanna rubbed her temples and looked back at the work she had done so far. It was pitiful. Transcription wasn't her favorite work, but she was usually pretty good at it. Today, she couldn't concentrate. She kept replaying the audio over and over again, and she just couldn't focus enough to get the words down. She could hear the words. She could understand them. She could type. But somewhere in between, there was a disconnect. She just couldn't do the job.

She wanted to take a break and go out shopping or check in with one of her friends. Even just to call Lydia or Erica. But she didn't have the time. If she took a break now, she wouldn't get the job done on schedule.

She just had to buckle down and focus, or she would lose the file and the client.

Eventually, Vanna gave up. After calling to cancel the job, she called Lydia to whine.

"Everybody runs behind schedule now and then," Lydia pointed out. "If you just tell them that you're going to take a few more hours, that it's a more difficult project than you expected."

"It's too late," Vanna said. "I already told them that I couldn't get it done. They'll have to get someone else to do it."

"Well, maybe they'll still call you for other jobs," Lydia comforted. "Just because you had problems with one job, that doesn't mean that you can't still do others. You just need to stand up for yourself. Explain that there are other things going on and that this one job, they need to get someone else for. But you can still do others. Be assertive."

"I told them," Vanna said.

"What did you tell them, though? You're always too polite to speak up for yourself."

"Let it go, Lydia."

Lydia laughed. "So much for not speaking up," she said. "All right, fine. It's your professional life, not mine. It sounds like you've got it under control."

"I just wanted to vent. I don't need any advice."

"Okay, got it." Lydia covered the phone while she gave instructions to the kids. Then she was back. "So you want to come over for a while? We'll make cookies."

"I still have other jobs lined up. I really should get onto some of them."

"You'll do better if you take a break. If you work all the time, you wear out. So come over and make cookies. Bring your laptop and then as soon as we put the cookies in the oven, you can do a couple of quick jobs. You'll do better in another setting."

Vanna could just about taste Lydia's gooey, warm, chocolate chip cookies.

She packed up her laptop.

———

Erica called Lydia while Vanna was there. Lydia raised her eyebrows at Vanna questioningly. Vanna shrugged.

"Yes, Mom. Actually, she's right here," Lydia told her. She listened to Erica for another minute, rolling her eyes. "Well, be nice to her. She's had a hard time at work today and she needs a little TLC."

This apparently raised further comments from Erica. Lydia stood holding the phone, waiting. Eventually, she smiled.

"Okay, Mom. Here she is."

She handed the phone to Vanna. Vanna took a deep breath and held it to her ear. "Hi, Mom. How are you?"

"Ivanna, how are you?" Erica purred. "Your sister says you had a bad day."

"I'm okay. Just needed to get out of the house. I couldn't get a job done today and I'm afraid I've lost that client. But… there are others. I'll be all right."

"Maybe… it's time that you got a *real* job."

"I have a real job, Mom. Just because I work for myself, that doesn't mean that I don't have a job. You don't have to go to the office every day to have a real job, you know."

"Of course I know that. Your father had his own firm for a long time. But that's not the same as your… *virtual* thing… you need to meet clients face-to-face and to have a dedicated office space. Equipment. Staff. Just floating around between home and coffee shops, dealing with everything by email… you're really only dabbling…"

"I make a good wage dabbling. I don't want to be tied down to a set schedule. And I certainly don't need the overhead of a physical office. It's still a real job."

"If you say so, dear. And you'll be okay? This client you lost today? It's not making you depressed?"

"Lydia and I made cookies. She always knows how to make me feel better."

"Lydia's a good girl. But what I called for today… I actually wondered… about your birth mom. If you don't want to talk to me about it while Lydia's around, you and I can talk later…"

"You want to talk to me about my birth mom?" Vanna repeated, opening her eyes wide at Lydia.

Christopher and Paul, sitting at the little table making their own cookies out of play dough turned around and looked at their auntie at the change in pitch of her voice.

"I don't mean to pry," Erica said, her voice strangely tentative. "I just wondered… how things were going. You haven't really said much about her."

"Well, there's not really much to say… I told her that I don't want any ongoing contact, but she is still calling me quite a bit. She doesn't have a lot to say… just apologizes for having given me up and wants to get together. She keeps asking for a picture, and I think I'm going to send her one. But…" Vanna trailed off, not sure what else to say.

"It's odd." Erica's voice was careful and measured. "People at the Country Club have asked me about your adoption or birth parents lately. People who have known us since you were a little girl, but haven't mentioned it in years. I haven't brought it up with anybody. It's just like someone has been talking about it and gotten people thinking…"

Vanna furrowed her eyebrows and bit her lip, thinking about it. "I haven't talked to anyone about it," she said. "Just you and Lydia. I don't think Lydia's said anything to anyone at the Club about it…?" Vanna looked at Lydia, who shook her head. "No, she hasn't, either. I haven't even seen anyone from the Club, much less been there lately."

"Well, that is odd. I supposed there might have been something on television lately. A documentary or one of those reunion shows. Something that has people thinking and talking about it without even knowing why."

"Yeah, maybe that's it," Vanna agreed.

She expected Erica to bring the call to a conclusion, but she didn't seem to be wrapping up. "What do you think this woman is looking for?" Erica asked. "Why does she keep calling you?"

"I don't know… I guess she just wants to connect with me… try to heal something from the past… It's kind of disconcerting that she calls me to ask how I'm doing, and then we spend the call talking about how awful she feels."

"Some people crave attention."

"I guess so. I don't get the feeling that she has any close friends. Maybe she's just moved back here from somewhere else and I'm the only one she knows."

"That's possible. I just think… you should be careful."

"Careful of what?" Vanna laughed.

"Careful who you let into your life. We don't know anything about this woman's past. What it was that got you removed from her care. She could have been a drug addict. A prostitute. Who knows?"

Vanna chewed on a nail. "I am being careful. Like I said, I told her I don't want a relationship. Sooner or later, she's going to get bored of calling me to spill all her woes and stop calling."

"You should tell her to stop calling. Period. Don't answer any more of her calls."

"I don't want to hurt her feelings. And if I ignore her calls, she just keeps calling back. Like T—but if I answer the phone and just don't engage with her… she'll get tired of it…"

Erica sighed. "Don't count on it."

———

Vanna didn't want to go back to her apartment. She would check the mail and there would be another letter from Julia. Or she would just get settled into reading a good book and the phone would ring, and it would be Julia.

Erica's warning not to allow Julia into her life was disconcerting and kept replaying in Vanna's mind. Erica had always encouraged Vanna to make friends, had pushed her to be more open, to go outside of her comfort zone and not be shy. It was strange, after years of 'open up to people' to hear Erica say 'don't let her into your life.' Vanna supposed it was just jealousy. Erica probably didn't even realize that she was worried Julia was somehow going to squeeze Erica out of her role as mother. Vanna should have expected it. It didn't matter how many times Erica said, 'I don't mind if you want to track down your birth family'; she wasn't a robot. She still had feelings. With how diffi-cult their relationship had been since Vanna's dad's had died, it wasn't any wonder that Erica was feeling anxious.

Even though Vanna had already eaten out the previous evening and spent the afternoon with Lydia, she was restless and avoided going back home. She had her laptop. She could work from anywhere. So she went to the coffee shop that was one of her favorite hide-a-ways and ordered a grilled cheese sandwich for supper.

She was just checking her email for any further jobs when someone sat down in the chair across the table from her. Vanna looked up, surprised.

It was Tino.

Of course. This had been a place where they had both come to eat and chat many times over the years. He would track her down there.

"Tino…"

"Don't say anything. I just wanted to apologize. Really, Van. I'm sorry. I really, really am."

Vanna opened her mouth to answer and he waved her into silence.

"I decided to look into that Rage Anonymous thing," he said.

Vanna had to pick her jaw up off of the floor. "What?"

"I looked them up and I found the local chapter, and found out where and when they meet. They said nobody can say if they saw someone they know there…"

"Well, yeah. That's the whole 'anonymous' part. You really did that, Tino? You're really going to go?"

"I'm going to my first meeting tonight. Last night I was a little… well, I wasn't ready. But I thought about it all day today and I looked them up." He reached across the table and took her by the hand. "Don't give up on me, Vanna. Please."

She swallowed and tried to figure out how to answer him. How many times had she capitulated and taken him back? She was always convinced by his remorse and got right back into a relationship. She knew better than to take him back just because of his words.

"I don't know, Tino. Let's see how it works out. I don't want to… I don't want to say no, but we don't know yet if you'll be able to stick with it and make changes…"

"You said I needed to get into a program. I got into a program."

"You made the first step. And that's good. I'm not knocking it. I just… don't want to commit to anything yet. Let's make sure that you can stick with the program…"

Vanna tried not to look at Tino's face. Those sad puppy-dog eyes would do her in. She had to stand firm and make sure that he followed through. He squeezed her hand.

"I will," he promised. "I will stick with it. You'll see."

The waitress came with Vanna's sandwich.

Vanna let go of Tino's hand.

Chapter Seven

She slept through the weekend. There were lots of things on her to-do list that she should have been doing. But Vanna was exhausted and she knew if she didn't get caught up on her sleep, she would end up being sick, and that would impact her ability to work and earn money. Too many nights tossing and turning, thinking about Julia and the events of the past that were missing from her memory. And time spent with her friends and Lydia, trying to relax and forget the stresses. Then she'd spent way too much time with Tino, downing coffee and discussing the past and the future, avoiding any reference to the present, late into the night.

So she slept in late Saturday and Sunday, not making it to the flea market or any of the meet-ups. When she got up, she had a lazy breakfast or brunch, watched TV for a while, and had an afternoon nap. In the evening, she tinkered a little with her pendant lights and some other projects that she had previously abandoned. When night rolled around, she'd had plenty of sleep and very little activity, but she still conked out almost the instant her head hit the pillow.

Monday morning came too soon. Vanna was taking a break

and looking over the priorities on her to-do list when Julia's number showed up on her caller ID. Vanna breathed a long breath out and tried to relax her shoulders and her tightening stomach muscles before picking it up.

"Hi, Julia."

"Vanna, thank you so much for sending me your picture," Julia was sniffling, her voice choked with emotion. "You are such a beautiful girl."

"I'm glad you like it." Vanna felt oddly empty. She knew she should feel something about her birth mom being so emotional over the photo, but she didn't. She just felt blank and empty. And she wondered just a little why Julia hadn't reciprocated and sent Vanna one of herself. Wouldn't it make sense for her to send her own picture to encourage Julia to send hers? Then they could look at each other's pictures and compare them for points of similarity. But so far, Julia had not sent a picture of herself. And Vanna hadn't asked her for one.

"You have such lovely features. You look so much like—" Julia cut herself off and breathed harder, making a confused sound in her throat.

"Like you?" Vanna suggested.

"Like your—my—mother. You have… a lot of her features."

"That's cool." Vanna wondered if Julia would send her a picture of her mother. She suspected not.

"We have to get together," Julia said all in a rush. "Please. Just this once. I've seen your picture and I just… I have to see you face-to-face. It all seems too unreal. Please. Wherever you like. Whatever's comfortable for you. But I have to see you. To touch you. Please."

Vanna cleared her throat. "I told you I don't want a relationship," she said. "This is already uncomfortable for me. I just want… to go back to my life."

"I'm not stopping you from doing anything," Julia protested.

"I just want a chance to see you, to meet you in person. How could you deny your own flesh and blood?"

Vanna was silent.

"Those people you grew up with are not your blood. Not like I am. Is it so much to ask? To see me once?"

"It isn't that it's a lot to ask—"

"Then you will?"

"No, I didn't say that."

"I know this must all be very weird to you," Julia's voice took on a sympathetic tone. "But you've spent so many years with them. Can't you spend a few minutes with me? Just a few minutes. Just *five* minutes!"

Vanna remembered how she used to beg Erica to let her stay up and watch TV or finish a project she was working on. 'Just five more minutes, Mom. Can't I stay up for just five minutes?'

But what kid didn't do that? Vanna had heard Christopher and Paul do the same thing. Begging for minutes, seconds even, desperate to be allowed to keep playing their video games or watching TV.

"Fine," Vanna gave in eventually. "Just once. I'm really not comfortable with it. This is going to be really hard for me. You have to understand that."

"Once we get together, it won't be like that. You'll see. Everything will just click and it will feel perfectly natural."

Vanna hoped that was true, but she doubted it. Nothing about this relationship so far had felt natural. And she didn't want to prolong it any longer. After they had met together face-to-face, she was going to have to be firm with Julia. Lay down the law and explain that there would be no more visits.

"You won't regret it," Julia promised. "You'll see. It will all work out."

———

In the hours before the meeting with Julia, Vanna paced. She couldn't sit down. She couldn't occupy herself with her crafts or any of the usual brain candy on the computer and TV. She couldn't stop thinking about Julia. Wondering what she would look like. How she would act. Whether Vanna would feel any kind of connection of any kind with her. Whether the meeting would trigger some kind of memory for her. She wasn't excited. In fact, she was dreading it.

Another trip to the bathroom. Her guts were so tied in knots over the whole thing, it would be a wonder if she could actually leave the apartment without cramping up. She considered canceling but knew that would just put off the pain. It would be even harder, anticipating it for longer.

At the appointed hour, she put on her rain jacket and left the apartment. The air outside was wet and clear, it smelled fresh like spring should. One thing you had to say about Birchdale—it was green. The rain had stopped, but Vanna wasn't sure it was going to stay stopped. She climbed into her car and turned it on, adjusted all of the air vents and mirrors, even though they didn't need to be adjusted. She was the only one who ever drove the car. Unable to put it off any further, she turned her keys in the ignition and drove at a very sedate pace to the Mexican restaurant that she had elected to meet at.

She was kicking herself now for picking Mexican. Why did she do it? Because Julia's name was Cortez, Vanna thought that she was Mexican? And that she would prefer Mexican food? There weren't a ton of Latinos in the city, but they ate just as many hamburgers as anyone else. Maybe it would have been less stereotypical to meet her at a grill or that new health bar that had opened up a couple of weeks previous. There was no reason Vanna had to pick Mexican.

At 'The Amigos' she looked around, trying to pick her birth mother from the unfamiliar faces. She should be able to recognize her own birth mother. Wasn't her face branded into

Vanna's infant brain circuitry? Nothing could erase that. It was permanent. Like facial recognition software, it should be in her genes to pick out a near blood relative. But she couldn't see anyone whose face rang a bell and she hadn't thought to ask Julia what she looked like or what she would be wearing. Vanna just assumed that she would know Julia when she saw her. There were a number of Latino women who looked like they would fit the part. The right age to fit the voice and fall into the window that would have made her a young mother when Vanna was born. Vanna assumed that she must have been a teenager or young adult when Vanna was born. That was why she hadn't known how to take care of Vanna properly. But all of the women who looked right were with larger groups, or were serving, or were occupied with other things, not looking toward the door to watch for her newfound biological daughter.

"Vanna?"

Vanna turned around and looked blankly at the young blond. "Yes?"

"It's me. Julia. Your mom!"

With her brain still chugging to catch up to this new revelation, Vanna reached her hand out to shake Julia's and forced a friendly smile. "Hi."

"Oh, come here!" Julia insisted, grabbing her hand and pulling her into a big hug. She squeezed Vanna tightly. She looked like a small, frail woman, but her grip was like steel.

Vanna squirmed to be released. Julia let go of her, laughing. "Oh, I can't believe it! You don't know how good it feels to hold you in my arms again. You look even more beautiful in person. And you're so… friendly. I just want to squeeze you."

Vanna held up her hands, guarding against another hug. "Let's see if we can get a booth," she suggested.

Julia fell back slightly, smiling and panting with excited emotion, like one of those sharp-nosed whippet dogs, ready to chase after a rabbit. Vanna tried to ignore Julia by engaging with the restaurant hosts to see if they could get a booth and how long the wait would be. Birchdale wasn't exactly a big city, and the restaurant was not filled to capacity, so they were shown to a table within a few minutes. Vanna sat down slowly, not wanting to look at Julia again. But she knew she had to. She was there with a job to do. A short visit with Julia, over supper, then break it off firmly and go home, free of her.

Vanna swallowed hard and took a sip of water, then forced herself to look at Julia again. Big, blue eyes, a face as young and innocent as a fawn, a slim but curvy body that Vanna found herself envying. The girl hardly looked older than Vanna. She must have been very young at the time of Vanna's birth. Vanna found herself trying to calculate. If Julia had given birth at fourteen, the youngest that Vanna could imagine, then she had to be thirty-six now and she didn't look a day over twenty-eight. And what were the chances that she had been as young as fourteen and managed to raise Vanna until she was two without any help?

Vanna looked away from Julia. "You're very pretty," she offered. "I'm surprised that you're so… fair." She didn't know what else to say. White? Caucasian? Non-Latino?

"Genetics does funny things," Julia said, flushing a little pink around her neck and ears. "My father was blond, so I guess I take after him. You look more like my mom. Your biological father was… darker too…"

"Oh. I see."

"Of course, my natural hair color isn't quite this blond… not anymore, anyway. It was when I was little, so that's the color I like…"

Vanna nodded. She didn't know whether she was happy that the hair color came out of a bottle or not. Julia's blue eyes and white skin were still shockingly non-Hispanic. She would be able to pass as Lydia's sister much more easily than Vanna could.

"My birth father," Vanna started out awkwardly, grasping

for a topic of conversation, "were you together, before I was born, or was it just… you know… a surprise."

Julia laughed. "We were together for a while," she said, evading the question. "But not for a long time."

"When I was born?"

She looked up toward the ceiling, searching her memory. "I don't remember."

She didn't remember whether her boyfriend was still around when her baby was born? Vanna shook her head, trying to understand. "Well, did he come see you at the hospital? Was he on the birth certificate?"

"No, I don't think so. There was a lot of stuff going on, though. It's hard to remember clearly."

Vanna passed on appetizers and desserts, hoping to end the evening as quickly as possible. Julia jumped from one random topic to another, from studying the shape of Vanna's ears to commenting on the shape and color of the placemats and the decor of the restaurant. Vanna talked about the lights briefly, mentioning the pendant light project. Julia nodded in all the right places and smiled at Vanna blandly, her eyes far away. Then she changed the subject to chicken fingers. Then a couple minutes later, she reverted to the decor.

"You make lights?" she questioned. "All by yourself?"

"Well… yes. I mean, I use fixtures and other existing materials… but I use them to make something new, these… hanging lights. They're not exactly chandeliers, but you get the idea."

"That sounds very cool. Your—my—mother was very creative. She liked to make things. Trying new crafts and stuff all the time. The house was full of them."

"But not you? It's not something you were ever interested in?"

Julia shook her head. Vanna studied her eye makeup. Her eyes looked so big, and Vanna couldn't figure out if it was because they really were large, or because her makeup made it look that way. Their dinner plates finally arrived and Julia looked at Vanna's fajitas.

"We should share," she suggested. "I'll take half of yours and you take half of mine. That looks really good."

Vanna opened her mouth and looked for a way to answer. They hadn't agreed at the beginning to share. She had ordered the dish that she wanted and had no interest in Julia's shrimp salad.

"I really don't like—"

"Come on, it will be fun," Julia encouraged. She reached across the table and helped herself to one of Vanna's tortilla shells and scooped vegetables into it. Vanna watched, her mouth open. Julia motioned to her own plate, indicating that Vanna should help herself. With reluctance, Vanna moved her plate closer and scraped some of Julia's shrimp salad onto her own plate.

They ate in silence for the first few minutes. Then Julia started with a round of what might have been a game of twenty questions. What was Vanna's favorite song? Color? What did she care about? What did she dislike? What school had she gone to? Who were her best friends?

Eventually, Vanna put down her fork. "I'm full."

Julia stopped chewing and looked at Vanna's plate, still three-quarters full. "Are you sure? Do you want something else? You don't like it?"

"I'm not feeling great."

Julia put her fork down. "Oh… I'm sorry."

Vanna scraped at the table with her fingernail. "Julia…"

"What is it?"

"I know that you want us to stay in contact, but…"

Julia's lips parted slightly. She didn't interrupt.

"I don't want you to call again," Vanna said, her mouth dry. She took a drink of her Perrier. "No more meetings or letters."

"But… why?"

"I just… it's very stressful… I just want my life to go back to normal."

"But I've enjoyed getting to know you so much. I'm your mother!"

"Maybe you were once," Vanna allowed. "But not now. I have a mother. I don't really know what it is that you want from me, but it isn't to be your daughter. You don't act like a mother and I don't want you to. I just want… I want us to live our own lives again."

"I do want to be your mother. I just don't know how. I haven't ever been a mother—for a long time. I can't make up for all of the lost years."

"No. I told you I don't want you to."

"Then let me be your friend! Don't shut me out, Vanna! I've waited too many years for this."

"Not now. Maybe in the future… I don't know… maybe. But I'm not ready for it right now. It's too… distracting."

"Distracting?" Julia's voice rose. "Being my friend is too *distracting* for you?"

Eyes turned toward them. People tried not to look as if they were watching and listening, but Vanna could tell from their covert looks that they were.

"Julia…"

A waitress hurried over to the table. She smiled at the two of them. "Can I help you out with anything? Would you like some dessert? Coffee?"

"No, just the bill, please," Vanna said in a quiet tone.

The waitress looked at her for a moment. Her glance flicked toward Julia, and then she nodded. "Yes, certainly. I'll be right back."

Julia stared at Vanna, her mouth a thin, bitter line. Vanna tried to think of something to say. She wanted Julia to feel better about it, but she couldn't figure anything out. She knew that if she gave in, like she had so many times with Tino, that Julia would just keep calling her, just keep trying to deepen the relationship, to pursue her further. And that wasn't going to work for Vanna.

"I'm sorry," she said softly.

"You're my daughter," Julia insisted.

"I'm not. You don't have any right to control me or demand a relationship with me. Please, I didn't want to hurt your feelings, but I don't know what else to say. I want you to leave me alone."

"Why didn't you just say that from the start, instead of leading me on? Why did you bother to answer my letters? Take my calls? Send me a picture? Why did you come here to meet me? If you didn't want to be with me, then why didn't you just make that clear from the start, instead of leading me on?"

"I'm sorry."

"I feel like such a fool. I thought that we were getting to know each other. To trust each other. I thought that you cared about me. But you don't. You were just getting some kind of weird kick out of leading me on just so you could push me down again."

"No—"

"You're not a very nice person, Vanna. I can't believe that you would treat your own mother that way. I feel sorry for your adoptive mom. Having to raise such an ungrateful brat. I'm glad that it was her and not me. Look at how you turned out."

Vanna couldn't help feeling guilty. A little sick to her stomach. She had to admit that she had led Julia on when she knew very well that she didn't want a relationship with her. She had thought that it would be easier, that she could give Julia just a little and then it wouldn't be so hard to say no. She thought that she was being nice. But was she being any nicer than Erica, when she lied about her own feelings and motivations, covering up what she was really thinking in an effort to make the other person feel better?

"I didn't want to hurt you," she repeated. "Please understand that. I just... I guess I misjudged. Please don't be upset with me."

"Why do you care whether I'm upset or not? You just said that you don't care a whit for me. So why act like you do?"

"That's not fair..."

"Life isn't fair, is it, princess? I thought that after all I've gone through, that maybe I could still have just a little bit of happiness. Just a little bit of peace in this life. But you couldn't do that. No. You just build me up and kick me in the gut. Thanks a lot, Vanna."

The waitress was there with the bill, looking at the two of them anxiously. Their discussion was drawing the attention of everyone within hearing. The other patrons didn't even pretend not to be listening anymore. They watched with open interest. The waitress held the bill between them, not knowing which of them to give it to. Vanna pulled it out of her hand.

"Thank you. I'll come up to the front to run this through," she offered.

The waitress nodded. Her face was flushed. She looked at Julia to see if she was going to go with Vanna. Julia stayed where she was. Vanna followed the waitress up to the register and paid for both of their dinners, adding a very generous tip.

"I'm sorry," she murmured to the woman. "I didn't now that this would happen. I didn't mean to disturb anyone."

———

Vanna was proud of herself. In spite of the previous evening's debacle, she had managed to focus on work and check a couple of big jobs off of her list. She had worked like a demon, focused hard on the tasks at hand, refusing to think over and rehash the conversations with Julia. They were there, in the back of her mind, but with narrowly focused energy, she was able to keep it all from coming to the forefront.

She was having a well-deserved cup of coffee and checking

the fridge for anything that might be good for lunch when there was a knock at the door. Vanna looked at her watch. She wasn't expecting any deliveries or company and it was too early in the day for solicitors. She had pressed the door release button when the buzzer had sounded a few minutes earlier, but she always did that. It was rarely for her, and it was easier to just press the button than to argue with the caller. She went to the door and looked out the peephole.

Vanna couldn't see the person who had knocked, but she could see a mass of roses. She opened the door cautiously. The delivery boy smiled at her and held them out. "Vanna Austin?"

"Yes, that's me," Vanna said, taking the big bouquet from him. A dozen red roses? On second thought, it looked like more than a dozen. Vanna did a quick count to see that it was actually two. Two dozen red roses. "Who are they from?"

"There's a card," he advised, and pointed to the small florist card taped to the plastic around the bouquet.

"Thank you."

IIe nodded and left. Vanna pushed the door shut and walked over to the kitchen table, pulling the tiny envelope off of the plastic and opening it up.

'I'm sorry. Can't we still be friends?'

There was no name. It had obviously been written by the florist, not the sender, so she had no hope of recognizing the handwriting. Vanna found herself frowning as she filled a big vase with water and cut the stems of the roses. She rubbed her forehead, trying to remove the frown lines. Her life could never be simple.

When she finished and went to her computer, she was worried that she wasn't going to be able to get anything else done in the afternoon. Her focus had been broken and now thoughts tumbled through her mind, multiplying more and more questions and worries. The phone rang and Vanna saw that it was Julia's number.

Vanna had been clear. She had asked Julia not to call her

anymore. She shouldn't even answer it. How was Julia going to understand that Vanna was serious about not having an ongoing relationship if she kept answering her every time that she called? But the roses worried Vanna.

"Hello?"

"It's Julia… I just wanted… is there any way that we could just start over again, Vanna? I don't know what it was that I did that offended you, but I don't want to lose you again…"

"Did you send these flowers?"

Julia didn't answer right away. Vanna frowned again. Was Julia trying to think up an excuse? Weighing how Vanna had reacted to receiving them? "What flowers?" Julia asked.

"You didn't send me roses?"

"No… you don't know who they are from?"

Vanna sighed. Tino. "Oh, I have an idea. I thought of you first, but if it wasn't you, then I know who."

"Red roses?" Julia asked wistfully.

"Yeah. Two dozen. There wasn't a signature on the card, so I wasn't sure."

"I *should* have sent you flowers… that would have been a nice thing to do."

"No. That's okay. I don't want you to. I just wanted to know if they were from you. I have to go…"

"I just wanted… I wanted to tell you how sorry I was for last night. I'm sorry I got mad. I'll do better. I can be a good mom. I'll show you."

"I already have a mom. I don't need another one. Let's just let it go now, okay? I'm not ready for this."

"Does that mean that sometime you will be?"

"I don't know. Right now… I don't think so. But I don't know. I can't speak about forever."

"We could be good friends. If you'd just open up and let me."

Vanna sighed. She thought about Erica's warnings. Something that happened in the past. This woman was unreliable or unstable in some way, or Vanna wouldn't have been taken away from her. Julia said that Vanna needed to open up, but she herself avoided any questions about the past. About what had happened when Vanna was little, before she was adopted. She demanded openness, but she refused to talk about what Vanna really wanted to know. She wasn't the type of person that Vanna like to spend her time with. Every conversation was fraught with tension and unanswered questions. It wasn't Vanna who needed to open up to make the relationship work. Though she admitted to herself that she wasn't prepared to share anything personal with Julia.

"I'd like you to just leave me alone," she said firmly.

Julia didn't explode. She simply hung up.

———

Vanna hadn't even had a chance to look at the meet-ups to see what was happening over the weekend when Muriel called her.

"Vanna, dear, it's been ages since I saw you last!"

"It has been a while," Vanna admitted, trying to remember the last event that she and Muriel had been at together. "Are you planning something?"

"I'm trying to get a group together to do some junkyard treasure hunting. I know I should use the computer meet-up thing, but I always get turned around and end up putting the wrong date or something. You can put it on the website if you want, but I just thought I'd make some quick calls to see who is available."

"What day are you going? This Saturday?"

"Yes. I thought a ten o'clock start should work for both the early birds and the ones who sleep in. Would you be interested?"

"Sure. I can put it up on the meet-up for you too. Who have you talked to?"

Muriel listed off a few of the group that she had called. "I think we'll get a pretty good group. We'll start at A&J at ten."

"That sounds good. Are you looking for anything special?"

"Yes, something that will net me about three million so I can retire and just diddle around all day with whatever I want."

Vanna laughed. "Save one for me too."

———

Vanna was bringing a few small items back from the junkyard hunt and ran into Mrs. Kingsley, one of her neighbors, in the hallway.

"Oh, you're home," Mrs. Kingsley said. "Can you wait for just a minute? I signed for a delivery for you this morning."

"A delivery?" Vanna was not expecting anything. "What was it?"

"Just wait."

Mrs. Kingsley let herself into her apartment and returned with a big vase of various colored mums. "They're so beautiful, you're very lucky," she gushed.

Vanna's heart sank. "Thank you. Would you like to have them?"

"No, no. They're yours, dear."

"I already have roses."

"You are a lucky girl! You take them. I don't need them. The roses won't last, but mums stay nice a lot longer."

It was true. The roses were already fading. Vanna juggled her junkyard finds in order to unlock her door, and then took the big vase from Mrs. Kingsley.

"Thank you very much."

On entering her apartment, Vanna immediately put everything down and called Tino. He answered after only a couple of rings.

"Hello—"

"Stop sending me flowers," Vanna snapped before he could even finish his greeting.

"What?" his voice was surprised. "You always like getting flowers. Weren't they fresh?"

"This isn't about whether they were fresh or not. Just stop it. We're not together and flowers aren't going to change that. You just work on yourself."

"I went to meetings twice." Tino's voice was eager. "So you see? I am committed."

"That's really good. Keep it up. But don't send me flowers."

"You used to like when I sent you flowers." His voice was pouty, like a little boy scolded by his mother.

Vanna had liked it. A long time ago, when flowers had been a romantic prelude, instead of the aftermath of another fight. "That was when we were together," she said. "And right now, we're not. I need some space, Tino. And you need to get your stuff under control."

"I told you I am."

"Yeah. And that's good. I'm really proud of you. But going to a couple of meetings doesn't change you. You need to put a lot of work into it."

"I'm not that bad. I know men with a lot worse tempers than I have."

"Like your dad?" Vanna suggested.

She knew that Tino had grown up terrified of his father. It was no surprise that he had inherited his father's fiery temperament and modeled his behavior. He still carried the scars of his childhood. Physical and emotional.

"That's not fair. I'm nowhere near as bad as my father."

"If you don't want to turn out to be like him, you have to work on it. Not just talk about it and go to a couple of meetings."

"I promise not to send you any more flowers," Tino growled. And he hung up.

Vanna put her phone down feeling guilty. She knew he

wasn't that bad. And that he was trying. It really wasn't fair of her to keep riding him about his problems when she knew it would just make him more defensive and angry. She couldn't just harp on his weaknesses and expect him to become a better person for it.

She reached for her coffee mug, but it wasn't there. Vanna glanced around the kitchen and didn't see it on the counter or in the sink. She tried to always put it in the kitchen when she was done so that it would get washed. But something could have happened to distract her. It often did. Vanna went back to her computer and looked around. No mug there, either. She looked more carefully, in case it was behind something, but was quite sure that it wasn't there, either. Vanna searched the rest of the apartment, an uneasy feeling growing in the pit of her stomach. Had someone been there? In her apartment? She went back to the front door and replayed the scene with Mrs. Kingsley in her head. The door had been locked. There had been no sign that the door had been forced or that anyone else had been there.

Her computer was still on her desk. Her stereo equipment and TV exactly where they should have been. Everything was in place except for her coffee cup. It seemed to have sprouted legs and run away. She even looked on the floors and behind furniture, in case somehow she had knocked it down and it had rolled behind or underneath something. But with no luck.

There was no sign of the coffee cup.

———

Vanna got a fresh coffee mug out of the cupboard. One of the mugs that she never touched unless she had company. She didn't want to be the slob who piled up dirty dishes while she worked. She wanted everything neat and tidy. So part of her discipline was only using one coffee mug and washing it before she used it again. No way that the dishes could pile up if you only used one set.

Even though no one else was there, she felt herself flush as she took the mug out of the cupboard. Not being able to find her coffee cup felt like a personal failure. She remembered losing things when she was young. How humiliated she would feel when Erica got after her for not being able to take care of her things. She was so flighty and disorganized. She remembered how things would just disappear and she would have no idea where they had gone or how she had lost them. Clothes, library books, homework assignments, her toothbrush, her key… She couldn't understand how Lydia always knew exactly where she had left things, yet when Vanna put something down, it was like it slithered away. She took to carrying everything that was really important to her in her pockets. They bulged uncomfortably and made it almost impossible to sit down, but at least she knew where everything was and they couldn't just slip away from her.

She had worked so hard to become organized. To have a place for everything. To follow checklists and procedures until she could complete things without getting distracted. She tried to be mindful every time she put down her cup or her keys or anything else that could go astray, putting it in its place so that she would be able to find it again. The fact that her cup seemed to have wandered right out of the apartment was terribly disconcerting.

The phone rang and Vanna looked around, disoriented, suddenly unsure where she had left that too. She followed the ring and found it on the floor next to the bed, where she had laid it down when she looked under the bed for any sign of the missing coffee cup.

"You're losing your mind, Vanna," she said under her breath.

It was Lydia's number, so she answered it, even though she was still feeling muddled and upset by the loss of the cup.

"Hi."

"Hey, Van. You know it's John Paul's birthday next week

and he's kind of decided last minute that we should get some friends together to celebrate…"

"Do you need someone to babysit?"

Lydia laughed. "No! We wanted you to come along. Would you?"

"Oh. Sure, of course. When and where? How big is this little group of friends going to be?"

"Mom has booked us a dining room at the Club, so it's no fuss, no muss. We'll just get together, have a good dinner and a few drinks and sing 'For He's a Jolly Good Fellow'. Then we're done for another year."

"Okay."

As they talked, Vanna noted the time on her calendar and double-checked that it was entered into the right week.

"Yeah, I can make that. Cocktail gown? Is there anything that John Paul wants?"

"Yes to the dress and no to a present. You don't need to bring anything. Just yourself."

"I've got it down. Sounds like fun!"

"Great, I'll see you there. And maybe sometime before that, too." Lydia sounded like she was winding up and then stopped. "Is everything okay with you? We haven't talked for a couple of days and I just wanted to make sure…"

"Sure." Vanna tried to convince herself that everything was okay too. "Everything is great."

"Did you sort things out with your birth mom? Did she take the hint?"

"Taking a hint is something that she is not good at," Vanna said ruefully. "I had to be pretty… assertive… and she still called me again. I hope that's the end of it…"

"What are you going to do if she doesn't stop?"

"I don't know. What can I do? Get her calls blocked, I suppose. But I don't want to hurt her. She gets so upset."

"There has to be something wrong with her, don't you

think? A normal person can understand when you tell them you don't want them to contact you anymore."

"I don't know." Vanna thought about Tino. He couldn't take no for an answer either. Maybe Vanna was just expecting too much. She wasn't being clear enough. It was her fault for continuing to answer the phone. That sent a mixed message. "She seems normal… but… I just don't know."

"Trust me," Lydia said. Her voice was far more sure than Vanna felt. "A normal person gets it when you say you don't want them to contact you anymore."

Chapter Eight

The party for John Paul was a lot of fun. As Lydia had said, with planning it for the club, there was no fuss and no muss, they could just enjoy the company without having to deal with logistics. Everyone had been cheerful and relaxed. John Paul told jokes and talked about the mischief he'd constantly gotten into as a child.

"At least Christopher and Paul come by it naturally," Vanna observed.

John Paul nodded, looking at his wife. "There really can't be any question that they're my children," he said dryly. "They do take after me…"

"I should have spoken to your mother before we decided to have children," Lydia said, nodding.

John Paul flushed a little pink.

"Who's got them tonight?" Vanna questioned. "Not Mom, I hope?"

"You know I wouldn't do that to her. I hired a girl down the street from us. Not a young girl… experienced enough to call us if the house is on fire…"

Vanna smiled at the warm memories of the evening and unlocked the door to her apartment. She kicked off her shoes immediately after stepping in the door and breathed in the warm, comforting scent of her own little space. It was all she could do to get to the bedroom before shucking off the cocktail dress and uncomfortable bra, hanging the dress in its place in the closet so that it wouldn't get wrinkled. Then she went straight to the bathroom and started the tub.

She hadn't spent much time on her feet. It hadn't been a dance. But her feet hurt and she was really looking forward to a nice soak in the tub.

———

Despite all of the dire warnings Erica had ever given her about falling asleep in the tub, Vanna found herself dozing in the soothing warmth of the bubble bath. Vanna yawned and tried to wake herself up, but it was a losing battle, and she decided she'd better get out of the tub before she drowned herself. Even getting out, she was still yawning and her eyes wanted to close as she dried herself off. She wrapped a bath sheet around herself and went back into the bedroom to get a pair of fuzzy pajamas from the dresser beside the bed.

Vanna's heart caught in her throat. The blankets had been turned back and a handful of red rose petals were strewn across the bared sheets. The air was cold on her warm, damp skin and she shivered, staring at the bed and trying to comprehend what was going on.

Someone had been in her apartment. The missing mug had been silly. She couldn't find any explanation, but assumed that it would show up in a few days in the freezer or a shoebox or some bizarre place that she had put it down. But this was differ- ent. This wasn't absentmindedness. Someone had been there. Someone had walked into her apartment and done this.

She looked around, her breathing strangled, goosebumps raised on her arm. Was he still here? Was he in the apartment even now?

There were no weapons. She didn't have a gun, a hunting knife, or even a baseball bat. The lamp by the bed was a frail, spindly little thing that would just smash to bits brought down on a hard skull. She had dropped her clutch purse with her phone in it somewhere along the way to the bathtub. Not in the bedroom, apparently. Probably on the catch-all table beside the door, or on the kitchen table.

Vanna looked at the closet. The door was standing open. She wasn't going to poke around in there, but there was no one obvious, standing there watching her like a bogeyman. She tiptoed toward the door, looking back over her shoulder to make sure there was no one crouched or laying on the floor on the other side of the bed waiting for her to turn her back. There wasn't anyone there. She didn't bend down far enough to look into the dark recesses under the bed.

The bedroom door was open part way, but not far enough for her to slip through it without touching it. And she knew the hinge creaked. She should have oiled it when she had thought about it the previous day. Or the hundred other times she had thought about it in the months that she had lived there. Vanna reached out a tentative finger and pulled the door open a few more inches, trying to keep it from squeaking. But she knew it would no matter how careful she was. And it did. The long, scratchy groan filled the apartment. Mrs. Kingsley next door could probably hear it.

Vanna couldn't hear any other noise in the apartment. If there was still someone else there, they were very still. Very quiet. Waiting for her.

It was several minutes before she was able to step through that door. She kept trying to slow and quiet her breathing, but there was no way. There was so much adrenaline pumping through her system that she would never be able to settle her heart and lungs back down again.

The minutes crept by. Eventually, Vanna steeled herself to step through the door, as quiet as a mouse. She was out in the open. Anyone who was in the kitchen, living room, or entryway would be able to see her. Her eyes traveled in panicked patterns around the rooms. The apartment was empty. She started to relax. She would have to make a more thorough search, but there weren't a lot of places that a person would be able to hide. Especially a big, threatening man.

Vanna slipped over to the door and checked it. It was properly shut and locked. She reached to fasten the chain, then decided against it. Until she was absolutely sure that there was no one else in the apartment, she needed to leave herself a quick exit. Sliding around the room, she stopped by the kitchen counter and hesitated between picking up her phone or a sharp knife.

Grasping the smooth handle of the knife that she had pulled out of the butcher block, Vanna made a tour around the apartment, checking every nook and corner large enough for a person to hide in. By the time that she was satisfied she had checked everywhere a person might hide, she was shivering, her tight stomach shuddering uncontrollably.

Vanna slid the chain on the front door. She put the knife back safely into the butcher block. She picked up her phone and started to dial, but stopped after two digits. She already knew who it was. Who else could get into the apartment? Who else would want to? The rose petals were his mark. His claim on her.

After their last fight, Vanna had demanded Tino's key back. He had thrown it away angrily. Out into the street. She hadn't seen where it landed. But he might have seen and he might have gone back to retrieve it afterward.

The chain would keep her safe overnight and she would get the lock rekeyed in the morning. Then he couldn't get in with the old key. If she went to the police, it would just escalate things further. Tino would be more angry and more upset that she wouldn't get back together with him. Even if he were arrested, they would let him go in a day or two. And then she would be just as vulnerable and he would be angrier. She wasn't about to make things worse.

———

At first, Vanna slipped into bed—after brushing the rose petals off the sheets—with her bath towel still on, too cold to take it off in order to get dressed. She shivered under the covers for a long time, listening to every creak and thump of the building around her. But eventually she warmed up enough to throw the covers back off and jump into her cozy PJ's. The pajamas were thick enough that she couldn't feel the damp spot she had left in the bed. She left the towel on the floor. She didn't turn off the light shining in the bathroom, but she turned off the bedside lamp.

Then she lay there, knowing that she wouldn't be able to sleep. She was in a strange place between being keyed up and being exhausted by the whole thing, after a full day of work and John Paul's party. Her brain was doing strange things, trying to shut down from exhaustion and overstimulation, but hyper-vigilant at the same time. It made her even more sensitive to the sounds around her, but she felt paralyzed, unable to do something with her fear. She wondered if half of the noises were even real, or if they were just hallucinations produced by her feverishly busy mind.

She lay for long hours, rigidly awaiting the breaking dawn.

Chapter Nine

In the morning, Vanna took stock. Yes, someone had been in her apartment but she knew who it was. No one but Tino would have a key. Or the building manager, in case of emergency, but he had no motive to sprinkle flower petals on her bed. Or to take her coffee cup. Though Vanna wasn't sure why Tino would want that either, except maybe to needle her. He'd always laughed at her using the same cup all day, day in and out, refusing to let any dishes pile up.

Yes, she knew who had been there. And he had no intention of hurting her. She wasn't in any kind of danger. Once she changed the lock, he wouldn't be able to get in again. She would quickly put a stop to any further visits.

Vanna wanted to call Lydia to tell her what had happened, but she was too embarrassed. Lydia thought that Tino was out of Vanna's life. That Vanna had kicked him to the curb. She didn't want Lydia panicking, thinking that Vanna was in some kind of danger. Or for her to take the opposite view, thinking that Vanna was overreacting over a schoolboy prank.

She made herself a cup of coffee and sat down at the kitchen table staring into it. In the light of day, her panic of the night before all seemed a little silly. She pictured herself creeping around the apartment, wrapped in a towel, knife in hand. What was she going to do? Would she really use it against an intruder? Especially if the intruder was Tino?

There was no menacing stranger. There was only Tino. And Vanna could handle him.

————

It was another gloomy, dismal day. She always said that she liked the rain and she liked the storms. Birchdale was the perfect place for her to live. But some days, it was too much even for her. She made sure that her laptop bag was properly shut before dashing out into the rain.

There was a letter from Julia in the mail. Vanna hardly cared. She shoved the envelope into her purse and headed to the car. The locksmith could not get to her until the afternoon, and she felt exposed waiting for him. Even though she had told herself that it was only Tino and he wouldn't hurt her, she still couldn't bear to sit there, working at the computer with her back to the door. She had her laptop and could work almost as well from the nearby coffee shop.

She had a lot of work to do and she had to be able to focus on it. She couldn't do that worrying about the locked and chained door behind her back.

————

When she got back to her apartment and was waiting as the locksmith rekeyed the lock, she remembered the letter from Julia and pulled it out. She thought maybe she should just mark it 'return to sender' and stick it back in the mail, but she was curious. Would this finally be a goodbye from Julia, a promise not to contact her again? She knew that it was unlikely, considering her experience with Julia, but she hoped that finally Julia would understand her need for freedom.

She knew that it wouldn't be a goodbye letter. But she opened it anyway.

It was five pages, front and back. Vanna sighed and scanned over it. More tears over missing Vanna's childhood. Begging for another face-to-face visit. The usual.

She looked up from the letter and watched the locksmith work on the door. At least she would be safe. There wouldn't be anyone else creeping into her apartment.

———

When Vanna walked by the mailbox, she saw that there was something else in her slot. She frowned looking at it. Had she picked up the previous day's mail rather than that day's delivery? She was sure she hadn't, but that was the only explanation she could think of. The mail was only delivered once a day.

She unlocked the mailbox and removed the package. It wasn't a letter, but something larger. Bulkier. It was very light, though. Vanna inspected it. It wasn't a parcel. It hadn't been sent in the mail. There was no address, no stamp. Just a brown paper bag. Vanna unrolled the top and peered inside.

She had been worried about what it might have been. But it was nothing. It was a small teddy bear. Just another unwanted gift from Tino. How he had managed to get it into her mailbox, she had no idea. He had never had a key to the box. Maybe he had bribed the postman.

The bear was cute, but she couldn't let him worm his way back into her good graces. This wasn't about flowers or teddy bears or romantic gestures. It was about Tino's behavior the rest of the time. It was about him not being able to keep from raging. She had to protect herself.

She stuffed the teddy bear into her purse. She would have to call Tino about it later. Unless that was what he wanted. Sending her flowers, stealing her mug, breaking into her apartment, sending her a teddy bear… all actions designed to get her to reach out to him, either in anger or romantically.

She couldn't call him because that was exactly what he wanted her to do.

———

It was still galling that she had to use a different coffee cup. Even as she settled down to relax before bed, wrapping her hands around the outside of the warm mug, she scowled. It might be part of the set and look exactly the same as the missing coffee cup, but *she* knew it was a different one and it irritated her.

The phone rang. She looked over at it, hoping it would be Lydia. But it was Tino. She snatched the phone up and answered the call.

"You need to leave me alone!" she snapped. "Stop calling me, stop coming over here and messing with my stuff and stop sending me things! It's not cute or romantic, it's creepy. Just stop it!"

There was silence for a moment while he considered her outburst. "Have you been drinking?" he asked finally.

"Have I been drinking? No! I just want you to leave me be!"

"All I did was call," he protested. "I was going to tell you how my group was going."

"You break into my apartment and take things and then turn around and send me a teddy bear? I told you I don't want any involvement with you. If you keep it up, I'm going to call the police."

"Someone broke into your apartment? Are you okay, Van?"

"*You* broke into my apartment. Don't act all innocent about it, because I know it was you."

"I would never do that. I swear it wasn't me."

"Who else would come into my apartment and leave rose petals on the bed?" Vanna demanded. "That wasn't just some random burglar or guy off the street. You are the only person who would do that!"

"I—Vanna, I swear, it wasn't me. What did he take?"

"You know what you took," she said firmly. "So just stay away from me and my place. Don't send me anything or call me!"

"But, babe—"

Vanna ended the call.

Chapter Ten

S he felt better after blowing up at Tino. At least for a while. Then she started to feel bad about it. All of the times that she had gotten after him for not being able to control his temper and here she was screeching like a banshee at him. She wasn't a very good example of maturity and self-control.

He really had sounded sincere when he said that he wasn't the one who had broken into her apartment or sent her the teddy bear. He had sounded surprised and concerned. But she knew that it was him. She wondered, not for the first time, if there was something really wrong with him. Was he psychotic, that he could lie to her so convincingly? Or maybe he really didn't remember what he had done, due to some kind of schizophrenia or Multiple Personality Disorder, or other mental illness. She knew childhood abuse could lead to multiple personalities, and she really had no idea as to the extent of the abuse he might have suffered as a child. Even having known him all these years, maybe there was still something lurking beneath the surface that she had never encountered. Something that was worse than the rages, because it was buried.

She got up and checked the door. The chain was on. The

locksmith had rekeyed it, so Tino couldn't get in using his old key. She had her phone if anyone came to the door. She could call the police.

But that didn't make her feel better. Nothing that she had done so far had helped. He had come into her apartment. Touched her things. It felt like he was in control of her life instead of her.

The phone rang again, making her jump. She looked down at it. This time, it was Lydia. It was after nine, so the kids would be in bed and they could have a quiet, uninterrupted chat. But Vanna didn't know what to say to her. She was embarrassed about how things were spinning out of control. She wanted to be strong and grown up, not to sound like a little girl who needed help and wasn't old enough or mature enough to be living on her own.

She almost let the call go to voicemail, worried about what she was going to say before she finally pressed the green button to answer the call.

"Vanna, are you okay?" Lydia's tone was worried. "Were you in the bath or something?"

"No… it just took me a minute to get to it. How are you?"

"Great. John Paul had such a great time at the party. I wanted to thank you for coming."

"It was really nice," Vanna agreed. The party seemed so long ago now. It was hard to believe that it had just been the previous evening. So much had happened since then. "I'm glad that he enjoyed himself."

"It's too bad that we can't enjoy our birthdays as much as our men do. Always too worried about getting older!"

"Yeah!" Vanna summoned a little laugh. She knew that Lydia worried a lot about wrinkles and gray hair, but they were really too young to start worrying about the big birthdays. Leave that to Erica and her peers.

"Vanny…?" Lydia's voice was concerned.

"I'm fine," she said immediately.

"Are you sick? Is something wrong?"

Vanna shook her head. "No, Lydia. Just feeling a little… I don't know."

"You sound down. Good thing I called! You want to talk about it?"

"No. I should just get to sleep. I didn't get much last night."

"Was it because of the party? Did we keep you up too late?"

"No. I don't want to talk about it right now."

"I'm going to pry it out of you. Do you want to go to the park tomorrow? We'll let the kids wear themselves out and you can tell me all about it."

"No. I should just go to bed."

"You're not going to bed, though, are you? Is it… Tino?"

"Lydia!" Vanna groaned.

"Is it? Is that it? What did he do this time? I thought you were getting rid of him."

"I am. I did. We're not together."

"What did he do?"

"He *says* he didn't do anything."

"Well, of course he says he didn't. But what did he do?"

"I don't have any proof."

"Tell me!" Lydia insisted, her voice taking on that 'mother' tone.

Vanna related the story of her return to the apartment the night before. Lydia made sounds of horror throughout, giving a little shriek at the end. "Vanna, you didn't report him to the police? You have to! This guy could be planning to kill you in your sleep!"

"Tino would never do anything like that," Vanna disagreed. "He would never try to hurt me."

"He *has* hurt you."

"Not planned, premeditated. Only when he's lost his temper. That's different. He'd never do something like that."

"You don't know. You have no way of knowing what's going

on in that sick brain of his. Vanny, you have to call the police. Get some protection."

"I can't prove anything. Someone came into my apartment. But I don't know who. I had the locks changed and the chain is on. I'll be fine."

"You know who it is. You don't need proof for them to talk to him, or come and take fingerprints, or to get a restraining order against him. Just call them."

"It's too late now," Vanna said, shaking her head.

"It's not too late. They're on shift all night. Call them and have someone come out to look at things."

"No, I mean it's too late to report it. If I were going to, then I should have last night. There's nothing to investigate today."

"Sure there is. It doesn't matter if it was yesterday. They investigate crimes that happened years ago."

"I just don't want to talk to them about it. I don't want to talk to anyone about it."

"Vanna… you don't know what Tino could be planning. This is really dangerous."

"He's not planning anything, he's just trying to be romantic and get me back. Like with the teddy bear."

"The teddy bear?"

Vanna explained about finding the stuffed animal in her mailbox. Lydia's voice rose several more tones. "How did he get into your locked mail slot?"

"I don't know." Vanna kneaded her tight forehead.

"He doesn't have a key to it, does he?"

"No. I never gave him one."

"You don't have a spare laying around the apartment?"

"No."

"Vanna… if he could get into your mail slot without a key, then what's stopping him from getting into your apartment?"

"I had the lock changed," Vanna protested. Then she realized that Lydia was right. How *had* he gotten into the mailbox without a key? The building manager had a spare key. But if

Tino had talked the building manager into letting him into the mailbox, what was to stop him from talking the man into letting him into Vanna's apartment? If he'd picked the lock, what was to stop him from picking the lock on the apartment door? Vanna was sure that the door had a more secure lock than the mailbox, but would that be enough to stop him? Where had he learned how to pick a lock?

"Vanna…"

"He's not coming back," Vanna assured Lydia. "Stop worrying. I've already talked to him tonight and he's not going to come by here. I told him I would call the police if he did."

"By that time, it may be too late."

"I know Tino. You're blowing this out of proportion. That's why I didn't tell you earlier, I knew that you'd get all freaked out about it."

"Have you told Mom?"

"Of course not! She'd insist on coming to pick me up and take me home. I'm staying here. You don't need to worry about me. Everything will be fine. It's just Tino showing off and I've set him straight."

"Why don't you come and stay here tonight?"

"No. I need to sleep in my own bed. I won't sleep well anywhere else and I need… I need to prove that I'm not afraid."

"*Are* you?"

"No. I'm perfectly fine here. All it would take is a scream and Mrs. Kingsley would have the police and half the building in here in five minutes. Honestly. I'm fine."

"I can't change your mind?" Lydia wheedled.

"No."

"If you decide you need to… just come over, okay? Even if it's the middle of the night, just come over and we'll put you in the baby's room. There's still a bed in there. Please tell me you will."

"I don't need to. But if I do, I'll come over."

"Okay. You be careful, okay? I love you."

"You too," Vanna said. "We'll talk tomorrow, okay?"

"Okay."

Vanna hung up. She hung onto her phone for a long time. She looked at the door, checking again that it was bolted and chained.

"I'm fine," she repeated aloud. "There's nothing to be afraid of."

———

It was a restless night. Vanna stayed up late, even though she was tired, knowing that she was going to be tossing and turning as soon as she went to bed. She hoped that if she waited long enough, she would be able to fall into bed and go to sleep. But she knew she wouldn't.

The sheets were too warm. The bed was too soft. Her brain wouldn't stop listening for footsteps inside the apartment. She wasn't afraid of Tino. She'd never been afraid of him except when he was angry. She knew that any other time, he wouldn't do anything to hurt her, just like she had told Lydia.

When gray morning light started to seep in through the blinds, she was still lying awake. There had been a few intervals during which she had dozed off, falling into restless nightmares of wolves stalking her in the woods. Not very restful.

Vanna knew there was no point in staying in bed, she would just get grumpier and more tired. She dragged herself out of bed and started the coffee maker. Usually, while it was brewing, she tidied up and made some breakfast, but today she just stood and watched it, with no energy to do anything else. She had two cups of coffee and no breakfast then packed up her laptop and headed back out to the coffee shop. She locked her apartment door behind her and did not look in her letter slot.

The coffee shop was already busy, which was good because she felt safer with people around her. She bought a mega cup and settled down in her favorite corner. She had just logged into her laptop and email when her phone started to buzz.

It was Julia.

Vanna let it go to voicemail.

Another call came through. Still Julia. Vanna ignored it and skimmed through her inbox. At least she hadn't had any more trouble accessing her online accounts. The phone started vibrating yet again. Vanna sighed and let it go through to voicemail once more. Her phone flashed a message that voicemail was full. Vanna swiped over to voicemail and saw that her voicemail box had been filled overnight with messages from Julia. Vanna didn't have time to check one of the messages before the phone started to buzz again. Julia again, of course. Vanna swore under her breath and answered it.

"Hello?"

"Well, it's about time!" Julia exploded.

"I've asked you not to call me."

"Didn't you get my messages?"

"No. My phone was on 'do not disturb' so that I can sleep at night and not be woken up by calls."

"What if it's an emergency?"

"Is it?"

"I needed to reach you and I couldn't. I thought something had happened to you!"

"I'm fine," Vanna said. "But I don't want to deal with these calls. I have work to do. And at night I need to sleep. Can't you respect that I don't want you to call?"

"I'm your mother, I can't help worrying about you. Are you sleeping?"

Vanna paused as she raised her coffee cup to her mouth. There was something more behind Julia's words. Why would Julia doubt that Vanna was getting enough sleep? Was Julia just assuming, like Tino would, that because Vanna hadn't answered her phone, she'd been off doing something else? Vanna sipped her coffee. She wasn't going to be able to stay on the phone with

Julia for much longer. The first two cups of coffee were making their way through her system at a lightning pace.

"I haven't been sleeping very well," she said cautiously.

"You see? I knew something was wrong. Are you sick? Maybe you should try some chicken noodle soup."

"Yeah, maybe I'll get some for lunch."

"You look so tired."

Vanna went rigid, her anxiety level shooting from sneaking suspicion to full-blown panic. She looked around the cafe, searching for Julia's face. Where was she? Inside? Outside? The place was so crowded. The small, blond woman could be behind a hundred other people milling around talking, lining up for their javas, browsing over donut flavors. Vanna stood up, looking for her.

"Where are you?" she demanded.

Julia didn't answer. Half the women in the place had phones up to their ears. Vanna thought she spotted Julia on the sidewalk outside the coffee shop and pushed her way through the crowd to get to her. She knew an instant before she grabbed the woman's shoulder from behind that it wasn't Julia. The woman turned, looking at Vanna with a questioning frown.

"Sorry. Thought you were someone else," Vanna muttered. She turned around and looked into the coffee shop. She had left her bag and her computer unattended at the table. She stepped back through the door and found herself nose-to-nose with Julia. "What are you doing here?" Vanna pulled the phone away from her ear and slid it into her pocket. "Are you following me?"

"You wouldn't answer your phone," Julia reminded her. "I thought something had happened to you. I thought you were in danger."

"Why would I be in danger?" Julia couldn't know about the trouble with Tino—unless she had been watching Vanna.

"I'm your mother," Julia repeated the refrain that had become an increasingly dominant part of her vocabulary since they had started speaking to each other. "I just… have a sense of these things. I thought… that you might be in trouble." She put her hand on Vanna's arm.

Vanna pulled back. "Don't touch me."

"You can't talk that way to me! I love you."

"Stay away from me."

The conversations around them were gradually quieting and dropping off as more people listened to what was going on. They kept their eyes away, but raised eyebrows at each other, indicated Vanna and Julia with little nods, and listened instead of talking.

"I won't stay away from you," Julia asserted.

"I'll call the police."

"For what? I haven't done anything. What would you tell them?"

"You've been following me. Stalking me. You have to stop."

"They won't believe you."

"You have to stay away from me," Vanna said, aware that her voice was rising to an angry yell.

"No, I don't. I'm your mother and—"

"You're not my mother!" Vanna shouted, so loud that it hurt her throat.

The coffee shop went silent. A couple of employees started to make their way through the crowds toward the source of the disruption. Vanna was distracted by them only momentarily, but before she finished turning her eyes back toward Julia, she took what felt like a hammer to the face.

In an instant Vanna was on the floor, tears flooding down her cheeks, her nose running or bleeding. Her head was spinning and she couldn't see for the dazzle of what seemed to be sunlight straight in her eyes. But it had been overcast, gloomy, only moments before.

"Are you okay? Ma'am? Are you all right?"

Vanna gasped for breath. "What happened? Where did she go?"

"The other woman took off. She's gone. Are you okay?"

Vanna felt for the place on her cheek that was throbbing. Julia packed a punch harder than Tino's. Or maybe it was just because Vanna hadn't seen it coming, hadn't been able to brace or turn aside. She dabbed at her nose with the back of her hand and tried to see if it was bleeding. Her eyes were trying to resolve, to piece together all of the information around her, but so far all she could see was white light and dark blotches. She thought the dark blotches might be people.

"We've called the police. You should just sit there…"

Vanna hadn't even considered getting up. She blinked a couple of times. Her eyes adjusted a little better to her surroundings. She could see, but it still seemed inexplicably bright inside the coffee house. Vanna squinted and looked around. She realized there was an empty cup in her hand and looked down at herself, realizing she'd just gotten a coffee shower.

"I must look like a mess," she mumbled.

"You took a pretty nasty punch. How are you feeling?"

"Like I got hit with a two-by-four. Was that her fist?"

There was a chuckle nearby. Lots of whispers. People probably hadn't planned on getting this much entertainment with their coffee.

Vanna was embarrassed. "Can I—can you help me up? I'll sit on a chair… over at my table… not here."

"I don't know if you should move around. You should probably wait until EMS gets here."

"I got hit in the face, not run over by a car," Vanna pointed out. "Help me up."

The Good Samaritan obligingly took Vanna's arm and helped to lift and steady her as she got to her feet. "There… now just wait for a minute before you try to go anywhere. Make sure you've got your balance…"

"I'm okay. Just help me over to my table." She squinted

around, trying to get oriented. "Over there, I think. Do you see my computer? My bag?"

"Is your bag made of... neckties?"

"Yes," Vanna giggled. "That's the one."

"It's very nice. Come on then, one step at a time..."

Vanna's steps were wobbly. Her knees were shaking like jelly. Then he helped lower Vanna into her chair. He drew another chair over and sat close to her, watching to make sure that she didn't topple over.

There were sirens, starting off faint in the distance and growing louder and louder until both a police car and an ambulance pulled up in front of the coffee house. The police came in first, looking around with sharp eyes, alert for any danger that might still be there. They made their way over to Vanna and her rescuer.

"Ma'am. Are you okay?"

Vanna nodded, but it sent her head whirling and she decided she'd better not try that again. "Yes, I'm okay. It was only one punch, but man, she packs a mean punch!" Vanna laughed weakly.

"Certainly looks like it," the woman officer said, stepping forward and shining her flashlight in several angles around Vanna's throbbing cheek. "Do you know the person who did this?"

"Yes. Her name is Julia Cortez."

"Do you know where to find her?"

"I have her number on my phone. Her address at my apartment, it's not far..."

"If you can give me what information you have..."

"You want to tell us what the fight was about?" questioned the male cop, towering over Vanna. He was young and his police utility belt sat on a surprisingly narrow waist. He was probably close to Vanna in age, but he acted like he didn't even really see her.

"She's been... she followed me here... I told her that I

didn't want her to call me or contact me anymore, but she wouldn't stop. And she followed me here, we had a confrontation… and she punched me."

"Did you have physical contact with her at any time?"

"No…" Vanna replayed the scene in her head. It had all happened so fast that she wasn't sure how accurate her recollection was. "She put her hand on my arm… I told her not to touch me… and she punched me. I didn't push her or hit her. I just… yelled at her." Vanna felt her face flush at the admission. At least with her complexion the blush wouldn't be obvious.

"Why is she following you?"

Vanna bit her lip. "Well, she's… she's my birthmother. She wants to have contact, but I don't."

The young cop raised his brow as he wrote this down. Obviously, that wasn't one of the usual causes of assault. "And how long has this been going on? Have you reported her previously? Taken out a restraining order?"

"No. It's been a few weeks… but I really didn't think I had any reason for a restraining order. I thought that if I just made it clear that I didn't want her to contact me anymore, that she would be reasonable… I kept hoping that she'd just give up." Vanna looked down at her phone, thumbing her way over to the missed calls and voicemails. Her eyes were blurring and she didn't want to cry in front of the policemen. The EMTs were moving into the coffee shop now, making their way through the still-gawking crowds.

"We're going to need to examine the victim for a few minutes," a tall, thin young man instructed, nudging the cops to the side. Vanna reached out and handed her phone to the policeman who had been questioning her.

"That's her number," she said.

He looked at the screen and wrote it down. Without asking, he tapped and swiped a few times. "And with this volume of calls, you thought she would be reasonable?" he inquired.

"Well, yes… I hoped she would. I thought it would wear off, that she'd just get bored or decide it wasn't worth it."

"But you were still answering calls from her."

"Not all of them. Just… I was annoyed at the phone ringing all the time."

"Contact your phone service provider for instructions on how to block her number. We'll follow up with her, charge her with assault, warn her not to contact you anymore. You should get a restraining order against her."

"Yes, I guess so."

"She knows where you live?"

"Yes. She sent me letters. Followed me here."

"Has she come to your door? Been hanging around the building at all? Any vandalism or anything else that we should know about?"

Vanna watched the finger of the EMT who was examining her. He moved it side to side, up and down, in and out, and had her close her eyes and touch her nose, which was surprisingly more difficult than she expected it to be.

"Well, I don't know…" she said to the policeman. "I've… been having some problems… but I thought it was Tino, my ex-boyfriend. I didn't think…"

"What kind of problems?"

"Somebody broke into my apartment. Well, not broke. Somehow got into my apartment when I was out. Took things. Left rose petals on the bed."

"That does sound more like a romantic overture," he agreed. "Maybe you'd better take out two restraining orders. Did either of them have keys to your apartment?"

"Tino did. I've changed the lock now."

"I'll need his full name and contact information. We'll need to follow up with him. See if he'll admit to being the one who broke into the apartment or not."

"You'll… be discreet?" The paramedic was poking and prodding Vanna's face and head. She winced and drew back. "I don't want him to think that I sent you. I don't want him… to be mad at me."

The young cop studied her expression. "Does he have a history of violence?"

"He—he does have a temper."

"Definitely take a protective order out against him, too. We'll be as discreet as we can, but he's going to know that it's about you. It will be easier to keep him away from you if there's a court order. Otherwise, we're just making empty threats."

"I'll think about it," Vanna said, looking down.

He handed the phone back to her. The EMT handed her an ice pack. Vanna juggled the phone into her pocket and held the ice pack to her face. The cold bit her skin, but it quickly soothed the pounding.

"I don't think you need to go to the hospital, but you should keep ice on that and take a couple of Aspirin. If you have a lot of dizziness or throw up, go ahead and have the emergency room do some testing for you. I think you'll be okay if you just rest for a few days, take care of yourself. Can you do that?"

"Yeah, sure. I will."

"All right. No need to incur any extra expenses, then."

He closed his kit again. The policeman took down Tino's contact information. When he asked for Tino's employer, Vanna shook her head. "No. You can't go to his work. That would be really bad. You'll have to contact him outside of business hours. He does some private work on the side, but he can take time away from that."

"If he's breaking into your apartment, it might be a good idea to throw a scare into him. Let him see how he's going to be treated if his employer or coworkers hear what he's been up to."

"No. No, I can't do that to him."

"Be careful. Can we drive you home?"

"Oh no, I can walk."

The woman cop, who had mostly remained silent and just

listened to the interview, immediately shook her head. "No, I think we'd better drive you. Come on."

Vanna looked for a way out of it, but the woman had obviously made up her mind. "You're in no shape to be walking even a block. So let us take you."

Vanna gave in and they helped her out to the police car.

There was a knock on the door. A persistent knock. Whoever it was would not just give up and go away. Vanna dragged herself out of bed and went to see who it was. Her head was spinning and she felt nauseated. It had not been a fun day and she had spent most of it passed out in bed, due to the combination of lack of sleep for the last couple of nights and the slight concussion from Julia hitting her. She didn't feel any better for having slept. The knocking on the door sliced into her head like a knife.

"Who is it?" Vanna demanded through the door, not even bothering to try to squint through the peephole. It was hard enough to see through at the best of times. With her current level of pain and nausea, there was no way she was even going to try.

"Tino."

"Tino!" Vanna leaned against the door. "What do you want? You're not supposed to be here."

"I need to talk to you, Van. I'm worried. Won't you let me come in?"

"No. Didn't the police come and talk to you?"

"Yes, they did… which is why I am even more worried than before. You need someone to protect you, Vanna. Let me in."

"No."

"You haven't filed a restraining order against me."

"No," Vanna admitted, "but that doesn't mean that I have to let you into my house."

"I think you didn't take out a restraining order because you know it wasn't me. You know you don't have to be afraid of me."

"You've hit me more times than she has."

His volume immediately dropped. "I'm not here to hurt you. I'm concerned. Come on, Van. All of your neighbors are listening to our conversation because I have to yell through the door. Just let me in."

Vanna really didn't want the whole building hearing about all of her troubles. She leaned there against the wall for a minute before finally sliding the chain off and turning the bolt to unlock it. She didn't open the door. After a minute, the door opened and Tino poked his head in, looking confused.

"Babe—?" He saw Vanna drooping against the wall and without hesitation, scooped her up in his arms.

Vanna tensed. "Put me down!" she insisted. "You can't do that!"

"I'll put you down where you won't fall down," Tino said, his long stride quickly eating up the living room before she could squirm away from him. He reached the side of the bed and transferred her to the bed as gently as possible.

"You're a mess! You look like you haven't slept in a week."

"Only a few days."

"Why didn't you call me? I could have come to help you. You need to take care of yourself."

Vanna let her eyes close, just swimming in the pain and nausea for a few seconds, wishing that she could just pass out and he wouldn't call anybody about it. But she knew that wasn't going to happen. "I didn't call you," she said, keeping her eyes closed, "because I thought that you were the one who was doing it."

"I told you I didn't. I never broke into your apartment. I didn't send you a teddy bear. Just flowers."

"The roses?"

"Yes… were there other flowers?"

"Yeah. Mums. And then rose petals on the bed."

"Romantic," Tino grunted, sitting on the side of the bed and making it sink down several inches. "You should have known that wasn't me."

Vanna laughed. "Yeah. I should know that."

Tino stroked her hair. She's always liked the way that he played with her hair. She loved the physical affection.

"Why don't you just tell this woman to take a hike?"

"The way I told you?" Vanna questioned.

"Well… yes, why not?"

"Did you stay away?"

"No, but…"

"Neither did she. And like I said. I thought it was you."

"The police will take care of it," he assured her.

"No," Vanna said. She wanted to shake her head for emphasis, but it would hurt too much.

"No? They talked to me. Why wouldn't they talk to her?"

"Because she doesn't exist," Vanna sighed.

Tino stopped patting her hair. "How bad is your concussion?"

"The cell phone number that I had for her was a throw-away. A burner phone, they called it. She registered it using a false ID. And after she hit me she ditched it. A few blocks away. They tracked it by GPS and found it in a garbage bin."

"Oh. They must have some other way to find her. They're cops."

"No luck. She's not showing up on their searches. As far as they're concerned, Julia Cortez doesn't exist."

"She's been sending you mail."

"The address doesn't belong to her. They went to the house, they even went in and looked around. The people there don't know her."

"But you wrote her back, right? You sent her mail back at that address, didn't you?"

Vanna had asked the police officers the same thing. They explained to her how it was done and she told Tino.

"Their mail is delivered to a mailbox outside the house, at the curb. You know, like the old style ones. Just a box, no lock. It's delivered at the same time every day, when the house owners are at work. So all she would have to do is go by during the day and check the box for anything that I sent her. No way to trace her. All they could do is watch to see if she shows up to get it. They don't have the resources to do that. Another dead end."

Tino was silent. Vanna opened her eyes to look at him. He gazed down at her, shaking his head. "But that's just… bizarre. Why would she…? What is she hiding?"

"I don't know."

"I'll stay with you tonight. Make sure that you're safe."

"No, Tino." Vanna moved to get up, to show him that she wasn't helpless and didn't need his help.

"Stay put. I'm not going to try anything. I'll sleep on the couch if you want. I have to make sure you're safe tonight."

Vanna didn't know what to say. She didn't want to be alone, but she knew that she couldn't let Tino back into her life. Tonight sleeping on the couch. Tomorrow, back in her bed. And after too many Friday night drinks…

"No. You have to go."

"She could come back here. You don't know."

"I'll be fine."

Tino shook his head. His eyes wandered around the room as he tried to think of some other way to persuade her to let him stay. He leaned over and picked up a photograph from her side table. His eyes went wide and he looked back at Vanna.

"Is this her? Is this who you are talking about?"

Vanna looked at the photo in his hand. Julia had finally reciprocated with a picture of herself. "Yes. That's Julia."

"But she doesn't look like you. There's no resemblance."

"I know she doesn't. But that's her. That's Julia."

He was frowning.

"Why?" Vanna asked. "What is it?"

"I know this face." He pondered over it. Then the scowl

faded and was replaced with a smile. "I towed her car the other day."

"What? How did you do that?"

"It was parked on the street, around the side of this building. I put it on the hook and she came running out screaming at me. I gave her the usual spiel. She gave me three hundred to get it back."

"You scammed my birth mother?"

He laughed. "I guess I did."

Vanna's head whirled. "When was this? She was here?"

Tino considered, tilting his head slightly. "A couple of nights ago…?"

"The night my apartment was broken into?"

"Well, I'm not sure, exactly."

"What was she doing here?" Vanna mused. Then she lowered her brows at Tino. "And what were you doing here?"

He shrugged, cheeks getting a little flushed. "I've had some good success around here. I like to… go back where the fishing is good."

"So it could have been either one of you. You were both here. I thought you told the police that you had an alibi. You were at work."

He grinned. "I was working."

"I'll bet you didn't tell them that you were 'working' the street outside my building."

"No, maybe not…"

Vanna closed her eyes again, fatigue washing over her. "You'd better be getting on your way. And I mean all the way home, not on my couch."

"I can't leave you alone when you're so vulnerable."

"You have to."

Tino sighed heavily, defeated. He stood up. "If there's anything I can do for you…"

"Tino?"

"What?"

"If you towed her, does that mean that you have her license plate number? That could really help in tracking her down."

He cleared his throat. "If I actually do the tow, then I record the license plates. But I only had her on the hook…"

"Waiting to see if she would show up and pay you not to impound it."

"Right. And she did. But I can tell you what kind of vehicle she drives. That might help… at least in keeping an eye out for her."

"Yeah. What was she driving?"

"A little black car. A Sunfire, I think."

"I'll keep my eyes out for it. And I'll tell the police."

"You can't tell them that I towed her, that puts me at the scene."

"Well, I'll tell them… I don't know. I'll think of something tomorrow, but right now I can't think."

"You need sleep." He bent over and unexpectedly brushed her cheek with a kiss. "You just rest, now."

"I will."

———

Vanna sat down at her computer and started going through her inbox and sorting out the jobs. She wasn't going to be able to concentrate on much, but at least she had been able to sleep. That helped, but she still wasn't close to normal. Her cheek wasn't throbbing anymore. But it was still pretty sore and had a visible bruise.

She emailed Sylvia Hartley after looking over her latest assignment, asking for an extension. Sylvia was nice and was pretty good about deadlines. Unlike some of the others who would get angry or dump her if she didn't get their jobs done within twenty-four hours.

Sylvia emailed back almost immediately, assuring her that she didn't need the spreadsheet immediately and wishing Vanna would get better soon. Vanna started to work on the Thorpe project instead. That was one that would not wait. She just hoped that she would be able to focus on it well enough to do good work. If she sent it back complete, but the quality was bad, they wouldn't send her anything else.

———

The work day seemed to take even longer than usual. There was a backlog of work to do. Combining that with her concussion, she could barely plow through. When she closed her work for the day, what she really wanted to do was to go back to bed. That probably wasn't a good idea. She would end up napping and then not able to sleep at night. And besides that, she was out of groceries and needed to go get some food. If she was going to eat for the next few days, she had to go out.

Driving was out of the question. But she had a cart and there was a small grocery just down the street. Walking that far wasn't usually a problem, but Vanna was pooped by half way. She stopped at the bus stop to rest on the bench. She closed her eyes.

When she opened her eyes, there was a little black car creeping down the street in front of her. The sun was glaring off the windows, but Vanna could see long blond hair through the driver's window.

She sat up straight, her heart pounding. Again? The very next day? Julia didn't even have the sense to stay away for a day or two to let things settle down? Vanna stood up and tried to decide whether to go back to her apartment or on to the grocery store. It was probably the same distance both ways. And either way seemed like a long distance today. She decided that the grocery store was probably the best. It was the opposite direction from where Julia was driving so she would have to flip a U-turn, which would give Vanna another minute or two of a head-start. And there were lots of people there. Witnesses. Her apartment was far more lonely. Even if her neighbors were home, they might not jump in to help out.

Vanna moved her feet as quickly as she could, fighting against a head rush, trying to keep her balance and keep moving and to get there ahead of Julia. She wasn't sure if Julia had seen her, or if Julia knew that Vanna had seen her. But she needed to get somewhere there were other people. It hadn't stopped Julia from approaching her at the coffee shop, but Vanna guessed that meeting her alone on the street would not be a good idea.

She was still half a block from the grocery store when Julia's car nosed up beside her. Vanna ignored the car and kept hustling. Julia honked. Vanna continued to ignore her, looking determinedly toward the grocery store.

"Vanna!"

Vanna didn't look at her. She kept going. Julia was insistent.

"Vanna, I want to talk to you."

Vanna finally looked toward her. "Leave me alone. I'll call the police."

"Vanna, just let me talk to you."

"I don't even know who you are," Vanna said, still approaching the grocery store.

"I'm your mother!"

Vanna looked sideways at her.

"You're not my mother. I don't even know who you are. Show me some sort of proof that you are Julia Cortez."

"What are you talking about? You know who I am. I'm your mother."

"No, you're not."

Vanna reached the parking lot of the grocery store, breathing heavily from the exertion. She was light-headed and weak-kneed. Julia pulled into the parking lot with a screech of tires and got out of her car. Vanna hurried toward the doors of the store.

"Come back here!" Julia insisted.

Vanna grabbed at the security guard near the door. "Please help me," she begged.

The security guard looked her over, his eyes widening. "What seems to be the problem, ma'am?"

"This woman, she won't leave me alone," Vanna gestured toward Julia.

Julia stopped in her tracks, her face getting red. "What are you doing? You're reporting me?"

"Yes. I told you I would call the police. You have to leave me alone."

The guard's eyes went from one woman to the other. "What is going on?"

"She's stalking me," Vanna said. "I'm trying to get a restraining order against her, but I don't know what her real name is." She shot a glance toward Julia, daring her to show her ID or to reveal who she really was.

"I'm stalking you?" Julia repeated. "You're the one who is following me, showing up everywhere I go. If you have a restraining order, then where is it? You don't have one."

"I said that I am trying to get one," Vanna repeated. "Not that I already have one. She assaulted me yesterday, sir," she told the guard. She pointed to the bruise on her cheek. "She hit me. The police were called."

"Well, if a police report has already been made, there's nothing more I can do to help you there. And if you don't have a restraining order, then I can't insist that this woman leave the store. There's really nothing that I can do."

"I don't want her near me."

"Ma'am," the guard looked at Julia. "The two of you need to stay away from each other. Just give each other some space."

"I would be happy to," Julia said. "But she keeps showing up in the places that I want to go to. Do you really think that I would hit her in the face like that? Do I look like a violent person?"

Vanna had to admit that Julia was very good at looking

innocent. She herself could hardly believe that this slim, petite blond had been able to knock her down like that. She was not what she looked like.

"Don't believe her," she said. "She's just pulling a fast one on you. You can't judge a book by its cover."

The guard looked from one to the other. It seemed like he was leaning more toward believing Julia, which burned Vanna up. She had seen this before. She had noticed the pattern while growing up with Lydia. Lydia, with her white skin and blond hair always got away with things that Vanna couldn't. If the two of them were having a disagreement over something, it was always Lydia that people would believe. At first, Vanna had thought it was just because Lydia was older, or a more convincing liar. But she had come to realize, over the years, that it was Vanna's darker skin that they didn't trust. They were conditioned to believe the pretty blond girl and distrust the Latino.

"I'm the one with a mark on my face," she pointed out, gesturing to her cheek again. "She did that. I didn't do that to myself. She is stalking me and I'm not safe while she's here."

"Maybe you should go home, then," he suggested.

"I can't. She has a car and I don't, she'll just follow me home and attack me there."

"I'm not going to *attack* you!" Julia said in an exasperated tone. "I just want to talk to you!"

The guard raised an eyebrow and he looked at Vanna. Julia had slipped up, admitting that she was the one who wanted to see Vanna.

"Maybe you'd better go home," he told Julia.

"I am not going back home. She is the one who is stalking me."

"Then I guess I'd better call the police," the guard said. He pulled out his phone.

"Go ahead."

He stopped, hesitating for a moment. Julia's eyes flashed. The guard started to dial. Julia backed up a step.

"Don't let her go," Vanna said. "The police have to be able to question her. Find out her real identity."

"I have no authority to keep her here."

"I told you that she assaulted me. And she stalked me here."

"But you have already reported the assault to the police. I haven't seen her commit any kind of crime. I can't perform an arrest or detain her unless I have seen her commit a crime. I'm afraid that your word isn't enough."

Vanna sighed in frustration. Julia was obviously backing off, obviously getting ready to take off. That was good for Vanna. But she still wanted to be able to stop Julia permanently. And she couldn't do that without even knowing for sure who she was or where she lived.

Julia went back to her car, looking back once at Vanna with a scowl. Then she got in and drove off. Vanna sagged against the wall. The guard looked at her with concern.

"Are you okay, ma'am?"

"Yes… I'm fine."

"Do you still want me to call the police?"

"I… I don't know. She's gone now… I don't know if she'll stay away. I mean, I know she won't. But maybe she'll stay away while I'm here."

"Do you want to sit down for a minute? Come over here." He took her to a bench against the side of the building and Vanna sat down. "There, just rest and get your energy back for a few minutes. I'll keep an eye open and make sure that she doesn't come back."

"Okay. Thank you." Vanna leaned back and closed her eyes, trying to relax.

———

"Is that her again?"

Vanna opened her eyes and looked where the security guard was pointing. It was Julia's black Sunfire. "Yes. That's her."

He dialed the police without any further discussion. By the time the police got there, Julia was not to be seen. The guard did his best to describe what had happened. The police officers looked at Vanna.

"And you filed another police report yesterday?"

"Yes."

"Why don't you describe, slowly, what happened and what your relationship with this woman is."

Vanna took a deep breath. She was starting to feel more like herself, more clear-headed now that she had been sitting for a few minutes. She outlined the situation.

"She's your birth mother?"

"She *says* she is my birth mother. We're wondering now because the police that were involved yesterday couldn't find any records in that name and she was picking up her mail at someone else's mailbox."

"Did you get the car's license plate?" the officer asked the security guard.

"Only partial… sorry. It was a black Sunfire. First letters MX. That's all I got."

"If we're lucky, that might be enough."

They didn't seem inclined to do anything. Vanna wasn't sure what it was that she would want them to do anyway. Julia was gone. They couldn't arrest her. They couldn't track her down unless the license plate panned out for them. There was no immediate threat.

"Did you need many groceries?" the other officer asked.

"No… not much."

"Why don't you go get it while we note up our report? Then we can at least see that you get home safely."

Vanna felt a warm flush. "That would be really nice," she said gratefully.

"Go ahead. Can you get around all right?"

Vanna stood up and made sure that she was steady on her feet. "Yes. I'm okay. I'll just be a few minutes."

"Go ahead. We'll wait for you. Watch to see if she happens to come by again."

"I don't think she will for as long as the police car is here."

"I suspect that she's pretty close by. They tend to stick pretty close to their targets. She'll be watching to see what happens. We probably won't see her… but you never know."

Vanna nodded and went into the store. She didn't need a lot. Just enough for meals to cover the next few days. She didn't want to be going out to restaurants for a while. Maybe if she just stayed at home, Julia would give up and leave her alone.

Vanna got checked out and went back outside. The policemen were leaning up against the building, chatting casually. They had obviously finished writing up their reports. Considering the pace that it took the average policeman to write a traffic ticket, Vanna was surprised that they were done already.

"Ready to go, ma'am?"

"Yes, thanks. I really appreciate you driving me. It's not far."

"Of course. We want to be able to do something for you."

"Can you tell me… is it possible to take out a restraining order when we really don't know if she is Julia Cortez or not?"

"Sure. They'll figure out how to note it up for you. Jane Doe, known as Julia Cortez. Something like that. Don't put it off just because you don't know how they'll issue it. You'll want to have something for the next time that this happens."

They walked Vanna to their car. The woman cop got into the passenger seat and turned partway around to talk to Vanna as they drove. "We don't think that there is really a lot for you to be worried about. The way that these things play out… studies have shown that the stalkers who commit violence, particularly homicide, are generally ex-intimates. You know, an old boyfriend or girlfriend. And this woman isn't. She's probably harmless."

"But she did hit me," Vanna pointed out.

"That was probably an anomaly. She felt cornered. I think that if you just keep it low key, don't worry too much about her, the visits will probably drop off." She took off her cap to scratch her head and put it back on again. "Woman stalkers are far less likely to be violent. And like I said, where she's not an ex-girl-friend, you probably don't have to worry about her escalating."

Chapter Eleven

She had so many questions about how to get the restraining order issued, it seemed like an insurmountable task. But the policeman who had driven her home was right. She couldn't afford to be caught out without one again. She needed to be able to pull out the restraining order if Julia showed up somewhere public and have her removed. She couldn't leave it to chance, to the hope that there would always be a guard or policeman around who could help her.

The court clerks were very helpful in showing her the paperwork that she needed to fill out and where to submit it, with what fee. A court date was set and she asked Lydia if she would get a sitter that day and go to it with Vanna. Lydia was happy to do it. More than happy, she seemed quite excited about the chance to go to court and see the wheels of justice in action.

Of course, Julia didn't show up at the court hearing. Tino didn't show up at his either, though at least they had been able to properly notify him. He was surprisingly calm and reasonable about it.

"I know that you have to do this, because of that woman," he said philosophically. "But I don't want them doing it at work in front of my boss or the other guys. I want you to be safe and if you don't want me there to protect you… I can at least make sure that you get your restraining orders."

It was surprisingly decent of him. Especially when, all things considered, his restraining order wasn't in any way tied to Julia's. Vanna could easily have gotten Julia's and let Tino off the hook. But not being one hundred percent sure which of them had actually broken into her apartment and the letter slot, Vanna wanted to cover all of her bases.

When no one showed up to contest the restraining orders, the elderly judge simply shrugged and signed them, handing them to the clerk of the court to take care of the final arrangements. Vanna turned and looked at Lydia.

"That's done," she sighed. It was a huge relief. Now she could be safe.

"It's sort of anti-climactic, isn't it?" Lydia said. "I kind of expected them to both be here to dispute the charges. Lots of yelling and having to prove that what you said was true. But nobody came."

"If Julia came, she'd have to prove who she is and where she lives," Vanna pointed out. "And Tino didn't want anyone to know what was going on. He'd be worried that someone he knew would be at the courthouse and word would get back to work."

"Yeah. It's just sort of weird, though. You could say anything you wanted to about them and neither one of them was here to argue it."

The clerk of the court came over and handed Vanna her copies, all properly signed, stamped and sealed. "There you go, ma'am. If you need additional copies, you can either pay for court-certified copies or have your lawyer produce notarial copies."

"Do I need to do anything else?"

"The final orders need to be served. You don't have a name or address for Jane Doe?"

"No… the police are still working on it, but haven't been able to identify her…"

"As soon as they make any identification, it will need to be served on her. Because of the nature of the complaint—there has already been violence or attempted violence—the court will attempt to serve it at no cost to you, but we can't do that without a name or address."

Vanna nodded. "I'll let you know if we find out."

"And this one you can have a process server take care of?"

"Yes." Vanna looked down at the top of the table. He didn't offer to serve that one at no cost. She hadn't listed everything in the protective order against Tino that she probably should have. She had only included the details tying him to the apartment break-in and not any previous violence. She wanted to keep Tino on her side. Putting it in the public record that he had hurt her in the past hadn't seemed like a good idea…

"Okay. This copy can be served on him."

"Thanks."

―――――

Everything was normal. Vanna tried to convince herself that her life was back to normal. She had a restraining order against Julia if she decided to show up again and cause trouble. Julia knew now that Vanna wasn't afraid to call the police and get them involved. She wouldn't risk getting caught by the police. Vanna could just go back to her life.

She had been putting off a big file management project for days, but the deadline was creeping up and she didn't want to risk losing any more clients. It was detailed, tedious work, scanning, converting and archiving hundreds of files. But she was feeling good, she was up for it. Turning off any distractions, she buckled down and focused on the mammoth task on hand.

―――――

It took a number of long hours to get the file management under control, but Vanna was pretty proud of the results in the end. Everything was neatly cataloged, tagged, and indexed so that the appropriate files could be found in no time. She was confident that Mario would be pleased with it.

She opened up the cloud account to upload the entire contents of the newly organized folder and saw that Mario's assistant had sent her a new message. She uploaded and then opened the new message while she was waiting. She stared at the contents of the message.

Two hundred more files to be integrated with the ones that she had just started to upload. Immediately. Before the end of the day. Vanna looked at the clock. She had already put six straight hours into the project. She was ready to sign off and relax for the evening. She hesitated. She could send a message back to Mario's assistant and say that she wouldn't be able to get to the new files until morning. But she hesitated to challenge the deadline. Mario could be pretty hard-nosed.

With a sigh, she started to download the new files.

———

Vanna checked her watch as she took the elevator down to the parking garage. She was running a few minutes late to meet the girls at the flea market. She would still get there in good time, but didn't want to keep anyone waiting or prevent them from finding their treasures. Treasures didn't last long, you had to be there early. But she could still make it.

As she reached the white Mazda, she pulled out her keys and searched through them for the right one. She wasn't sure why she had so many keys on her key chain. How many did a single person with just a car and an apartment need? She realized that the one her fingers had landed on was Tino's. Why hadn't she ever given him back the key to his apartment? He hadn't ever asked for it back.

She looked up and was startled to see a figure blocking her car door. Dressed in dark clothes, with a cap pulled down low and shadowing her face, it was a split-second before she realized that it was Julia. Vanna pulled out her phone to dial nine-one-one. There was no cell signal in the underground parking. Julia smiled at this.

"I just want to talk to you," she said.

"No. I don't want to talk to you. I have a restraining order. You can't get within one hundred yards of me."

"I haven't been served with it."

"You would be if you were using your own name. Who are you really and where do you live?"

"So that you can stalk me?" Julia mocked. "Where I live is my own business, not yours."

"Why would I stalk you? You're the one who has been following me!"

"I just want to talk," she said reasonably. "I think you've misunderstood. I don't want to hurt you. I never meant to hit you. I just want to talk to you. To be your friend, part of your life. I don't understand why you would want to hurt me like you did!"

"I hurt you?"

"You think your words don't hurt? That your rejection doesn't cut me to the heart? How would you like it if your own flesh and blood rejected you, refused to even talk to you? We've hardly had any time to get to know each other. If you took the time, you would like me. You'd find out how much that we have in common and how many things we could enjoy doing together. You need me, Vanna and I need you."

"I don't need you. I have done just fine without you the last twenty years. And you've survived just fine without me. I don't know why you came back, after all of this time, and why you think that I have to be part of your life. Why don't you just carry on with your own life? Start another family. One that you can take care of." Vanna felt a little twinge of guilt for suggesting this. Did she really think that bringing an innocent little child into the world for this woman's gratification was a good idea? How would she treat a child? If Erica was right, and she usually was, Vanna's first couple of years might have been pretty bad. "You don't need me," she repeated. "You are a strong, beautiful woman. You have so much potential. I think that you could succeed at anything you tried." That might be laying it on a little thick, but one thing about Julia, she had lots of persistence and a strong mind. Vanna had a good suspicion that she got pretty much everything she put her mind to.

"How could you know any of that?" Julia demanded. "You haven't taken the time to get to know me. You never ask me how I am or ask me about what I've gone through. You think that the past twenty years were a walk in a park? I have waited and waited for the day when I could come and find you. My little girl. My special daughter. The one who was ripped from my arms. Seeing you with that other woman…! Socializing with the muckety-mucks, like it makes you better than me. I know where you came from. You're not any better than me. All the money in the world couldn't make you something different."

Vanna glanced down at her useless phone. She looked at the keys in her other hand, just as useless with Julia standing right in front of her door. She only had one defense left and that was her mind. She had to out-think Julia. Out-talk her. Figure out what it was that she wanted and give it to her. Or hold it in front of her like a carrot. Something.

"So why don't you tell me," she suggested. "What have you been going through the past twenty years? What was it that happened? I can't remember what happened when I was a baby."

"You weren't a baby. You were so smart, watching everything with those big, brown eyes. You were always watching everything. I knew you were smart. I knew you knew everything that was going on around you. Understood more than any other little two-year-old could have. Oh, no, you weren't a baby."

"You thought I was smart?" Vanna was a little surprised. She had never done well at school. She was scatterbrained at home. She flitted from one thing to another and couldn't 'apply' herself. She had gone through years of therapy. There had been speech therapy in those early years that she couldn't remember. She did remember playing in the psychologist's office, but could never really understand why she had gone there. She had had tutors of all sorts, summer school, special intervention programs to try to help her with her reading, writing, and math. None of it had come easy.

"I know you were smart. The smartest little thing around. That's why I thought that you would remember me."

Vanna shook her head. "I was just too young. I'm sorry I don't remember. I have tried. You're very different than I imagined you would look when I used to try to picture my birth mother. Very… different."

Vanna shifted, looking around for help. Where was everyone else? Did everybody sleep in on a Saturday morning? Wasn't there anyone who got up for early-morning karate or something? She could really use a witness.

She tried to keep her focus on Julia's face. Was she really Julia? The cops didn't seem to think so, but Julia really did have memories of Vanna. Or she seemed to. Was she remembering someone else and had just obsessed on Vanna because of some perceived similarity? Or was she really Julia? Vanna still couldn't believe that this tiny blond could really own the name Cortez.

"You hurt me so much when you went away. I wanted to know you, to raise you. It wasn't fair that you went away. And now, when you could be my daughter again, when I could have a relationship with you again, then you turned against me. Called the police. Tried to have me arrested, thrown in jail. What kind of a daughter treats her mother that way?"

"It was just… a misunderstanding. I was scared. I didn't know how to react to you coming back. I was… I was just confused by the way that you were acting. You can understand that, can't you?"

"Everybody turned you against me." Julia's voice was a plaintive whine. "You are my daughter and they all taught you to hate me. It's not fair. I've been treated very unfairly."

"Yes. You have. And I should have understood that, but I didn't. I should have seen through it all. I'm sorry I didn't."

Julia didn't seem to be reassured. Vanna felt like everything she said just wound Julia up tighter. She couldn't seem to find the magic key that would turn Julia's reactions down instead of up.

"Could we… go for a walk? I'd like to go to the park… the playground… couldn't we go do something like that together?"

Julia seemed unsuspecting, but not assuaged. "Everybody turned you against me," she pouted.

"Didn't you ever wish you could go to the park with me? Let's go for a walk. Just you and me."

Julia turned to the car. "We could take your car," she said.

"No… there's a park that's really close by. I'd like to go there." Getting in a car with this woman would not be a good idea. An enclosed area. With a weapon, Julia could take her hostage. Maybe take her out to some lonely road on a pretext and kill her. Bury her in the woods. Beside a pretty pond some- where. Somewhere she could go back and visit whenever she wanted to talk to Vanna. No one would ever know what had happened. "I need to stretch my legs, don't you? How long have you been waiting here?"

"I suppose we could walk," Julia conceded.

Vanna motioned toward the elevator. "I'll show you where it is."

Julia moved toward her, walking away from the car. Vanna had a strong impulse to run to the car and try to get into it and drive away before Julia could stop her. But she knew that Julia was still too close and she didn't have a hope of unlocking the car and getting into it and locking the door before Julia could follow. It wasn't like she was some old senior. She was young and powerful. Trying to overcome her or to race her was impossible. The idea of outsmarting her seemed similarly impossible. She kept waiting for Julia to grab her by the arm, or to go back to the car to prevent her escape. But Julia walked with her to the elevator calmly.

Vanna wondered if she had a gun. If it were a movie, she'd have a gun. But Julia had never shown or used any weapon. Somehow, that didn't make Vanna feel any safer.

They both got into the elevator when it dinged and the door opened. Vanna pressed the ground level button and Julia didn't do anything to stop her.

Her stomach was already feeling unsteady and the jerk of the elevator threw her temporarily off-balance. She grabbed onto the railing, and Julia stared at her suspiciously, as if Vanna might be trying something. She looked back away.

"Did you used to take me to the park?" Vanna questioned.

"No."

Vanna wondered at the curt response. What mother didn't take her child to the park? But she already knew that she hadn't had a normal childhood. Julia offered no excuse or explanation. They arrived at the main floor and waited for the elevator doors to open. Vanna's phone was still in her hand, but she couldn't look at it, draw Julia's attention to it.

"This way." She led Julia down the street toward the park. Maybe she should have asked Julia to go for coffee and they could go back to the coffee house. Maybe one of the baristas would recognize them and realize that Vanna needed help. But it was too late to change her mind now.

Anxiety was eating a hole in her stomach. Vanna winced at the pain. So much for everything being back to normal now that she had a protective order.

They walked in silence. Vanna was desperately trying to come up with a topic of conversation that wouldn't set Julia off. Something that would relax her and reassure her.

"Did you send me the teddy bear?" she asked suddenly.

Julia looked at her. "Of course I did."

"Was it a teddy bear I had when I was little?"

"No. It was new. You had a teddy bear when you were little… a different one… It was a bigger one, didn't look like that. You loved that teddy bear. Did you take it with you?"

"No, I don't think so. I don't know. I had teddy bears growing up, but I don't know if I had… a special one. I'd have to ask my m—Erica."

"I thought it would make you feel better. Not so scared. Not so threatened. I know what it's like to be scared."

Vanna swallowed. "What is it that scares you?"

"I've been in places you couldn't even imagine. You'd have to be crazy not to be scared."

Vanna wasn't so sure that Julia wasn't crazy. It wasn't exactly reassuring. She looked down at her hand involuntarily. The phone was still clutched there, but she couldn't dial. Not without looking at the screen and drawing Julia's attention to it. She'd never identified it as a problem with smartphones before. Not being able to use touch to find the keys. She dialed that phone every day. Her thumb should know where the keys were instinctively. But she wasn't confident enough in being able to hit them square on without looking at the screen. Even if she tried, she was bound to look toward it, risking discovery.

"What places have you been?" she probed further.

"Is that the park up there?"

Vanna nodded. "Yeah. I come here to eat my lunch sometimes. To get a breath of fresh air. It's good to get away from work now and then and reset."

"You want to sit down?" Julia suggested, motioning to a bench.

"Yeah."

They sat. Vanna watched the playground. It was a busy little place. The only playground in the area, it was always crawling with kids until dark. Mothers sat around the perimeter, some of them with babies in strollers. Dogs on leashes. A couple of dads. Vanna's mouth was dry. She swallowed, but couldn't work up any saliva.

"I'm going to go get a drink," Vanna said, motioning to the water fountain.

Julia nodded. Vanna walked across the park and bent over the fountain, sipping the water. She turned her head to look at Julia. Julia was looking at a little girl playing in the sand a few feet in front of her. Holding her phone on the other side of the fountain where Julia couldn't see it, Vanna dialed nine-one-one.

She couldn't put the phone up to her ear, or Julia would see. She turned her head away from Julia as if she was taking another drink. "I need help," she said. She gave the address and mentioned the restraining order, hoping that the dispatcher would be able to hear and understand her.

Vanna slid the phone into her pocket without turning it off. Hopefully, the dispatcher would realize what was going on and wouldn't try to talk to her, or if she did, that it wouldn't be loud enough for Julia to hear. Vanna walked back over to the bench and sat down by Julia again. Now all they had to do was wait until the police came. They would arrest Julia under breach of the restraining order, or if they couldn't do that, at least find out her name and address. Maybe this nightmare would come to an end.

Julia looked at Vanna when she sat down. "I'm not here to hurt you," she affirmed.

"No, I understand that now," Vanna said. She felt a flush creep along her throat. Erica could always tell when she was lying. Hopefully, Julia hadn't yet figured it out. "You just want to spend time with me."

"That's right," Julia agreed.

"Why don't you… tell me about what things were like when you were a little girl," Vanna suggested. "What kind of a home did you grow up in?"

"No, none of that matters anymore. I have a new family now. I have you."

"I just wondered… what your parents were like. Did you have a mom and dad?"

Julia studied her suspiciously. "What are you up to?"

"I'm not up to anything. I'm asking you about your family. Getting to know you, like you said."

"No… something is wrong. That's a lie."

Vanna swallowed. She didn't want to turn her head to look around for the arrival of the police. But the impulse to do so was very strong. Where were they? Had the dispatcher not been able to understand her? Didn't know where to send the police? Didn't understand that it was really urgent?

Where were they?

Julia stood up abruptly, her body coiled tight like a spring. She looked around for the danger like a dog scenting the wind. Her eyes went back and forth wildly. Vanna spotted a police car crawling along the road on the other side of the park. What was she going to do? Stand up and wave? How would they have any idea which two women to be concerned about?

Julia spotted the police car as well, and she was moving away from Vanna, her face a bitter scowl. "Why do you hate me?" she demanded. "What have I ever done to you?"

Vanna opened her mouth, but she was at a loss what to say. That Julia had phoned her? Had sent her a teddy bear? She'd brought this all on herself, by her unwillingness to connect with Julia. If she'd been more accepting, they could have just had a regular relationship. She'd misjudged everything, making the worst choice possible by rebuffing Julia's attempts at friendship.

Julia quickly lost herself in the foot traffic out to the city sidewalk. Vanna pulled her phone out of her pocket. "She's leaving now… she's on the sidewalk. Headed… west down fifth… she's wearing black pants and a dark jacket."

"Are you okay, ma'am?" the dispatcher's voice queried. A woman, middle-aged, her voice calm and businesslike.

"Yes, I'm fine. She's blond. Her car must be somewhere between here and my apartment. It's a black Sunfire, license plate starts with MX."

"We have a police car at your location, ma'am. Please flag them down, if you can."

"But you need to catch her. If we can't even identify who she is…"

"The officers will talk to you, ma'am. They're looking for you now."

Frustrated, Vanna waved her arm at the police car and walked toward it. She stopped by the driver's window.

"Everything okay, ma'am?" the beefy cop behind the wheel inquired.

"She went over there, that way. She'll have to go back to her car, which has to be near my apartment, that way. It's a black Sunfire, license plate MX—"

"Just slow down, there." He put the car into park and pulled out his notebook. "Name?"

"I don't know her name. She is going by Julia Cortez, but no one can find anything under that name. We don't know where she lives, but her car—"

"Yes, ma'am. I mean *your* name." He looked at his partner. "Initiate a search on Julia Cortez."

"But she's not in the system, the police have already searched!"

"Your name," the man insisted.

"Vanna Austin."

His eyes widened slightly. "Are you Donny Austin's daughter?"

Vanna nodded, surprised. "Yes. Donny was my dad."

"I heard a little about this case. Well, don't you worry. Violence is pretty rare in stranger stalkings. We'll put out an alert and see if anyone can pick up her trail, but chances are, you're perfectly safe."

Vanna rolled her eyes. "They keep telling me that. But

she's already hit me once. She probably broke into my apartment, she knows where I live. She was waiting for me today, by my car and wouldn't let me by. I was afraid she might have a gun."

"Did you see a weapon?" he asked, looking up from his notebook.

Vanna shook her head. "No."

"Did she make any verbal threats?"

"No. She said she didn't want to hurt me. That it had been a mistake before."

"There you go," he nodded. He looked over to his partner. "You getting any hits on the name? Put a BOLO out on the car. I think it's actually already on the watch list. Double-check."

Vanna leaned against the car, finding that her legs were shaking. "You're not going to do anything? You aren't going to try to catch her?"

"We're not the only officers in the area. Relax. You're safe here with us."

"Do you think that you'd be relaxed if you had a psychopath after you?"

He waved his hand in a calming gesture. His tone was intended to soothe, but she felt patronized. "Stalkers are not usually mentally ill. Most can be persuaded that it is in their best interests to stop and leave the quarry alone."

Vanna did not like being referred to as quarry. "Most, but not all."

He shrugged. "Most. They aren't usually psychopaths. I'm just trying to reassure you. People hear 'stalker' and they think Fatal Attraction or Single White Female. But that's not the way it really happens. Not in ninety-nine percent of cases."

"Can I maybe… sit down?"

He looked up quickly. "Yes, of course," he opened his door and got out, opening the back door for her. Vanna lowered herself onto the seat.

"I'm not just some hysterical woman," she said, putting her

face in her hands and closing her eyes. "You don't know what it's like to have someone like this after you day in and day out."

———

Vanna was escorted into a conference room and sat down with her coffee to wait. She was tired and a little on the chilly side by the time that an officer whose name bar said 'Sweeny' joined her. He wasn't in a full police uniform. It looked like he had probably come to work in a suit, but had since removed the jacket and tie and rolled up his sleeves. The shirt was neatly pressed, but he smelled a little musky, like he'd been working hard all day and his deodorant was just starting to give out. He gave her a polite nod and sat down, putting a stack of papers and folders on the table in front of him. He was just a couple of inches taller than her, probably in his early thirties and a few pounds overweight, but in a comfortable way. No belly hanging out over his belt.

"Miss Austin. My name is Officer Sweeny. Sorry to keep you waiting."

Vanna shrugged. "Vanna."

"Vanna." He gave her a small smile. "Pretty name. I've been assigned to your case. We'll be working together to try to get this sorted out."

"Sorted out?" Vanna repeated.

"We want to charge the woman who has been stalking you and to have enough evidence to turn over to the DA for prosecution."

"Sounds good to me."

"Good. Have you been given your case number?"

Vanna shook her head.

"Let's start with that, then." He produced a small notepad and with deliberation neatly wrote the number out and tore off the page. "That's the magic number. If you have anything further to report, or any further incidents, then you reference that number. Of course, a dispatcher or officer can search by your name as well, but that never seems to work as well as having the case number. Computer systems. Not quite up to the level of efficiency that I'd like to see."

"Okay."

"I'm going to give you my number. That will route to me even if I'm off-duty, anytime night or day. You can put it on your phone and set a speed-dial."

Vanna took her phone out and entered the screen lock code, then nodded to him. He dictated the number. Vanna input it and added his name.

"How long do you think this will take?" she asked.

Sweeny considered the question, scratching his ear. "You don't know the identity of this woman. That makes it harder. Sometimes these things can be… protracted."

"Okay. What are you going to do? The other officers said that there was nothing that they could do if her name didn't show up on any of their searches and didn't catch her in the act. So what can *you* do?"

"I and my officers will investigate further. That will include interviewing you, maybe members of your family, neighbors, building manager, witnesses from the other day, any way that we can get more clues. Trust me, we haven't found everything there is to find yet. Something more will turn up."

Vanna nodded.

"In the meantime, we'll also want to step up patrols in your neighborhood. Help you to feel more secure. Be here to answer questions."

"Up until now… it seems like everyone just wants to brush it off. She's a woman so she won't do anything. She's not an ex-girlfriend and it's only exes that are dangerous. No one will take it seriously."

"I'm taking it seriously," Sweeny promised, looking her in the eye. "I am not going to just put this on the back burner. We're not going to just sit back and wait for her to make the next move. I want you to tell me everything that you can about her. And we'll do whatever we can to find her and to protect you."

Vanna breathed out, her stomach muscles a little shaky. She'd been holding herself tense a lot lately. But she liked this new officer. Maybe there really was something that he could do. Even just having his number made her feel more secure.

Chapter Twelve

G et your shoes on. You're coming with me."

If the words had come from anyone but Lydia, Vanna would have freaked out. But she had already gone into panic mode when Lydia arrived unannounced, certain that it was going to be Julia. Or even Tino. She couldn't handle dealing with either one of them. She had been so relieved when she looked through the peephole and saw Lydia.

"I buzzed and buzzed," Lydia complained. "I had to follow someone else in who had a key. Is it broken?"

Vanna shook her head. "I didn't want anyone to know that I was home."

"You could at least answer to see who it is. You don't have to let them in."

"If they know I'm here, they could just follow in someone else who has a key," Vanna pointed out. "If I don't answer, they at least don't know that I'm here."

"Oh. Well, I'm sorry, I wasn't trying to scare you. But come on. Get your shoes on."

"Why?" Vanna moved slowly. She didn't really want to leave the safety of the apartment. When she went out, bad things happened. It felt safer to just stay home and not worry about the outside world. She could do all of her work from the apartment. She could order in groceries. People could come to visit her if they made arrangements ahead of time, or they could video conference with her on the phone or computer. There was no need for her to leave the apartment at all.

"You've been holed up here for too long." It was as if Lydia was reading her mind. "You need to get out."

"Actually, I'm okay. I don't need anything."

"Come on," Lydia insisted. She stood waiting, jiggling the baby. Christopher and Paul weren't with her. "They're at my neighbor's," Lydia said, reading her mind. "We trade off babysitting sometimes."

"Mandy's sure getting big," Vanna said. She bent over to tie her shoes, wondering why they had to go out anywhere. She was hoping that Lydia hadn't been sent by Erica to bring Vanna to see her at the Estate or at the club. Vanna didn't need the extra pressure from Erica.

"She is. She's sure getting heavy," Lydia agreed.

"She'll be walking around before too long. Chasing around after the boys, getting into mischief."

"Don't remind me. Maybe she'll be easier. I'm told that not all children turn into little hellions."

Vanna giggled. She started to gather things together to put in her purse. Lydia watched the painstaking progress, jiggling the baby and tapping her foot.

"All you need is your wallet and keys," she said. "Nothing else, I swear. Even that much is overkill because I'm driving and I'm paying."

"I don't know how long I will be. Or what I might need, since you haven't told me." Vanna wondered whether she should take along some fruit roll-ups or crackers for a snack. She wouldn't want to go hungry.

"We'll get lunch," Lydia said, trying to move Vanna along.

Vanna grabbed her water bottle anyway. There was no telling whether she would be thirsty before they got to the restaurant. Or Lydia might want to go for a power walk while they talked. She could be impulsive. And even post-baby, she was in better shape than Vanna.

"Is that everything?" Lydia demanded.

Vanna looked down at her bag and nodded. "Okay. But I wish you would tell me what this is all about."

Lydia smiled. "Would I do anything to hurt you? Come on."

Vanna followed her out of the apartment and carefully locked the apartment door behind her. She had to be really aware of that now. No more walking off and discovering when she got home that she had left the door unlocked the whole time. No more forgetting anything important.

When they got out of the building, Vanna's head swiveled back and forth as she looked for any sign of Julia. No black car. No blond-haired or hooded figure. Everything seemed entirely normal. But she couldn't get past the sick feeling of dread that something awful was going to happen. Lydia led the way to her car and let Vanna in. Vanna got settled while Lydia put Mandy into the baby seat and got her all strapped in.

"There you go, baby. All nice and safe," she comforted while Mandy squirmed and fussed at having to sit still.

"I know the feeling," Vanna whispered to Mandy while Lydia was still outside the car. "Trust me."

Birchdale wasn't a big city, but Vanna didn't know every street and she didn't recognize the route that Lydia was taking. It wasn't to any of the stores that they usually frequented. Lydia stopped in front of a little cafe Vanna had never been to before. Probably they were famous for their tetrazzini or something. Vanna waited while Lydia got Mandy back out of the car seat and they went in together. Vanna hung back and let Lydia enter first.

The place was clean but obviously didn't get a lot of business. It wasn't rush hour, but Vanna would have expected there to be a couple of other tables occupied, even during off-hours. Instead, there was only one woman there. Late thirties or early forties, with naturally graying hair, pulled back in a rather severe hairstyle. She sat with a book but looked at Vanna and Lydia as they came in through the door. Lydia looked around.

"Suzanne?" she said to the gray-haired woman.

"You must be Lydia."

"I am. Hi." Lydia tugged Vanna over to the table. "This is my sister, Vanna. Vanna, this is Suzanne, she is a member of a support group for woman who have been stalked or harassed."

"Oh!" Vanna looked her over, surprised. "I didn't know that there would be enough people in Birchdale to have a support group."

"You'd be surprised how many of us there are," Suzanne said, smiling. "I'm very glad to meet you, Vanna. Lydia's told me a lot about you."

Vanna's eyes slid over to Lydia. Lydia looked up at the ceiling as if admiring the single, slowly-turning, five-bladed fan.

"Come have a seat," Suzanne suggested. "We'll have some tea and talk and then we can have lunch once you're feeling better."

Vanna glanced at Lydia again and sat down in the chair across from Suzanne. Lydia sat down on the side between the two of them.

"Do you have a Safety Plan?" Suzanne asked.

Vanna shook her head slowly, her forehead wrinkling. A Safety Plan sounded like a good thing to have. All at once, she was glad that Lydia had forced her into this meeting. She probably would not have agreed to come if Lydia had told her ahead of time. Which Lydia had obviously guessed. Or maybe Suzanne, the experienced one, had known.

"What's a Safety Plan?" Vanna asked. "How do I make one?"

"The first thing you need to do is to make sure that everyone knows what's going on. I'm talking about family, friends, co-workers, neighbors; the people that you spend time with, not just the police or the court system. The police and the courts are not going to be watching you at ten o'clock at night. But you can bet that if your neighbor hears shattering glass and knows that you have been threatened, they will take action. You need to tell them everything you can, including names, your police case file number, and pictures of your subject if you have them."

"I have one," Vanna agreed, nodding.

"Take it down to the local print shop and run off a whole bunch of copies. Give them to everyone. Put them up by the mailboxes in your building and in the elevator. Even if they get taken down in a day, at least people will have a chance to see and know what's going on."

Vanna squirmed. She didn't want to be in trouble with the building manager. She would ask him if she could put a picture up…

"Does she know your phone number?"

"Yes… but I can't block her because she just calls from other phones. She got rid of her first phone. The police said it was a burner. She didn't use her real address."

"Get your number changed right away. Make sure it is unlisted. Only give it to people who absolutely have to be able to reach you. If you have any common acquaintances with her, don't give the number to any of them."

"I don't know anyone she knows."

"That helps. But numbers still get shared, so make sure everyone that you give it to understands that it is life and death that they do not give it to anyone else. Even someone who says they know you and just lost your new number, or are related to you and need to reach you because it is an emergency."

"Life and death?"

Suzanne gave her a steely stare. "Well, it is, isn't it? No matter what the police say, no one can predict which stalkers will be violent. No one."

Vanna nodded slowly. "Yeah."

"It is life and death. If you don't follow your own Safety

Plan and if you don't do everything that you can to persuade other people to follow it…"

"Okay. I will."

"You need a 'go bag.' Do you know what that is?"

"No."

"If you need to leave the house quickly, or if you are away from home and can't go back, you need a ready supply of cash, a credit card, any medication you need, keys, important papers, and so on. If you couldn't go home from here, what would you need to live on for the next week? What if your bank account was frozen? I'm not talking about food and clothing because you can buy those if you have cash. But what can you not live without?"

"That won't be a problem for Vanna," Lydia laughed. "She practically carries the house around in her purse!"

Vanna glared at her.

Suzanne merely nodded. "Good. And you should keep a second bag stashed at someone else's house, away from yours. Again, with everything that you would need in it. If your pursuer manages to snatch the first one from you or you end up having to leave a house on fire without anything at all, you still have somewhere to go where you are safe and can take care of yourself. Remember that you need to have cash, not just a credit card. You don't know whether you'll be able to get to the bank and credit cards can be traced. If you want to be untraceable, you have to have cash."

"But a regular person can't trace your credit card, can they? Just the police?"

"These people are very resourceful. They can talk their way into anything they want. They'll call the bank, or the police, or hire a hacker. Any trail that you leave can be followed. So don't leave a trail."

"Okay."

"I have a list of emergency numbers for you." Suzanne slid a trifold photocopied page across the table to Vanna.

"Assistance agencies, emergency shelters, people in our network. There are places for you to write down the officer assigned to your case, your court and police case file numbers, the woman's identity and description. Keep a copy of her picture with it. There are places to write down your friends' and family's phone numbers. Don't assume that you'll be able to remember them in a panic. Don't assume that you'll have your phone to look up their numbers, it can be pulled out of your hand and tossed in the river or down a grate. Get a money belt and keep it there, on your body, at all times. Put a bit of cash and a key in there too. Not a key to your house. An unidentifiable key to somewhere you can stash your second go bag, a locker, a safety deposit box, something like that. Not your mail box. Not your car."

Vanna nodded. She fingered the paper. She had the compulsion to fill it out immediately, without delay. She wanted to do everything that Suzanne had advised, right away, so that she could feel safe again. She wanted to be able to feel that she was now safe.

Suzanne took a deep breath and let it out slowly. "We're not done."

Vanna smoothed her forehead with the pads of her fingers. She nodded. "Okay. What else?"

"You need to vary your daily schedule and the routes that you travel. Don't go to work at the same time every day. Don't go shopping the same day every week. Take a roundabout route. Go to grocery stores you've never gone to before. Make it hard for anyone to predict where you are going to be at any particular time."

"Right. Okay."

"You should have a secret code word or phrase for the people that you talk to regularly. Your sister, your mother, your friends. A word or phrase that the person you are talking to knows means you are in danger and they should call nine-one-one right away. 'I love broccoli' or 'remember that road trip to

Canada?' or 'I am waiting for a delivery.' Something that sounds pretty normal, that you can slip into a conversation and they know that you need help."

"Custard," suggested Lydia. "It's a family tradition and Vanna can't stand it. If you ever slip that into a conversation, I'll know something is going on."

Suzanne nodded. "Keep a log of all contacts or suspected contacts. Write them all down, with the date and time and all of the details you can think of."

"Is that it?" Vanna asked, her head whirling with all of this information. "Please say that's all."

Suzanne shook her head and raised her brows. "I'm sorry. But we haven't gotten to the hardest one yet."

"Uggh."

"Your online activity."

"She doesn't have my email address. And all my social networks are private."

"Don't you believe it. There are ways around those privacy protocols. Have you had any problems the last few months with email passwords or verification?"

Vanna looked at Lydia. There was no way that Julia had access to her online accounts as well! "Well… I got locked out of my email account. I had to prove my identity to get it unlocked again."

"She hacked it."

"She couldn't have."

"Don't bother trying to figure out how," Suzanne said, waving this idea aside with her hand. "She would date a support rep at the email provider if that's what it took to get access. But she did get access. And that means that she knows a lot more about you than you could ever guess. How many other places do you use the same password?"

"I did use it at a lot of places," Vanna admitted. "But after my email account got hacked, I went through and changed all of the important ones…"

"By that time she might have already installed a key logger on your computer. She could have access to every single key you press. Did you change them all to the same new password?"

"No."

"You're learning. But with a key logger, she has them all anyway. You need to get a new computer, or else totally wipe the one you've got and start fresh. You have no way of knowing how many trojans may be residing on it right now. New computer. Set up new accounts for everything. Everything. Don't use the same password on two of them. Get a password program that sets a random password for every site and saves each one in a separate, encrypted file. After you've set up all of your new accounts, you will have to contact each of your people and give them the new information. It's going to be a huge pain in the neck."

Vanna tried to fathom how she was going to get it all done. It would take hours. Days. And transferring all of the information…

"That's the worst part," Suzanne commiserated.

"I hope so."

"Are you ready to eat now?"

Vanna stared down at the table, shaking her head.

"You can do it, Vanna. You're not the only one who has had to go through this. There are others who are here to support you. Lydia's here. I'm here. I'll tell you about our support group meetings."

"Okay."

Suzanne ran through the details. Vanna couldn't stop thinking over all of the things that she was going to have to do to protect herself. All because some lunatic decided that they should have a relationship. She thought about other people she had heard of who dealt with stalkers for years. Years! She couldn't manage a few days, a few weeks, without feeling like she was going to have a nervous breakdown. How could anyone survive such an ordeal for a year? Three years? Seven years? It was unfathomable. She wasn't even sure how she was going to make it through the next week.

Suzanne reached across the table and touched her hand. Vanna looked up.

"You will survive," Suzanne told her. "You are strong and you will fight, and you will survive. Because you are a survivor. You'd be amazed at how strong you are when the chips are down."

"I don't know," Vanna confessed. She shook her head. "I'm feeling pretty weak right now."

"That's because you need food," Lydia inserted brightly. "I know I do. What should we get?"

"Something with lots of sugar," Suzanne suggested. "Good for alleviating stress."

"I don't really feel like anything," Vanna said.

"You just wait. I'll get you something. Once you wake up your stomach, you'll realize how hungry you are."

Lydia and Suzanne both walked up to the counter. Vanna stayed where she was, all of the energy just seeping out of her body. Suzanne looked at Lydia and nodded. Nothing had been said, and Vanna wondered what thought the nod communicated.

Chapter Thirteen

I have been trying to get a hold of you!" Maria Sandusky shrilled. "Your phone was disconnected. Your emails are bouncing back. I was starting to wonder if you got hit by a bus!"

Vanna took a breath, shaking her head at the woman's near-hysteria. The closer they got to the wedding, the more freaked out Maria became. Instead of being calm and satisfied that everything had been arranged as it was supposed to be, she was convinced that everything was spinning out of control and that the wedding was going to be a disaster. It didn't matter how much Vanna tried to reassure her that everything had been done as requested, Maria just didn't get it.

"I sent you an email with my new address and phone number, Maria. I sent it out to all of my clients. I've had some issues with my previous account getting hacked and I wouldn't want to take the chance of not getting one of your emails because of that."

"Why didn't you call me?" Maria demanded. "I don't always get to my email. Or stuff ends up in spam. You can't just assume that someone got your email."

"Since we usually work with each other by email, I didn't

think that would be a problem. And I am calling you right now, to follow up and make sure you have all of my new contact information."

"I thought that everything I have been working for was down the drain! All of that work! All of that money! You can't imagine how I felt."

"You must have been pretty stressed out. But rest assured that everything has been taken care of. Even if I was hit by a bus tomorrow, everything is already in place. The florist and the dressmaker and everyone are all contracted directly with you. You have all of the information. They would take instruction from you without any word from me. I'm just here as your assistant, everything has been taken care of in your name."

"I wouldn't know where to start."

"Well, if you didn't know where to start, then you could get a wedding consultant or another assistant to go through your file and pull out all of the relevant information."

"I don't have a file!"

Vanna rolled her eyes. Heaven help the groom who was going to have to take over from Vanna and handle Maria after the wedding. She was so helpless. And so frantic about being helpless. Vanna suspected that Maria liked to be the center of attention, just a little. She liked to show off how horrible her life was turning out, just a little. It was pretty hard to pull off when a person was as wealthy as Maria, but then, people were well-paid to hold her hand and act sorry about her latest disasters.

"Did you need me to do something for you today, Maria? Or did you want to check on something?"

"I'm worried about the wine," Maria fussed.

"What about the wine?"

"I know that I told you I wanted the nineteen forty-five, but I'm thinking now that the nineteen forty-seven would have been a better choice. Betty—you know, from my show—she had the nineteen forty-seven at her wedding. I think that if people see that I brought in the nineteen forty-five, they'll think that I didn't provide the best experience. They'll think that the nineteen forty-seven is better, just because that's what Betty had at her wedding."

Vanna was well familiar by now with Betty, the actress from Maria's favorite soap. She couldn't count the number of details in the wedding that had been modeled on what Betty was planning, or was rumored to be planning, for her wedding. Or what she had done for her character's fictional wedding. And now that the real wedding had, in fact, been pulled off just days before, there was going to be a whole avalanche of last-minute changes based on what Betty had actually done.

"If you want to change to the nineteen forty-seven, I don't think it's too late," she said. "But I should call and arrange it today. Is the nineteen forty-seven your final pick?"

"Oh… I don't know… my fiancé says that the nineteen forty-five is definitely better… I don't know what to say. I don't want people to think that I couldn't do just as well as Betty…"

"Either one is excellent. You remember what the sommelier said. They were both fabulous vintages. I think that if your friends really pay attention to vintages, they'll know that."

"Do you think so?"

"Yes. I do."

"I wouldn't want anyone to think that I picked an inferior wine…"

"No."

"Ooooh…" Maria squeezed the syllable out in agony. "I don't knooooow…"

"Do you think that Betty made the best choice?"

She could practically hear the gears turning. Surely nobody could choose better than Betty. Betty couldn't make a mistake and if she thought that the nineteen forty-seven was the better wine, then she had to be right.

"Go with the forty-seven," Maria said with confidence.

"Now, you're sure. You're not going to change your mind again? We have to give him the final pick today."

"Yes. Yes, of course, I am. The nineteen forty-seven is definitely the better choice."

"Okay."

So much for her fiancee's opinion. Vanna again felt a pang of sympathy for him. Did he know what he was getting into by taking Maria on? Or would they be divorced again within a year and Maria would be planning her next, even more fabulous wedding?

"Was there anything else?"

Maria hummed and hawed for a minute or two. Then she seemed to make up her mind. "Well… about the cake…"

"Yes…?"

"It's only five layers…"

"Five layers plus the topper," Vanna said. "Just like Betty's."

"Betty's had real roses instead of sugar roses."

"Do you want real roses?"

"I don't think we'd ever get a match to the wedding colors with a real rose…"

"No, I don't think so. With the sugar roses, we can."

"Yes. And Betty had special lighting on her cake."

"Yes. You know that will be extra. Higher cost, more wiring, more set-up time, and another thing that can go wrong. And it means that people can't get as close to it or take pictures from all angles."

"That is true."

"I think the full-spectrum lighting you've chosen for the event will really make it pop without any special equipment close to the cake."

"You think so?"

"You can call the wedding planner and ask her. I'm just an assistant."

"Oh… she is irritated with me," Maria said with a pout that Vanna could hear in spite of the poor call quality. "She says I mustn't change anything else this late, or call her about little things that were supposed to be decided weeks ago. No one will talk to me, Vanna. No one except you."

"I think she's right in this case. I don't think you want to be changing anything about the electrical or the cake this late in the game. It is coming up, you know."

"I know, I'm getting so nervous about it. What if something goes wrong?"

"It will be okay, Maria. It has been planned down to the last detail. There may be a couple of little hiccups, but honestly, it is going to be a lovely day. Your dream wedding."

"Okay. You're right. Will you go through the RSVP list one more time? I'm worried that the caterer doesn't have the final numbers and somebody will be short."

"They will provide a slight overage, just in case. But I'll check."

"Thank you, Vanna. You really are a lifesaver."

"You're welcome. Remember to look for my email and update your contact list."

"I will."

Maria rang off. Vanna put her phone down and stretched out her neck and shoulders. She was holding herself stiff. That had been happening a lot lately. She'd never had much sympathy for Erica's myriad of aches or tension headaches, but she was starting to develop it now. She'd never realized how crippling stress could actually be.

———

Vanna had not picked up her mail for several days. Her version of Suzanne's 'vary your schedule, don't do everything at the same time or on the same day' was not to go out at all. She didn't pick her mail up at the same time every day anymore. She left it as long as she possibly could and then picked it up at some random time. She stayed in her apartment and didn't go out. Then she couldn't be followed. Julia hadn't come up to the apartment and Vanna believed that if she didn't go out, Julia wouldn't.

She pulled a small sheaf of letters out of her mail slot. It was mostly bills and junk. One cheque from a client, which she needed desperately.

She went back up to her apartment, shuffling through the letters as she went. Vanna was doing her best to ignore one envelope. But by the time she got to her door, she could no longer ignore the fact that Julia had sent her yet another letter.

"No, no, no," she whispered. She threw it on the table and went back to her new computer.

Working, knowing that the letter was sitting there waiting for her to open it, was impossible. She couldn't work while it pressed down on her consciousness. Suzanne had told her never to engage with Julia. Not to answer phone calls, letters, emails, or face-to-face contact out on the street. But she hadn't said what Vanna should do when she got letters. Was she supposed to read them and give them to the police? File them? Mark them 'return to sender' and throw them back in the mailbox? She had no idea what method would be the most effective in getting Julia to stop.

Without being able to get any work done, she eventually walked back into the kitchen and looked at the letter sitting so innocently on the table. She knew that she couldn't return it to Julia. Not without knowing what Julia had said. She sat down and stared at it for a while longer.

She knew Julia's handwriting from all of the previous letters. The envelope and notepaper were from the same box as the last one she had received. Vanna slit it open carefully and pulled out the three sheets of notepaper. Covered with Julia's careful writing front and back.

The letter started differently than any of the others. With the words, 'I am so sorry.' Vanna blinked, not quite believing it. The first full page was a series of apologies, seemingly sincere.

'I don't know how things got so out of control. All I wanted to do was to meet my daughter, and I don't know how I let it all get so out of hand. I never meant to hurt you, either physically, or emotionally. I realize now how it must have scared you. I came on too strong and didn't give you any space to get used to the idea of having a birth mom.'

Vanna touched the words and read them again. Was it possible that Julia finally had come around? Maybe the police officer was right and Julia just had to be persuaded that it was in her best interest to leave Vanna alone. Maybe the close calls with the police had finally made her realize how much she was risking by continuing to contact Vanna. Maybe it was finally all coming to an end.

Vanna turned the page.

'I just feel so lost and out of control and I don't know how to fix it. I know I've been away from you for a long time and you don't remember me. A few times you have asked me what happened and I realize now that you were trying to connect. But at the time I thought you were just being intrusive, that you wanted to know what had happened so that you could blame me. That didn't seem fair to me. I wish that I could tell you about what happened in the past, when you were a baby. But that is in the past and we can't change it.'

Vanna could relate to the feeling of powerlessness, of everything falling apart. She read the passage again. Julia still wasn't telling her anything about the past, but at least she was acknowledging that Vanna was just trying to build a relationship.

'A lot of bad things happened back then and when I was a little girl. Life isn't really fair. I never had a chance at a normal life, just being home with my baby. Things didn't work that way for me. I never really had a chance at happiness. I wanted you to be happy. All of these years, while I've had to be away from you, that was all that I wanted. I just had to know that you were safe and happy, that things had worked out.'

Vanna didn't turn the page for a long time. She skimmed

over the repeated refrains of how Julia had been done wrong, to the final page.

'I will honor your wishes and not contact you again. I'm sorry that things didn't turn out. I hope that you will be ready in the future. But I will leave it up to you to decide.'

Vanna closed her eyes. It was over.

It was finally over.

Chapter Fourteen

You think that she's telling you the truth?" Suzanne questioned.

Vanna could tell that Suzanne was trying to keep sarcasm from entering her voice. Her stomach made a low gurgling noise and her heart started to pound faster.

"She apologized," Vanna said. "She's never done that before. It's a change in her behavior. That's good, right?"

"Don't count on it. It probably just means that she's trying a different tack. The direct approach hasn't worked, so she's going to try the opposite and see if you will let her get closer if she backs off. It's not a change in her attitude. It's just a change in approach."

"But it sounds real," Vanna insisted. "It doesn't sound like she's just trying the words that she thinks will work. There's real emotion in it. It sounds totally sincere."

"And does that mean that she isn't going to stalk you anymore? Does emotion equate with truth?"

"I think she really does want to change."

"Maybe she does. But that doesn't mean that she has changed or that she will change."

Vanna wanted to just end the call. Here she had called Suzanne to tell her the good news, that Julia was going to stop. She had called to share and to be reassured, and Suzanne was throwing cold water all over Vanna's party.

"Don't tell me that," she groaned. "Please, I just want it to end!"

"I know you do, Vanna," Suzanne agreed. "Remember, I've been there. I'm still dealing with those feelings. I want my life back too. But if you reach deep down, you'll recognize that it's not true. You know just as well as I do that she's not going to change. She's not going to stop tracking you just because she says she is. That's why you called me and not your sister. You know that Julia's not stopping."

"I'm calling Lydia too," Vanna said lamely, wondering why she had called Suzanne before Lydia and Erica. After all, they were the ones who really cared about her. Not Suzanne. Suzanne was just a third party, a bystander. And not one who was sending a lot of lollypops and rainbows her direction, either.

"And what are you going to tell her? Are you going to tell her that it's all over, or that Julia says it's all over? Because I think you know which one is the truth."

"Can't I pretend, just for a little while, that it is true?"

"That depends on whether you are going to let down your guard or not. If you can pretend for a little while without letting down your guard, then go ahead. Enjoy your little fantasy. But stay on guard until the next letter shows up, or she finds your new email address or phone number."

Vanna swore under her breath. "I happen to think people can change," she said firmly to Suzanne.

"So do I. But stalkers don't stop stalking until they are forced to, one way or another. And Julia hasn't been forced. She is sitting safely in her own house, safe from police or prosecution, thinking about what she can do to get under your skin. She is living in her own little fantasy world, where she can control you, make you do whatever it is that she wants you to. Have whatever relationship it is that she wants. Yes, people can change. People change all the time. Sometimes on purpose, and sometimes they change because of outside circumstances, like being stalked. Are you telling me that you haven't changed? Because I know that I have."

There was a bang in the hallway and Vanna just about jumped out of her skin. "Oh!"

"What's wrong?" Suzanne questioned immediately. "Are you okay?"

"I'm fine. I just was startled by a noise. The neighbors. It's nothing."

"Do you want to check? I'll stay on the phone with you while you make sure it's okay."

Vanna shuddered. It was just Mrs. Kingsley getting a delivery or the guy from down the hallway bringing in yet more new furniture. She was sure the guy got a new couch every month. And she never saw him get rid of one. It was always new and she pictured his apartment packed wall to wall with couches, stacked on top of each other. He would have to crawl over them through tiny spaces between them to get from one room to the other.

She went to the door and squinted through the peephole. She couldn't see anything. That meant that Julia wasn't standing in front of her door. If it were Julia, Vanna would be able to see her.

"It's okay," she said to Suzanne. "There's no one out there."

"She could be standing against the wall, out of view of the peephole. Did you get the wide angle that I recommended?"

"No… not yet."

"You need to do that. You need to protect yourself. Are you sure there's no one out there?"

"I can hear people next door. They must have gone in there. Don't worry about it, I'm fine."

"Okay. But if you hear anything else that you're worried

about, you call the police right away, okay? Better to end up calling them when there's nothing than not calling them and getting yourself hurt. You have your go bag ready?"

"Yes. I did all of that stuff. I have my bag ready." Vanna was actually pretty proud of how well she had packed the emergency kit. She had done a bunch of online searches for ideas and had thought through every facet of what she would need if she had to leave in a hurry. She enjoyed the feeling of being totally prepared and organized. It gave her a feeling that she was in control, in a time when she felt completely out of control.

"Good," Suzanne approved. "I guess I'll let you go; but please don't let your guard down. Stay alert and aware."

"I will. Um… thanks."

Suzanne laughed softly. "I know you think I'm just a downer, but… you wouldn't really believe me if I told you it was all over anyway."

———

After hanging up with Suzanne, Vanna tried to go to bed. She kept telling herself that she was safe now. She could finally get a good night's sleep without having to lie awake worrying about every sound in the apartments around her. Or to wake up in a cold sweat after having finally drifted off.

But Suzanne was right. Her body and her brain simply didn't believe her. She considered taking a sleeping pill, desperate to get some shut-eye. But Suzanne had warned against taking anything that might make her groggy, might keep her from waking up when she was in danger and had to run. Just thinking about it made her that much more wide awake.

Vanna roamed around the apartment, making sure that the door was locked and chained and that her go bag was in place by the door. She stood at the big living room window and looked down at the street, glistening wet.

There was a figure on the street below. Standing and waiting, then pacing back and forth. Who would be out there now, in the rain, in the dark of night?

Just standing there, as if waiting for someone to come out.

Chapter Fifteen

Vanna jerked out of her restless sleep, arms flailing, and just about fell off of the couch. She caught herself and looked around, disoriented. Somehow she had fallen asleep watching out the window, her head resting on the back of the couch. Vanna looked down at the street.

There was no one standing down there now. Her mysterious figure must have eventually been picked up, or gone on her—or his—way.

On autopilot, Vanna got up and started the coffee maker going. Her head was thick and muzzy and she wished that she could just lie down and go back to sleep. She wandered to the bathroom and then into her bedroom to get dressed. Noticing her bedside clock, she realized that it was still early and she could catch a few more winks if she wanted to. She stretched out under the covers and closed her eyes to go back to sleep.

But sleep didn't return.

———

Obeying Suzanne's dictate not to always do things at predictable times and places, Vanna had met her mother at the

Country Club in the morning instead of at the Estate during the afternoon or evening. Erica had ordered tea, and Vanna sipped at it even though she was in the mood for something much stronger.

"What is it that you hope to find, digging into the past?" Erica asked, adding a small spoonful of honey to her tea and giving it a couple of swirls. "How is that going to stop this woman from harassing you?"

"I don't know… maybe nothing at all. But at least I would know. Right now there is just a huge hole in my past. If she really is Julia, maybe I can figure out why she is doing this. Figure out what motivates her and how to stop her. If she isn't Julia, then maybe I can figure out who she is. Then the police can talk to her… it would be better to at least know who she is."

Erica inclined her head in a brief nod of agreement and took a sip of the tea. "I can check in your father's files for the information that we have on your adoption, but I don't think it will be helpful. We weren't given any identifying information, or information about where you had come from. The social worker won't still be there; nobody who knew anything at the time will be."

"I know. I don't expect there to be anything in your files. I'm hoping that the government adoption files haven't been destroyed. I have no idea what their retention policies are for adoptions."

"Probably five years," Erica said with a shrug.

"I hope not…"

"It is probably going to take a lot of digging. We don't even know what your name was before the adoption. It was redacted from all of our documents."

Vanna sighed. "There should be some kind of guidelines online for how to get records opened up. The adoption itself is a court order; they don't destroy court documents, do they?"

"I remember a few years ago, a whole bunch was

damaged by black mold. Thousands of dollars to clean them up and salvage what they could. A lot can happen in twenty years."

"Thanks for the optimism."

"I just don't want you to get your hopes up and be disappointed. Even if you find out all of the details of why you were adopted out or what happened before that, there's no guarantee that it will be any help to you. This could just be some random woman with nothing to do with the adoption."

"I know… but I can't help thinking that this is all because of what happened in the past. That the key is there."

Erica reached over and patted her hand. "You are looking so worn these days. You have dark shadows under your eyes."

Vanna rubbed them. They were puffy and congested. "I know. I can't sleep. I just want to figure this out so that I can go back to my normal life."

Lydia had offered to help Vanna out with some phone calls and research. Vanna didn't know how Lydia managed to do so much in between keeping the boys from burning the house down, nursing a new baby, putting dinner on the table every day, and all the rest of the work that she had as a busy stay home wife and mother. Sometimes Vanna could barely manage to find time to feed herself and she didn't have anyone else to look after.

"Where do you want to start?" Lydia asked, having laid Mandy down on a blanket to gurgle contentedly. "Google? Public records search?"

"I don't even know what to look for," Vanna said, feeling her way through all of the questions that vied for her attention. "I don't know if Julia Cortez is the name of my birth mother, the stalker, or neither, or both. It could just be a random name, a red herring."

"Then the first task should be to find out your birth mom's name. Right?"

Vanna dangled a toy over Mandy and the baby grabbed it and pulled it into her mouth. Vanna smiled. "I guess so, yes. So how do we do that?"

"Call the adoption agency?"

"It was DSHS. Not a private agency."

"So is there a public information line?"

They both had their laptops out and tapped in a few searches. Lydia got the first hit. "Here, try calling this one."

Vanna keyed the phone number in. She swallowed hard and licked her lips. Lydia gave her an encouraging thumbs-up. A harried-sounding woman answered the call rather abruptly. Vanna was taken off-guard for a minute and tried to collect her thoughts. She started to explain the situation.

"You need to file a DOH 102," the woman interrupted.

"What is that?"

"A request for Original Birth Certificate."

"Oh, okay." Vanna tapped the form number into her computer. "Where do I get that?"

"It's on our website. Do you have access on your computer?"

"Yes…"

"Just go to Adoptee Request for Original Birth Certificate. Submit the completed form with the fee and we will mail you your results within six weeks."

"Six weeks? I need something a lot sooner than that! Is there a fee for priority service?"

"No. Requests are processed in the order that we receive them. You will get the results within six weeks."

"This is a very urgent case."

"Talk to your lawyer. The only other option is to make an application to the court. And it will take you a while to get a court date too."

Vanna wrote this down. She gave Lydia a frown and headshake. "I guess I'll have to try that. I just… it's really important to get my birth mother's name as soon as possible. Is there any chance that when I fill in the form, I'll find out that it's not even on your records?"

"Of course it will be on our records," the woman said impatiently. "Fathers are not always listed, but mothers are."

"Is there any way you won't release it to me or won't be able to find it? I don't know what my birth name is, only my adoptive name."

"Sometimes searches fail, for different reasons. Your birth parent may have requested that no identifying information be released. You don't need to know your birth name. The form only asks for your adoptive name."

"Okay. Thank you for your help." Vanna hung up and shrugged at Lydia. "Fill out a form and wait six weeks. Hopefully, they'll find it. But the birth parent can request that no identifying information be given out. What do you think are the chances that Julia will block it?"

"If she's really Julia."

"Even if she's not—she won't want me to know anything. She won't answer any questions about the past. She hasn't told me anything, not even made up. She'll have checked the law. She'll know what she can do. She'll forge a request or will have made sure she picked someone who had already requested no identifying information be released."

Lydia shook her head. "So—a court order?"

"Yes."

"Did Mom give you the name of the attorney she was thinking of?"

"Yes." With heavy warnings not to expect anything good to come of it. "I guess I'll give him a call and see if he can help me get information any faster."

"Yeah. Sounds good. Maybe we should write up a summary of what we know so far. That might help pull things together."

"But I don't know anything about her," Vanna protested. "Not even if she is who she says she is."

"You know more about her than you think. Come on. Let's do it." Lydia tapped a few keys. "You know she has a black Sunfire with license plate MX."

"But how is that going to help?" Vanna reasoned.

"I don't know yet. Let's just write it down, because you know it's true."

"Okay…"

"What else?"

"Not anything, really. I know she should be Hispanic, not white."

"Good," Lydia nodded her approval and typed something in. "With a name like Cortez, and your features, you would expect your birth mom not to be Caucasian."

Vanna nodded. "And she's too young. I mean, it's possible, I know, but I think if she kept me until I was two, she should be at least thirty-eight."

"Right. Unless there was a grandma or someone who was raising you."

"I guess. Yeah."

"What else?"

"I don't know. She writes a lot of stuff in her letters…"

"But you don't know that any of that is true. What do you know?"

"She's strong… she can fight. She's smart enough to hack my email or to persuade someone else to do it for her."

Lydia noted these points. It lifted Vanna up a little to be able to write down concrete things about Julia.

"She talks about having such a hard life… but she has really neat handwriting."

Lydia stared at her. "What do you mean? Someone who grows up poor or underprivileged can't have neat handwriting?"

"Well, I suppose they can, but I just feel like… if she's uneducated or has had to deal with learning disabilities or alcoholism or something… you don't expect nice handwriting, you expect… something like mine. Chicken scratch."

Lydia pursed her lips and thought about this. Mandy fussed a little and Lydia played with her fingers to quiet her.

"You have all of those sample letters," she said slowly. "Why don't we get a graphologist or whatever to do a handwriting analysis? Maybe we could even get some kind of psychological profile from what she says or the words she uses."

"Can they do that? I have lots of letters."

Lydia typed for a couple of minutes, her cheeks turning a bit pink. "I think that's a good idea, Vanna. Really good."

Chapter Sixteen

Vanna was feeling pretty good before she walked into her apartment. She felt like they were finally making some progress. She had the number of the attorney to make a court application for her. She had Lydia's list of the things that they knew for sure about Julia, and Vanna was hoping that if she thought about it some more, she might be able to add some more to it. The more that they knew about Julia, the better the chances were that they'd be able to figure out who she was and stop her.

But the instant she walked into the apartment, she knew that someone had been there. There was a faint scent of perfume in the air. That was something else to add to the list. Julia wore perfume. With a few minutes of work at the makeup counter in the department store, they could probably find out which one. It wasn't likely to be anything rare, but they would know one more thing…

Vanna looked around, trying to figure out what Julia had touched or moved. Had she taken anything away? Left anything? She knew for sure it wasn't Tino this time. It didn't smell like him.

Vanna's go bag was in her hand and one part of her brain

was yelling at her to get out of the apartment to somewhere safe. But this was her territory, her safe place, and she hated to have to leave.

She had known that as soon as she left the apartment, Julia would be back. She knew that something bad would happen if she did. And she had been right.

She wasn't safe there anymore. But Vanna was pretty sure that Julia was gone. There was no sensation that there was anyone else in the apartment with her. It was empty and had been for some time. She took a slow circuit around, looking for anything out of place. Nothing jumped out at her. She locked and chained the door. She knew that she should call Sweeny right away and put them on alert that someone had been in her apartment, but there was nothing missing and she would just come off as a hysterical woman.

Vanna sat down at her computer and opened up her email to review anything that had happened while she was away. She couldn't afford to spend many days chasing around trying to turn up clues. She wasn't a detective. As she reviewed her emails, she remembered that she needed to pull a file from the old computer. It was available in the cloud, but a direct transfer would be faster. She looked up to grab the old laptop and her hand hovered above the desk.

It wasn't there.

Vanna's heart beat wildly. It wasn't there. She had done as Suzanne had said and started everything on a clean laptop so that she would know it was secure. But she hadn't gotten around to cleaning everything off of the old one yet. She'd left it available, just in case there was something that she'd forgotten about. Some file that wasn't stored somewhere else, or some setting that she needed to double-check. She hadn't wiped it clean and now it was gone. Vanna swore and slapped her hand down on the desk.

"No!"

Her voice echoed around the room and Vanna suddenly

panicked, wondering if there was a bug planted somewhere in the room. Or several of them. Julia had been in her apartment at least twice now; she could have left some kind of listening device, so she'd be able to monitor Vanna's mood and communications. She lowered her voice and swore fiercely several times.

Vanna grabbed her computer and got up. She picked up her go bag before ducking out the door. Now she needed to report this to Sweeny for sure.

———

"Why didn't you just call me from your apartment?" Sweeny asked. "Call nine-one-one. They would make sure that I got the message."

"I couldn't," Vanna said. "I was worried that she might be listening with a bug. And I didn't want her to know that I realized she was there and had called the police. I don't know. I guess she could have followed me here in the car, too, but I just felt too… exposed there. I didn't feel safe staying."

He nodded. "You gotta listen to your gut. If it tells you that you're not safe, then you bug out. Are you okay?"

"I'm pretty shaky. And just… so… frustrated and angry. I just want her to leave me alone. And she said that she would. I thought it would be the end."

"Of course you do." Sweeny bent over his keyboard, pecking at the keys with two curved fingers, looking like some bizarre eagle or vulture hovering, claws extended. "Let's get started, then. Any idea how she got in?"

"I can't figure it out. I had the locks changed. I know I locked it when I left. So how is she getting in? There is no sign of a break-in."

"She's picked the lock. Or someone let her in. Have you talked to the building manager?"

"I talked to him before. He said he wouldn't let anyone in. I gave him her picture. He wouldn't have done that."

"Then I guess someone has taught her, or she has taught herself, how to pick a lock. Was it bolted, or just the handle lock?"

"It was bolted. I bolt it every time."

"You might want to consider moving. But when she's still following you… she would just follow you to your new house. That wouldn't help us at all. You have it chained when you're home?"

"Yes."

"That's good. Have you considered taking any self-defense classes or getting a gun?"

Vanna drew in her breath sharply. "My friend Suzanne said that I should take self-defense. But she said that any weapon could just be used against me so a gun might not be a good idea."

"Those are good points. If you get a weapon, you need proper training in how to use and handle it, too. Just buying it doesn't give you any protection. You can well imagine, this woman doesn't have any scruples. She will grab it out of your hand and use it if she can."

"Yeah." Vanna remembered how Julia had hit her. It had been so sudden and violent and unexpected. She couldn't be fooled into thinking that it couldn't happen again. She knew from her years with Tino that an apology, no matter how sincere, didn't equate to a change in a person's nature or behavior.

"Did she leave you a message when she broke in? A note that made you feel threatened?"

"No. Nothing that I saw."

"I'll have some officers give it a once-over, just in case there are fingerprints or anything else that might give us a clue as to this woman's real identity."

"Okay. Thanks."

"Tell me about the computer. It was a laptop?"

Vanna nodded and gave him the details that she could remember. She hadn't stopped to get the warranty papers out of her file cabinet before leaving, so she didn't have the model or serial number handy, but she gave him everything she could remember.

"I have more paperwork at home. I just didn't stop to bring it," she explained.

"You can get it when the officers go over. Not to worry. Chances are, it isn't going to be recovered until she is arrested anyway. What kind of information did you have on the computer? Anything like social insurance or passport numbers? Other personal papers?"

Vanna rubbed her temples. "I kept everything on that computer. I wasn't planning on it getting stolen. It has a password on it, but I assume those can be hacked. I don't even want to think about everything that was on it. Family pictures, journals, passwords, everything."

"But you said you've changed all of your passwords when you got the new computer."

"*Most* of them," Vanna corrected. "The big ones."

"You'd better get around to changing the rest today. Before she has a chance to get access to them."

"Yeah."

"We'll watch for it in all of the usual places, but you and I both know that she didn't steal it to hock at the nearest pawn shop. It wasn't for money. It was for information. With that computer, she can get right into your psyche."

———

Dr. Dent was the graphologist that had been hired to look over Julia's letters and to give them an analysis. This time, Vanna was glad for her family's money. She would not have been able to afford even ten minutes of Dr. Dent's time on her own account.

But Erica was generously picking up the tab and Dr. Dent had moved quickly on his analysis.

"She is a very interesting subject," Dr. Dent observed, looking over his notes and then looking up at Vanna's face to give her a huge smile. "I like interesting subjects."

"What was interesting about her?"

"She is very intelligent. Not highly educated, I wouldn't think, but very smart. She has tried to make her writing perfect, like a schoolteacher's script, but her personality still shows through to the expert."

"Like?" Vanna wrote down 'intelligent' in her notes.

"Her writing shows a high degree of deception."

Vanna snorted and wrote it down. "I would say you're right about that one," she agreed.

"Glad that my analysis matches what you know. It is very self-centered and yet insecure. Not someone who has a lot of confidence in herself. I might go so far as to suggest that the deception might include self-deception."

Vanna nodded. She wondered as she wrote the words down what her handwriting would reveal to Dr. Dent. Would he immediately spot how scared and anxious she was? Or would he just see chicken scratch and declare that he couldn't read a thing, as Vanna's schoolteachers had usually done?

"I would say she is introverted, closed off. Great attention to detail. And, as I said, highly intelligent."

"Right."

Dr. Dent tipped his chair back and watched her as she caught up with him. "I will give you a written report, of course. It will take a few days to get it written up properly."

"I know. But this is sort of urgent."

"As you say. She may come across as cold or disconnected. But she is very passionate. Very emotional."

"Can you tell from her writing if she is someone prone to violence?"

He studied her over the top of folded hands. "Interesting that you should ask that."

"Well…?"

"I do see several red flags for violent or angry behavior here. This is somebody that you would want to be very careful around. The combination of attributes… smart, careful, closed off, violent or angry… not a good person to cross."

"And what would you do if she was already after you?"

He scratched his chin, looking down at his notes. "You realize I am not a psychologist."

"Maybe not, but you're creating a kind of psychological profile."

Dr. Dent nodded and continued to rub his chin. "I'm sure there are people who are far more qualified to give an opinion than I. But I would suggest… you stay as far away from her as possible… don't give her any information about yourself or your family… don't get into an argument with her."

Vanna rolled her shoulders, trying to relax. Her back and chest were tight and sore. "I'm doing my best," she said.

Don't give her any information.

With Vanna's computer, Julia had all the information that she could possibly want. She knew everything about Vanna, and Vanna still didn't even know Julia's real name.

———

It had been a long day, but Vanna knew she had to get back to her apartment to get some work done. She was falling behind with several accounts. Too much time spent on amateur detecting. Too many sleepless nights killing off her brain cells. She just couldn't keep up with it all.

She wasn't paying much attention when she got back to the apartment building. A wave of fatigue passed over her and she put her head down on the steering wheel, closing her eyes.

When she opened her eyes and sat back up, she saw Julia. She was standing over by the elevator.

Vanna moved her elbow a few inches back to lock her door. She pulled out her phone and saw that this time she had a signal. She dialed Sweeny's number. He answered it within a three rings.

"Vanna?"

"She's here, Sweeny. At my apartment building. In the parking garage."

"Are you safe?"

"I'm in my car. Locked. I don't think she knows that I've seen her."

"She'll figure it out before long. Don't unlock your door. Don't engage with her. If she approaches the car, keep the windows up and don't talk to her. If she touches the car, drive out of there. I'm sending units over."

"Okay."

He clicked off and Vanna looked at the phone, unsure whether he had hung up or put her on hold. Sweeny's number was still on the screen, so she was just on hold. She waited.

She watched Julia. Julia stood there for a few minutes, waiting for her to get out of the car. When Vanna didn't, she walked over to the car. She looked in the window and saw that Vanna was on the phone. She tapped on the window. Vanna didn't respond. Holding the phone to her ear, she didn't know whether she should hang up and drive away. Julia was touching the car, but she wasn't violent or threatening. Vanna thought that she should probably stay there and wait for Sweeny's officers to show up. If she left, Julia would leave, and they wanted Julia to stay, so she could get caught this time.

Julia tapped again. Vanna rolled down the window a crack.

"Have a good day?" Julia asked.

Vanna swallowed and didn't answer.

"You were out for a quite a while," Julia observed. "Don't

you worry about not getting your work done? Or did you get work done somewhere else? In a coffee shop or at your mom's?"

She still wasn't sure what to do next. Sweeny hadn't come back on the line. The police hadn't yet shown up. Her heart was pounding hard. Where were they? Busy somewhere else?

"Get away from her!"

Vanna's head snapped around as she looked for the source of the voice. She instantly recognized Tino's roar. He had come in from the street and was headed straight for Julia.

"You just leave Vanna alone! Get out of here! I don't want to see you hanging around here again!"

Julia's face turned red as she faced off against Tino. "What makes you think you can order me around?" She spat like an angry cat.

"You're not supposed to be around her. You're not supposed to be within a hundred yards of her. You get out of here!"

"I'm not supposed to be within a hundred yards of her?" Julia repeated. She laughed without humor. "I could say the same about you, couldn't I? She filed a protective order against you, Mr. Valentine Peak. She said that she thought you had broken into her apartment."

"That was you, not me, and you know it."

Tino was shifting back and forth, sizing Julia up, trying to figure out how to approach her. His hands were open wide like he was getting ready to grab her if she ran. Julia's eyes were blazing. Vanna breathed with her mouth wide open, unable to get enough oxygen.

"What's going on?" Sweeny questioned urgently in her ear, suddenly coming back onto the line.

"Tino confronted Julia. They're arguing…"

"Tino? Who is Tino? My officers are going into this and will have no idea what's going on. Is he armed?"

"No, he's not armed. He doesn't use weapons…"

"Who is he?"

"An ex-boyfriend…"

"Ex-boyfriend? What's he doing there?"

"He's… I don't know… I have a protective order out against him too… I didn't know if… I thought that he might have been the one to break into my apartment, to start out with."

"Why is this the first time that I am hearing about this?"

"I talked to other officers about it. I thought it was passed on to you."

Vanna saw Tino and Julia draw closer together and then suddenly Julia was running, out the door and gone, too fast for Tino to catch. Tino watched her go. He turned back toward Vanna in the car puffing out his chest proudly.

"Got rid of her," he boasted.

"Tino… what did you do that for?"

His eyes widened. "She's the one. You have a restraining order against her. She was in breach of it. I got rid of her for you. Protected you."

"No, you didn't. You chased her off before the police could get here to arrest her."

"What?"

Two police cars sped into the parking garage, engines roaring, echoes bouncing from wall to wall. The color drained from Tino's face. Vanna put her hands over her face. "Oh, Tino!"

"I didn't know!"

"Why couldn't you just stay away from here? She's right, I do have a restraining order against you too. You shouldn't even be on this block. You're supposed to be leaving me alone."

"I have been leaving you alone. I haven't contacted you, have I? But I couldn't just let her threaten you."

One of the cars screeched to a stop beside Vanna's car. "Are you okay, ma'am?"

"Yes, I'm fine."

A heavyset cop jumped out of the passenger seat, approaching Tino with his hand on his holstered weapon. "Please put your hands on the car, sir," he barked.

Tino looked at him. "I'm not doing anything! What's the problem?"

"Put your hands on the car, please."

Tino opened his mouth to protest again.

"Do it now!"

Tino moved to obey. The cop pushed him into place, patted him down and handcuffed his hands behind his back.

"He wasn't the one who was harassing me..." Vanna protested. "She went out—"

"You're under arrest for breach of a protective order," the cop growled. He proceeded with the Miranda warning.

"It's not him—" Vanna tried to protest.

"You have an order against him," the other cop said.

"Well, yes, but—"

"He's breached it by being in here. We are required to arrest him. You need to just stay out of it."

"But he wasn't doing anything wrong, he was trying to help me!"

"Ma'am, guys like this can seem charming, they can wheedle their way back into your favor, but that just makes them more dangerous. It's women like you who get killed because they can't uphold the restraining order and they let the guy back into their lives and their homes again."

"But..."

"Just stay out of it. Let the wheels of justice turn the way they are supposed to."

One of the officers from the other car, a young man who barely looked old enough to be out of high school, walked over to talk to Vanna.

"You can hang up the phone," he advised, a smile quirking one corner of his mouth.

Vanna looked down at it. "Oh. Um, bye, Sweeny. I guess I'll talk to these guys here."

"Maybe they can still track her down," Sweeny said. "Chances are, she hasn't gone very far. I've got a couple more units patrolling the neighborhood, seeing if they can spot her." He paused. "Is there anyone else who you have a restraining order against? Anyone at all?"

"No, that's it." Vanna's face felt hot. "Bye." She ended the call and looked at the young officer. "Sorry. She got away before you got here."

"Which way did she go?"

Vanna made a motion. "Tino scared her off. He thought he was doing the right thing, but…"

"Tino?" he questioned, jerking his head toward the car where Tino was sitting.

"Yeah."

"He should have just stayed away. What's he doing hanging around here?"

"I dunno… I guess he's trying to keep an eye on things for me."

The boy-cop looked at her for a moment and then made some scribbles in his notepad. He turned his head to talk into his radio and walked over to the exit that Julia had used, looking around attentively.

The big officer who had put Tino under arrest returned to Vanna's window. "Sorry we got here too late, ma'am. Maybe they'll still find her. Are you feeling all right?"

Vanna took a deep breath and tried to relax her body. She realized that she was shivering. "I'm a little… a little shaken," she admitted. "After all of her apologies… she just walked right back in here like nothing had happened."

He nodded. "They'll do whatever they think they can get away with and act like it's perfectly reasonable. Look at some of these sickos who stalk celebrities. The police can warn them off again and again and they keep showing up. Some of them have been doing it for years. But since they are not a big threat, all judges can do is put them in jail for a few days or give them a fine and then they're free again to continue."

"If you arrested Julia… it would be for more than a few

days, wouldn't it? She wouldn't be able to keep coming back here after that?"

"I can't speak for what a judge would do. If you have bad luck and end up getting one who decides to be lenient because there was no actual threat made…"

Vanna hadn't thought about this before. She had just assumed that the main hurdle was getting Julia arrested. Having the police catch Julia in violation of the restraining order. Vanna had assumed that would be the end of it. Once they caught her, they wouldn't let her go again. But now she thought about it. She didn't imagine that there were a lot of people sitting around in prison because they stood there and talked to someone. Asked them how their day was.

The people that were in prison were the ones who had tried to kill someone.

Or succeeded.

Chapter Seventeen

S haking her head, Vanna made an irritated noise in the back of her throat.

"I don't *want* to go to the support group," she said into the phone. "It just makes me more depressed. There are people in that group that have been stalked for years. Eight years, one of them. Eight!"

"That doesn't mean that's how long yours will go on for," Lydia said. "I would say that's pretty unusual."

"Yeah, most women get killed in the first four," Vanna snorted. She stared at her computer screen, trying to sort through the email that was piling up, but unable to focus on it.

"Don't talk like that! The stats say that most stalkers are harmless. Just annoying."

"Annoying. That's a word that only someone who hadn't been stalked would use. You don't know what it's like. I can't relax. I'm worried that everything I say is being listened to. That every time I step outside of my apartment, she's watching me. She knows everything about me. She has my laptop! My whole life was on that laptop!"

"But you'd copied it all onto the new one." Lydia completely missed the point.

"I'm not upset because I don't have a copy. I'm upset that she does! It's… it's an invasion of my life. Like… a psychological assault. Like she's stripped off all my clothes and I'm exposed to the world."

She could hear clinking dishes in the background as Lydia washed up or unloaded the dishwasher. Lydia paused, thinking about this. "If you went to the support group, there would be people there who could understand that feeling and help you through it."

"Why do you care if I go to the support group or not? If it's not helping me, I shouldn't have to go." Vanna recognized that a whine had crept into her voice. Not exactly pretty.

"I think it would help you if you'd give it a chance. I'm worried about you. Mom's worried about you. We know what a toll this is taking."

"I don't feel like I belong there. Everybody else, they're either being stalked by ex-lovers or by strangers. There's nobody being stalked by their mother!"

Giving up on her email, Vanna went out to the kitchen to refresh her coffee.

"She *is* a stranger," Lydia pointed out. "She hasn't been part of your life, you don't know her. And you said yourself that even if she's your birth mother, she isn't your mother."

"It's just weird. I'm an anomaly."

"What if I came with you? Would that help? What day of the week is it?"

"That's the other thing. Any other support group meets at the same time and place every week. But we're not supposed to follow a predictable schedule, so it's all over the place. Different days of the week, different times of day, different locations. I can't keep track of when and where the next meeting is. There's not a published schedule or a call-in number. It's all cloak and dagger."

"So how are you supposed to know where and when the next meeting is?"

"I can't tell you. We're not supposed to share it with anyone outside the group. But suffice to say… it's very complicated and includes public advertisements with keywords."

"That sounds like fun! So cloak and dagger. When is the next one?"

"I haven't checked. It's too much of a pain. Really, Lydia, I don't want to go. And even if I did, you've got the kids, you don't need to be running around to my meetings."

Lydia was silent.

"It's not helpful for me," Vanna repeated.

"Okay. If it's not working for you, then it's not working. I'll just have to accept that. But I still think you need to get out. You're pretty much a recluse these days. You used to always go out to events with your friends. Meet-ups, dinners…"

"There just hasn't been anything going on lately."

"Try to get out to something."

"We'll see. It… makes me nervous to leave the apartment, knowing that she could be here while I am gone. I never know what I'm going to come home to."

Vanna picked up her bag and stepped out the door. She only got a few steps down the hall before it hit her. First, a wave of dizziness, like a head rush from getting up too fast. She wondered for an instant if she was coming down with a cold and had triggered the rush by bending over for her bag. But the wild thumping of her heart against her ribs told her that there was more to it than that. She steadied herself with a hand on the wall and looked around carefully. *Trust your instincts,* Sweeny had told her. Listen to your body. Look around, be alert. Pay attention to what your conscious self might have missed.

The hallway was empty. No neighbors, visitors, or repairmen. Just Vanna. She looked at the video surveillance cameras that the building manager had recently put up. They were supposed to make her feel better. But rather than feeling safe that the hall was being monitored and recorded, Vanna was paranoid that Julia would hack into the system and use the cameras to watch her coming and going. She didn't want to feel like someone was watching her. Not the building manager or security contractor, not Tino stopping by to make sure she was safe, and not Julia. She wanted to go back to the time when she could come and go as she pleased, with no one paying any attention.

Her heart gave a series of three throbs that hurt so much they made tears come to her eyes. She broke out in a sweat and breathed harder, trying to get enough air. Was she having a heart attack? People could have them young and Vanna had no way of knowing if there was a family history. Her family doctor, still the one she had used when she was at home with Erica, was very thorough and assured her that she was in perfect health. Other than that she could stand to lose just a few pounds. She wasn't huge, but ten pounds wouldn't hurt. Of course, that was before Julia had started contacting her. Vanna's clothes were pretty loose now and she knew from looking at her face in the mirror that she had lost a little of the roundness of her cheeks.

The throbbing had stopped, but her heart was still racing. Sweat slid down her back. She wasn't exactly feeling dizzy, but definitely light-headed. Maybe she was coming down with something. She turned around and went back into her apartment. She locked and chained the door and stood there leaning against it for a moment, the feelings of queasiness and distance gradually melting away.

She pulled out her phone to call Sue Anne. She'd have to get together with them another time.

―――――

The lawyer Erica had retained, Mr. Wright, of Wright Law LLC, had left a voicemail message for Vanna that he had made some progress and wanted to speak with her. She wondered what exactly that meant. He hadn't had any doubt that he would be able to get somewhere on her case. But he wasn't sure *exactly* how much information he would be able to get the court to release in light of the fact that everything had previously been redacted and kept so quiet.

She waited to be connected. It was a while before the secretary came back on the line. "It's only going to be about ten more minutes until Mr. Wright gets out of his conference. Do you mind waiting? Or do you want me to have him call you back?"

Vanna glanced at the time. "Yes, I'll just hold."

While she waited, she put on another pot of coffee and tried to catch up on a little of the filing that had gotten so behind the last few weeks. Whatever had happened to a paperless society? If anything, she was sure that she had increased the amount of paper she was handling. It could be overwhelming. And how much of it would she really ever need again?

Thinking about throwing out or destroying any of her files, though, just made her think more about the court documents. It didn't seem right that the DSHS could just destroy their records after five years as if it meant no more than a sale of shares or a housing purchase. They had thrown away important details of her life. Of who she was. All without any regard to whether she would ever want it.

Of course, she hadn't wanted it until the stalking had begun. If they had asked her permission, she would have gladly given it. She hadn't wanted anything to do with her birth family. It meant nothing to her. Less than nothing, because it detracted from her adoptive family. She didn't want them to think that there was anything more important to her than them. She was horrified by the thought that her father, or Lydia, or even Erica would ever feel crowded out or displaced by her birth family. She would never let that happen.

"Miss Austin? I'll put you through to Mr. Wright now."

"Thank you."

But her voice was drowned out by the ring tone, the secretary had not waited for her answer. The elderly Mr. Wright answered. She knew there was a younger Mr. Wright too. There might even be three generations of Mr. Wright at Wright Law LLC, but she wasn't one hundred percent sure.

"Miss Austin. Thank you for calling me back and for waiting so patiently."

"I don't know how patient I've been," Vanna confessed. "I'm pretty anxious to hear what you've found out."

"Not a lot yet, I'm afraid. There will be the need for some further court applications and orders before we have the full story. Judges are very leery of opening up sealed files, under any circumstances."

"What did you find out? Did you at least get a name?"

"I don't yet have confirmation of the name. It may or may not be Julia Cortez, no one has disclosed that yet. But I did get one piece of information that they hoped would satisfy us."

Vanna held her breath. She wondered if Mr. Wright realized how much he was teasing her, if he was intentionally drawing out the tension.

"Your birth mother is dead."

Vanna gasped aloud. It was a good thing that she was already sitting down because black blotches crowded out her vision and she was afraid that she had fainted for a moment. Holding onto the desk in front of her, she breathed in a few long, deep breaths.

"Miss Austin? Vanna? Are you still there?"

"I'm here." Vanna's voice was strangled.

Her birth mother was dead? The real Julia, or whatever her real birth mother's name was, was dead.

"Are you okay? I'm sorry, it must be quite a shock to you." His tone was concerned. "Are you by yourself? Maybe we should send someone to be with you."

"No. No, I'll call someone. My sister or my mom. Are you sure? They're sure that my birth mother is dead?"

"That's the information that the court released. Their hope is that that is all that we will need and they won't have to release any more information. But of course… you wanted more details than that. Don't you?"

Vanna's head was whirling. Julia wasn't her birth mother. There was no doubt now. But who was she? Would digging into Vanna's past reveal any clues? Or was Julia just a random stranger who had pulled her name off of an adoption database somewhere in order to masquerade as her birth mother?

"Yes…" Her voice came out in a croak and she cleared her throat and started again. "Yes, I think… I think we are still going to need more. If my birth mother's name is Julia Cortez, then this woman—this impostor—still knows more about me and my adoption than even my mom does. She has to be involved somehow. Even if she just knew the social worker who handled it. There is some kind of secret that everybody is trying to keep. Why was the file sealed by court order anyway? What happened that made them put me into adoptive care? Was it when my mother died? Is that when I went up for adoption? Because my mom says I had gone through some kind of trauma." Vanna barely paused for breath. "How did she die? Was I there?"

Wright chuckled. "I have no idea as to the answer of any of those questions. But you raise some good points. I will draft up a new application explaining the need for real details. Her name and the circumstances of her death, if they are on the file."

"Okay. Yeah. That would be good. How long do you think all of this is going to take? I feel like they're just trying to screw me around. Don't they understand that it's not just curiosity? I'm being stalked by this woman!"

"I'll get it drafted up today. I'll have a junior take it over for filing tomorrow. But as far as how long it will take to work its way through the system… I can't make any promises."

Vanna sat staring down at her hands. They seemed paler than usual, with striations across the nails that she hadn't noticed before. She rubbed the ridges on her index fingernail with her thumb.

"I'll be waiting."

Chapter Eighteen

It was dark. The phone was ringing. Vanna reached for it groggily, trying to push restless nightmares of crying babies from her mind and to focus on what was going on. *Who was calling her in the small hours of the morning, when she had just barely drifted off to sleep? Was it Erica? Was everything okay?*

She thumbed the on-screen button to answer the call without being aware enough to focus on the phone number to identify the caller. She realized as the call clicked through that it was probably some drunk who had called the wrong number and she should have just let it go through and then blocked the number from calling back again. But it was too late.

"Why are you doing this to me?" Julia whined in her ear. Her voice had an uncontrolled quality to it like she was drunk or hysterical. Or both. "How can you treat me this way?"

"What are you talking about?"

She realized too late that she was supposed to hang up. Not to engage with Julia. She was supposed to hang up and then call the police to have them trace and track the phone that had called her.

"You treat me like some freak!" Julia wailed. "You act like

you don't know me. Like you hate me! I'm not a horrible person. I love you!"

"Who are you?" Vanna questioned. "Tell me your name."

"You know my name!"

"Your real name. I don't want to hear that you are Julia Cortez. Julia Cortez is dead. Tell me who you really are."

For a moment, there was no response. Vanna could hear ambient background noise. Maybe a restaurant or a club. Not really loud music, but loud enough for her to identify the song. Then the call clicked off and she was left looking at the phone's wallpaper. Vanna bit her lip, thinking about it. Then she called the police. Not Sweeny's number, because there was really no point in getting him out of bed for this, but nine-one-one. She gave her case number and explained that she had just received a call from her stalker and needed it traced and, if possible, GPS tracked to its current location. The operator took down her information and promised to get someone started on it. They would call Vanna back in the morning if there were anything to report.

———

It was Sweeny who called Vanna in the morning to get the rundown from her on the early-morning call from Julia.

"You're not supposed to answer or engage with her," he reminded her.

"I know. But I was half-asleep. The phone woke me up and I haven't been sleeping a lot lately, so I wasn't really in the best state of mind. It's unlisted, I didn't think she had the new number yet."

"Did you learn anything new?"

Vanna considered. It was good of him to ask her and not just to lecture. So far, he hadn't told her what he had found out, but she hoped that he would share after she did. "It wasn't a very long call. She sounded upset, wound up about something.

Accusing me of treating her badly. Like an animal. I think she might have been drunk, but I don't know for sure. Just a sense. She wasn't slurring her words, but she was… emotional."

"Uh-huh."

"I asked her what her real name was. I told her that I knew that Julia Cortez was dead and I wanted to know who she really was."

Sweeny's voice was cautious. "That's provocative. You don't actually know that Julia Cortez is dead."

"The court record said—"

"The court record said your birth mother was dead. We don't actually know that her name was Julia Cortez until the court releases that information."

"Oh. That's right."

"But she appeared to be affected by your question?"

"Yes. She didn't have an answer. Usually, it doesn't matter what I say, she'll just keep getting more and more upset with me. But asking her what her real name was, or telling her that Julia Cortez was dead, that seemed to stop her in her tracks. She didn't say anything else and she hung up."

"I think we can infer from that that she knows Julia Cortez is dead. If Julia Cortez was just a fictional name, or if it was her real name, I think that she would have argued that she was Julia Cortez. Challenged you to prove that she wasn't."

"So my birth mother's name was Julia Cortez?"

"Maybe. I'm thinking it probably was."

"Then… she's getting her information from somewhere. She must have known my birth mother or her family. How else would she know that Julia Cortez was my birth mother? It's not publicly accessible information. And how did she track me after the adoption?"

"There's a small possibility that she was someone who was involved in the case at the time on an administrative level. A secretary or court clerk or social worker who knew the details of the case. But I don't think so. I think she was more intimately involved. This doesn't strike me as the behavior of an outsider who just happened to latch onto a couple of names and obsess a little over the case. This feels much more… personal."

Vanna shuddered. But she nodded in agreement. Sweeny, on the other end of the phone, couldn't see either reaction. "Yes, I think so too," Vanna agreed, her voice controlled and dispassionate. "I've thought so from the start. That's why I thought she really was my birth mother and I was so thrown when they said that she was dead. She really sounds like she believes that she's my birth mother when she talks to me. She says 'I am your mother' a lot and it really sounds… genuine."

"Maybe she is someone connected to the court case," Sweeny said. "Like a social worker. Someone who was a little unbalanced and she had some kind of psychotic break… because you were someone she had always felt sorry for, because of the case, she stepped into your mother's place. Assumed her identity."

"Maybe," Vanna agreed. She let out a long, pent-up breath. "I hope that we can get more information from the court soon. Wright said that they asked for priority service, but I'm still waiting to hear back."

"The department made an application as well. But sometimes these things do take weeks to get back, even though you ask for priority."

"I guess all we can do is wait. Did you find anything out about the phone? Who owns it or where she was?"

"It was a burner, like the previous one. She turned it off, so we don't know where it is right now, but she was at a bar when she called you. We've flagged it in the system, so when it comes back online, we can try to track it again."

"Okay. What name was it registered in? Was it a name you know or the address that she used before?"

"She used an alias. Not one that shows up on our files. Used fake ID when she bought and registered it. Different address, one that didn't exist. Not the one from before."

"Do you think she still watches that mailbox?"

"I wouldn't be surprised. But don't you get any ideas. I don't want you writing to her to try to draw her out."

"I won't. But maybe you guys could watch the mailbox… set up surveillance for the time between when the mail is delivered and when the owners get home to check it."

"We have had it watched. Not the entire time, but at random intervals. She may not be checking it every day anymore. Or she may have spotted the surveillance and waited until we weren't around."

"She's too smart."

"She's a canny one," Sweeny agreed. "I prefer the stupid ones. They're easier to catch."

———

Vanna looked up the upcycling group's meet-up page. She should really go out to something again. It felt like it had been months since she'd had face-to-face contact with any of her friends. Some of them had called or emailed, but mostly she had just cocooned herself in her apartment, keeping all possible interruptions or intrusions to a minimum. But she was starting to feel antsy. She needed crafting supplies. Even though work on the pendant lamps was slow because she was so tired all the time and had little interest in things creative, she felt like she had to get more supplies and move them forward. She had to stop herself from being isolated all the time and take back up some of those things that had once brought her happiness.

But as she looked at the meet-up page and started to make plans to join up with the others on some of their outings, she had a sinking feeling.

Julia had her old computer. Which meant that she had all of Vanna's bookmarks and web history. She would know that Vanna often met up with the group, and there was nothing to stop Julia from going to those meet-ups to see if Vanna showed up. They were happy to welcome any new members. It wasn't like there was some vetting process to see if new people were really interested in upcycling, or if they had criminal backgrounds or could pass some sort of security check. It was just a casual group of like-minded individuals.

She couldn't go to the meet-ups.

She couldn't go anywhere that Julia might expect her to go.

Chapter Nineteen

Y ou are so pretty. I am lucky to have such a gorgeous, sexy daughter.'

Vanna's stomach turned over as she read the latest letter from Julia. The letters from Julia had gradually been changing, but the latest was the most obvious. They had been getting shorter. Less personal information. Not so rambling. The handwriting growing a bit larger over time. This one was the shortest yet, only one page, front and half the back. There were extra loops in the writing that she would have to ask Dr. Dent about, and big loopy descenders on the letters that went below the baseline.

But she didn't need Dr. Dent to tell her that the latest letter sounded less like a letter to a long-lost daughter and more like a letter to a lover. The not-so-subtle shift frightened her. Was Julia losing her grip on reality? Or maybe it was a good thing. Maybe Julia didn't believe that Vanna was her daughter anymore. Maybe she would just let go and move onto other things.

But in her heart, Vanna knew that it wasn't true. Julia's shift of focus or new reality wasn't a good thing for her.

It was very, very bad.

———

The collection of undeposited checks was getting too large for Vanna to keep holding onto, and her bank account was dry, begging for more funds. She had to deposit them or she would be unable to pay her bills. Rent was coming due, as well as her internet provider's bill, and half a dozen other assorted bills that she would need to pay. So she finally decided that she couldn't avoid going out any longer and got on her raincoat. The day was dismal and gray. Not just wet, but cold and gloomy. The kind of day that didn't use to bother Vanna at all.

She used to laugh at people who got depressed by the weather.

She wasn't laughing any longer.

Vanna picked up her bag and headed out the door. She carefully locked her door and looked up and down the hallway. Her heart started racing and palpitating, but she held firm.

She could go out if she chose to. It was up to her whether she wanted to or not.

She was safe and in control of her own life.

The affirmations didn't help much. But she knew that if she gave in, she would have to pay a courier to take the checks to the bank. And she didn't have any deposit slips. And she didn't want to have to open a door to a stranger when the courier came to collect them. She needed to go to the bank and she needed to do it in person. So she held firm and forced herself to continue down the hallway, to the elevator and across the echoing parking garage to her car. It looked forlorn sitting there, where it had sat almost untouched over the past few weeks. Vanna looked around for Julia, but she wasn't in the parking area today. Neither was Tino, apparently. Tino had been pretty embarrassed by the arrest for breaking his protective order. He was worried that it was going to get back to his employer and he would get fired over it. They wouldn't understand why he had been there even though he knew about the restraining order. They would think that he was a bad person, psychotic.

Vanna felt bad for him. But he *had* breached the protective order. He should not have been there to interfere.

———

She made a quick stop at the pharmacy first and Vanna was just stepping out the door when she heard her name called. She turned around and saw Kelly, from the flea market.

"Vanna! I haven't seen you forever, where have you been hiding?"

She gave him a weak smile. "I've been having some problems. I haven't been able to get out."

"I heard… I think it was from Sue Anne… she said that you were being stalked?" Vanna nodded and his eyes widened. He shook his head. "That's horrible! Are you okay? Are you safe?"

"Nothing *really* bad has happened… I mean, it makes me really anxious, but they say that I probably don't need to worry… she'll just get tired of it and back off eventually… they say that most stalkers aren't violent."

"She?"

Vanna nodded. She didn't explain that Julia was her birth mother. She didn't want all of the details out there and Kelly was a horrible gossip.

Kelly looked slightly relieved by this. Apparently, he too bought into the idea that if it was a woman, Vanna didn't really have anything to worry about. "Do you need anything? Can I help in any way?"

"No." She touched his arm. "Thanks, but I don't think that there's anything that you could help with."

"You're sure…? You let me know if you think of anything. Really. I'd be happy to help."

"No, really. I'm fine."

"Okay." He leaned in and kissed her cheek. "You take care of yourself. Hope to see you soon."

Vanna smiled at him, appreciative of his concern. He gave her a friendly half-hug squeeze and went into the pharmacy.

———

It was only a short drive to the bank. When she got there, she looked around again. Nothing seemed out of the ordinary. Everybody went about their own business, ignoring Vanna. No black Sunfire. She went into the bank and used the ATM, trying to get it out of the way as quickly as possible.

As she punched the numbers in, the two sides of her brain were warring over whether she should stretch her luck and go to the grocery store as well. She could save on delivery charges. She could pick out her own produce instead of them delivering green, plasticky tomatoes.

But would that be pushing her luck?

She should get back to her apartment, where it was safe. Make sure that Julia wasn't there, touching her things and moving them around. Maybe stealing something else that mattered to Vanna, or leaving an unwanted gift for her.

Vanna was distracted by the argument in her brain as she moved back across the parking lot toward her car. To go to the grocery store, or not to go to the grocery store. Would it be safe? Was it wise? Was she just being paranoid?

She looked up at the sound of a racing engine and realized that the low, black car was coming directly for her. She hesitated, the proverbial deer in the headlights, unsure of whether to run across or back. The car would stop, wouldn't it? At the last second, Vanna tried to retreat. She heard a scream and knew by the roar of the engine that she wasn't going to make it in time. Unlike on television shows, you couldn't outrun a car in real life. She was not going to make it. Vanna felt a burst of pain in her leg and she knew she was falling, but she didn't remember hitting the ground.

———

Vanna awoke groggily, feeling like she'd been asleep for a very long time. She wondered how she had managed to sleep for so long when sleep had eluded her so much lately. Her body felt like it was floating. It was a long time before she managed to open her eyes.

"Ivanna. Ivanna… are you awake?"

"Mom?"

"Wake up, sleepyhead." There was a smile in Erica's voice. Vanna had been notoriously hard to get out of bed in the morning as a teenager. Lydia seemed to have no problem jumping out of the bed in the morning, fresh as a daisy. But for Vanna, it had been hard. Erica had been patient, trying everything she could think of to make the transition easier for Vanna and still to get her to school on time.

"I'm awake," Vanna murmured. She blinked, trying to clear her vision. What was Erica doing there? The room wasn't familiar and Vanna looked around, disoriented. She tensed to get up. "What happened?"

"Shh, stay put. Just lie still."

"What happened?"

"You had a little accident."

"I did?" Vanna tried to remember. "How? Did I fall?"

Nothing hurt, exactly. Her body was sort of achy, but in a far-distant way. She supposed she was pumped up with painkillers.

"No, you were hit by a car. In the bank parking lot."

"I was?" Vanna pressed her memory, but couldn't call it up. There was a blank. "That was pretty stupid."

Vanna knew she was too easily distracted. She had probably been looking at her phone while crossing the parking lot or been watching a mother pushing a baby carriage. Or she just had her head in the clouds thinking about Julia or a problem with a client or event.

Erica reached out and touched Vanna, but Vanna didn't feel it. Maybe Erica hadn't really touched her. Maybe her hand merely hovered over Vanna and she was afraid to touch Vanna for fear of hurting her.

"It wasn't your fault," Erica said. "It was Julia. People described her car. Someone saw the driver had blond hair. She ran you down."

"Ran me down? Why would she do that?"

"Nobody knows… that policeman Sweeny said it is 'anomalous' behavior. She didn't exactly wait around to explain herself. They got the rest of the license plate, but it turned out to be a stolen car."

"Oh."

Erica sat looking at her, concern in her eyes.

"How badly am I hurt?" Vanna asked.

"No broken bones. Lots of bruises and scrapes. The doctors said that you'll be pretty sore for a few days. You'll have to take it easy. I should probably set up an appointment for you at my chiropractor. Something like this can really throw your body out of alignment and if we can get it worked on right away before it starts causing major issues…" Erica trailed off.

"Sure," Vanna agreed. She could see the relief on Erica's face. Erica had been afraid that Vanna would rebel against this advice. Vanna was… independently minded. She had not appreciated Erica trying to interfere with her life, especially since leaving home. Vanna should be showing a lot more appreciation for her mother. This woman had saved her from whatever horrible beginning she had suffered, had patiently worked with her as a traumatized child, loving her and nurturing her. Vanna had grown up feeling secure and cared for. She couldn't remember the fear that she had experienced in those early years.

Erica stroked her hair, nodding and smiling. "I'm sure you'll recover quickly. You're young and healthy."

Vanna nodded slightly in agreement. She closed her eyes, resting.

"There was a court order issued in response to your application and the police application."

Vanna's eyes flew back open again. "There was? What did they say?"

Erica took a long time to answer. "Your mother's name was Julia Cortez," she said.

Vanna breathed out a long sigh. Now she knew for sure. Knew where she had come from. It was only one tiny piece of information, but it was important. Something to hold onto. "Anything else?"

There was another pause as Erica considered her answer. "She died before you came to us. She fell off a balcony."

"Fell off?"

"That's what the adoption file says."

Vanna rested, thinking about this. "What else does it say?"

"You were not found until several days after her death."

"What does 'not found' mean? Someone would have to check her apartment after she fell, right?"

"The police thought that you had been abducted. You turned up in a children's play place in the mall. You know—those places with slides and a ball pit and that kind of thing?"

"But that wasn't until a few days after she died."

"Yes."

"And they don't know where I was in between?"

"No."

"And do they think I was with Julia? Or whoever this woman is? Do they know?"

"There's no details on the adoption file. There are a few people that DSHS talked to at the time, but the names are redacted."

"Still?" Vanna's frustration seeped into her voice.

"The court believed that those people still had the right to their privacy."

Vanna growled in frustration. "Honestly! Is Wright going to do another application?"

"He doesn't believe that the court can be persuaded to release the documents with the names of the involved parties. There were no findings. DSHS wasn't able to discover what had happened in the intervening period. There are general descriptions of the people they talked to, like 'an ex-boyfriend' or 'maternal grandmother'."

"No 'blond female stalker'?"

Erica laughed. It wasn't her polite social laugh, but a giggle of genuine amusement. She'd obviously been under some stress and Vanna's question had taken her off-guard. Vanna smiled in appreciation at her mother's laughter. For a while, she lay there quietly, her thoughts drifting from one thing to another with the muddling effects of the painkillers.

"What was my name?" she asked. "Did they redact that too?"

"Amelia," Erica said promptly. "Amelia Cortez."

Vanna didn't feel any stir of recognition at the name. It seemed strange that she wouldn't recognize her own name. "Did you know that before? I mean, did they tell you that my name was Amelia, but you could call me what you liked?"

"They said that you were young enough that if we just started to use another name, you would respond to it soon enough. They never told us your name or called you Amelia in front of us. They'd say 'sweetie' or 'honey' and you didn't seem to mind. Within a day or two, you knew that we were talking to you when we said 'Ivanna.' You were very bright."

Past tense. She *had been* very bright. The intervening years had proven that early judgment to be incorrect. Too many years of the other students calling her a dumbo, or worse names and spending half of her time in the resource room. Vanna knew that she could get by if she worked hard, but high intelligence wasn't on her resume.

"With Lydia dragging you around by the hand all day, you couldn't help but learn your name," Erica said, her head tilted to the side slightly. "Ivanna this and Ivanna that. It was all we heard all day long."

"I'm lucky to have her as a sister," Vanna acknowledged. "Where is she? Does she know about my accident?"

"Yes. She's at home, but she'll come later on this evening when John Paul is home to watch the boys. She sends her love. She's worried about you. But I told her you were going to be okay."

"Yes, I'm fine," Vanna agreed. "Just tired, really. I'm not in pain. When will they let me go?"

"Not for a while. They want to make sure there are no unidentified problems or concussion."

"I want to get home. And lock the door," Vanna felt her consciousness starting to fade. It was getting harder and harder to keep her eyes open and attention fixed on Erica.

"Your apartment is locked up safe and sound."

"What about me?" Vanna looked around blearily. "What if Julia comes here?"

"I'm sitting with you and then Lydia will sit with you. The doctors and nurses all know to report anything unusual. And Sweeny put an officer on detail to watch your room. He knows that only Lydia or I or the medical staff are allowed in the room."

"Okay." Vanna yawned. "I think I'm going to sleep for a while, then."

"You go ahead. Your body needs sleep to heal."

———

Vanna drifted in and out of consciousness. The hospital wasn't quiet, with public address pages, nurses coming and going, and a patient down the hall shouting in what Vanna thought was Portuguese. Vanna was aware that Erica had traded shifts with Lydia and gone home. But it was all a blur.

She awoke in the night to a nurse taking her pulse and temperature. The nurse bent down to whisper close to her ear.

"I killed her," she said, her warm, moist breath on Vanna's cheek. "She thought that she could cheat on me. That she could kick me out. But she *couldn't.*"

Vanna stared at the nurse in horror. In the dimness of the room, she could just make out Julia's blond hair and profile. Vanna opened her mouth, but couldn't speak.

No sound came out.

She was paralyzed.

Julia stroked her hair and then left.

Chapter Twenty

Lydia had fallen asleep in the visitor's chair, in a position that was bound to give her a crick in her neck when she woke up. She moved around restlessly and gradually became aware of the sun starting to peek in through the windows and Vanna's open eyes.

"Hey, sis'," she greeted softly. "How are you doing?"

Vanna tried to speak, but still no sound would come out. She moved her lips and tried to force the words out, but nothing would come. Tears started to leak out the corners of her eyes.

"Vanna?" Lydia moved in closer, her eyes worried. "Are you okay? What's wrong?"

Vanna couldn't get a word out. She heard a sob, a choking noise. It couldn't have come out of her mouth. Because nothing was coming out of her mouth. Nothing at all. Lydia grabbed Vanna's hand and gave it a comforting squeeze.

"Talk to me, Vanny. What's the matter? Are you hurting? Do you need more painkillers?"

Vanna was able to shake her head. At least the paralysis of the midnight dream had left. She held tightly to Lydia's hand.

"Are you scared?"

Vanna nodded.

"Oh, honey. You don't have to be scared. Everything is okay. Do you know where you are?"

Vanna nodded. She motioned to the doorway and mouthed 'help'.

Lydia let go of her hand and hurried out the door. Vanna could hear her calling out to the nurses. "I need help. Something is wrong with Vanna!"

The nurse's voices were too low to hear. There was a flurry of activity, Lydia and a couple of nurses and a uniformed policeman all coming into the room at once. Vanna focused on the policeman and tried to speak to him. She couldn't think of what to say. More sobs came out of her. He could see that she was trying to tell him something and got closer, his brow furrowed.

"You want me? What's wrong? Did something happen?"

She nodded. All at once, the dam burst and the words came pouring out, along with a flood of tears. "She was here! She was here in this room! You let her right in!"

"Here in this room? When? Who was here?"

Vanna tried to speak around the choking sobs. "She was dressed as a nurse. In the night."

"You had a dream, Vanna," Lydia comforted. "That's all it was. A nightmare. The trauma from your accident, thinking about Julia, and being here with all of the disruption and the painkillers… you just had a nightmare."

The policeman nodded his agreement.

"There was a nurse," Vanna insisted.

"There have been a few," the officer agreed and looked at the two nurses who had come in. "You see? One of these?"

"No. It was Julia. The one who says she's Julia. She said… she said she killed my mother!"

Lydia took Vanna's hands and tried to comfort her. "It's okay, Van. It was a dream. Just a dream!"

"No, it wasn't. She was *right here*."

The police officer frowned at her, shaking his head. "The

only people who came in here were doctors or nurses. No one else."

"She was wearing scrubs. And a stethoscope. But it was Julia!"

"When, Vanna? I was here with you the whole time," Lydia pointed out.

"You fell asleep. It was in the night. It was still dark."

"You just dreamt it."

"No!" Vanna insisted. Her throat hurt, she put so much force into the word. "No, it was Julia! And she said she murdered my mother!"

"Your mother was just here yesterday," the cop said. "She just went home for a rest. She'll be back any minute now."

"No, not Erica. My birth mother. My birth mother was murdered. Julia did it!"

"Who told you that?" Lydia asked. "Did Mom tell you that? I thought that all we knew is that she is dead. I thought she fell."

"She must have been pushed. Julia pushed her."

Lydia touched Vanna's forehead, checking for a fever. "Do you think you could give her something?" she murmured. "Or is she reacting to the painkillers?"

"She probably just had a dream, like you said." The heavy Asian nurse moved closer and poked her electronic thermometer into Vanna's ear. "I think once she's been awake for a while, she'll be fine."

"I want Sweeny," Vanna told the officer. "You tell Sweeny I want him here. I need him to come and talk to me!"

"He'll be by later," the officer agreed. "He wanted to wait until you were lucid." A shadow of concern flitted across his face. "You can tell him all about what you saw."

"There was a blond nurse," Vanna said. "Right? Did you see her? A small, blond nurse? Very pretty? Like... in her twenties or thirties?"

He nodded. "Sure."

The nurses exchanged looks.

The policeman looked at them. "That would have been nurse…"

"We only have one blond in the unit," the smaller brunette said, shaking her head. "Berit. She's Norwegian and she's…" she made a 'big' gesture and giggled a little. "Her hair is ash blond, turning gray. She's not little or young."

Vanna raised her eyes meaningfully at the policeman. He chewed on the inside of his cheek, turning this over in his mind. He walked back to the door, looked up and down the hall and then pulled out his cell phone. Vanna relaxed back into her pillow with a deep sigh.

"I told you. I didn't imagine it. She was right here. You were asleep and she was standing right here, whispering to me."

"I'm sorry, Van," Lydia's face was turning pink. Her voice cracked. "I'm so sorry. I didn't mean to fall asleep, but I thought it was okay. There was a guard at the door. I had no idea… she shouldn't have been able to get in here."

"It's not your fault. I just… I'm not going crazy. It really happened."

"I… I guess it did. I'm sorry I was asleep and I'm sorry that I thought you were dreaming. I… just jumped to conclusions."

"I'm not going crazy. I'm not imagining these things. It's really happening."

Lydia nodded in agreement. "You're right, Vanna. I'm sorry. Really."

"What's going on here?" Erica asked, striding into the room and looking around at the obvious tension in their faces. "Is she worse? Ivanna, are you okay?"

The nurses made their escape.

"She was here," Vanna said. "Julia. Masquerading as a nurse. She said that she killed my birth mother."

Erica's eyes widened in shock. "Did they catch her?"

Vanna shook her head. "She got in and out without the cop realizing it. She was gone…"

"Why didn't you call for help?"

"I… I couldn't. I couldn't say anything. I was… I don't know. I was too scared."

"Oh…" Erica's voice went down. She looked at the tray in her hands. "Hot tea. Do you want some?"

Vanna nodded and Erica handed one of the disposable cups to her and another to Lydia. Vanna took a sip of the tea and breathed deeply in, trying to relax her body. The tea warmed her, the familiar taste soothing. She closed her eyes.

"Thanks, Mom. That helps."

Erica sat down beside the bed. She rubbed Vanna's shoulder. "Did you get a good sleep last night?"

"Yes. Mostly. Until Julia got here. Then… I didn't go back to sleep. I couldn't speak or move. But I didn't go back to sleep."

"Poor Vanna," Lydia moaned. "I feel so bad that it happened on my watch and I didn't even know. I didn't even wake up."

"She's very crafty," Erica said. "I don't know how she got in here, but she's very smart."

"The handwriting guy said that she was very intelligent," Vanna said. "She has to be. I don't know how she's done any of these things. How she could just walk in here."

"We'll figure it out," Erica assured them. "Everything will be sorted out."

It was what Vanna wanted to hear. She wanted to believe it. So she didn't question it.

"She said that she killed your birth mom?" Erica's voice was tentative. Delicate. She didn't want to upset Vanna any more than she already was.

"Yes." Vanna's throat felt tight and hot, even though she didn't know her birth mother.

"The DSHS file said that she fell off of the balcony."

"Maybe someone helped her off."

They all sat considering it.

"Why wouldn't that be on the file?" Lydia asked.

"At the time that the file was opened and the report was

made, they might not have known," Erica pointed out. "They would only be able to report the facts that they knew for sure at the time. If there was any allegation that it was murder—and we don't know, maybe there was and maybe there wasn't—then they might not have even been allowed to put it on the file."

Vanna closed her eyes again, exhausted. "We'll have to find out."

———

Vanna was able to get into her apartment under her own power. She told Erica and Sweeny that she was perfectly fine. Sweeny could see that she was in physical pain and Vanna thought that Erica recognized the psychic pain. But neither of them could persuade her to stay at the hospital any longer. Sweeny promised that she would be safe. He would post two guards this time and nobody would be allowed in unless they had been officially introduced to the guards. No nurses just walking in and out.

Sweeny confirmed that Julia had actually had a hospital ID tag clipped to her uniform. There had been no way for the police officer to realize that she wasn't a real nurse. She was dressed the right way, had a stethoscope and hospital picture ID had completed the disguise. She had smiled at him, walked confidently into the hospital room, and appeared to be performing a routine check on Vanna. No matter that he should have recognized her picture. The halls were only dimly lit at night and she had fooled him.

No new security measures could make Vanna feel safe at the hospital. Nothing Sweeny said could talk her into it.

Erica had offered to stay with Vanna at home for a day or two until she was feeling better, but Vanna knew how crowded the apartment would feel. She wouldn't be able to put up with Erica intruding on all of her routines and invading her space. Everything at her apartment was arranged to help her to stay focused on her work and not to lose things or get distracted. But it wouldn't all make sense to Erica. She would start to rearrange things in ways that she thought were more efficient. Putting things away when they needed to stay in sight. Moving the bowl she put her keys in over to the other side of the counter. Lecturing Vanna about putting her toothpaste tube away when she was done brushing her teeth. It would drive Vanna crazy and she wouldn't be able to get back on track for weeks after.

So she had told Erica no, she was all right. Thank you, but she didn't need anyone there to look after her. Vanna had promised to call Lydia before bed, but as soon as she walked in her front door, an overwhelming sense of fatigue washed over her. She put down her bag, placed her keys in the bowl, and staggered to her bed. She slid under the covers and closed her eyes, her body shutting down.

She slept for a long time. The pain, the after-effects of the painkillers that the hospital had her on and the days and weeks of oppressive stress all combined with her sleep-deprived state and drowned her with sleep.

Vanna recalled waking up to answer the phone once to reassure Lydia that she was okay. She had reached home and she didn't need anything. But now that she thought about it, she wondered if it had even been Lydia on the phone at the time. Had she actually known that it was Lydia or had she just spoken to Lydia, knowing that was who she was supposed to call before she went to sleep? Maybe it had been a telemarketer, or a client, or even Julia. Vanna couldn't remember one way or another.

She couldn't even rouse herself to find her phone and look at it to check. The fatigue still held her a hostage, kept her from rolling over to grab it. She felt like she had been sleeping for days, but there was no end in sight. She couldn't see ever being able to get enough sleep to overcome the overwhelming need.

———

When Vanna had finally gotten up, groggily, in the middle of the night two days after she had gotten home, there was a long list of missed calls on her phone. She knew that she should call her clients to start with. Reassure them. Tell them that she would get right on their projects. But she didn't. She couldn't face work yet.

Her body ached from the cramped position that she'd been sleeping in, or maybe it was from the accident. The pain, together with a new sense of wakefulness, kept her from being able to go back to sleep again.

Vanna called Lydia in the morning. Lydia confirmed with amusement that they had, in fact, talked on the phone. "You were a little… slurry," she laughed. "I thought maybe you took a couple of sleeping pills."

"No. I didn't take anything. I was just… exhausted."

"How do you feel now?"

Vanna yawned. "Tired."

"Why don't you lie down again for a while?"

"I've done nothing but sleep this week. I need to get up and do something."

"Well, remember that you were hurt. Sometimes it takes getting hit by a car to remind us that we need a little vacation now and then…"

"No, too much to do. Everything is falling behind and there isn't anyone else to take it for me. It's just me, Lydia, so I've got to focus on it."

"Be careful. Don't try to do too much. Remember the doctors said it would be a while before you were feeling quite up to par again. Did you call Mom?"

"No, not yet. Why, what did she say?"

"I don't know. She wanted to talk to you. She said she had called a bunch of times, but you hadn't answered."

"Yeah, I saw her on my caller ID. I'll give her a call. Probably just that chiropractor appointment."

After hanging up with Lydia, Vanna prepared herself mentally and called up Erica.

"Ivanna, I've been trying to get a hold of you! Are you all right?"

"I've just been sleeping, Mom. My body wouldn't let me do anything else."

"Your body has been through a lot," Erica agreed. "It's good that you're listening to it."

"Yeah." Vanna stifled another yawn, trying not to think about going back to bed again. She needed to stay focused on her work and what needed to be done. "So why were you calling? Was it just to check up on me?"

"No. I've been going through your father's old files and I found the name of the social worker who placed you with us."

"Oh! That's great!" Vanna's mind immediately overflowed with all of the questions that she wanted to ask the social worker. All of the things that she wanted answered. If they had a person, a real live person who had been involved in it all, they could get all of the questions answered. "We'll have to get a detective to try to track her down. Do you think they'll be able to?"

"I already tracked her down," Erica said, her voice dry and amused.

"What? You did? How?"

"I do know how to use the internet when I have to. It wasn't that hard to track her down, she was still living in the city."

"Is she retired? What's she doing?"

"I wanted to talk to you before setting up a time to meet with her," Erica said, bulldozing past the questions and into the heart of the matter. "Are you up to it?"

"Yes. Absolutely. I have to talk to her."

"I'll tell her. Any particular time? Do you have any appointments?"

"No, I'm flexible. I won't set up any appointments until you've set it up. What's her name?"

"Faith Cuthbert."

"Faith. I hope she lives up to her name."

Erica sighed. "Don't get your hopes up, dear. I don't know how much she will remember. Or how much she knew at the time. I haven't asked."

"I'll try not to. But I really hope that she has some answers."

Chapter Twenty-One

F aith Cuthbert was a woman around Erica's age. Graying gracefully, with her hair gathered back into a wavy ponytail instead of a perfect coif like Erica's. Just a little makeup, which didn't attempt to hide the wrinkles that were making their appearance. She looked Vanna up and down and shook hands with her, then they all sat down around Erica's coffee table. Erica picked up her tea. Faith picked hers up, but sat with it in her hands, not actually drinking it. Vanna didn't pick hers up at all. She knew that she would just fiddle with it and Erica would glare at her for fidgeting. This meeting needed her entire attention.

"You grew up," Faith observed with a wry smile.

"I guess I did. Sorry, I don't remember you."

"Don't be silly, I wouldn't expect you to. So how are you doing? This is all very exciting, I don't usually have anything to do with any of the kids that I placed or supervised."

"Vanna is going through a very difficult time," Erica cut in. "You can see some of the abrasions. She was recently hit by a car."

"Oh my! I'm so sorry!"

"By a woman who claims to be my birth mother," Vanna filled in.

The ex-social worker's eyes widened. "Your birth mother? But that's impossible."

"According to the court files that we've been able to access, Vanna's birth mother died before she was placed with us."

"Yes, that's right. It certainly wasn't her!"

"But she claims to be," Vanna inserted. She looked at her teacup and again decided not to pick it up. It would rattle in her shaky hands. "So we need to figure out who she really is."

"She hit you with her car?" Faith asked.

"Yes. She's been… stalking me for months now… and she showed up when I was in hospital. She said that she killed my mother."

The woman's wide-eyed surprise was taken over by a shocked, horrified expression. At first, she couldn't find any words. "That's… horrible," she said finally.

"Thanks. Yeah. So I was hoping that it would be someone that you investigated, during the foster-adoption placement."

Faith put down her teacup and saucer and sat back. She seemed overwhelmed by the whole thing. Her face was as white as one of those drama masks of a crying or laughing face.

"I couldn't tell you anything about the investigation," she said carefully. "It's all confidential. All of those records should have been destroyed by now."

"They were," Vanna confirmed. "We got the court file opened but they still aren't making very much available and everything is redacted. All of the names are blacked out, so we can't see the names of the people who were interviewed."

"That is a problem."

"I was hoping that you could fill us in a bit."

They all sat in silence while Faith considered this. "I really can't say anything," she protested.

"This is a life and death situation. If this woman killed

Vanna's mother, she could easily turn around and kill Vanna," Erica pointed out.

"But what reason would she have to kill Vanna?"

"So you know who it is."

Erica and Faith both turned toward Vanna when she spoke. Faith frowned, her eyebrows drawing down. "I didn't say that."

"You questioned her motive to kill me. You didn't say that you didn't know who it was. You didn't say that you didn't know why she had killed my birth mother. You implied that you knew why she had killed my birth mother."

"I did no such thing," Faith sat up primly, closing her mouth firmly.

"You have someone in mind," Erica said. "Do you know who killed Julia Cortez?"

"I went away soon after placing Vanna with you," Faith said, not answering the question directly. "My husband was in the military and we had to follow his deployment. So I wasn't here for the trial."

"What trial?" Vanna questioned, turning her head to look at Erica. Erica shook her head and Vanna looked back at Faith. "What trial?"

"The murder trial."

"There was a trial? You knew it was murder?"

"It was suspected pretty early on. It was obvious that there had been a struggle in the apartment. And you were missing for a few days. There was a lot to be suspicious about. But I was just the social worker. I wouldn't have been involved in the murder trial even if I had stayed around."

"But you must know what the outcome was."

"I wasn't here. We were stationed in Germany for ten years. When we came back here… the trial was long over and I never looked it up. It was ancient history."

"But you must have had your suspicions," Vanna pressed. "If you think you know what the motive for the murder was, then you must have had your suspicions about what was going on in her life around that time."

"I don't know anything for sure. And what I do know is confidential. I swore never to reveal private information to the public."

"But now that private information is destroyed. We have no other way of finding out."

"It was destroyed for precisely that reason. It was an investigation. Lots of things turn up that are private, that people want to be kept quiet. You can't just disclose that information to the public. The people who were involved in the Cortez case are still alive. You don't think they would want me revealing their private information, would you? I can't give you names or tell you what we suspected was going on. That would be a privacy breach. We're not allowed."

"What about public information?" Vanna pressed. "I thought that government files were opened up to the public after a certain length of time."

"Not the details of investigations like that. Those people have reputations that could still be damaged. We swore to keep it confidential."

Vanna sighed in exasperation. She looked at Erica. Erica would be able to wheedle something out of this woman. Vanna couldn't believe that they had found the social worker, only to run into another barrier.

"What do you know about the murder trial?" Erica asked. "That's not private information. You weren't involved in the murder trial."

"You'd have to look it up," Faith said. "I don't know what's on the public record and what's not. I was in Germany, I wasn't able to follow it. I don't even know what the outcome was."

"The court record that we got shows that there was an ex-boyfriend." Erica took a sip of her tea. Her eyes were intent on Faith. "That was in the court documents. The public court record."

"Yes," Faith agreed. "Obviously there was an ex-boyfriend if there was a child." Her eyes flicked toward Vanna.

Vanna felt like she'd been kicked in the stomach. "Are you saying the ex-boyfriend was my birth father? Is he still alive?"

"I couldn't say whether you are the child of the ex-boyfriend or not. Only Julia Cortez knew that, and maybe even she didn't know. But there were obviously men in her life at some point."

"Right," Vanna agreed, rolling her eyes up to the ceiling. She shook her head. She looked at the social worker and looked back at her mother, waiting for the next step.

"Was the ex-boyfriend investigated for the murder?" Erica asked.

"Anyone who was closely involved with Julia Cortez was investigated. That's the way it works. The closer you are, the bigger a suspect you are."

"But he wasn't the one who was charged," Erica finished.

Faith shifted, considering her answer, before finally answering. "No."

"Was it a woman who was charged?"

"I wasn't here—"

"But you know who was charged. You know it wasn't a man. So if there was a murder trial, then it must be a woman who was put on trial for it."

Faith shrugged, accepting this.

"Was she convicted?"

"I don't know."

"Are you sure? You never even heard a whisper of what the verdict was?"

"You would have to look at the public record. I wasn't here."

"Does that mean you don't know, or you don't want to tell us?"

"I'm not in a position to tell you anything."

Vanna looked back at her mother.

"We will find out," Erica assured Vanna. "Don't you worry."

Vanna nodded. It shouldn't be hard to find. Unlike a sealed adoption record, the verdict in a murder trial could not be obfuscated. It was either guilty or not guilty, and it was probably in all of the newspapers at the time.

"And you think that this woman took Vanna?" Erica asked. "That's where Vanna was, those first few days? With her mother's murderer?"

"We don't know. No one was ever prosecuted for that. Vanna just turned up at the mall, by herself."

"But you had suspects…?"

"I suppose there were a few people that we suspected might have something to do with Vanna's disappearance. But since she was never found in their custody and there was never any proof, there wasn't really anything that we could do about it."

"Who did you suspect?"

Faith raised her eyebrows and just sat there. Obviously tired of arguing the point, she had decided that maybe silence would be a better answer to their repeated demands.

"What else *can* you tell us?" Erica asked.

Faith pursed her lips. "I don't think I can help you. Not about this."

"What can you tell us about Vanna? Maybe something that you didn't tell us when she was first placed?"

Faith glanced over at Vanna and back at Erica. "We told you everything that we could at the time."

"But maybe now that it is twenty years later and the murder trial is long since finished, there are other things that you could tell us," Erica suggested, her words slow and precise.

Faith looked at Vanna uncertainly. Vanna tried to look open to hearing whatever she had to say. If Faith was basing what she should say on how Vanna would take it, Vanna needed to look as stable and calm as possible. She had turned out well. There was no need to keep anything else a secret from her.

"The apartment... Julia Cortez's apartment... I told you that there were signs of struggle. Signs that it was murder and not suicide or accident."

"Yes," Erica agreed and she and Vanna both nodded expectantly.

"And Vanna was missing. Of course, she wasn't Vanna yet, she was Amelia, but we never called her by that. We tried to prevent it from leaking out that Vanna was Amelia. We wanted Vanna to be stable in foster care or adopted into a family, not tainted by the murder trial. We didn't want there to be any association, because we knew that murder trials take years. She didn't need to be growing up in the shadow of the trial. To be known as the child whose mother had been murdered."

"I appreciate that," Erica agreed. "It would have been nice if you had at least shared that information with us, but that's neither here nor there. DSHS did what they thought was the best."

"Well... Vanna was missing from the crime scene..."

"Because she *had been* at the crime scene," Erica said.

Faith nodded. The impact of the statement didn't hit Vanna. She heard it, but it didn't really mean anything to her. It wasn't new information.

Erica picked up her tea and took a sip. She looked at Faith over the brim of the teacup. "Vanna witnessed her mother's murder."

"Yes."

They both turned and looked at Vanna. She looked back at them. She repeated the words in her mind, but they still didn't mean anything to her. She had seen her birth mother's murder. Was Julia's—fake Julia's—face imprinted in her brain somewhere, because Vanna had seen her wrestle Vanna's birth mother off of the edge of the balcony? Surely that would make some sort of permanent impression on her. Surely she would know Julia's face when she looked at it again. She'd recognize her as a murderer, as a threat.

Vanna hadn't connected with Julia when she saw her face or looked at her picture. She hadn't felt that feeling of 'my mother.' But at the same time, she didn't connect the woman's face with danger, either. It meant nothing to her. It was all just a blank.

"My poor girl," Erica murmured. "No wonder she was so traumatized."

"There was no way she could testify as a witness. She was so young, and when we got her back, we discovered that she couldn't—or wouldn't—speak. That clinched it. If she couldn't be part of the trial, we didn't want her to be associated with it in any way. The sooner we could start the healing process, the sooner she would be on her way to growing up to be a successful woman." Faith smiled at Vanna. "The successful woman we see that she has become."

Vanna wanted to argue with her. Successful? While she was happy with the way that her business had grown and of being an independent woman, an entrepreneur, all of Erica's criticisms over the years had lodged in her brain. She knew she was a failure in Erica's eyes. Erica believed that she should be working at an office somewhere. She could be a high-powered businesswoman. A socialite pushing the needs of children, or battered women, or some other important cause. She should live in a big estate like Erica and do the same kind of work that she did. Vanna knew that she would never live up to Erica's assessment, because she could never be a woman like Erica.

"Vanna has grown into a lovely woman," Erica said, confirming Vanna's assessment.

Ignoring the sting, Vanna pressed ahead. "Can you tell us anything about the ex-boyfriend?"

Faith looked surprised. "Why the ex-boyfriend?"

Erica turned to Vanna as well. They all knew that it was a woman who had been tried for the murder, so why would Vanna care to know anything about the ex-boyfriend?

"I don't know. I just wonder if he is a key. You know the

usual motives for murder: money and jealousy. If there was an ex-boyfriend, then maybe there was a new boyfriend. Or maybe the ex-boyfriend had a new girlfriend who was jealous of my birthmother, or something like that. We know from the court files that they talked to the ex-boyfriend. Those relationships might be the key."

"I don't know what I can tell you," Faith said. "He was a boyfriend for a while and then he wasn't."

"Was he seriously considered for the murder?"

"I think that he actually had an alibi."

"Did he have a new girlfriend?"

"I don't know of anyone. He might have, or he might not have."

Vanna was disappointed. She had hoped for something to hold onto. Some way to identify who had killed the real Julia. The new girlfriend of an ex-boyfriend made sense. Jealousy. But if there was no new girlfriend, then that was out.

"And was he my biological father?"

"I don't know. Honestly. I didn't know your birth mother before she died. I never talked to her. I only became involved in the case after you were found. I never even heard of Julia before that. I know that there was an open DSHS file. They were already monitoring the situation. I had to make an attempt to track down any biological family before putting you into the system for foster and adoption. But I wasn't able to find anyone. Julia Cortez had left home very young. She didn't know her own father. Her mother was still around, but she didn't have any… interest… in adopting Julia's child. We wanted a permanent solution, not just moving from one home to another. There was no father listed on the birth certificate. We advertised, but no one stepped forward."

"You talked to the ex-boyfriend, though. Did you ask him if he was the father—my father?" Vanna stumbled.

"I don't remember," Faith evaded. "I'm sure I talked to him.

Maybe just on the phone. But he wasn't ever identified as the biological father. Not that I remember."

"Thank you for coming to meet with us," Erica said, standing up.

Vanna stood as well, a little surprised that the interview was over. But they weren't getting anywhere. Faith had made up her mind not to tell them anything revealing, and she would just continue to duck their questions.

Faith got to her feet now, also looking a little startled at the abrupt close of the interview. "It has been nice to meet you," she said. She put out her hand hesitantly. Erica shook it. Then Vanna. "You've really grown up to be a lovely girl," Faith said. "I'm glad that things worked out well for you. I was really happy to find your family. I knew they would be good parents."

Vanna nodded, smiling. "They have been," she agreed. "I wouldn't even be asking anything about my life before I was adopted… except, with all of this stalking stuff…"

"Of course," Faith agreed. "You feel like you need to know about the past to unlock the future."

"Yeah," Vanna agreed. "Exactly. And especially… where she said she killed my mother… if it was murder, then we can at least find her name, identify her."

Faith held onto her hand for an instant longer. "You should be able to find what you need in the public record."

She released Vanna's hand. Erica offered to escort Faith to the door and Vanna sat down again to think about her birth mother and the unknown woman who had murdered her.

———

"Will you be okay, dear?"

Vanna looked up from her phone, where she had been concentrating very hard on her email while Erica escorted Faith to the door.

"Yes, I'm fine," she said automatically.

"No, not fine. You are still looking very fatigued and this can't have been easy for you. I had hoped that this would provide the answer to all of our questions, but it seems to have just generated more questions. We will have to go to the newspapers, look at old stories. Pull the old court record. All we should have to do is search Julia Cortez and the date of the murder, right? Will the internet have all of the old articles?"

"I don't know. Maybe some of them. A lot of newspapers are putting their old archives up online for those who want to access them, but I don't know if they will go all the way back twenty years. That's a long time."

"Why don't you leave it to me? I will take care of it."

"Mom, you don't have to do that. I'm perfectly capable of doing my own research."

"You have other things that you need to attend to." Erica gestured to Vanna's phone. "I know that expression…"

"Mom…"

"I know you haven't been able to take care of your… fake clients the last few days. I'm sure the work must be piling up…"

"Virtual clients."

Erica's face cleared and she nodded, giving a little laugh. "Your virtual clients. They'll be wanting you to do things for them."

"Yeah. They are. I just don't know if I am up to it."

"You have to," Erica said. "If you don't do it, someone else will. You have to be responsible, Vanna. You can't just flit from one thing to another and still keep clients. They will know if you haven't put the time into their work. The quality has to be outstanding for them to keep giving you new things to do. You don't build a business by neglecting people's needs."

Vanna sighed. "I have a few things to attend to," she agreed. "But I'll be able to do some research later on today. Tonight. Sometime."

"Why don't you let me get a head start on it? If I don't find anything, you haven't lost anything. And if I do, then you have something that you can dig your teeth into."

Vanna nodded. "Yes… that would be good. It's just that… I don't know. I guess I want to be the one to find it. The identity of my stalker. I want to be the one to take it to Sweeny and say 'there she is, go arrest her.'"

"You still can. I'll just gather articles and order the court records. I won't read them. I won't have time to. Then you can be the one to discover her identity. But you don't have to do all of the work all by yourself."

Vanna knew that Erica wasn't going to let this go. She wanted to be involved in the investigation and she had been helpful so far, with turning Faith up, even if Faith hadn't been as helpful as they had hoped.

"Okay, you're right. It's just… I was raised to do things by myself," she told Erica. "You can't just be lazy and expect people to do things for you."

Erica smiled. "You have done so much for yourself. I'm proud of you. Now let me help."

"Okay. But you aren't allowed to read them."

———

It sounded so easy. Vanna would just leave her mother to do the initial research, while she put out some fires, taking care of any burning projects for her clients.

But even as she turned on her computer and logged in, she had a headache. She was already reviewing the emails that she had read in her head and trying to set up an order of functions. But her brain just kept tempting her toward bed.

The more she stared at the screen, trying to move past her inertia and figure out what to do first, the more tired she got and the more the headache grew. She could barely even see the screen anymore. It was hopeless. There was so much to do and she couldn't even get started.

Vanna got up. She would brew some coffee, take something for her head and check again to make sure that the chain on the door was fastened. Then she would go back to her computer and start on the first task in the oldest email. She could do just one task, focusing hard on it, and then she would worry about the next after that. Just one at a time.

She stood in the kitchen watching the coffee brew. She knew that she should do something else while it was brewing. Wipe down the counters. Make herself a sandwich. Send out a couple of emails to clients explaining why she was going to be experiencing delays. Where she had been and why she hadn't gotten back to them as quickly as she usually did. But instead she just stood there, staring at the machine.

When the coffee mug was full, Vanna carefully took it out and dumped the filter and grounds in the garbage so that they wouldn't drip. Then instead of walking back to her computer and sitting down at her desk, she walked into the bedroom and lay down. She propped herself up like she did when she was going to read a book before bed and took a few swallows of the scalding hot coffee. She didn't pick up her book and take out the bookmark. She just lay down and went to sleep.

———

"Did Mom tell you what she found?" Lydia asked. Vanna could hear the boys squabbling in the background, but Lydia wasn't distracted by them. She was focused.

"No… she was going to do a bit of research for me, but she wasn't going to read any of the articles," Vanna said. "I wanted to do that part."

"She said that she found lots. When they weren't online, she went down to the library and searched the microfiche."

"Did she?" Vanna pictured her mother in front of the big microfiche machines, twirling the knobs to go from one page to the next, stopping to print out the occasional article. "Wow. I didn't know she knew how. I guess I'd better call her."

"She didn't want to bother you with it until you were ready. She said that you had a bunch of work to do with your clients and she shouldn't interrupt you."

Vanna let out a moan. "She's right. But all I did was go to sleep. I couldn't do anything else."

"Well, you're still recovering from being run over. They'll just have to understand that."

"I wish it was that simple. I committed, I really do have to find a way to get the work done."

"Well…" Lydia trailed off. She covered up the phone and said something to the bickering children and their noises faded away.

"What did you do with them?" Vanna questioned.

"Oh, I just sent them outside. I'll have to check in a couple of minutes, though. See what they're doing and tell them to stop it."

Vanna laughed. "Good thing we weren't like that. I don't know if Mom could have handled it."

"Give her some credit. I don't think we were angels. I'm starting to find that she was a lot more skilled at the parenting thing than I ever thought she was. Really. Sometimes the solutions she came up with to deal with you and me were brilliant."

"Like insisting that we could only whisper when we were fighting?"

"Yeah. Like that." Vanna could hear Lydia opening and closing cupboards and then the microwave beeping. She must be heating herself up a late lunch or early supper. "There's just one more thing, Van."

"What?"

"Tino."

Vanna stared at the phone. Tino? She hadn't even thought of Tino in a week.

"I saw him at the hospital," Lydia said. "It was just for an instant; I don't know if he even realized that I had seen him."

"He didn't come to visit me."

"He couldn't. Because of the restraining order and armed guard, right? But he was there. I think he might have dropped off a card."

"I didn't get one."

"Would Mom have given it to you?"

"No, I suppose not."

"Just… be careful, okay? I know you're worried about Julia right now and I think she's the one to watch out for the most. But Tino… I want you to be careful of him too, okay? Don't tell him it's okay to come over."

"I won't," Vanna agreed.

"Do you think that's who did it?" Lydia said suddenly.

Vanna tried to quickly replay the conversation in her head to see what she had missed. "What?"

"Do you think that Julia—or at least the one we call Julia—do you think she was the murderer? And if so, why? There was an ex-boyfriend, he had to be the prime suspect. Or the current boyfriend, if she had one. You always look at the people closest to the victim."

"Yeah, I don't know."

"Let me know what you find out, okay?"

"I will," Vanna agreed.

She just had a couple more dictations that she needed to work on and then she would call Erica.

———

It had been a long day and Vanna didn't really want to have to get up and go to the Estate again.

"Can you send them to me?" Vanna asked. "Fax or scan them? Or do I need to come there? It's just that I'm sort of tired…"

"I'd really like to go over them together," Erica said. "They look really interesting. I could bring them over to your place if you don't want to come here. That would make more sense, really. You need to get some rest. You don't need to be running around the city. I can bring something over for supper, too. Subs? Spaghetti and meatballs?"

In spite of her best intentions, Vanna was still in bed, and having dinner come to her, along with the articles and Erica, sounded heavenly.

"Ivanna?" Erica prompted.

"Okay," Vanna agreed. "Bring them over here. We'll look at them together."

"Good. I'll be there in an hour or so, then. All right?"

"Okay, Mom. Thanks."

Chapter Twenty-Two

She hadn't planned to fall asleep again while she was waiting for Erica. She had actually planned to get up, freshen up a little bit, check her email and maybe do a small job or a chore before Erica got there. Her kitchen was badly in need of a sweeping and there was unopened mail on the kitchen table. But the next thing Vanna knew, her phone was ringing over and over again, even though she let it go through to voicemail. She finally picked it up and put it to her ear.

"Yes?"

"Ivanna! Thank goodness, I thought something had happened to you. I was getting ready to call Sweeny, or get the building manager."

"What is it?"

"I'm here. You need to buzz me up and let me into your apartment."

"Oh. Yeah. I'll be right there. Hang on."

Vanna hung up and staggered out to the door to hit the release button and then to watch for Erica through the wide-angle peephole.

"Sorry, Mom. I just fell back asleep. I didn't mean to."

"I'm just glad you're all right."

Erica swept into the room. She put a takeout bag that smelled of spicy Italian tomato sauce on the kitchen table and moved a pile of mail and other junk out of the way.

"Let's get something nourishing into you, before we get started."

"I had nourishing food at the hospital," Vanna pointed out. Erica always thought that she couldn't take care of herself properly.

"You didn't have anything like this at the hospital!" Erica pulled the Styrofoam boxes out of the paper bag. Vanna had to admit that the spicy, meaty smell was nothing like any of the bland, tasteless, purportedly healthy meals that she had been served at the hospital.

"I didn't think I was hungry," she said. "But smelling that, I think I changed my mind. I'm actually starving."

As Erica set the food out, Vanna locked the apartment door and chained it. She stood at the door for a minute looking out the peephole, looking for any sign of movement. When she walked over to the table, Erica's eyes were on her.

"Just making sure," Vanna murmured.

"Why don't you come back home? Just for a while until they can sort this out and get her into custody. I'm so worried about your state of mind."

Not worried about her safety, Vanna noted. But worried about her state of mind. As if Vanna might just lose it. She might not be keeping up very well with work, but she was still alive, and she wasn't crazy, even if Lydia *had* thought so for a while at the hospital.

"It will be okay. I feel safe here."

"Are you sure?"

"I'm sure, Mom. It's good. I like having my own place and I don't feel like anyone is going to hurt me. The security here is probably better than out at the Estate."

"I could fix that," Erica said. "I could make it Fort Knox."

"No, that's okay. I want to just stay here. But thank you for the offer. Again."

Vanna pulled out a chair and sat down. She picked up one of the plastic forks and sank it into the nearest meatball. It was tender, spicy, and hearty. Just what she needed. For a while, they didn't say anything, just eating. Vanna tried very hard to pace herself according to the size of bites and frequency that Erica was taking, rather than wolfing down the food as fast as she could, as she was prone to do.

"Mmm," Vanna said. "This really hits the spot. You know, I probably would have just had more coffee and gone back to bed."

"I know," Erica said, raising her eyebrows.

Vanna felt her cheeks flush. She nodded at Erica's valise. "Can we look at the articles now?"

"We should wait until after we are finished. We don't want to get sauce on them."

"They're just photocopies, not priceless originals. Let's get them out and take a look."

Erica let out a little sigh and bent over her bag. She took out a file folder nearly half an inch thick.

"Wow, that's a lot. It must have really been in the news."

"I guess it was. I don't remember hearing much about it at the time, but I guess we were busy raising two girls and didn't pay much attention. You had your needs and therapies and Lydia was in school…"

"You didn't read these?" Vanna fanned through the pages, letting them fall before her eyes at high-speed, like the little animated pictures that they used to draw in the corners of notebooks to amuse themselves.

"No, I didn't. But I couldn't help seeing the headlines and pictures."

Vanna stopped at one page with a big, above-the-fold picture and headline. It was Julia. Or the woman that they knew as Julia. "Abigail Stone." She looked over the page at Erica. "Her name is Abigail Stone."

"Yes, so it would appear."

"I have to call Sweeny."

Erica didn't say anything. Vanna pulled out her phone and pressed the speed dial for the policeman. It didn't take him long to answer.

"Vanna. How are you feeling?"

"I'm good. Look—we found something out."

"We?"

"Mom and I. Mostly Mom, I guess. She found the social worker that placed me and we talked to her."

"You might have brought me in on that."

"I guess so… I didn't really think about it. Mom can give you her contact information and you can go see her. She wasn't very helpful because everything was confidential, she didn't want to reveal anything private."

"I might be able to get something more out of her."

"But we did have a breakthrough. She said that there was a murder trial. My birth mother falling off of a balcony wasn't an accident or suicide, it was murder."

"Murder!" There was a change in his voice and a shift in how far he was holding the phone from his mouth. She pictured him straightening from a slouch like he was sitting up and taking notice for the first time. "*That's* something that I can look up. We can pull the old police investigation files. And the court files shouldn't be sealed. Not for a murder."

"Mom asked Mr. Wright to look into it. And she went to the library and looked at microfiche."

"And what did she find out?" Sweeny demanded.

"Her name. My stalker. It is Abigail Stone."

"Abigail Stone." There was a pause while he wrote it or typed it somewhere. His voice in her ear was musing. "I've heard that name. Recently."

"Do you think you can find out where she's living?"

"I'll get some inquiries made right away. We'll certainly have better luck finding Abigail Stone than a dead woman."

"Yeah." Vanna paged through the articles while she talked to Sweeny. "Wait."

"What is it?"

She stared down at the headlines in disbelief. "Abigail Stone was convicted."

"Of the murder?"

"Yes."

"That's why she didn't show up in your life until now," Sweeny suggested. "She's been in prison. But it's twenty years later, now. And she's been released. That must be where I read her name. We get briefings, sometimes, when potentially dangerous criminals are released or known to be in the area. Or there might have been a bulletin if she breached the terms of her parole."

Vanna looked at Erica to see if she was understanding the half of the conversation that she could hear. "She went to prison. That's where she's been for twenty years."

"And that's why they tried to keep you from being associated with the trial," Erica said. "They didn't want outsiders to connect you with this big public trial, but they also didn't want to give Abigail your new identity."

Vanna felt a shudder. Goosebumps stood out on her arms. "Sweeny…" She was aware that her voice had dropped to a breathy, tentative tone, like a little girl. "She's killed. She admitted it to me. She was convicted. It's not just a possibility anymore. She really did it."

"I'm going to see if I can get the patrols around your building increased. I'm not sure what else we can do. I can't give you a twenty-four-hour guard. You might want to think about moving. Going under the radar for a while."

"I can't. I can't leave my home. And I would still have to tell my clients where I was. I need to make a living."

"She already has all of your clients' names and contact

information from your old computer. I think it would be a good idea to… find something else to do. Make a course correction. A change to your career path."

"You think I should give up my VA work altogether and find something else to do?" Vanna couldn't believe it.

"It might be a good idea. I know it's not a nice thought, being pushed into this sort of a situation…"

"No, I can't do that."

"Hey… I just got that."

"What?" Vanna asked tiredly, putting her forehead in her hand, braced on the table.

"VA. Virtual Assistant. Vanna Austin. That's clever. Is that why you go by Vanna instead of Ivanna?"

"I've always preferred Vanna, but yes, that part works out nicely."

"Huh. So," Sweeny gathered his thoughts. "I'm going to get an APB out on Abigail Stone. Start some searches and see what we know about her. I'm going to increase the patrols in your neighborhood and I'm going to send someone inside the building just to check out the locks on the doors and everything. He'll be in uniform, so he'll be easily identifiable, okay? I just want to be sure that she hasn't tampered with any doors or isn't squatting in the basement. Some of these stalkers can be pretty resourceful."

"We already know she's smart. We have to make sure not to underestimate her."

"Right. Is your mom going to stay there tonight?"

"No. Why?"

"Just checking. She is a small blond, like Stone. I wouldn't want there to be any confusion; one of my officers sees Erica leaving your apartment or building and thinks it is Abigail. We'll have to make sure they know about your mother as well, so they don't get thrown off the trail."

"Oh. Okay. Yeah, she'll be here a little longer, but then she'll be headed home. Nobody shoot her."

Erica raised an eyebrow inquiringly and Vanna giggled. It was all just so ridiculous. Ridiculous to have this woman stalking her, claiming to be her mother, when she was really Vanna's mother's killer. Ridiculous to have to worry about Erica being mistaken for a psychopath leaving the building. And Vanna was tired. Her stomach was full and happy. They had solved the mystery of her stalker's identity. And her body was telling her it was time to go back to bed.

She said tired goodbyes to Sweeny and he rang off to do his work.

"Are you done with this?" Erica asked, gesturing toward Vanna's unfinished spaghetti and meatballs.

"Yes. I can't eat anymore tonight. And I'm too tired to think about anything else."

"Do you want me to put it in the fridge? Save it for tomorrow? I didn't finish mine either."

"Yeah, put them in the fridge. I can manage the microwave."

"Put them on a plate before you put them in the microwave. You know better than to microwave Styrofoam. You don't want toxins in your food."

"Yes. I'll put them on a plate."

Vanna watched her mother put the takeout containers in the fridge. Vanna tapped the stack of newspaper clippings straight. "I'll read these in detail later. Thank you so much for your help, Mom. I don't think I could have managed all the microfiche work. That was brilliant."

"You're very welcome," Erica said, with a surprised note in her voice. She actually blushed, though she turned away to hide it and retreated to the bathroom to check her hair and get herself back together before she left.

"Now, is there anything else that you need?" she asked as she got on her raincoat. "You've been through a traumatic time and your body is still recovering from the car accident. Incident. Collision."

"No, I don't need anything." Vanna got up and kissed her mother's cheeks, both sides. "Just more sleep, apparently. It seems my body wants to make up for all the sleep I've been missing lately. All at once."

"You listen to it," Erica advised. "Otherwise you *will* end up being very sick. You never did well as a little girl if you were short on sleep."

"I know."

Erica headed for the door. She stopped with her hand on the knob. "Did Lydia tell you that she saw Tino at the hospital?"

Vanna nodded. "Yes. She told me."

"I wasn't sure if she would. You will stay away from him, won't you? You won't call him because you're lonely or scared? He's not good for you."

"I know. I won't call him. One stalker right now is enough."

Erica frowned at this. The worry lines between her eyebrows deepened.

"It's okay, Mom, really. I was joking. Tino won't bother me. But I'm not going to invite him in, either. You don't have to worry about him."

Erica nodded and let herself out. She closed the door firmly behind her.

Vanna shot the bolt and fastened the chain. She looked down at the thick stack of papers in her hand. "One psychotic killer is quite enough."

———

Vanna slept late again. But at least she didn't sleep for two days straight this time. By late morning, her body was starting to make noises like it was alive again. She needed to use the toilet. Feed herself. Have a tall glass of water and brush her hair. Then maybe she'd feel human again.

She couldn't get her mind off of the newspaper clippings.

The whole time that she had been sleeping, she had been dreaming about them, her restless brain speculating what details she would be able to glean from them.

What more was there to find out? Abigail Stone had murdered Vanna's birth mother and now she was after Vanna. Did she really need any more details than that?

In her dreams, Erica, Julia, and Abigail had morphed together and swapped in and out. It had been impossible to tell which woman was which. She would think she was talking to the one and she was talking to the other. She was running away from Abigail to Erica, and running to Abigail. Julia's face was shadowy, unknown. A dark shape in the night or a heap on the road. She needed to know what Julia really looked like.

Vanna pulled one of the takeout boxes of spaghetti and meatballs out of the fridge and started to eat it cold. In spite of her assurances to Erica that she could manage a microwave and that she would put the spaghetti on a plate before reheating it, the whole thing was just too much bother. She didn't have the energy for all of that. So she sat down and ate it cold while she started to flip through the newspaper articles, skimming head-lines and looking for a picture of Julia. And it wasn't long before she found one.

Julia was really gorgeous. She wasn't definably Latino. As far as Vanna could imagine from the black and white copies, her skin was a golden tan and her hair in most of the pictures was a long, straight black or dark brown. Her facial features and eyes were exotic. Big, dark, arresting eyes. Mysterious, teasing eyes. Her hair framed her face and long bangs tickled her eyes. Smooth skin. Full lips. A funny little snub nose that she would have thought was Asian more than Hispanic. But somehow it all pulled together to form a girl who was effortlessly gorgeous in all of the published pictures. Maybe just like anyone else, she had other pictures where she looked like she had just gotten out of bed, had a big zit on her nose, or looked tired and pouchy. But the papers hadn't chosen to publish those pictures.

True or not, they had chosen to portray Julia as a poor single mom. Down on her luck through no fault of her own, just struggling to get from one day to the next with all of the weight of the world on her shoulders. Chances were, that wasn't the whole story. Chances were, there was a story behind the out-of-wedlock child. An abusive boyfriend, a night out partying, some series of poorer and poorer choices. The faithful social worker had said that there was already a file open on Julia before the murder. They had already been watching the situation. That meant that someone had reported Julia for neglect or abuse, or some community service organization had raised concerns over red-flagged behaviors or situations. It wasn't usual to open a file on a family just because they were a poor or single parent family.

Vanna's eyes skipped down the page, picking out words and phrases here and there, initially skimming, but then working her way deeper and deeper into the story that the articles told.

Abigail had pled 'not guilty'. She initially denied being anywhere near the apartment, until they had managed to prove through witnesses and evidence at the scene that she had been there. Then she switched to a claim that it had been an accident. Involuntary manslaughter. She gave no explanation for the fight that had trashed the apartment before Julia went over the railing.

The investigators had initially thought that they were looking for a man, due to the weight of the furniture that had been thrown around. It would have been difficult to force Julia over the railing and off of the balcony. It seemed inconceivable at first that this diminutive teen could have been the one responsible. But people could do things when they were angry or scared that they wouldn't normally be able to. Vanna knew that Abigail was much stronger than she looked.

There had been some reports on Vanna's disappearance and her surprise appearance at the mall. Abigail said that she had wanted to take care of Amelia until Julia recovered from her fall. But as the news broke that Julia was dead and people were looking for Amelia, she decided that she'd better find a way to return the girl.

Exit Amelia and enter Vanna.

Abigail had asked several times during the trial where Amelia was and how she was doing. The newspaper reporters had obligingly done 'where is she now?' articles and tried to track her down, two years after the murder. But the DSHS had not been helpful and all they could do was speculate.

———

Sweeny had brought donuts. He disclaimed the stereotypical donut-eating-cop image. "I just hit my ten-pound weight-loss milestone, so this is my reward for being good. And you looked like you could use some nourishment."

Funny how his idea of nourishment and Erica's were so different. But both of them had noticed Vanna's weight loss and felt the need to encourage the consumption of calories. Even so, he had only brought two donuts, not a whole box. They each took a donut on a napkin and sat down to review developments.

"Abigail was released from prison just a few weeks before your stalker showed up," Sweeny advised. "She didn't take very long to track you down. I'm not sure how, with how carefully the adoption record was sealed up. I think she must have worked some kind of inside source. Maybe some office worker at DSHS who knew where you had gone."

"I've been reading through the news articles on the trial. She asked a number of times where I had gone and how I was doing. So maybe someone finally gave her an answer, thinking that she was just concerned for my welfare."

"I think she must have been convinced when she let you go that you couldn't be a witness against her. But maybe as the years in prison went by, she started to worry about what you might remember as you got older."

Vanna frowned. "But she'd already been convicted of Julia's murder. So why would she be afraid that I could identify her? She couldn't be tried for it again."

"No. That's true. But I can't think of what other motive she could have for stalking you."

"She never acted threatening toward me. Not until she ran me down in the car. It was always about unwanted attention, her giving me gifts and always wanting to be in my life."

"Then maybe it's guilt," Sweeny suggested. "Maybe she didn't take you from the apartment because she was worried you would identify her, but because she felt guilty. She took away your mother, so she needed to take care of you. She still feels like she needs to take care of you."

"Yeah, that makes more sense. That's how she acted."

He took a small bite of his donut and dabbed his lips with the napkin. "But what changed? Why go from trying to take care of you to running you down with her car?"

"Maybe she just finally got the message that I didn't want her in my life. And she felt rejected."

Sweeny sighed noisily. "Maybe. At any rate... we are not having any more luck tracing her as Abigail Stone than as Julia Cortez. Not yet. As you probably guessed, she broke the terms of her parole and disappeared. Stole the car. They don't know where she is living. We've published a request for assistance for the public to help, hoping that someone will see her and report it. At this point, we don't have any leads on where she is."

"I can tell you where you'll find her. Here. She has to be somewhere close by."

Sweeny looked around the apartment thoughtfully.

"I requested a twenty-four-hour guard, but like I figured, they denied it. Hugely expensive to put a twenty-four-hour guard on someone, especially when it is for an indefinite period. We know that Julia can hide out for weeks and then pop up as soon as we remove the guard."

"She comes here whenever I go out," Vanna said. "I'm sure

of it. I come home and things are out of place. She must pick the lock. Why don't you just put a couple of policemen here? I'll go out and she'll walk right into the trap."

"Or come after you with a car again."

"So guard me too. It's not indefinitely, just for… a sting."

"I'll see what I can do. It will take time to get through the bureaucracy."

"You know, those television cops, they can always pull together something like that in a few minutes."

Sweeny laughed. "I'll do what I can, but I'm not promising anything. It may sound like nothing; a couple of cops in the apartment, a couple on your tail, but these things are unbelievably expensive. Especially if she doesn't show up like you expect her to."

Chapter Twenty-Three

Vanna was worried about Abigail showing up and worried about her not showing up. She didn't want to get hurt. She didn't want anyone in her apartment. And she didn't know how she would handle a face-to-face meeting with Abigail if she appeared.

Everything seemed quiet. Vanna looked around the parking garage before stepping away from the safety of the elevator. There was no one waiting for her, as far as she could see. The place was as quiet as a tomb. Slowly, Vanna crept from the elevator to her car. Her body still hurt and she had some ugly scrapes and bruises, but considering that she had been hit by a car not that many days ago, she was actually doing pretty well. She could have been lying dead in the morgue.

Vanna turned the key in the lock, taking a brief second to look in the back seat of her car to make sure that no one was hiding there waiting to surprise her once she got out onto the road. The back seat was empty. She breathed a sigh of relief, slid quickly into her seat and locked the door.

For a few minutes she just breathed, waiting for the wild beating and palpitations of her heart to calm down again. She was safe. She was in her car. Julia—Abigail—couldn't hurt her there. Vanna's hands were shaking. She wanted nothing more than to go back to her apartment and just to burrow down under the covers and close her eyes.

But she had to be strong. She couldn't let Abigail control her life.

Taking a deep breath, Vanna turned the key and listened to the engine come to life. There was no explosion. Nothing moved in the parking lot. She was perfectly safe. She was just as safe in the car as she was in her apartment. There was nothing to be worried about.

After checking her rear-view mirror, she backed out of her parking space and navigated out of the underground parking.

It was a gloomy, drizzly day. The kind of day that she used to love. But she needed the extra boost that the sunshine could have given her. It was amazing what a difference a little depression could make on your view of the weather.

She headed the car toward the grocery store. It practically knew the way by itself. She didn't have to think about it and just let her mind wander, particularly avoiding the topic of Julia or Abigail. She had to focus on her life, get her goals back on track.

Vanna was almost to the grocery store when her phone rang. She looked at the hands-free display and her stomach clenched. She answered the call.

"You are being tailed," Sweeny announced without introduction. "I'm going to give you some instructions and we'll see if we can make the pursuer the quarry."

"Okay," Vanna's voice was tiny and she was worried that he wouldn't be able to hear her. She cleared her throat and swallowed, trying to calm herself down.

"First of all, relax. You are safe. You're in your car, she is in hers. My officers have her in sight and they're not going to let her run you off the road. So breathe. I don't want you to do anything desperate. Just follow my instructions."

"I'm good." Good was far from what she was.

"All right. You're headed for the grocery store?"

"Yeah."

"I don't want you to turn in there. Look around for somewhere that you wouldn't normally go. A strip mall with a parking lot that is mostly empty."

"Okay."

Vanna looked around. There were a few likely spots. It was a semi-industrial area, a lot of small offices for coal-mining companies, tour companies, and so on. She glanced in her rearview mirror, but couldn't see Abigail's black car or the police officers. They probably weren't in marked cars. That would be an obvious red flag to Abigail. Forcing herself to keep her eyes on the road instead of in the mirror, Vanna selected one of the strip malls with a store front, not sure what Sweeny's plan was.

"I'm pulling in," she told him. There was a lot of background noise, Sweeny talking to people who were with him or talking on radios to the pursuit cars.

"Great. I want you to go around to the back lane behind the building."

"What?"

"You are off of your usual routes. She doesn't know where you're going. When you go out of sight, she has to follow or she's going to lose you. She will have to close in a bit and keep you in sight."

"Okay." Vanna nodded. She took a turn around the side of the building and scanned back and forth. There were several directions to go. "Do I just keep going straight? Or do I stop?"

"Don't stop," he snapped. "It doesn't really matter what direction you go, as long as you keep moving and don't take any dead ends. Go a direction you can see is clear."

"Right."

Vanna kept going. Was she going too slow? Too fast? She didn't know if Sweeny wanted her to pull out ahead so that Abigail would be forced to close in further, or if he wanted her to slow down so that she wouldn't lose Abigail.

"Sweeny—"

"Just keep going, Vanna. You're doing fine."

"Okay."

She couldn't help checking the rear-view mirror again, looking for the black car.

"She's still in pursuit," Sweeny confirmed, as if he could see what she was doing. "You're just fine. My cops still have her in view."

Vanna blew her breath out. She seemed to be significantly short on oxygen. "What do you think she's doing? What does she want?"

"She wants to know what you're up to. You've broken your pattern and you've got her worried."

"What if she sees the police cars?"

"They're unmarked. Just regular civilian cars, nothing suspicious. She might wonder, and as we close in, she'll know, but she's not going to get away. We have cars out ahead of you as well. She's not going to get away from us this time."

And then Vanna could go back to living her life. She could go back to working and crafting and going out with friends whenever she wanted to. She could go back to sleeping eight hours every night; not two and not fourteen. She could be the person that she had been before it all started. Provided they could put Abigail in jail for long enough and didn't just let her out in a few days.

Vanna caught a movement in her rear-view mirror out the corner of her eye. She looked in the mirror and recognized the pursuing vehicle.

"Sweeny—"

"It's okay. They're right behind her. Thirty seconds and it will all be over."

"But, no—"

"When you cross the next street, a couple of police cars are going to pull in to block her escape. You can pull into the next back lane and just stop and watch it go down. Stay in your car until an officer comes up to your vehicle and tells you that it is safe."

"Sweeny, it's not—"

"Stay with me." His voice was smooth and calming, but he wasn't letting her finish.

Pulling out of the back lane, Vanna watched the two marked cars with lights flashing turn in and close it off. She pulled into the next lane and stopped the car. She got out and hurried toward the police barricade.

"Stay in your car!" one of the cops yelled at her, looking over his shoulder briefly. They had their car doors open and were sheltering behind them, guns drawn, aimed at the pursuing vehicle.

"It's not her! It's not Abigail!"

He looked back at her again. "Get down! Now! You need to follow instructions."

"It isn't Abigail Stone! Don't shoot him!"

The cop spoke into the radio mounted on his shoulder. Vanna couldn't hear what he was saying. She had left her phone in the car and was no longer in contact with Sweeny. She was in a panic. "Don't shoot!" She repeated. "Please don't shoot!"

"Calm down. Get down on the ground. And shut up."

Vanna finally obeyed, getting down low behind the nearest police car, peeking over it anxiously to see what was happening.

The pursuing vehicle, a beaten-up tow truck, had come to a stop. Other vehicles had pulled in behind him, blocking his retreat. He hadn't gotten out of the truck.

"Tino!" Vanna groaned. "Dammit, Tino! Why do you have to keep doing this?"

"Driver, turn off the engine and put your hands out the window!" a voice on a bullhorn commanded.

The engined quieted, the window was laboriously rolled down, but it stuck half-way, as it always did. Tino's beefy hands and forearms appeared out the window.

"Open your door using the outside handle. Keep your hands out the window!"

It was a struggle, with the window only able to go down half-way. Tino had muscular biceps, and his elbow and shoulder were not that flexible. It took a few minutes of groping and twisting before Tino was able to pop the handle on the outside of the door and open it. It would have been comical if Vanna hadn't been so terrified that they were going to shoot Tino if he made a wrong move.

"Step out of the vehicle. Keep your hands through the window."

The door was pushed open further and Tino was looking out, estimating the distance to the ground and whether he could actually keep his hands through the window when he stepped down. He did his best and the cop on the bullhorn didn't censure him.

"Now lace your hands behind your head and lie face-down on the ground. Keep your hands behind your head."

Vanna put her hands over her face, but still watched Tino through the cracks in her fingers. He obeyed and once he was face-down on the ground, several uniformed officers swarmed over him, searching him for weapons and handcuffing his hands behind his back. Once he was secured, the officers sheltering behind the doors of the marked police cars stood up and the one who had shouted at Vanna marched over to her. He grabbed her arm and pulled her roughly to her feet.

"You put yourself and everyone here in danger with that stunt," he growled. "You were given specific instructions. You were to remain in your car."

"But I had to tell you—"

"No. You didn't. Nobody here was planning on a shoot-out. The only thing that was different was the identity of the pursuer. Nothing else."

"I'm sorry… I thought…"

"You weren't supposed to be thinking. You were supposed to be following the instructions that you were given."

Vanna nodded. She looked down at her feet. "I'm sorry."

"Get back on your phone and give Sweeny an update."

Vanna walked back to her car. It seemed a lot further away than it had been a few minutes ago. She could feel the cops watching her go. They were talking about her. About how stupid she was to not follow Sweeny's instructions and to try to interfere with the takedown. She could have gotten someone hurt. She didn't know how, but she could have gotten someone hurt. But if Tino had come out of that stupid tow truck rip-roaring mad, unable to control himself, then they could have killed him. She knew that he didn't carry a gun, but the cops didn't know that, and if they had judged that he was a threat, they could have shot him dead and asked questions later.

There were tears on Vanna's cheeks when she climbed back into her car. She wasn't sure how they had gotten there.

"Um… I'm back," Vanna offered to the air.

Sweeny growled in his throat. "Are you kidding me, Vanna? Are you bloody kidding me? You're going to discount every-thing that I said to keep you safe and run into a potential fire-fight? Could you have chosen a stupider thing to do?"

"I didn't run into the middle of it," Vanna corrected. "Just… to the edge of it…"

"How am I supposed to protect you if you won't listen to me?"

"I don't know." Vanna's stomach was twisted into a hard knot. She felt like throwing up. He may have thought her flaky before, but now he'd downgraded his opinion. Now he knew how stupid she was.

When Vanna thought back, she wasn't sure how long Sweeny had raked her over the coals. It felt like an eternity, but when she tried to reconstruct what he had said, she couldn't remember more than two or three sentences.

She had left her door open when she slipped back in to talk to him and that turned out to be a good thing. Because she didn't see her physical reaction coming. She knew that she felt sick. But she felt sick so often lately that she had assumed it would just stay with her the rest of the day. If she were lucky, it would be less in the morning. The big lump of anxiety that she carried around with her seemed to grow every day.

But it reached critical mass during Sweeny's lecture. She barely had time to turn her head to the side when vomit rose up in her throat and she started spewing everything she had eaten in the last twenty-four hours out the door and onto the pavement. Her whole body convulsed with the effort and she hung onto the door frame to keep from falling out. Sweeny's voice cut out abruptly and she was left to puke in peace.

When her body was totally wrung out and she was able to stop, she found one of the police officers standing a respectful distance back from the car, looking a little green at the gills. He was young; they had obviously given the rookie the worst job.

"I'm sorry," Vanna apologized, wiping her mouth weakly with the back of her hand. "I don't know… I guess I've got a bit of the flu."

"Can I help you with anything? Get you something?"

"No. Thanks."

"We'd like to talk with you. If you're done."

"I don't know what I can do at this point."

He took another step closer, carefully staying back of the puddle of sick. "Why don't you drive forward a few feet?" he suggested. "It will be easier to talk to you that way."

Vanna put the car into drive and coasted forward a few feet. She put it back into park. The officer came up to the car to talk to her. Closer this time, his nostrils flaring at the smell of the vomit on Vanna.

"You know this Valentine Peak that we arrested?"

"Yes. I think if you look, you'll find that I have a restraining order against him too."

The boy's brows drew down. "You have two stalkers?"

"Well, two… I don't know what you'd call Tino… he's not really a stalker, but… I mean, he doesn't want to hurt me, but… he won't leave me alone."

"That meets the qualifications for stalking in this state."

"He just wants to keep me safe. He knows about Abigail. That's why he was following me. Probably. I guess."

"He botched up our operation and the boss isn't very happy about that. He's going to go to jail for a few days."

"I know. It's… the second time he's breached the order."

"The second time? There may be a pretty hefty penalty this time. Can't you tell him to just stay away?"

Vanna favored the young officer with a glare. "If a restraining order and the threat of arrest don't stop him, then what makes you think I can just talk him out of it? That's why I got a restraining order in the first place!"

He got a little bit red around the neck. Vanna assumed that a police officer's training with regard to restraining orders didn't include telling the victim that it was her fault or that she could do something about it if she were just persuasive enough. He should know better, even if he was a rookie.

"Yes, ma'am," he agreed. "I'm sorry."

"I hope you don't ever have to deal with a stalker. Or your mother or your sister. It really isn't a barrel of monkeys. I would put a stop to it if I could."

"Yes, ma'am."

Vanna swallowed. There were still bits of vomit lodged in her mouth, throat, and nasal passages. She didn't think she was going to throw up again, but she didn't want to hang around talking to the police about everything that had gone wrong in the operation.

"Can I go home now?"

"I'm not sure about that. Let me just check."

He walked back away from her. Vanna leaned her head back on the headrest and closed her eyes. She wasn't sure how much time passed before another officer came over to talk to her. She might have fallen asleep there while waiting.

"Miss Austin?"

Vanna opened her eyes and looked at him. "Yes?"

"Do you want to slide over to the passenger's seat and I'll drive you home?"

"I can drive."

"You've been through a pretty rough time. We'd like to make sure you're okay and get there safely. And without picking up another tail."

Without picking up another tail. Abigail was still out there. Still in the shadows, watching her, waiting for her opportunity… to do what?

"Well… I suppose," Vanna agreed. She didn't like the idea of someone else driving her car. Not an insured driver and all that. But she supposed that if it were an on-duty police officer, then if anything untoward happened, the police insurers would have to cover it. And nothing was going to happen.

He waited patiently while she got out of her seat and walked around the side of the car to the other door. It felt strange, sitting in the passenger seat of her own vehicle. She'd never really done it. She rarely had any passengers and she never let anyone else drive it. It was a comfortable seat. She could get used to sitting there.

The officer got in. "My name is Officer Tetrault, ma'am. I'll get you home and make sure you're safe there."

Vanna sniffled, her nose running, still trying to clear the burning acid from her passages. "Thanks. So… she didn't show up at the apartment either?"

"No. She didn't show up, and they've done a sweep to make sure that everything is secure. They, uh, found a couple of listening devices. Someone's been bugging you."

Vanna stared at him. She remembered the feeling that she

had before, that even when she was alone in her apartment, Abigail could still hear her. It turned out she was right. Abigail could hear everything. Including Vanna and Sweeny trying to set up a sting to catch her if she either followed Vanna or returned to the apartment while she was gone.

"So we just ruined that whole operation by letting her listen in," she observed.

"After I drop you off, we'll do a sweep of your car too. See if she has a bug inside or a GPS tracking device on the outside. But your parking garage is not secure, so even if we sweep it today, she could still bug it tomorrow."

"Thanks for the encouragement."

He looked over at her and shrugged uncomfortably. "Sorry. You just may want to move somewhere more secure."

"Sweeny thinks I should move. But I just… can't."

"Maybe stay with someone else. Once we've swept the car to make sure that you can't be tracked easily. If you go today, before she realizes that you have plans to move, you might be able to get established somewhere without her knowing where you've gone. For a while."

"I don't know. Right now I just need to be home. In my own bed. I'm not feeling very well."

"Sure. Well, if you need any help you be sure to let Sweeny know. We can help to move you, or make sure that you can't be followed wherever it is that you choose to go."

"She'll still find other ways to track me down. Watch my mother's house. My bank. All of the places that I go to regularly. I'd have to move across the country and assume a different name and never use a credit card again. Maybe then I'd be safe."

He nodded. They pulled into the underground parking and Vanna pointed to her parking place.

"I know," he acknowledged.

Vanna guessed that he had been on duty checking out the building before. He pulled smoothly into the parking spot without scraping the door on the pillar. Vanna opened her door and got out.

"I'll walk you up," Tetrault said.

"I don't really need you to. I'm okay."

"And I'm under orders. So I will be walking you up and checking the apartment one more time before I leave."

Vanna shrugged. "Okay. Whatever."

They proceeded in silence. Vanna wasn't in much of a mood to talk and he apparently didn't find it necessary. They took the elevator up and he held his hand out for the key when Vanna moved to unlock the door. He stood to the side as he unlocked it and then he pushed the door open without standing in the doorway. Vanna stepped forward to go inside, but he shook his head. He entered the apartment with his gun drawn and completed a security sweep before returning to the hall and allowing her to enter.

"Everything looks clear. Do you want to take a look and make sure that everything looks normal?"

Vanna gave a cursory glance around the apartment. She already knew that the police had been there and that they had found two bugs. She didn't know where they had been found, but she assumed that they would have moved a number of objects during their search. She straightened out a few things that were slightly off position and nodded at Tetrault.

"Yes, it looks fine. Thanks."

"I'll take off, then. Be sure to call if anything worries you. Bolt and chain the door."

"I know."

He gave her a sloppy salute and left, pulling the door shut behind him. Vanna locked and chained it.

After rinsing her mouth and brushing her teeth, Vanna headed for her bed. That was where she felt the safest and she really didn't think that she could manage anything else, even just logging into her email. It would just be too much.

But she was too restless when she lay down. She didn't want

to do anything else or go anywhere else, but her body had other ideas. She felt like there were bugs crawling under her skin. She couldn't lie still. She couldn't think straight. Even closing her eyes was just too difficult. She had to get up again and move around.

She hoped that a coffee might help settle her nerves. She couldn't sleep anyway, so it wasn't like it was going to keep her awake. Vanna went into the kitchen and pushed the button to start the coffee brewing. As she was standing there, her mind wandered to the bottle of wine in the lower cabinet that a client had given her for Christmas. She hadn't been sure how to refuse it, and so she had accepted it and just stored it away out of sight until she figured out what to do with it. To regift or take to a party. Alcohol always made her sleepy. She avoided it as much as she could in the past few years because she didn't like the dopey way it made her feel.

But now… maybe that was exactly what she needed. One glass would do it. Maybe two with her current anxiety level. She could never drink to excess with the way that it affected her. There was no chance of her becoming an alcoholic.

But she could sleep. And sleep was all that she wanted.

———

Lydia stopped by in the middle of the afternoon to bring Vanna a care package. She said casually that she had left the boys at Erica's so that they wouldn't get into Vanna's things. By which Vanna knew that it had been Erica who had sent Lydia over on the errand of mercy. Lydia would never leave the boys with Erica without a specific invitation to do so. And even then…

Lydia had brought along a big, deep-dish, supreme pizza. There was no way that the two of them could eat more than one or two slices, so the rest would go in the fridge to be eaten cold the next time that Vanna got around to eating. Vanna sat slumped at the table and munched on a steaming hot piece.

"This is great. Even better than the meatballs that Mom brought."

"Good. Are you okay?"

"I'm not great. But what do you expect?"

"I know. I'm just worried about you. You seem really... withdrawn, I guess. It's getting to you, huh?"

"I don't think they're ever going to be able to find Abigail. I really don't. They can't watch me all the time. But I can't go out anywhere without worrying that she is going to follow me, or try to run me down. Or how long is it before she gives up on the cat-and-mouse game and just breaks into my apartment while I'm still here? And throws me off the balcony?"

"You're only on the third floor. I'm not sure it would kill you."

"Well, great, I could just be crippled for life instead. Or maybe I'd get a head injury and not even know that I was being stalked anymore. Maybe she would stop stalking me once I was brain dead."

Lydia frowned, studying her. She picked up Mandy, who was fussing, and took a minute to comfort and settle her. "That's pretty bleak."

"I'm sorry. I don't want to bring you down. I'm just feeling a little... hopeless right now."

"The police haven't made any progress on finding Abigail?"

"No. She's below the radar. She seems to have plenty of criminal skills... stealing cars, picking locks, hacking computers... so she doesn't need to do all of those things that would give her away, like worrying about driver's license and car registration or filing taxes."

"You'd think that they'd still be able to find her," Lydia grumbled.

"Where? Where would you look?"

"I don't know. Wherever the criminal element hides out. She must have old friends around, don't you think? If she lived here before your birth mom died, she must have contacts from back then. Have they looked them up?"

"I don't know. You'd think Sweeny would know all of that. I never asked."

"You should. I really think that they should have found her by now."

Vanna shrugged. She was going to avoid Sweeny as much as possible for the next few days. Give him a chance to forget how she had disobeyed his orders.

———

After Lydia was gone, Vanna had another drink and sat down to look over the newspaper articles. She frowned, trying to sort out the events that had led up to Julia's murder.

Julia was a single mom, around Vanna's current age, rather than a teen. Abigail was younger, a fresh-faced sixteen-year-old. Vanna couldn't find any reference to how they had met. Maybe Julia had needed help with child care. Someone to look after Vanna—Amelia—while she was going to night school. Or to pick her up from daycare if Julia had to work late. It seemed like there had been a close relationship between the two girls. From what Vanna could read between the lines of the news stories, Abigail sometimes stayed overnight with Julia. Maybe when Julia needed extra child care, or maybe when Abigail was having problems at home. Vanna could imagine Julia reaching out to a young abused or neglected girl, trying to give her a hand up, not realizing she was inviting a viper into her home.

Then what had happened? They had argued over something. The argument had turned into a full-fledged, knock-down drag-out fight, with Julia ultimately being pushed over the railing to her death. Abigail, in an apparent panic, took the baby and ran.

It didn't take the police long to figure out who they were looking for, in spite of initially being misled into thinking that

Julia had fought with a man due to the violence of the fight. Within a day, they seemed to have honed in on Abigail. She hadn't gone home to her family. Various members of her family were quoted saying that they had no idea where she was and really didn't care. Vanna noticed that they all had different last names. Multiple marriages or relationships, Abigail had probably grown up without any kind of stability. Who knows what kind of abuse might have been inflicted by the constant stream of men in and out of her mother's life. Abigail had complained about never having a chance as she grew up. Maybe she hadn't.

There had been various bulletins and pleas made to the public to assist in bringing Abigail in 'for questioning as a person of interest' in the case. They never said that she was a suspect, but it was pretty obvious from the slant of the articles that the newspaper reporters, at least, hadn't believed that line for a second.

Eventually, the missing baby had turned up at the play center at the mall. If Abigail had hoped that this would reduce the heat, she had apparently been disappointed. Now that they no longer had to worry about the safety of a child within their suspect's care, the police turned the intensity of the manhunt up instead of down. Within forty-eight hours of little Amelia being abandoned at the mall, an arrest had been made. Abigail had been spotted and arrested at Corban's, a disreputable downtown bar.

In the beginning, she proclaimed her innocence. She was just a bystander or a witness. She would never have done anything to hurt her friend, Julia. She would never have put the baby's life in danger. She was devastated by Julia's death and blamed it initially on an accident, then suicide, then on the ex-boyfriend. Partway through the trial, she switched from 'not guilty' to 'guilty of manslaughter' in an attempt to get a shorter sentence. But by the time the offer was made, the prosecution felt they had already convinced the jury of murder. And apparently, they made the right call. Vanna was glad that they had done so, or Abigail might have shown up much earlier. As horrible as it was to be stalked by the woman at the age of twenty-two, it would have been much worse for a ten or twelve-year-old. At least she had been allowed, by DSHS and the courts, to grow up oblivious to the drama that had plagued her early life. She had been allowed to grow up loved and nurtured in the Austin home.

They managed to try and sentence Abigail as an adult, being seventeen at the time of the murder. Another good call and one that Vanna was grateful for.

But now, here Abigail was. The justice system had done its job in punishing her for the murder, and when they were done, they had released her. Now she was Vanna's problem. Sweeny's too, but mostly Vanna's. Sweeny would sleep nights, whether Abigail was brought in or whether she stalked Vanna for the next twenty years. Or found a balcony to push her off of.

Vanna had started a list as she went through the clippings. She had hardly even been aware of what she was doing. But she looked at it now and swallowed, her throat dry. It was a list of the words and phrases that people had used to describe Abigail. Of course, some of them were the reporters' own words. But most of them quoted Abigail's family and friends, or the lawyers, police officers, or counselors who had spoken with her during the time leading up to and during the trial.

Psychotic

Pure evil

Immature

Tantrum-prone

Brilliantly bad

Child murderer

Crazy

A mass of festering fears and fury

Psychotic

Stunted sense of morality

Sick

Not right in the head

Vanna realized that she had written down 'psychotic' twice and crossed out the second occurrence.

———

Vanna wondered who was calling her in the middle of the night. Why couldn't people just wait until morning? And why wasn't her phone's 'do not disturb' feature working so that she could get the proper rest that she needed?

But when she pulled down her blanket to find her phone, she found that the bedroom was bathed in light. So much for it being the middle of the night. Hopefully, it wasn't a client hoping to get a job back right away. She pawed the phone off of the bedside table and took a look at it. The number was unfamiliar. Which didn't mean anything; Abigail did just fine at finding new phones to call Vanna from. She answered it and held it up to her ear, bracing herself.

"Hello?"

"Vanna? How are you? Are you okay?"

Vanna rolled her eyes at the familiar bass. "Tino. You're not supposed to be calling me. You'll get thrown back in jail and neither of us wants that. Honestly, when I got the restraining order, I thought you understood how it worked."

"I won't get thrown back in jail," Tino's voice was amused. "Because that's where I am now."

"They let you call me?"

"They don't know that's *who* I'm calling. I wouldn't exactly tell them that, would I?"

"Why don't you call someone else? If you're lonely, call someone who doesn't have a restraining order against you. Or isn't there anyone?"

"I'm not lonely. I want to know that you're okay. It's been so long since we got together… I just want to know that you're still all right. Do you know I tried to come see you at the hospital?"

"Yes, and do you know how stupid that was?"

He chuckled. "Well, I didn't get arrested, but if that cop at the door had seen me, I suppose I would have. But how was I supposed to know it was a sting on Wednesday? I had no idea that there were cops watching your tail. That's the kind of thing you might think to tell me!"

"You are supposed to be staying away altogether!" Vanna retorted. She knew the frustration was not just creeping into her voice, but rushing full-force. "Stay away from me and they'll stop arresting you!"

"I don't trust them to be able to protect you. Where were they the other day when I chased her off? Where were they when she ran you down in her car? I'm only one guy, but I'm doing a better job than they are to protect you."

"What does that mean?" Vanna asked.

"I can do a better job—"

"No, you said you *are* doing a better job. How do you know that?"

"I've tailed her twice from your place. I haven't found where she's living yet, but I'm close. And if you think that those occasional patrols past your building are doing any good, you've got another thing coming. She knows they're coming by before they do. She always scrams before they show up."

"How would she know they were coming? And exactly how much time are you spending watching my building?"

"She probably has a police scanner. I've been thinking of getting one myself to avoid these… misunderstandings. And as to the other question… I plead the fifth."

"Tino. Stay away. Please. You're going to end up in real trouble."

"I like that you care. But I'm not going to stop. Not until this nutcase is in jail and I know that you're safe. Then maybe you and me can talk…"

"No. Just—no. Listen, I'm going to call Sweeny to tell him about your… surveillance findings. So there will probably be someone by to talk with you. Will you cooperate with them? Please?"

"Of course, babe," he agreed. "You know I'd do anything for you."

Growling in frustration, Vanna hung up the call before she could blow up at him. She put her phone firmly face-down on the side table. Tino was so infuriating. It was comforting, and at the same time laughable, that he was singlehandedly trying to protect Vanna from Abigail. At least he was more invested in it than the police force. Sweeny had to go through all of the red tape and convince them that it was worth their budget money to put light surveillance on her. Tino didn't have to persuade anyone else. He just decided he was going to do it and he did. And he was right; so far, he was doing a better job than the police force at it, too.

Chapter Twenty-Four

So far, no one had spotted Abigail. Sweeny had talked the court into keeping Tino in jail for a while longer so that he couldn't get in the way of their investigation and surveillance. Vanna thought it was a little silly of them to be so concerned about him keeping an eye on Vanna. Why didn't they just step up their own surveillance a little bit? Then they would know when Abigail was lurking about and Tino too. It was an embarrassment to them that a private citizen could do more about it than the whole department.

The long period of quiet didn't help Vanna to feel better. There was no question in her mind that Abigail was still around and still a threat. Only now, Tino wasn't watching out for her and the cops couldn't seem to get eyes on her, even after switching from radio contact to telephones to try to keep her from finding out the locations of the cars via a scanner. Vanna just kept waiting for the other shoe to drop. For the next attack.

She had no doubt that it would come. Abigail wasn't giving up that easily.

———

There was a sharp knock on her door that made Vanna jump and look toward it wildly.

"Ivanna? It's your mother," Erica's voice carried through the door before Vanna could even get there to look out the peephole.

Vanna opened the door. "Mom. What are you doing here? You didn't call."

"I didn't want to give that woman a heads-up. In case she's still listening, you know. Someone could be listening to your phone. They have apps for everything these days."

Vanna nodded stiffly. "Yeah, they do."

"I came to take you shopping. I know you're not going out and you'll starve if you don't buy some good, nourishing food."

"Mom. I can order grocery delivery. It's really not hard. You don't need to worry about that."

"When was the last time that you put in an order?"

"Oh. Well… I was going to make one today or tomorrow…"

"Let's go, then. I'll take you. There's safety in numbers."

Vanna couldn't think of an argument. Not a good one, anyway. Not one that was anything other than that she just didn't feel safe and didn't want to go. Erica stood waiting for her. Gradually, Vanna forced herself to move, gathering up her things, including her go bag. Erica shook her head, looking Vanna over.

"You always were such a clutter bug. You don't need all that."

"I do. If something happened and I couldn't come back here, this is everything that I would need to get on for a few days."

"You could just come to the Estate and you'd have everything you needed."

"Not copies of my ID and pictures. Not my laptop. There are things that are important that you can't provide."

Erica's lips pressed together. She looked like she had just

sucked a lemon. Very sour. Vanna considered trying to reword the statement. But while it might have been blunt, she didn't think that it was inaccurate or hurtful. It was just the truth. Vanna had a life of her own. Erica didn't have everything that she needed. That was just the truth.

"You ready to go, then?" Erica asked.

"Yes."

Erica stepped out into the hallway and waited. Vanna checked the hall before stepping out into it. She pulled the door shut and locked it. She tested the handle and door before stepping back. Though she didn't even know why she bothered anymore. She might as well just leave it wide open with a welcome mat out for Abigail.

She had asked the building manager for a copy of the surveillance camera footage to her apartment for a couple of separate times when she had been away from her apartment and suspected that Abigail had been there. And sure enough, they had a clear picture of Abigail approaching, blocking the view while she picked the lock to let herself in. There wasn't anything special on the film. Nothing that they could use to track her. They already knew her name and her face, and she didn't reveal anything else about herself by walking down the hall to the apartment.

Whenever they had tried to use the apartment as a lure, Abigail had not shown up. Like she knew their plans ahead of time. Vanna wondered how many more electronic bugs there were that no-one had yet found. It could be her phone, as Erica had suggested. Abigail was just a step ahead of them whatever they tried. Vanna didn't think that Sweeny would ever work out how to catch her. They had to rely on her making a mistake and it didn't seem like she was making any.

"Come on," Erica encouraged, motioning for Vanna to come with her.

Vanna stood there for a moment, immobilized. Erica didn't have any idea how difficult it was for her to leave her apartment. Erica thought it was just laziness or a mild concern that kept Vanna from leaving her apartment more often than she absolutely had to.

"Are you okay?" Erica prompted when Vanna still didn't move.

Vanna leaned against the door, taking deep breaths and trying to relax. She pressed one hand to her chest as if she could reach through to her heart and touch it, quieting it like a frightened animal. She fought against tears, hating the look that Erica was giving her.

"Ivanna?" Erica moved toward her and took her arm gently. "What's wrong?"

"I can't do it," Vanna said, struggling to keep the sob out of her voice. "I want to stay here."

"You can do it. You are safe with me. Nothing is going to happen. Come on. You definitely need to get out."

"I can't breathe."

"If you couldn't breathe, you wouldn't be able to talk either. Just slow your breathing down so you don't start hyperventilating. How long has this been going on?"

She rubbed Vanna soothingly on the shoulder and back. Vanna tried to obey and slow her breathing down. She wiped a layer of sweat from her forehead with her sleeve, closing her eyes for a moment.

"Months," she confessed. "A long time."

"Why didn't you tell someone? The doctor can give you something. A tranquilizer or anti-anxiety pills. You don't need to suffer like this."

"I don't want pills."

"You want to feel like this?"

"I don't need pills. I can still go out. It's just… hard."

"Well then, once you have collected yourself, we will go out. Since you can."

Vanna didn't think she had exactly won that point. She shrugged off Erica's hand and pulled her bag up onto her shoulder like she was a soldier getting dressed for battle. She snapped the strap into place and took her first step forward.

Erica knew better than to coax Vanna along any further. Vanna was fully capable of walking by herself. She didn't need any babying and Erica seemed to sense that. Tough love. That had always been Erica's approach. She had nurtured Vanna and Lydia, but never babied them. They were expected to be mature and responsible and they did their best to step up and do what was required.

"We should probably start with a meal plan for two weeks," Erica decided. "That way we can be sure of getting everything that you will need, with the least amount of fuss. But that doesn't mean that you are hibernating for the next two weeks. You are still going to need to push yourself to get out and get some fresh air and exercise."

They were just stepping off of the elevator into the parking garage and Vanna breathed in the cool, moist air. It was only mid-afternoon, but the dimness of the light coming in from downtown seemed more like twilight. It did feel good to get out into the air. It was easier once she broke free from her apartment and got out of that hallway. Once she got on the elevator, she felt better.

"I do sandwiches for lunch," she told Erica, just as briskly as Erica was speaking.

Erica glanced sideways at her and allowed a small smile. "Good. Do you have a notebook? Let's make a chart for you."

Vanna waited while Erica unlocked the passenger door to her car and got in. "I've got better than a notebook," she announced as Erica got in. She pulled out her laptop.

"That might be overkill. It's sort of awkward to carry through the grocery store."

"When it's done, I'll send it to my phone."

Erica raised her brows. "You can do that?"

"Easily."

"Make a chart, then. Fourteen rows for the days and

columns for breakfast, lunch, supper, and whatever snack times you usually observe."

Vanna was already working on it. It was good to do something specific, but that she didn't really have to think about too deeply. Just a mechanical exercise.

"If you want sandwiches every day of the week, then just fill that in down the board for your lunches. What kind of sandwiches do you eat? The same every day?" Erica knew that for three years, Vanna had refused to take anything but peanut butter and strawberry Smuckers jam sandwiches in her school lunches. Vanna couldn't remember Erica ever trying to talk her out of her PBJ lunches. It was a good thing that the school had allowed peanut butter. A lot of them didn't anymore.

"I rotate through about three different kinds," she advised.

"Write down the ingredients that you will need for those lunches and the number of loaves of bread that will take. There are usually about twenty-four slices per loaf, so that will give you one sandwich for eleven days."

Vanna noticed that she automatically discounted the end slices. "I know, Mom."

"How about breakfasts? Cold cereal? Toast?"

They continued on like that, working through each meal and the ingredients that Vanna would need to add to her list. It was a mechanical exercise that Vanna could have managed on her own, but she wouldn't have done it if Erica hadn't been there. She would have just gone to the store, or ordered groceries online, without considering what she would actually make each day and if she would have everything that she needed.

Vanna just hoped that everything would be as she left it when she got back. And there would be no new surprises.

———

The bills were probably piling up in the mailbox, so Vanna decided she'd better check. She had been diligently sending Abigail's mail back marked 'return to sender' as Sweeny had advised her to do. She didn't have to open them and wonder over the contents and try to figure out how to respond or not respond. She didn't have to decide what was important and what was not. She just had to mark them and send them back. It was a much better procedure, over in a few minutes and forgotten in a few hours.

But as she pulled the stack of mail out of her lock box, Vanna saw that there was an oversize envelope with Abigail's writing on it. And not only was Vanna's name and address printed on it, but in big block letters, the warning: 'Send this back and DIE!'

She caught her breath. That was a new approach. Instead of going through the stack to find all of Abigail's letters and send them back, Vanna went back up to her apartment and put the whole stack on the table. She pulled out her phone and tapped Sweeny's speed dial number.

"Are you okay?" he asked.

Vanna haltingly described the letter and its message.

Sweeny was quiet for a minute, considering it. "I'll come over," he said. "We'll need to examine the envelope and letter, make sure there are no contaminants on anything. Please don't touch it or open anything, especially if it looks like it might have been tampered with or has her writing on it. Okay?"

"Okay."

"Promise me that you won't open it."

"I'm not even going to look at it. I'm going to go in the other room."

"Good. I'll be there as soon as I can, but I might be a couple of hours. I'll want to get a couple of techs to come along with me and sometimes they're in the middle of another job."

"Okay."

"See you soon, then."

Vanna looked at her computer and felt guilty. She knew that more and more emails and requests were building up in her inbox and she just couldn't handle them. There had been some pretty terse conversations with clients lately.

Instead, she put the bottle of wine she had opened the day before on her side table, along with her coffee mug. She tried to read for a few minutes to distract herself, but eventually was forced to consider the drink again. She poured herself an inch or two in the bottom of the coffee cup and sipped it slowly. After a few minutes, she noticed her heart rate slowing and knew that the alcohol was having the desired effect. By the time Sweeny finally got there with his techs, she was feeling nice and mellow.

"Are there any more letters, or just the one?" Sweeny asked, approaching the table and poking at the larger envelope with the end of his pen.

"I don't know. I didn't look. I just put everything on the table the way I took it out. I don't know what else is in there. I didn't go through them."

"Keep your pen out of there," one of the techs ordered. "If there is some contaminant in or on these envelopes and you go poking in them with your pen, you could have a nasty surprise next time you put your pen in your mouth to pick something up with both hands or to chew on it while you think."

"I don't chew on pens," Sweeny retorted. But he withdrew the implement and wiped it on his pants.

The two techs, both wearing glasses, moved in. They were also both wearing gloves and they worked together like they were part of the same unit. Some kind of synchronized forensics performance team. With barely a word passing between them, they carefully went through the rest of the mail, putting it into separate piles on the table.

"That's quite a bit of mail," Sweeny observed. "Is this just one day's worth?"

"No. I haven't checked it for a while. Maybe a week's worth."

He nodded. His eyes lingered on her for longer than they usually did. Vanna checked herself over covertly, making sure that all of her buttons were done up and she didn't have a big ketchup stain down her front or something caught in her teeth.

The techs continued to sort and examine the mail. They used various swab tests, shone lights on them, looked at them with portable microscopes and other instruments. It would have been interesting if Vanna's life didn't hang in the balance. As it did, she felt a little queasy watching them.

There was a machine in a big, rolling, aluminum briefcase that Vanna watched the techs unload and set up. It looked oddly familiar.

"Is that an x-ray machine?"

"Yes," one of the techs answered, as they both donned lead aprons. "We'd ask you to go in the other room as we take a quick run through these envelopes."

"Uh, okay," Vanna agreed. The two techs continued to get the machine ready, and she looked at Sweeny. "I guess… you need to come too."

He nodded and followed her, taking it as his invitation.

Vanna stepped into the bedroom ahead of Sweeny. It was pretty much a disaster area. She hadn't been keeping on top of things like laundry and making the bed. The room was close and messy and a little smelly. And on the table beside the bed was the open bottle of wine.

Sweeny looked at it but made no comment. Vanna sat down on the end of the bed.

"You don't know what it's like," she said. "Being stuck in the middle of something like this. How it affects you."

"I've seen how it affects people. And I've seen how it has affected you."

"But you haven't. You don't know what I was like before it all started. And you don't know… all of the things going on inside. You really can't know what it's like."

"Okay, maybe not completely, but I understand the best I can. I am sympathetic, Vanna."

"You think that I'm ruining my life."

"This isn't a choice that you made," Sweeny said firmly. "This is something that happened to you and you're dealing with it the best that you can. I think that there are some other things that you could try that might help you a bit, but I know you're trying your best to just hold things together."

Vanna rubbed her eyes. "What things could I try?"

"You've already heard them. Go to the support group and talk to other people going through the same thing. Move out of here. In with your sister or something. See a therapist. Get some medication for the anxiety and depression. We're doing everything that we can, but we can't fix you. We can try to prevent any further damage, but you need another kind of help."

"I've always been strong. My mom made sure that we were. She didn't coddle us. She expected a lot from us. And even though I hated it, especially during high school, I know it was the right thing. If she'd let me just coast through on school and let me use my learning disabilities as an excuse, or if she'd said that it was just in my genes or history and I was managing the best that I could… I never would have become the person that I am. If she'd let me be lazy, I would have been. I'd still be at home, just taking an allowance from my dad's estate, sitting around all day."

"Getting help doesn't mean you're weak. Admitting that you can use help isn't being weak. Everybody needs help. Pretending that you don't is a sure path to misery."

"Do you ever need help?" Vanna challenged him.

"Sure. I ask for help every day. From my officers and my superiors. From my family. Even from God. Every day. I know I can't make it all work without help."

"But that's not the same. That's just regular, everyday stuff. That's not like… therapy. That's not like having to go back home because I can't hack it on my own. Those things are hard. They're not normal, everyday things."

"Why should it be okay to ask for help on little things and not big things?"

"There are some things it is okay to ask for help for. And some things that are not."

"And who decides what those things are?"

"I don't know. Society. There's a stigma attached to some kinds of help."

"Vanna. Who cares about stigma? Is stigma going to save your life?"

"Is therapy?"

"Maybe." He looked at the wine bottle on the bedside table. "You never know."

———

The techs had taken their x-rays and called Sweeny and Vanna back out again.

"We haven't identified any kind of threat. We are going to proceed to open the envelope."

Vanna looked at Sweeny, her heart thumping. Was he going to let them do that? Right here in her apartment? Shouldn't they open it in a lab somewhere, with a fume hood and the proper materials to contain a spill, if there was something toxic inside?

But Sweeny just nodded. "Let's have a look," he agreed.

But she noticed that he didn't get close to the table. He stood well back and let the techies debate the best way to open the envelope and then to proceed with their oddly synchronized dance. The envelope was slit open. Nothing happened. They carefully slid the contents out of the envelope. There was no powder. No explosives. No electronic switch. Just pieces of paper. Some were apparently a letter, on foolscap instead of pretty notepaper and some were blown-up photos.

They separated the pages and laid them out individually on the table. They again went through the motions of shining lights, swabbing pages and examining each one minutely. After a while, they nodded to Sweeny.

"You can come have a look, now."

Sweeny stepped forward and surveyed the contents. He nodded to the letter. "They are double-sided?"

One of the techs used a pair of tweezers to turn the first page over. Sweeny read through each of the pages in order. He looked dispassionately at the pictures.

"Do you want to see?" he asked Vanna.

"No, probably not."

He nodded and turned back to the table to give the techs instructions.

"Do you think I *should* see?" Vanna asked. "At least the pictures?"

"If you want to. It is addressed to you."

"Do I want to?"

Sweeny looked at her for a minute. Eventually, he nodded. Vanna walked up to the table and looked down at the pictures. Of course there were a couple of her, looking tired and drawn, in her car or at her window. Candid surveillance photos. There were also pictures of others. Her mother. Lydia and the children. Tino sitting in his tow truck. Sweeny talking to Vanna, with another of the officers in the background.

"She's right there all the time," Vanna said. "How could she be this close and we never saw her?" She tapped the picture with Sweeny in it.

"Telephoto lens. It can make it look like you're really close when you're far away. Chances are, she was two or three blocks away, out of our sightline. Maybe sitting in a car or behind a tree."

Vanna looked closely at Sweeny's dispassionate face. "Doesn't this upset you?"

"Of course it does. Everything about this case upsets me. But I have to stay objective and keep working on it."

"She's telling me that she could go after my mom. Or my sister. Nobody in my life is safe."

"I'm afraid so. We can't watch everyone. We can't even keep a full-time watch on you. She'll just wait us out. She'll just watch and wait."

Chapter Twenty-Five

The day of the Sandusky wedding, Vanna knew that she had to get out of the house and be on hand in case Maria needed her or anything went wrong. Everything was dealt with, but there were bound to be last-minute panics, things that needed to be adjusted. Adaptations. Someone would be late. Some table would not be set up the way it was supposed to be.

She set several wake-up alarms for herself and as a last-ditch effort instructed Lydia to call her and not to give up until she got through to her. She didn't need it, though. She was up and ready before Lydia's call. She felt good, for once. It was like her old life was back again. She felt alert and awake, super-focused, calm and ready for anything. She was going to be just what Maria needed. She would blow them all away.

There were a few minor issues. The photographer was late, arriving about three minutes behind schedule and causing a panic. The flowers were on time, but two bouquets were missing and Vanna had to drive down to the flower shop to replace them. Which she did in plenty of time for the ceremony, even though they would be missing in a couple of the early pictures.

The ice sculpture had a crack and had to be repositioned slightly so that it would not show.

The cake was beautiful and Vanna was sure that Maria would be delighted with it when she saw it on display.

Vanna wasn't involved with the ceremony. She had made all of the initial arrangements, but she wasn't needed at the church. That gave her some extra time to take a stroll around the reception room and to make sure that all of the decorations were perfect. The name cards were all set up correctly. Not a thing was out of place. There were more pictures after the ceremony, so the bridal party didn't show up at the dining hall until half an hour before the dinner. They walked around to check out the ice sculpture, cake, and waterfall, and to ooh and aah over everything. Maria's face was glowing. She looked like a princess.

It was just as everyone sat down for supper that everything fell apart. The groom grabbed the bottle of wine at his table and prepared to pop the cork. Maria gasped and grabbed it out of his hand. There was a ripple of whispers and laughter that went around the room. Maria stared at the label in her hand and then raised her eyes to look at Vanna. Her face turned a deep shade of red. Vanna hurried across the room, a great hole in her stomach, her heart thudding fast.

"What is it? What's wrong?"

Maria turned the wine bottle around and Vanna stared at it. She couldn't see the problem immediately. She wasn't a big wine person. Then she focused on the year on the label. Her dyslexic brain slowly untangled the numbers and sorted them properly from left to right so that she saw them as they were rather than as she assumed them to be.

Not nineteen forty-seven, as they should be. But nineteen seventy-four.

Nineteen seventy-four.

That was *not* a good year for wine.

And more importantly, it was not the year that Maria had ordered. It wasn't the vintage that Betty had used.

Vanna dragged her gaze back toward Maria. The girl's face was nearly purple with rage.

"There's nothing we can do now," Vanna told her in a low murmur. "I don't know how this could have happened, but it's too late to change it now. You will just need to be gracious and continue with the toast as if this was the wine that you planned all along. Most of the guests won't know the difference."

"How could this happen?"

"I don't know. I'll find out. But in the meantime, betray nothing. Stiff upper lip. Big smile. And just go on."

"You have totally ruined my special day."

"I'm sorry about that."

Vanna turned and walked back away from Maria, giving calm and collected smiles to anyone who tried to make eye contact with her on her way out of the room. She walked to her car, got in, and banged her forehead against the steering wheel.

When Vanna got back to her apartment, she went first to her email and searched up all of the correspondence with the vintner. There it was in black and white, her order for nineteen forty-seven. She breathed a sigh of relief. That was proof that she had not made a career-ending mistake. It wasn't her sleep-deprived brain that had caused the hiccup. It was the vintner's fault, not hers.

She gave him a call after a few calming breaths.

"Ah, Miss Austin. The Sandusky wedding today, is it not? Everything arrived safely, I trust? No breakage?"

"No breakage," Vanna confirmed. "But there seems to be a miscommunication about the year. I ordered nineteen forty-seven and what arrived was nineteen seventy-four. The client just about blew a gasket."

"But Miss Austin… you changed that order."

"I changed from the nineteen forty-five to the nineteen forty-seven. Yes. But what we got was seventy-four."

"No, no. We already had this discussion. You sent me an email after that. She changed her mind, she wants the seventy-four. I protested. The seventy-four vintage is inferior. No one would change to the seventy-four. It would be ridiculous. Back to the forty-five, fine. But not to the seventy-four."

"I didn't send an email like that."

"I remember it quite specifically. You think I would forget that?"

"I don't know what you're talking about. Send me a copy of that email."

"Certainly, Miss Austin. I am happy to. And you can have a talk with your assistant about it too. She was quite emphatic that they wanted the seventy-four. Some long windy story about a grandfather and good luck and a bunch of sentimental hogwash. No one orders the seventy-four because of a bunch of sentimental hogwash. But she was quite insistent. And it is what the client wants. I cannot change their mind."

"My assistant? I don't have an assistant."

There was silence from the vintner. Then a protest. "Miss Austin…"

"I do not have an assistant," Vanna insisted. "Who did you talk to? I never ordered the seventy-four and I don't have an assistant. Who exactly did you talk to? Did you call her, or did she call you?"

"She called me after I sent you back an email protesting that you must have been mistaken when you typed nineteen seventy-four. It is an easy mistake. It's just a reversal. She called and said most emphatically that it was not a mistake and that was what the client wanted. It didn't matter what I thought was better." He gave a long, injured sniff.

He had forwarded his email. The beep brought Vanna's eyes up to the top of the list and she clicked to open the forwarded mail. It was her email address and her usual signature. But the words on the screen hadn't been typed by her. She had never sent him a follow-up email changing the order.

Vanna moaned and swore under her breath. The offended vintner did not respond. "Marcel… Marcel, I never sent you this email. Somebody spoofed my address. Someone who wanted to ruin the wedding. To ruin me."

"It was not an email from you?"

"No. No, oh Marcel—no, never."

"I am so glad!" he sounded relieved. "Miss Austin, I hear rumors that you are having problems. That your business is not going well. I did not want to believe that you could have… that you could have made such a devastating mistake as this."

"No, it wasn't me. But it may as well have been because it is going to affect me the same way. It is going to ruin my business either way."

"Surely not," Marcel argued. "Everybody knows that you are dependable. Efficient. You get things done and done right. Nobody will believe that you made this mistake. Tchht." He made a noise that Vanna wasn't sure was a word, but might have been. "You will see. People will rally behind you."

"I wish I could say that I thought that. But since I got run over, I have hardly been able to do any work. People already know that I am having problems getting things done. This will just confirm it. Vanna is a deadbeat. Don't give her any work."

"No. No, no, my dear. I will speak for you. You were run over? But what a terrible thing to happen! You must let me help you."

"No, Marcel." Vanna sighed. "No one can help me now."

Vanna couldn't think of what else to do. As much as she hated to leave her home, she didn't have much choice anymore. Not only was it not safe, but she didn't have enough money for the rent. Her work had always paid the bills before, but since Abigail had started to stalk her, things had gone gradually downhill, and now she had no work and no money coming in. The spectacular wedding fiasco had lit up her clients' world like fireworks. No one was sending her anything anymore. Not even short, simple clerical jobs. It was completely dry.

The wine mistake had actually gotten into the papers. Granted, it was just a small social column, but it was read faithfully by many of the Birchdale elite, including her mother. The fact that Maria Sandusky had served a poor seventy-four vintage at her wedding had been widely circulated and Maria was holding Vanna accountable for her horrible day, filing suit against Vanna the very next day. Vanna had no idea what she was going to do about the lawsuit. She didn't have money for a lawyer or a settlement. She knew that Erica would step in if she needed it, but she desperately needed to retain some independence. Some semblance that she could handle her own life.

It was partly this desperation that made her go to Lydia instead of Erica. Erica thought that it was ridiculous, when she had that great empty mansion, that Vanna wouldn't come and stay with her. Lydia had a house full of little people, without even a spare room for Vanna to call her own. The spare bed was in Mandy's room.

Lydia assured her that Mandy was a good sleeper and rarely woke up in the night. If Mandy did wake up, there was a baby monitor and Lydia would come in and get her. Vanna didn't have to worry about a thing.

Sweeny would have preferred that Vanna went to the Estate too. The security measures already in place were better and Erica could have pumped them up even further. But to Vanna, going back there would be admitting defeat. It would mean that Erica had been right all along about Vanna not choosing her career path wisely and not having the skills or maturity to live on her own yet. At least with going to live at Lydia's, she could claim that she was helping out with the kids and that it was only a temporary setback.

It wasn't admitting final defeat.

Not yet.

Chapter Twenty-Six

This is going to be so much fun!" Lydia enthused. "Just like a sleepover, every night. And the boys are so excited about auntie coming to stay."

Christopher and Paul were currently being airplanes, their arms extended as wings, racing back and forth in everyone's way as they made loud motor and diving noises with their mouths. Vanna laughed.

"They're excited, all right."

"I had such a hard time getting them down for bed last night. They wanted it to be today so that they could get up and see their Auntie Vanna. Christopher called to me at eleven o'clock wondering if he could get out of bed yet."

Vanna smiled at them affectionately.

"It will be great," she agreed, but without Lydia's enthusiasm. She felt like she was being sucked down a whirlpool. There was no getting out, and when she got to the bottom, she was going to go under into the darkness and drown.

Still, she tried to smile and act like it was just one great adventure. All of her furniture and files were moved into a storage locker. She wouldn't even store those at the Estate, trying to hang onto a few last vestiges of dignity. Most of her clothes and personal belongings went into the storage locker as well. She had only what could fit in two suitcases, her laptop bag and her go bag. Even that made Mandy's little nursery room seem crowded. Vanna realized that this last-ditch effort wasn't going to work for long.

She looked out Lydia's big kitchen window, which looked down on the side street. Vanna scanned it for black cars. Of course, if Abigail was smart, she might have switched cars by now. The little black Sunfire was probably getting too hot. Too much on the radar of the police.

Lydia saw her eyes searching the street below and she looked up and down it. "What? Do you see something?"

"No… just checking."

"Sheesh, don't do that, Vanny. You scared me. I thought that she had followed you here."

Vanna hadn't told Lydia about the photos that Abigail had sent. Lydia was worried that Vanna might have been followed to her house during the move. Not realizing that it was way too late for that. Abigail already knew where everybody important in Vanna's life lived. Vanna warned Erica and Tino, but she couldn't bring herself to tell Lydia. Lydia knew security had been amped up around her house because Vanna was moving in there. She didn't know any further details.

Vanna scanned the road again. She walked out to the living room and scanned the front street as well, looking for any sign of Abigail. She couldn't see anything and that just made her feel worse. How could she guard against something that she couldn't even see? Abigail lurked like a ghost around the edges of her life, watching with telephoto lenses or binoculars, with the glowing bright eyes of a cat in the darkness. Wherever Vanna went, Abigail was watching, whether Vanna could see her or not.

"John Paul doesn't mind?" she asked Lydia, for the umpteenth time. She felt like such an intruder in their cozy little life. She felt guilty for bringing the danger nearer.

"John Paul thinks he just acquired a live-in babysitter for free. And he loves you, Van. You know that. He's always considered you his own kid sister, ever since we started dating."

"He's a wonderful man. He really is."

"I agree," Lydia smiled and lifted her chin proudly. "And one day, you'll find one of your own."

"I don't think so." Vanna shook her head, still scanned the street anxiously. "I think I'm doomed to only attract men like Tino. There just aren't that many John Pauls out there."

"Don't give up. You'll find your prince one day."

Maybe.

If she lived that long.

———

Vanna checked her timer to see how long the hair dye had been in her hair, resisting the temptation to remove the towel and look at it.

"What color is it going to be?" Christopher demanded again, dancing around Vanna. "I want to see!"

"It's going to be light. Like your mom's. Not quite as blond as your mom's. But lighter."

"Like mine?"

Vanna looked at Christopher's medium brown hair with blond highlights.

"I hope so. I really like yours. I'm not sure what mine will look like. I haven't tried this color before."

"What color have you tried before? Hasn't it always been black?"

"When I was in high school, I did red. Even some purple."

"Purple hair!" he squealed.

Paul ran into the room at top speed.

"Purple hair? I want to see! Is it purple?"

"No," Vanna laughed at his excitement. "I was telling

Christopher that once I dyed my hair purple. But not this time. Sorry."

He sighed and stuck his lip out in a dramatic pout. "I like purple."

"I like purple too, but I'm not coloring my hair purple. Not this time. Maybe Mommy can find a picture of when I had purple hair."

"Yeah!" He bounced off to go ask her.

"Is it time?" Christopher asked again, looking at the timer.

Vanna looked at it. There was only one minute left. "Yes, that should do it," she agreed.

Christopher watched with fascination as she unwound the towel and shook out her hair. He frowned. "It's darker than mine," he pointed out.

"It's still wet. It will dry lighter." Vanna examined her reflection in the mirror. "Doesn't yours go darker when it's wet?"

"Yes. Paul's too."

"That's right. So we won't know how light it will be until it dries."

"Are you going to dry it now?"

"I'm going to rinse it out and then I'll dry it."

Christopher alternately watched Vanna and ran to his mother and Paul to report each development. Vanna had to laugh at his fascination. She waved off Lydia's attempts at getting him to leave Vanna alone.

"It's okay, he's not bothering me."

Lydia shook her head. "Well, you be sure to tell him if he's getting underfoot. He can be a bit of a pest with his questions." She looked at Christopher with affection.

He shook his head. "I'm just curious, Mom."

"Yes, you are a very curious boy. Be sure not to get in auntie's way, then, okay?"

"Okay. But do you like her new hair, Mom?"

Lydia studied Vanna's new look as she curled and dried her

hair. "I think it's a good look, but it's going to take me some time to get used to! You've never done blond before."

"I knew it would never be like yours."

"That doesn't mean that you couldn't have your own look."

"Oh, I did! But I didn't want to look like I was trying to be you."

"Oh." Lydia nodded. "I get it."

Vanna wasn't sure that Lydia really did. Looking in the mirror, Vanna had always known that she was different. Her hair color and texture weren't the only thing. Nor was it just skin color and features. She was fundamentally different from Lydia. Inside and out. She felt close to Lydia. They were best friends and shared almost everything. But she had never felt like they were the same and came from the same place. She'd always felt like an interloper.

Vanna caught Lydia's eyes on her, a small frown line between her eyebrows like Erica got. "What?"

"Do you think it will make a difference? To Abigail, I mean?"

Vanna looked up at the ceiling. "No. Not really. It's all sort of academic, moving here and changing the way I look. Because she already knows where to look for me. Even if I don't look the same, she won't be fooled for long."

"No, I guess not. Are you going to do like Suzanne says and get a different car?"

"I actually did already. I went to an internet cafe and I bought it online. Sweeny is going to bring it by… trying to keep the switch from being obvious."

Lydia giggled. "It's like a spy movie."

Sweeny's officers had swept the car and her baggage for bugs before Vanna had left. And had followed her to make sure that Abigail couldn't follow her. But as Vanna told Lydia, it wouldn't really make much difference. When Vanna didn't return home, Abigail would watch Lydia's house, Erica's estate, and Tino's apartment, and she would find Vanna again, new hair color and car or not. If she hadn't already tracked Vanna's new computer or phone or some other method.

Vanna had shut down the business and not given her clients any forwarding address. Her apartment mail would be forwarded to a box and Erica would pick it up. The chances of losing Abigail were nil. Especially with moving in with Lydia. But where else would Vanna go? She had no money and as yet no way of making money. Even starting a regular nine-to-five job was out of the question right now, when all she had the energy to do was nap and eat the occasional meal.

"It's like a nightmare," she told Lydia in an undertone. "Only I can't wake up."

———

Erica was by the next day to make sure that Vanna was settled in and to give her a pep talk. She took in Vanna's new appearance with raised eyebrows. "It's not really your style, is it?"

Vanna felt a stab of disappointment, even though she had been prepared for rejection. She tried to push the feelings aside. "My style is going to have to change if I'm going to have any chance of avoiding Abigail."

"Of course. It's just… I like your natural look. You don't look like my little girl."

Vanna rolled her eyes. "Why don't we sit down? Lydia's just trying to settle Mandy down for a nap."

There was a shriek from the two boys, followed by running on the stairs and a slammed door. Erica shook her head, smiling. "Girls were much quieter."

"I don't imagine all girls would be. I have a feeling that Mandy will give the boys a run for their money, once she gets a little bigger."

"Lydia says she's pretty mellow."

Vanna shrugged. Erica pulled out an Italian leather writing

portfolio from her briefcase and laid it across her knees. "So. We should discuss your needs and a budget."

Vanna bit the inside of her lip. Mentally, she felt herself sliding down a long hole, into darkness. Her stomach took a dive like she was on a roller coaster. She found herself glancing around the room for John Paul's liquor cabinet, wishing for something to numb the pain that constricted her heart.

"I don't need anything. Really. It's covered. And I'll find some job that I can do to help Lydia out."

"Nonsense. You're being silly. You've already lost your apartment, let's protect what you have left. You're going to have to pay for that storage unit."

"I've paid the three-month deposit. I don't need to make another payment right away, so that can wait until I find a job."

"What about your car?"

"It was mostly a straight-across trade. I didn't owe anything on the Mazda. So just a few hundred dollars."

Knowing that she wasn't likely to get an exact number from Vanna, Erica scribbled down her best guess at what 'a few hundred' might be. Vanna didn't correct her.

"And was that from savings or on credit?"

"Credit," Vanna admitted.

"How much is on your credit cards?"

"Not that much. I usually pay cash for everything."

"Good girl. We can check the balances later. Make sure that it isn't more than you think. Then there's the lawsuit from Maria Sandusky." Erica said Maria's name with distinct distaste, her tongue reminding Vanna of a cat trying to lick peanut butter from it's paws. The image was faintly amusing and she had to stifle a noise in her throat. Erica frowned at her. "Clearly you are not at fault, but we will still need to pay an attorney to file the appropriate documents and possibly a settlement to keep the whole stalking story from getting into the papers. You don't need your private life smeared all over Birchdale's society pages."

"You don't think it will just go away? If she doesn't get a good reaction, won't she just let it die?"

"I don't think we can count on it. The Sanduskys are notoriously hard-headed and vindictive. You don't go halves on a Sandusky. So we'll have to set some money aside for that." Erica scribbled down a rather breathtaking sum. "Now, what about your living arrangements? You are not going to live here."

"I am for now."

"I understand you want a place of your own. I would have paid to keep your last apartment, only it was safer to have you out of there anyway. You really shouldn't impose on your sister."

"She's not imposing," Lydia corrected, coming down the stairs and catching Erica's words.

Erica blushed pink.

"Don't go telling her that she's not wanted or has to move out," Lydia warned. "Vanna's going to stay here with me, where I can keep an eye on her and she can help me out with the boys. That's our arrangement. When she's ready, we'll talk about the next step. But not now. She's just moved in and she needs some time to get her legs back under her."

Vanna was grateful for the words but felt a little ashamed too. She looked down at her feet. Lydia sat down on the couch next to Vanna and rubbed her back.

"So where are we?" Lydia asked. She looked at Erica's notes. "John Paul is looking into getting a better security system. Tightening it up a bit, which will also keep the boys safer and hardwire us into the fire department and everything too. I think..." she glanced sideways at Vanna and didn't ask her opinion. "Some new clothes. The hair color and style isn't going to fool anyone for long. I can lend her a few of my things, but we're not the same size. Even if it's just outerwear for now; it's still the rainy season. A couple of new raincoats and umbrellas. Maybe some heels to disguise her height. What do you think? I mean, we don't need to totally make her over, but I think we can do better."

Erica nodded agreement. "Right." She wrote down another figure. "You can come with me, Vanna. My car has tinted windows and we'll go shopping at places you don't normally go. Some new clothes probably wouldn't hurt your outlook, either. I'm worried about her mood," she said to Lydia as if Vanna was no longer even there.

Lydia looked at Vanna and didn't comment.

"Are you going to your support group?" Erica turned her questions back to Vanna. "And what about therapy? I think a couple more trips to the chiropractor for your back would be good, but I'd like you to see a psychologist too. Someone that you can talk to about all of this." She pursed her lips. "Even about reconciling the past. This must have stirred up a lot of that old trauma."

"I'm fine. I don't need to talk to anyone. And I don't remember what happened when I was little."

"You aren't going out with your friends."

"No. Not much. But that's just so that Abigail can't use them to find me. Really. I'm okay."

"We all need help sometimes, Ivanna."

"I'll let you know if I need therapy," Vanna said, careful to keep her voice completely even.

"You don't worry about the cost. There is plenty of money left in the estate to help my children. There's no point in new cars or houses or other things if your mental health is an issue. You can't be happy with *things* if you are not happy as a person."

Vanna shrugged and didn't argue any further. Erica pressed her lips together and jotted a couple more notes to herself on the notepad. "Now, why don't we try some retail therapy?"

———

It had been a long day and the 'retail therapy' *had* helped raise Vanna's spirits much more than she had expected. As much fun as buying new clothes was, it was even better, because it made her feel more secure. Maybe Abigail wouldn't recognize her. Maybe she'd just think that Lydia had gotten a new nanny for the boys and not even realize that it was Vanna. She did look very different with her blond, wavy hair, high heels, and differently styled clothes. Vanna had always chosen her own style, ignoring any advice from Erica, so she did the opposite this time. She didn't want anything to be in her style. She wanted to look like a different person. She would go with her mother's suggestions on style as long as it fit and wasn't too overpriced, letting Erica play dress-up-doll to her heart's content.

Vanna went back to Lydia's house exhausted, completely bone-tired-drained-to-the-last-drop. But she was confident that she could start over. She could stay out of Abigail's line of fire and start a new life for herself. Maybe even a better life. She had to admit, she did look good in spite of the bags under her eyes, carefully concealed by an expert.

"I just put Mandy down," Lydia whispered. "So any time you want to go to bed is fine, I won't be interrupting you. Do you want a sandwich before bed?"

"Mom took care of that already," Vanna advised.

"I'll bet she did. Can I get you anything? Anything at all?"

Vanna painfully drew off her new heels and massaged her toes. "I have everything I need," she assured Lydia. "Really. Just a quiet place to lay down my head. That's all."

Lydia nodded and gave her some space. Vanna hung up her coat and carried her shopping bags upstairs—anything that Erica hadn't taken to be altered—and dropped them on the floor. She reasoned that she couldn't hang them up in the dark anyway and didn't want to wake up the baby by turning the light on. A quick trip to the bathroom with her overnight bag to swish some mouthwash around, skipping the flossing and only brushing for about ten seconds. Toilet and jammies, and off to bed.

She didn't even remember laying her head on the pillow.

———

When she awoke, she realized that Mandy must have started to fuss because it was still dark and she could hear Lydia singing softly. Vanna closed her eyes again, rolling over to the other side and seeking to sleep again. She was starting to drift again when the soft singing changed abruptly to whispered curses.

She'd never heard anything so foul come out of Lydia's mouth.

Vanna was instantly wide awake. She turned around and searched the room wildly. Lydia was not there. There was no dark form bent over the crib. No one sitting in the rocking chair. There was only Vanna, and Mandy making whimpering noises in the crib. Vanna tried to clear her head. Had she been hearing things? Had it been a dream?

The voice started again. This time, it wasn't aimed at the baby, but at Vanna herself. "Mealy Amelia. You think I don't know you? You think I wouldn't recognize you if you color your hair? You're still the same little girl you always were, crying for your mama."

Vanna was frozen for a few seconds, unable to move or to utter a sound. Abigail was there, in the room with her, in the room with the baby. She knew it wasn't possible, but it was true. She wasn't imagining it. She tore the blankets off of herself and dashed over to the crib. She slid her hands under Mandy and raced out of the room.

Startled out of sleep, Mandy started to cry. A choking protest at first, and then rising to a shrill fire-engine yell. Vanna blundered down the hall to the master bedroom.

She could see Lydia in the moonlight, climbing out of bed

with a disoriented expression. "Vanna? What's wrong? Mandy woke up?"

"She's in my room. Abigail. She was in the room!"

John Paul was getting out of bed now too. "She couldn't be in the house. The security alarm didn't go. You had a dream."

But he wasn't waiting around to find out. He hurried out of the room and down the hall to the baby's room. He threw on the light and looked around. Lydia took Mandy from Vanna's arms and tried to calm her. The baby was nearly hysterical, jolted from a sound sleep and now having the lights turned on as well. Vanna was feeling a little hysterical herself. She and Lydia followed John Paul at a distance. He looked around the room, shaking his head and putting out his arms in a wide, questioning shrug.

Then Vanna heard the voice again. Another lullaby. Lydia gasped. John Paul whirled around. The voice was coming out of the baby monitor on the dresser. He picked it up and yanked it away from the wall, disconnecting the power. It apparently had a battery backup in case of power failure, because it kept going, Abigail's laugh coming from his hand. John Paul switched the power switch off. He opened the battery door in the back and pulled the batteries out, letting them fall to the floor.

They all stood around, looking at the baby monitor like it was some predator that they had just killed and gutted. They waited for it to come back to life. It remained silent.

Vanna raised her eyes to John Paul. "How did she do that?"

"I don't know." He shook his head, looking down at the lifeless monitor. "She hacked into it. I don't know how."

"Did she come into the house?" Lydia asked. "Did she have to go into the baby's room to do that?"

"We'll have to ask someone who knows more about these things than I do. I just followed the instructions to install it."

"I'll call Sweeny," Vanna said. "Do you think I should call him? Is it an emergency, or should I call in the morning?"

Lydia looked around anxiously. "I'm really nervous. Could

you call him? He can at least send someone over to make sure…
I don't know… someone who can make sure she isn't in the
house. That everything is still secure."

Vanna nodded. She went back into Mandy's room to
retrieve her phone. Then she left the room again, feeling
exposed. Her stomach was quaking. Her whole body was shuddering and raised in goosebumps.

"You're cold," Lydia said. "Let me get you a wrap."

Vanna hit Sweeny's speed-dial. He answered after a couple
of rings.

"Vanna? What's wrong? Are you okay?"

"Yes. Everybody's okay. But… Abigail hacked into the baby
monitor. I thought she was in the room. She was singing to the
baby, and threatening, and swearing… I thought she was right
there." Vanna tried to control the wobble in her voice but was
unsuccessful. A sob escaped her throat.

Lydia wrapped a housecoat around her, giving her a
comforting hug.

"I'll send someone over," Sweeny promised. "We'll make
sure that the perimeter hasn't been breached. Is the security
alarm on the same network as the baby monitor?"

Vanna looked at John Paul, who could hear Sweeny's
booming voice from the receiver. John Paul gave a wide shrug.
"He doesn't know. We don't know how anything is set up."

"We'll take a look and see what we can figure out. You
should have the security company out by morning, if not
tonight. They need to know that the system may have been
breached. They may leave a private guard overnight to keep
watch."

"Yeah, okay."

"I'm sorry, Vanna… this is crazy stuff. I know that you were
hoping that Abigail wouldn't be able to trace you there."

"How am I supposed to get away from her? I can't make a
move without her knowing. She's watching everything I do!"

"I know. I'm sorry. We're doing everything we can to help,

but if we can't find her, put her under arrest, we can't keep her away from you."

"It's not fair." Vanna sniffled and broke out into regular sobs. "I don't know what to do."

"It's not fair," he agreed. "I'm going to get off now so that I can get some officers over there. Don't open the door to anyone but uniformed officers in a lit-up police car."

Chapter Twenty-Seven

Vanna hadn't slept again, in spite of being exhausted. She couldn't lie down again. She sat on the couch in front of the television and a couple of times nodded off for a minute, but no more than an instant or two at a time.

The police and security men were in and out of the house. Vanna tried to keep her eye on them, afraid that somehow, Abigail would insert herself into the mix; that with all of the coming and going, she would walk right into the house, right under everyone's noses. There was one security woman, but she was too big to be Abigail. Vanna took a good, long look at her face to persuade herself that it couldn't possibly be Abigail in disguise.

She was sure it wasn't, but she still watched. She was still afraid that somehow Abigail would slip past them.

The various public and private investigators were there almost all day. Lydia managed to catch a nap when John Paul took the boys out and Mandy went down for a sleep. John Paul hadn't gone in to work, too worried about something happening to his family while he was gone.

Lydia ordered pizza. They were all too tired to cook. The boys were excited and got all wound up about it, jumping off the furniture and running around pretending to be spies. Vanna wasn't sure what spies had to do with pizza. Maybe just having all of the police around had inspired them.

The police had promised that everything was secure. After Lydia put Mandy down for the night, she made a motion toward the bedroom.

"She's down for the night. You can go to bed any time you like."

"Do you think… I could flop on the couch, instead?"

Lydia looked at her for a long moment. "Sure, Vanny. I'll get you some blankets."

"I know where everything is. You just let me get it myself."

"Oh, it's not a problem. Let me do it for you."

"You've had to put up with all of this stuff all day because of me. I can get my own blankets. Let me feel like I'm doing something other than being a burden to you."

"You're not a burden!"

"If I'm just a housemate, then let me do some of the work."

Lydia leaned against the doorframe, looking suddenly tired. "Okay. Help yourself. I am going to bed."

"See you tomorrow."

Lydia retreated to her bedroom. John Paul was already up there, reviewing some work papers while sitting up in bed. Vanna heard the bedroom door click shut, and their low, murmured voices.

She never did get up and get the blankets. She couldn't seem to lever herself up from the couch. It was too hard physically and mentally. She just sat there, watching TV and occasionally changing the channel. She didn't fall sleep until the room was filled with early-morning sunlight. It seemed like about ten minutes later that the yells of Christopher and Paul awakened her.

"Shhh," Lydia whispered as she descended the stairs. "Auntie may still be sleeping."

She got to the bottom and looked at Vanna on the couch.

She had Mandy in one arm, but put her other hand on her hip as she looked at Vanna with a frown.

"I'm up," Vanna offered.

"And I see have already made your bed," Lydia observed ironically. "Did you get any sleep?"

"No… not really."

"Why don't you go up and lie down now? It won't be quiet, but maybe quiet isn't what you need."

Vanna nodded. "Yeah. Maybe."

She didn't like to think of lying down on that bed again, with the baby monitor still in there. It was just too creepy. She couldn't be in there without feeling like Abigail was watching her. The security crew had confirmed that Abigail had merely hacked it through their wireless network. She had never been in the house. But that didn't make Vanna feel any better. Lydia went into the kitchen and worked on breakfast for the children. The boys thumped down the stairs behind her and started bickering over the remote for the TV.

"It looks like John Paul will go into work today," she called back over her shoulder to Vanna. "Things should be quieter today."

"Okay."

"Maybe you and I could spend some time—"

The shriek this time was not from the boys, but from Lydia. Vanna was immediately on her feet and out to the kitchen. Lydia was standing at the back door with a garbage bag in her hand. The door was open, and lying before the threshold was a large dog, a german shepherd. The eyes were open and sightless and it lay in a large pool of blood. There was an envelope, smeared with bloody fingerprints, tucked under the dog's collar.

Vanna pulled Lydia back away from the door and slammed it shut again just as the children tumbled into the room, wanting to know what was going on. Lydia looked at Vanna with horrified eyes.

"What is it? What happened?" Christopher demanded.

"Go get your daddy," Vanna told him. She pulled out her phone and called Sweeny. Before he could even greet her by name, as he usually did, Vanna rushed ahead. "She's been here. She didn't trip the proximity alarm even though she was in the yard. She's…" Vanna looked at Paul, who was still watching her with bright, eager eyes. "She's left something behind."

"Are you okay? Is everyone safe?"

"Yes. Everyone is okay, but they're not safe. Not with her getting that close to the house. Someone needs to come and… clean up this mess. And I… don't know what to do…" She felt her throat tightening with tears and was angry with herself. It seemed like she was crying about everything lately.

"Lydia? Lydia, what happened?" John Paul was coming down the stairs, his voice full of concern. Vanna ached for it to be for her instead of his wife. When he saw Lydia's expression, he pulled her close in his arms. "What is it?"

Vanna had no one to hold her. She sniffled into the phone. "Are you coming?"

"Yes. I'll be there as soon as I can. A few minutes."

"Thank you."

She knew that Sweeny was busy. She might not have gotten him out of bed, but hers wasn't the only case that he had. It both soothed and worried her that he was going to come himself. Lydia was murmuring to John Paul about what she had seen outside, but refused to let him open the door again. He took the garbage bag from her hand and set it on the floor. He took Mandy out of her arm and he hugged her again.

"You sit down," John Paul told his wife. And taking note of Vanna for the first time, he included her as well. They both sat at the table. "I'll put some coffee on. It will all be okay. He's coming?" The last question was aimed at Vanna.

"Yes."

"Okay. Let's just act as natural as we can." He nodded significantly at Paul.

Vanna couldn't help but think about her own past. How she

had come into her family, damaged and traumatized and they had acted natural, had provided the simple, normal family setting that she needed to heal again. No matter what she had gone through, theirs was a normal, everyday family, going through normal, everyday actions.

"Who wants cereal?" she asked Paul. "You know what, I think I saw some really unhealthy-looking kids' cereal in the cupboard the other day."

That piqued Paul's attention immediately. "That's the *Saturday* cereal," he explained. "Is today Saturday?"

"You know what? It isn't. But I'm going to get it out anyway, because I'm the fun auntie."

He half-giggled and half-shrieked, and ran off to find Christopher.

"Thanks!" Lydia's tone was mock-disapproving. She moved to get up.

"Stay there," John Paul ordered. "I told you I'm getting breakfast."

"Well, that's not acting naturally," Lydia pointed out.

John Paul laughed good-humoredly. "Well, other than that."

Paul returned to the room, looking more subdued. "He won't come."

Again, Lydia moved to get up, but Vanna beat her to it. "I'll go get him."

Vanna went upstairs and found Christopher sitting on the edge of his bed. He was looking down, unusually still and somber. Vanna sat down next to him. "What's up, bud?"

"Bad things are happening." His lip quivered and he glanced at her. "Why are so many bad things happening?"

Her first instinct was to ask him what he meant and to try to explain it away. But that wasn't honest and she didn't want to minimize what he was feeling. Even if he hadn't seen the dead dog or heard Abigail's voice on the baby monitor, he was still sensitive enough to sense the atmosphere of the adults and to hear enough to know things were not right. She put her arm around his shoulders and hugged him to her.

"I know, Chris."

Normally a driven, physically active child, it was rare for him to stay and cuddle with her, but he nestled against her without talking.

"I'm sorry for everything that's happening," she told him.

"Why is it?" he asked, still pressing against her.

"There is a lady whose… I guess she's sort of mad at me. She wants to scare me, I think."

"Is she a bully?" He looked up at her face.

"I guess she is, kind of," Vanna agreed. "What do you know about bullies?"

"On TV. On my shows. Sometimes there are bullies."

Vanna nodded.

"Sometimes bullies just want attention," he offered. "Or they might just play too rough. Not on purpose."

"Yes. Some bullies might just be… misunderstood. But this lady… she really is just being mean."

Christopher snuggled back against her side. "Sometimes bullies are mean because someone else was mean to them."

"Yes. Maybe that's what happened to her."

That was how Vanna pictured Abigail. Bullied, maybe even physically abused by a drunken father. Mother negligent, scared, or just not in the picture. Maybe there were other children that Abigail had tried to protect, taking the brunt of the abuse, eventually boiling over with the suppressed rage, aiming it at someone else, an innocent bystander. But she didn't really know anything about Abigail's family or formative years.

"Paul said we're having Saturday cereal *today*."

Vanna looked down at Christopher's mischievous smile. "That's right. Because Auntie's here, and Auntie said 'let's have something full of sugar!'"

"Okay!" he crowed.

Having had his sad time, he was now ready to move on and

tackle the day. Vanna stayed sitting on his bed for a few seconds longer, wishing that she could move on just as quickly.

———

Lydia took the boys out after they had their breakfast. They would go to the play place and try to burn off the sugar before returning home. Hopefully, by that time the police would be done and everything would be cleaned up.

Sweeny arrived just as they were leaving. He nodded to Lydia and didn't stop her to question her on what had happened. Instead, he went directly to the house and was examining the security panel beside the front door. Vanna opened the front door to allow him to enter. He straightened up.

"Was the system armed last night?"

"Yes. Of course. After everything that happened yesterday?"

"That's exactly my point. You had a lot of people in and out of here. You were all exhausted from the night before. Who armed it?"

"John Paul. I'll get him."

Vanna turned to fetch her brother-in-law and just about ran right into him as he approached her from behind.

"Sorry," he murmured, grinning.

Vanna turned back around, stepping to the side so that the men could talk.

"You're sure it was armed yesterday?" Sweeny repeated.

"Yes. Before bed. Absolutely."

"You armed it yourself?"

He nodded.

Sweeny looked at the two of them. "And this morning? Did someone have to disarm it? Or was it already disarmed?"

"Lydia said that she didn't get a warning beep when she opened the back door," Vanna confirmed. "I'm the one who shut the door and neither of us turned off the alarm. When John Paul checked it, it had been disarmed."

Sweeny shook his head. "So she's hacked your system that quickly. Did you change the code yesterday?"

"Of course," John Paul leaned against the doorway. "Do you want to come in?"

"I'll go around back first and see what we're dealing with. Who chose the code?"

"Lydia."

"Is it the same code that she uses on anything else? Or completely unique?"

John Paul grimaced. "She does use it for some other things," he admitted. "I know you're not supposed to use birthdays, but it's not like it's ours or one of the kids'…" His eyes turned to Vanna and his brow wrinkled. "Oh…"

"Don't tell me," Vanna groaned. "Tell me she didn't use *my* birthday."

Sweeny shook his head at John Paul's stricken expression. "You used the birthday of the person the woman you are trying to keep out is obsessed with as the security code."

"We… I… it's just a combination of numbers that we use sometimes. I didn't even think about where it came from… I never even considered it."

"You *need* to be thinking. About everything. This woman will do whatever it takes to get to Vanna. You're lucky she didn't decide to enter the house once she took the system down."

"I was watching TV on the couch," Vanna said. "No one came in."

"But she could have."

Vanna and John Paul both nodded. Sweeny took out a notepad. "How many digits?"

"Six."

He wrote out a number. "I want you to change it right now. That's your new code."

John Paul looked at it, opening his mouth.

"Don't say it out loud," Sweeny snapped. "We'll have to do a sweep to make sure she hasn't left a bug. Memorize it. When

Lydia gets back, she memorizes it. Then you destroy that paper. And I don't mean tear it in half and throw it away. I mean burn it. And flush the ashes. Don't tell the number to Vanna."

Vanna looked at Sweeny, startled. "Why…?"

"If she gets to you somehow, you don't want there to be any chance that you could give her information that would make your family more vulnerable. You don't know that she'll stop at you. She didn't stop with your birth mother."

Vanna nodded. "Yeah. You're right. I didn't really think about that."

———

Sweeny hadn't wanted Vanna to read the note from Abigail. And she probably shouldn't have. Abigail's letters had, despite the neat, familiar handwriting, descended into rabid, vitriolic rantings. Vanna remembered the letters from those early days with something like fondness. Why hadn't she appreciated the sweet, concerned birth mother that Abigail had played back then? Maybe a few kind words of encouragement would have sent Abigail down an alternate path. One where she didn't turn back into the murderous monster who had killed Julia. Vanna felt as though Abigail had killed Julia twice. Once the actual, physical murder. But then again, twenty years later, Abigail had again killed the uncomfortably-friendly woman who had been Julia to Vanna for a short length of time.

Sweeny watched her eyes and spoke to her when she reached the end of the short note.

"I told you that you didn't need to see that. You can't get anything out of it."

"I just… I don't know. I used to know what to expect. Now… she's changed from the way she was, in the beginning. I wish I'd done something to dissuade her back then, before she became… this."

"She didn't become this," Sweeny corrected. "She always

was this, underneath. That's why you felt so uncomfortable with her. Because, in spite of all of the window dressing, you could tell that something wasn't right underneath."

"I didn't know, I just… I didn't want her intruding in my life. I wanted her to leave me alone."

"The same as now. Only then, you felt guilty about not wanting her there, because she seemed nice on the surface. Now, you're feeling guilty because you think you could have done something to stop it from happening. If you had just done something…"

"How do you know that?" Vanna looked at him, surprised at his insight.

"Because they all feel guilty. We're social animals. It's in our nature to interact with each other, to provide benefits to each other. When that mutual benefit model fails, we feel bad."

Knowing that everyone felt guilty about their stalkers was little consolation. She was glad to know that she wasn't the only one and that there was a logical reason for the feeling, but it didn't change the feeling. She still felt like she should have been able to manage it. She should have been able to fix it, somehow.

"She killed your birthmother," Sweeny said. "You can't fix this. She was already broken twenty years ago. It was too late then."

"But, why?"

"I don't know. I'll see what information I can find you about her history, but I don't think you're ever going to be satisfied with the answer. She's an outlier. Whether it's genetic, or a choice, or the way that she was raised, we may never know. But she doesn't play the mutual benefit game. She just takes."

"Is that normal?"

"No, I just said that's not the way that our society is set up."

"No, I mean is that normal for… stalkers."

He shrugged. "Nothing is normal for stalkers… but the percentage that we identify as mentally ill is very small." He anticipated her next question. "I can't tell you if Abigail is technically mentally ill or not... it wasn't used as a defense and she wasn't treated for anything in prison, as far as I can tell."

"I just don't understand. I don't get why she killed my birth mom. I don't get why she's threatening me. Does she really believe that I've done something to her to harm her?"

Sweeny shrugged a little. "Yes, She probably does."

———

Once again, all was quiet. Vanna had decided that a bubble bath might soothe her nerves, and she was stretched out in the tub, as much as she could stretch out, with a warm washcloth over her eyes, thinking about Julia.

At first she had tried not to think about Julia and Abigail. But her mind kept going back to them and eventually, she just let it, wallowing in her grief.

She had never known her birth mother. Had never missed her. Not in memory, anyway. It was odd that she should mourn Julia now. Yet she couldn't deny that was what she was doing. She was deeply sad for what Julia had gone through. There was an almost-physical pain that made it hard to breathe. Had Julia tried to reject a relationship with Abigail too? Tried to get the young girl out of her life, only to find that there was no way to keep her away? No way to protect herself? During those last few minutes, when they fought... how had she felt? Was she angry? Terrified? When she fell, was she relieved that the night-mare would finally be over?

Vanna shifted. She longed for the day when it would all end. She wasn't sure that it was going to end during her lifetime. But she so much wanted it to be over. She wanted to live in her own apartment again. Not to have to worry about her own or her family's safety. Anything was better than sitting awake all night, listening to every creak and groan of the house, wondering if Abigail was there, or if she was going to come. Waking up in the morning, on only an hour or two of sleep and feeling that dread fill her stomach.

Vanna shifted her weight and tried to find a more comfortable position in the unforgiving shape of the tub. She knocked something into the water and ran her fingers under the water looking for it. It took a few swipes before she was able to find the object and scoop it out of the water. It was Lydia's safety razor. Vanna shoved it back into the corner beside her. The skin on her thumb was rough on the handle as she put it back into place and Vanna looked at it. She had managed to run her thumb along the blade when she was feeling for the razor in the water, forming a couple of shallow cuts along the tip. She smoothed them with her index finger. They would sting later on, but right now, warm from the bathtub water and not in contact with the air, they didn't really hurt. She pressed her thumb against her knuckle, making the cuts spring open again, and a drop of blood oozed to the surface.

Vanna rinsed the blood off in the bath water.

Chapter Twenty-Eight

Vanna? Are you all right?" Lydia knocked on the door.

Vanna opened her eyes, sluggish and groggy. It took a long time for Lydia's words to penetrate her brain, where they swam around for a longer time in the murky soup before they started to make sense. Lydia was knocking again, louder this time.

"Vanna! Vanna, did you fall asleep?"

Vanna tried to sit up, but her body wasn't obeying very well. "I'm up. I'm okay," she croaked.

There was a noise on the door, Lydia brushing against it. Pressing her ear against the door to hear Vanna's answer better. "You're all right?"

"I'm okay."

"Okay. Why don't you get out and we'll hang out for a few minutes before going to bed?"

"Sure."

Lydia stopped talking, but Vanna could still hear her pressed against the door. Her feet blocked the light under the door, throwing a shadow. Vanna took a while to pull the drain and climb out of the tub. It wasn't as deep as hers, but she was so groggy, it could have been a swimming pool. Vanna intentionally knocked over the kid's soap squirter on the counter as she picked up her towel. Hearing that she was out of the tub and moving around, Lydia finally moved away from the door. There was a long line of unblocked light under the door.

Vanna tried not to take too long getting dressed and ready for bed. The air was cold on her skin and made her shiver before she was dried and dressed. When she got down to the living room, Lydia looked drowsy in front of the television.

"Sorry, I was falling asleep in there," Vanna explained, sitting down with her.

"I hear you. It's been an exhausting couple of days." Lydia got to her feet. "How about a nightcap? I know that you're not a big drinker, but I could use just half a glass of wine. How about you?"

"Can you do that when you're nursing?" Vanna asked, surprised.

"I'm not nursing right now. I've already put Mandy down for the night, she probably won't nurse again until morning. And I'm only drinking half a glass. That will be out of my system within a couple of hours." She took out a bottle and examined it. "So? Will you have one too?"

"You're going to open a bottle just to have half a glass?"

"Yes."

"Okay. I guess I'll have a taste too."

She wouldn't mind having more than a glass. Not after everything that had happened. Vanna watched Lydia uncork the bottle. She poured a very small glass for each of them. When she handed Vanna her glass, Vanna could see something there, around her eyes. More worry than usual. Lydia was tired, but it was more than that. She had been really worried about Vanna. Worried about more than just her falling asleep in the tub.

"I'm okay," she assured Lydia. "Really. I am."

Lydia took her hand for a minute. "Don't do anything

desperate. Please. There are lots of people who will help you. We'll work it all out, somehow."

Vanna nodded, not sure she trusted her voice. She took a sip of the wine. Lydia let go of her hand and sat back again. She put her feet up beside her on the couch and wound a fuzzy velour blanket around her.

"I didn't realize how bad it was," Lydia said. "It was different when you were in your apartment and I was just seeing you now and then. I didn't really know how it was affecting you. I didn't realize how… it just ends up consuming your whole life. I'm sorry."

"You've been great," Vanna protested. "Both you and mom. You've both been very supportive, in different ways. I know you can't understand completely. I don't expect you to. I just appreciate the support."

"The security code has been changed, so we should all be safe tonight. No more unwelcome guests."

Vanna looked over at the front door, which she could just see from where she was sitting, to verify that the chain was on. She relied on that chain a lot more than she did the electronic security. It would make a noise if anyone tried to come in the door, security alarm or no security alarm. And it would hold—hopefully—for long enough for Vanna to get out of the room safely and call for help.

Lydia followed the direction of her eyes and didn't comment. "Is there anything else I can do for you? You have to sleep tonight."

"I think I will, between the bath and the wine."

"And not having slept last night."

"Yeah, well, it's not the first time."

"I didn't think so."

Vanna leaned against her sister, enjoying the warm feeling that she only got from snuggling up with someone else. All the blankets in the world couldn't compete with a warm body. She wondered how Tino was. He was out of jail again, which just confirmed to Vanna how little the system actually cared about stopping stalkers. She hadn't shown up to testify against him, and even though they knew it was at least his second time violating the restraining order, they had just let him go again. How many people would go appear in court to testify against their stalkers? She wasn't sure she'd be able to testify against Abigail.

———

The phone was ringing. Vanna pulled herself out of sleep and snuggled under the covers. She was comfortable and didn't want to move. Eventually, she managed to grab the phone off of the coffee table and answered the call before it went to voice-mail. Except she didn't have voicemail anymore. What was the point?

Vanna raised the phone to her ear. She didn't say anything.

"I know what you're doing," Abigail whispered in her ear. "You think that you're fooling me, pretending that you're inno-cent? Acting like there's nothing going on? I saw you. I know what you're doing."

She still didn't say anything, waiting to see if Abigail would run out of things to say.

"I know where you are," Abigail said. "I know everything. You can't hide from me. You can't get me."

You can't get me. Vanna shook her head. *She* couldn't get *Abigail?* The whole world was tipped on its head. Did Abigail really believe that Vanna was plotting something against her?

———

In the morning, Vanna was laying on the couch, trying to decide whether to bother calling Sweeny about the phone call the night before, when he called her.

"Hey," Vanna greeted. "I was just thinking of calling you. How did you know?"

Sweeny didn't answer right away.

"What were you going to call me about?" he asked finally.

"She called me in the middle of the night. Raving about how I was plotting against her. Pretty twisted, huh?" She said it lightly like it didn't bother her. Like she could be amused by the whole thing.

"Yes, she's pretty disturbed."

Something about his tone warned her what was coming. Vanna's heart beat so hard it was hurting her. She was forced to put her hand over her chest while she tried to pretend that nothing was happening. This was just a normal, everyday conversation with Sweeny.

"Has something happened?"

"There was a call early this morning from Egret Road."

"My mother?" Vanna gasped. Her head started to spin. "Tell me… tell me she didn't kill my mother like that dog!"

"No," Sweeny said. "As far as we know, Erica is still okay."

"As far as you know?" Vanna repeated faintly.

Lydia started to walk by and Vanna waved her over. Lydia took one look at Vanna's face and sank into the nearest chair, the color draining out of her own.

"It was an abduction call. I'm sorry, but Erica is missing."

"Abduction? Kidnapped?"

"Yes."

"And you don't know where she is?" Vanna's voice rose, siren-like. She couldn't stop it. "She was kidnapped and you don't know where she is?"

Mandy started to cry.

"We're working on it. We're doing everything we can. The Chief of Police is doing a press conference in ten minutes. I didn't want that to be the way you found out."

"When did it happen? Why didn't you call me sooner?"

"Things have been happening pretty quickly around here. It

was more important to identify the perpetrator and get alerts out than it was to call you. Since I already had a pretty good idea who it was, I just came here to verify the details and get the things rolling as quickly as possible. It was early this morning, three-thirty or four as near as we can tell. We were called at five-thirty."

"Why didn't you get called until five-thirty?"

"The assistant, Mrs. Chatsam. She was the one who called it in. And she didn't call it in at three-thirty because she was knocked out cold for the intervening period."

"Oh. Poor Misty. Is she okay?"

"On a cursory check, yes. We've sent her to the hospital to be examined. She didn't want to go."

"No, she wouldn't. She's been with mother for more than twenty years. As long as I can remember."

"Vanna?" Lydia spoke up. "What's going on?"

Her sheet-white face and wide eyes told Vanna that she'd already understood most of the conversation, but didn't want to believe it.

"Abigail has kidnapped Mom. They're looking for her." She switched back to talking to Sweeny. "Was my mother hurt? Did Misty think that she was okay?"

"There's no indication that she has been seriously injured. There was a small amount of blood in the bedroom." Vanna gasped and covered her mouth, her brain instantly jumping to a hundred different scenarios, all of which involved Erica being mortally wounded. "Not high-velocity spatter. Not like she was shot. Not a large amount. Just a few drops, like she had a nosebleed."

That was a little more reassuring. But still… Vanna pictured her mother with a bleeding nose, hand held up to her mouth and nose, the sparkle gone from her eyes…

"You look like you've seen a ghost," Lydia said. "Are they sure she's all right?"

Vanna forced herself to nod. "Just a nosebleed or

something."

"And Misty?"

"Knocked out. But okay. She went to the hospital."

"We'll have to send flowers," Lydia said automatically, sounding remarkably like the ever-efficient Erica. Always making the appropriate social gestures. Lydia lowered her head and covered her face with one hand, the one that wasn't holding Mandy. She sobbed. Vanna juggled the phone to her other hand and went over to hug Lydia. To try to comfort her.

Vanna had done this. It was her actions that had led to Erica being threatened, being kidnapped. If she hadn't been adopted into the family, they would have been safe. But because they had taken Vanna in and nurtured her, they were now at the center of Abigail's crosshairs.

"Are you going to come over here?" she asked Sweeny. "Or do you want me to come there? I want to help, but I have no idea what to do."

"If you could come up here, that would be the best. You can have a look around, tell me if there is anything that seems odd or unusual. Something missing… something out of place…"

"Misty would be better at that than I would. She's there every day. Puts things away, tidies up. I'm only there for occasional visits and trust me, I don't mess with any of Erica's stuff."

"Still… Mrs. Chatsam might have missed something, in her state."

"Okay. I'll come up right away."

"I'll send a car for you."

"Why? I can drive up faster."

"Because I want to ensure your safety. First from Abigail, and also from causing an accident because you are upset. It's not the time for you to be driving. I'll send someone."

Vanna wanted to leave immediately. She didn't want to have to wait for someone to come pick her up. So she grumbled, but she didn't argue any further. Vanna didn't think that she would have an accident, she was still collected. Focused. But Sweeny was in charge, and if Vanna ran into Abigail now, it might complicate the search for and rescue of Erica. Vanna didn't want to put that in jeopardy for anything. It was bad enough that she had caused this in the first place.

She hung up and filled Lydia in the best that she could, suddenly realizing how many gaps there were in the story. She hadn't asked about anything. She didn't really know anything about what had happened. Lydia nodded and swallowed.

"Well," she said, her voice forced calm, "first things first. We need to eat and get the children fed. John Paul will have to stay home or arrange for a sitter for the boys. If we're quick, we'll be ready when the police car gets here to pick us up."

"You're going too?"

Lydia's brows went up. "Of course I'm going too. She's my mother! If anyone should go, it should be me. I'm the elder, it's my responsibility. And you should be staying as far out of the spotlight as possible so that nothing worse happens."

"I'm still going!" Vanna objected.

"Of course you are. I wouldn't stop you. I'm just pointing out, it's my job. Not yours."

"Because I'm not really her daughter?" The words came spitting out of Vanna before she could stop them. All of the bitterness that years of being the baby, the ugly daughter, the second thought. All of those thoughts that she had pushed away, locked up in the back of her heart. She knew that Erica had never intended to favor Lydia over Vanna. She knew that Lydia considered Vanna a 'real' sister. She had never held Vanna's parentage over her head. She'd never claimed priority. But Vanna was so scared, so off-balance, that it came out without any thought.

Lydia opened her mouth, shocked. At first she couldn't seem to find her voice. Then, jiggling Mandy on her hip, she turned to face Vanna square on. "Don't you ever say that again! I told you, it's my job because I'm the older child. Not because of my birth."

Vanna nodded, looking at the floor. "I'm sorry. I didn't mean that. It just came out."

Lydia's voice was light and casual, a break from the worried, serious tone she had been using. "You always were a blurter," she said. Something Erica had pointed out many times and tried to break Vanna of. How many times had she been lectured on thinking before she spoke? "Now, let's get a quick breakfast on, before that policeman gets here."

As it turned out, they were only halfway through their hurried breakfast when the doorbell rang. Vanna hurried to open it, but John Paul stopped her. "Check first," he reminded her. "Only open it if it's a uniformed officer."

"Oh. Right."

Vanna checked the security monitor for the front door. The picture was broken up into several different squares. Various angles on the guest and on the car parked below the driveway. Definitely a cop and not Abigail. Vanna opened the door.

"We'll be right with you. Let me just grab my toast."

Not because she felt like eating. Every bit went down in a choking lump, no matter how much coffee she tried to wash it down with and then it sat in her stomach, unmoving, as heavy as a piece of iron. But she knew that she needed the nourishment or she would crash all too soon.

Erica needed her.

———

Once in the car, Vanna had to think about what was going on. Since receiving Sweeny's call, she had been avoiding it, focusing on helping Lydia with breakfast and the kids. But once she got into the car, there was nothing else to think of.

"She'll be okay," Lydia assured her. "Mom may look vulnerable, but she's a tough bird. Abigail may have bitten off more than she could chew."

Vanna shook her head. "If Mom makes it too hard for her… you know what happened to Julia. She fought back."

"Don't say that."

Vanna didn't say anything. They rode the familiar route to the Estate, each looking out their own windows instead of at each other. The officer driving them made no effort at conversation. The ride seemed to take both longer and shorter than usual. When they got there, they both got out of the car and went into the house without a word to each other. Sweeny was talking to other officers, but he broke off when he saw them.

"Ladies. I'm sorry to have to ask you to come here. Are you okay?"

Vanna and Lydia both nodded. Lydia looked around, all business. "So what happened? What do you want us to look at?"

Sweeny nodded his appreciation at the direct approach. "Come with me. I'll show you around."

Vanna had a weird sense of unreality as he escorted her through the house. He didn't belong. It was her mother's house, her childhood home. The policeman didn't belong there. As they walked through the home, everything seemed perfectly normal. Until they reached Erica's suite. Misty's room came first. There wasn't much to see. Her bed was rumpled and unmade, but there was no apparent violence. No blood. Nothing else out of place. She had never seen Mrs. Chatsam's unmade bed before, but that was the only thing. Misty had always been sort of a robot or a vampire to Vanna. Always up early before anyone else, not retiring until after Erica and Vanna's father had gone to bed. As far as Vanna could tell, Misty never actually slept. So it was sort of a shock to see her bed like that. Lydia looked at Vanna and she could tell that Lydia was thinking the same thing. But it wasn't appropriate to smile or laugh at it, in spite of the weirdness of the shattering of their shared childhood perceptions.

Erica's sitting room was in disorder. Things had been knocked down. Furniture pushed aside, books thrown on the floor, broken glass and porcelain from some of her mother's treasures. When they got to the bedroom, Vanna had to lean on the doorframe for support, her stomach lurching and threatening to return the toast she had eaten on the way over.

She had been prepared for another rumpled bed, a turned-over chair, and a few drops of blood. But the entire room was in chaos. It looked like there had been an earthquake, everything pushed out of place or on the floor. Even the bed itself was off-kilter, pushed askew several feet from where it usually was. And it wasn't just a few drops of blood. There wasn't really enough to qualify as a pool, particular having soaked into the carpet, but it was more than just droplets. Sweeny grabbed Vanna's elbow as her knees buckled and he and another officer got her into one of the Queen Anne chairs before she could faint completely away.

"It's not as much blood as it looks like," Sweeny told her. "I've been at a lot of crime scenes. It always looks like more than it really is. That's not from a mortal wound. Likely just a nosebleed or superficial cut. Scalp wounds, in particular, bleed like the dickens. If Abigail tried to hit her over the head like she did Mrs. Chatsam, she could have hit a glancing blow and caused a wound that looked nasty but was really just a surface cut."

Vanna breathed, holding her hands over her face and closing her eyes.

"This is a mess," Lydia said. "I don't know how we're supposed to tell anything from this."

"I don't expect you to," Sweeny agreed. "The forensics guys are giving us as much direction as they can. I'm only wondering whether there is anything weird. Something missing. Something that's been tampered with. Try to look past the blood and the furniture being moved around. Picture how the room looked before. Is there anything wrong with the picture?"

Vanna opened her eyes to look at the room again, trying to

remain clinically detached. She avoided picturing what had happened and just looked for what might be out of place.

"It's so long since I've been in my mother's bedroom," Lydia confessed. "We didn't usually hang out here. We usually met in the arboretum or the hall. Maybe her sitting room. This was the inner sanctum."

"Chances are, not a lot has changed in the last few years. If it is the inner sanctum, it has probably been kept the same for a long time," Sweeny countered.

"Okay."

Lydia walked around, avoiding anywhere there was blood or the numbered yellow evidence tags. Vanna wanted to warn her not to walk through the room, in case she disturbed some kind of evidence. A hair, or the impression of a footprint in the carpet. But the lab boys had already been through. They had already gleaned everything they could from a physical examination of the room.

"There was a picture here," Lydia said, frowning at the side table. She looked at the matching side table on the other side. "I'm a bit disoriented. It's…"

She walked over to the side table's mate and looked down at the contents that had been knocked to the floor.

"Can I touch things?"

Sweeny moved over, snapping a glove on over his right hand. He turned over the face-down framed photo. It was a picture of Lydia, about four or five years old, in a frilly dress and tiny, elegant gloves. Vanna remembered its mate.

"There was one of Vanna on the other side," Lydia said. "She was two or three."

Sweeny nodded. "Abigail is still stuck twenty years ago," he murmured.

"You said it all happened around three thirty," Vanna said.

Sweeny cocked his head at her, a frown of concentration on his face. "Yeah."

"But she called me." Vanna pulled out her phone and located the call log. "She called me at three thirty-two."

"Maybe from outside the building, or even once she was inside. What did she say? Any clues as to what she was doing or thinking?"

"She said that she knew what I was doing. That I couldn't get her."

Sweeny pulled out his notepad and made a note. "We'll try to get some kind of psychological profiling… figure out where her head is."

Vanna nodded. "Okay." She didn't have any other suggestions for him.

"How did she get in?" Lydia asked. "I thought Mom was going to tighten security. She knew what happened… at my house."

"The system was down when we got here. Erica may have forgotten to turn it on, or Abigail might have hacked it. The security company is going to give us a log for the last twenty-four hours of activity. And do an audit of the system." He chewed on the inside of his cheek. "Tell me she didn't use your birthdate too."

Vanna let her shoulders rise and fall in a shrug. She'd never had the security codes. As a teenager, if she was past curfew, she had to ring the bell to be let in. She looked at Lydia. "I don't know what she used. Do you?"

Lydia shook her head. "I don't have any idea."

"Is there anything else missing or odd?" Sweeny asked.

Lydia and Vanna looked around. Lydia had already made one find, which put Vanna at a disadvantage. It was her turn to find something, to offer Sweeny something that was helpful. The things that had disappeared from her own apartment had seemed random. The computer. Her coffee mug. A tube of toothpaste. And there had been additions, little things left behind to throw her off-balance. Vanna squinted in concentration.

"Did she leave anything behind? Have you swept for bugs?"

Sweeny made a sour face. "We haven't checked," he admitted. He took a covert look around. "I'll have a crew run through. I don't like the idea of her listening in on the investigation."

They continued to look around the room, silent now, aware that there might be other ears listening in.

Chapter Twenty-Nine

They waited until they got outside again before speaking, and even then, waited for Sweeny's signal, aware that there could be listening devices anywhere in the house or yard. Sweeny took a careful look around and motioned them into one of the police cars, where they sat down. Or Sweeny and Lydia sat down. Vanna stayed standing, facing into the police car, her legs feeling too twitchy for sitting down.

"I wish I knew where she was," she growled at Sweeny. "I'd punch her in the face!"

Sweeny looked surprised at her outburst. He gave her a slight smile. "Well, something has come out of this. She's got you angry instead of scared."

"I'm still scared. But angry doesn't even begin to cover it. She kills my birth mother and now she's taken away my adoptive mother? What kind of a game is she playing at? I just want to…" she fought for some vestige of self-control. "I just want to hit her!"

Lydia was smiling. Not a small, cautious smile like Sweeny, but a real smile of enjoyment. "Mom always says it takes a lot to get Vanna's dander up, but when she does… look out!"

Vanna remembered schoolyard fights and other times when she'd gotten in trouble for letting her anger get the best of her. She wasn't sure she agreed with the assessment that it took a lot to get it up. She always felt that her temper got away from her way too fast.

"Right now, there's nowhere to focus that anger," Sweeny said, a little apologetic. "You'll have to convert it into some other kind of energy if you're going to avoid exploding. There are some things that you can do. A media appeal. Maybe go through your mother's personal files to see if she has any information on Abigail that she might have withheld or forgotten until now. It's not a lot, I know…"

"I have to do something," Vanna said. "This is all my fault."

"It's not your fault," Lydia objected. "It's Abigail's. You didn't do anything to make this happen to Mom. You would have done anything to avoid it."

Vanna shook her head. She looked at Sweeny. "You haven't found anything out from old friends or family? Places that she used to hang out?"

"Sorry. No." He shrugged widely and sighed. "Twenty years later, everything has changed. And she never did have the support of her family. There's a brother who is still around, but he hasn't seen her since she went to prison and makes no bones about the fact that she was a black sheep. He doesn't want anything to do with her. There have been a lot of changes in twenty years."

"What about Abigail's lawyer?"

"What about him?"

"Has he had any contact? Does he know where she might go?"

"There's no reason to think that he does. But if he does, it's under lawyer-client privilege."

Vanna shook her head. She looked around. "I want to go home. Are we done here?"

"Yes. I'll have an officer drive you back. Oh, I'll be pulling the phone records on your cell. That's where she called, right?"

Vanna nodded. "Yeah. Of course. But it will just be another burner."

"I would be negligent if I didn't follow up every time. One day she may get careless and hang onto it for too long. You can't predict."

———

Lydia tried to get a casual conversation going several times in the car, but Vanna couldn't concentrate on what she was saying. Her own thoughts were too scattered. Or too focused on other things. Whichever way you looked at it, she wasn't in any shape to be having a light, carefree conversation. In spite of what anyone else said, she knew that the abduction was her fault. She had set this off and she was the only one who could stop it.

Eventually Lydia gave up on trying to engage her and just gave her a hug around the shoulders, giving a brief squeeze and then letting go. "We're going to find her, Van. I promise."

"I'm not going to let this woman take another mother away from me."

Lydia nodded, not sure what to say to that. They continued the rest of the way home in silence. On reaching Lydia's house, Vanna waited for a few minutes until the police car was out of sight and then she headed for her own vehicle. Lydia looked surprised.

"Where are you going?"

"I'm going to find her."

"But… where are you going to look?"

"Wherever I can think of."

"Vanna!" Lydia tried to catch up with her before she got into the car. "You can't, it's too dangerous. The police are looking. They'll find her. You need to stay here where you're safe."

"I'm not safe here. I'm not safe anywhere. Haven't you

figured that out? I'm not safe until she's behind bars. Permanently."

"Vanna, you can't! Stop and think about it!"

Vanna pulled her door shut. Lydia stood there watching as Vanna jammed her key into the ignition and roared away.

She regretted having to worry or upset Lydia, but that wasn't her main concern. She had to find Erica. She had to confront Abigail and save Erica before it was too late.

At first she just drove. She drove around, trying to spot a car tailing her. She knew that Abigail was good at this, but reasoned that sooner or later she would have to risk becoming visible to keep Vanna in sight. But several long hours of driving around didn't entice her out and Vanna's mind was working on other approaches. She went back to her old apartment building. She sat in front of it. Drove around to the parking garage and waited there, searching the shadows for any sign of her nemesis. She went to her bank, her grocery store, everywhere she could think of that Abigail would know that she frequented. She kept watching, waiting for Abigail to appear, but she didn't.

After several long hours, Vanna's phone started ringing and wouldn't stop. It was Lydia. Vanna switched her phone off. That would mean that Abigail couldn't reach her by phone either. Maybe Abigail would get mad. Maybe she would start looking for Vanna. Show her face.

Eventually, Vanna found herself at the building where it had happened. She had seen pictures of the building in the news clippings that Erica had researched. It hadn't really changed. A new marquee, a different name on the bodega on the main floor. Other than that, the brick building looked the same as it had then. It hadn't been new when Julia had lived there. Vanna didn't know what the neighborhood had been like then. Probably pretty much the same as it was now. Not quite skid row, but not an area that Vanna would have chosen to live in. She looked up at the apartments above her. There was no sign of the accident that had once occurred here. No broken railing. No police tape. No boarded-up window. Why would there be? It had all happened twenty years ago.

Vanna went in and managed to track down the building manager. A graying man with a two-inch swathe of bare belly showing under his stained, inadequate t-shirt. She avoided shaking his hands and showed him a picture of Abigail on her phone.

"I'm looking for a friend. Does she live in this building? I know it was this street, but I can't remember what building."

He looked her over for a long moment, considering, before he finally turned his eyes to the girl on the phone.

"No, don't recognize her."

"Are you sure? I thought it was this building. She just moved in a few months ago, she hasn't been here long."

"I haven't seen her around here."

"Okay, thanks." He started to walk away. "How long have you been here? You weren't here twenty years ago, were you?"

He favored her with a suspicious glare. "No."

"Oh, okay. I just remember… there was a murder here, in this building, a long time ago. I wondered if you remembered it."

"You aren't old enough to remember that long ago."

"No. My aunt told me about it. She used to live down here. Not in this building," Vanna said lamely, "just in the area." Every scenario she came up with made her sound more like a flake. "Sorry. I just wondered whether any of your tenants lived here that far back, when it happened."

"I have no idea."

"Okay. I just wondered."

"You can do the rest of your wondering outside," he gestured to the main entrance.

Vanna nodded and left quickly. He watched her the whole way out. Vanna moved out of view of the doors and after a moment of consideration stepped into the little bodega. She knew the name had changed, ownership was bound to have. But she was there. She might as well ask.

The small, dark man that was standing behind the counter looked like he was probably the owner of the shop. Not a teenage employee. His face was wrinkled and weathered. She wasn't sure from his features whether he was Hispanic, Middle Eastern, or something else.

"Hi, there. I'm wondering if you can help me," she turned up her smile as much as possible, but he didn't respond with one of his own. "I'm looking for anyone who might have lived or worked in the area twenty years ago."

He shook his head. "Before my time."

She struggled to place his accent. Not Indian. Not Latin. What could he be? Egyptian?

"Ah. Just my luck. How long have you been here?"

"Fourteen."

"Fourteen. Anyone around here before you?"

"No," he snapped. He pushed a couple of random buttons on his register as if he was in the middle of a transaction that she had rudely interrupted. "I don't know anyone here longer."

"Okay." She gave him another friendly smile, not pushing him further. "Thanks for your help."

He didn't move and neither did Vanna.

"I used to live here."

He looked her over, brows raised.

"Right in this building," Vanna said. "I was born here."

"Good for you." His eyes were on her, steady, challenging. "You don't belong here anymore."

It wasn't just a statement of fact, an observation that she had moved somewhere else. It was a judgment. She didn't belong anymore. They were of different social strata. He knew, just looking at her, that she wasn't from the neighborhood. She had moved up the social ladder and she wasn't accepted there.

"No," Vanna agreed softly. "I guess not." She paused before turning around to leave. "Thank you."

He offered nothing else and Vanna walked out into the cool, misty air. She hadn't really noticed earlier what a dark, drizzly day it was. Now that she did, she pulled her hood up and looked around for any other likely targets. Surely someone in the neighborhood had lived there for twenty years.

———

When it started to get dark, she was forced to admit that she had made no progress. Discovered nothing helpful. The few residents that she had managed to find who had lived in the area for long enough to remember the murder hadn't had any connection with Abigail. They shook their heads remembering those dark days. Vanna had come up with nothing useful.

But she wasn't going home. She wasn't going to go back to Lydia's to admit defeat. She had to find something. She had to be doing something. Because she couldn't just go home and sleep, or toss and turn, for one more night. She couldn't go to bed not knowing where Erica was.

She went to the mall next. Vanna had no idea what part of the mall the kids play place had been twenty years ago. It was long since gone. But she walked around anyway. She tried to picture how it had looked to Abigail back then. A teenager who had just made the biggest mistake of her life. She had killed a person. A close friend, if Vanna was to believe the news reports.

Abigail had tried to take care of the baby. Maybe to make up for what she had done. Maybe just because she had panicked and taken Vanna before she could cry. But a few days trying to take care of the little girl on her own, it had been too much. Vanna had cried too much or had refused to eat or sleep. Had looked at her in a way that made Abigail feel guilty.

And the police were looking for her. A pretty blond with a dark little girl. Too visible. She couldn't go anywhere without people noticing them and wondering if someone was going to turn her in.

So she had come here to escape. Maybe she went window shopping, pushing a cart or stroller from one shop to the next, gazing wistfully over all of the pretty things that she could never afford. Maybe she had watched clusters of other teenagers walking around together, chattering like magpies, apparently without a care in the world. And always, she would be afraid of a security guard's eyes lingering on her for a minute too long. Of an old lady who had watched the news the night before studying her face, comparing it mentally to the picture on the TV.

She wondered if Abigail had originally taken Amelia to the play place as a reward for good behavior. Or to play at being a good mom or fun auntie. Had Abigail pictured herself as the ideal caregiver? Or had she gone there knowing that she couldn't manage it anymore? That she would abandon the baby there in the hopes that the police would stop looking so hard, stop making all of those news flashes on the television. In the hopes that Abigail would be harder to spot without the baby. She could dye her hair. Change her clothes. Hide out somewhere. She couldn't stay hidden with a baby constantly in need of supplies and attention.

There was a little-kid corn maze set up in the middle of the mall and Vanna stood there, gazing at the mothers, imagining their stories. How many of them were struggling, wishing that they could just walk away and leave their children. What would happen if they did? They wouldn't all go to homes as good as Vanna had. She had been lucky. Others went on to languish for years in foster care, never being adopted. Never having a permanent family. Maybe hopping from one abusive or negligent home to another.

"You didn't cry," a voice said in her ear.

It was very soft, but still made her jump, Abigail had crept up on her so silently, like a shadow. Vanna turned her head very slightly to look at Abigail and swallowed.

"When you left me here?" she said.

"At all. The whole time I had you, you never cried once."

For a moment, Vanna fumbled with her phone in her pocket. But she couldn't dial without looking at the screen. And she needed to talk to Abigail. She had to find out what Abigail had done with Erica.

"Then why did you leave me behind?" Vanna asked. As if she would have liked to have stayed with Abigail. She just wanted to keep Abigail talking. It didn't matter what she said. She needed to bridge the gap. She needed to forge a relationship with Abigail, no matter how tenuous. That was the only way that Abigail was going to back off, to give her what she wanted. Vanna had to get Erica back.

"Too many cops looking for you," Abigail said. "And I couldn't stand your eyes, watching me all the time. All sad and wise, like you understood what had happened."

"I don't remember," Vanna said apologetically.

"I thought you would. But you were only two. Most people don't remember much about when they were two."

Vanna reflected on this. "Do you?"

Abigail didn't answer right away. They both stood there, watching the happy children shrieking and playing in the maze, watched over by their parents.

"I can remember some things," Abigail said. "I didn't grow up in a nice place like you."

"I'm sorry."

"You should be happy that I let you grow up in that home. You didn't have to go through all of the crap that I did. I hated them all. Hated my family."

"I love my family," Vanna murmured. "Very much."

"The way that they dote on you and smother you all the time. I couldn't stand that. I'd want to punch someone in the nose."

"There's only one person I want to punch in the nose right now."

Abigail laughed loudly. "I wonder who that would be! Well,

why don't you take your best shot, baby? I'll just stand here and you can hit me however hard you want to."

Vanna looked Abigail full in the face. Something that she had been avoiding doing. "No. I want my mother back."

"Your mother is dead."

Vanna swallowed the lump of fear that swelled up in her throat at the assertion. "Not Julia. My real mother."

"I'll be your mother. I don't understand what I did wrong in the beginning. Before you knew that I wasn't Julia. Why wouldn't you let me be your mother?"

"Because I already have a mother. And I want her back."

"You're not getting her back. I want to be your mother."

Goosebumps rose on Vanna's arms. She shook her head, blinking her burning eyes. "I need her back, Abigail. Please. Just let her go and I'll call off the cops. I'll do whatever you want. Just give Erica back."

"You'll do whatever I want?" Abigail repeated.

Vanna's breath was coming in gasps. "What do you want?"

"You said you'll do whatever I want. Will you really?"

"I… I don't know."

"Why don't you come with me? To my house. And you can be my daughter like I wanted in the first place."

Vanna's stomach was queasy, writhing around like she had food poisoning. "You'll let her go if I come with you?"

"Of course."

Vanna made her decision, quickly, like ripping off a band-aid before she could think about how much it would really hurt. "I'll come."

Abigail didn't respond. She just stood there, watching the children in the maze. A little boy started wailing and had to be rescued by his mother. Vanna looked at his miserable face, at the tears streaming down it and at the mother who cuddled him close, laughing at his panic. Didn't she know how he felt?

"Come with me, then," Abigail invited. She turned away and Vanna followed her.

Vanna knew it was stupid. She knew how Sweeny would react. He would not be impressed. But she had to do something. Finally, she was doing something about it. There was no guarantee that it would actually help Erica, but there was a chance and Vanna had to take it. She had to do everything she could for the mother that had saved her from a life of poverty and loneliness. From the specter of abuse and neglect that Abigail and so many others like her had suffered.

Was it Abigail's own fault that she was the person she was? Vanna didn't have the answer. Vanna had grown up privileged and could be kind and understanding. Abigail had not had that part of her nurtured. Maybe she had never had an example of kindness, couldn't understand what it meant or how it worked. Sweeny said that she didn't understand the reciprocal nature of society. She only knew how to take, not to give.

All kinds of random, inconsequential thoughts raced through her mind as she walked with Abigail as if they were friends. There was no gun or knife at her back. Nothing to signal to any policeman or security guard that she was in trouble. And if they were stopped, she would deny it. She would say that she wasn't being forced or coerced. She was going with Abigail of her own free will. She had to.

When they reached the parking lot, Abigail turned and smirked at her. "You want to go see your mommy?" she asked.

Vanna swallowed and nodded. "Yes."

Abigail set out again. Vanna stuck to her. Abigail walked through the parking lot and started trying the handles of each car that she passed. She found one with a backdoor that had been left unlocked and unlocked the front. She climbed into the driver's seat, motioning Vanna to the other side and leaning over to unlock it for her. Vanna frowned at the sight of Abigail sitting in the driver's seat with no key. How did she think she was going to drive?

Abigail took her time doing up her seatbelt. She smiled at Vanna coyly, like they were the best of friends. Vanna did up her seat belt. Abigail reached down behind her leg and pulled out a screwdriver. Vanna couldn't tell whether it had been secreted in her boot or a sheath, but she pulled it out like a magician making the grand reveal. With a proud smile, she shoved the screwdriver into the ignition slot and with a bit of wiggling and twisting, the engine roared to life.

"Where did you learn how to do that?" Vanna asked.

"Maybe I learned it in prison. You can learn a lot of stuff in prison. It's like university."

Vanna noted that she didn't say that she had learned it in prison. It was a demure answer. A non-answer. Abigail backed the car out and drove out onto the street. Vanna watched the streets go by. She was surprised that Abigail hadn't blindfolded her, or at least told her to close her eyes. She didn't drive in circles or switch directions to try to confuse Vanna.

They were almost at the destination before Vanna understood where they were going. They turned in and drove under the wrought-iron archway with the words "Garden of Peace".

Vanna's stomach clenched. *What had Abigail done?*

Abigail drove calmly, following the posted speed limit, which was a crawl. It was dark, though there were some street lamps. Vanna could have jumped out of the car and run away. But that wouldn't help her to find Erica. Wherever Erica was and whatever condition she was in.

Abigail seemed to know where she was going. All of the rows and pathways looked the same to Vanna. Row after row of gravestones in all shapes and sizes. After taking a number of turns, Abigail pulled over. She got out of the car and Vanna followed her.

Abigail's heels sank into the soft turf. Vanna was wearing sneakers and didn't have much trouble making it across the grass. There was only a small marker where Abigail stopped. Not even a simple tombstone. Vanna looked around before zeroing in on the marker. She didn't want to be surprised and she wanted to know where Erica was. Was she here, somewhere? Tied up in one of the tiny mausoleums? In a closet or groundskeeper's shed?

She looked down at the marker, but it was overgrown and encrusted with dirt. In the dim lighting, she had to crouch right down and scratch the debris away to make out the words.

Julia Cortez.

No date, no epitaph. Just the name. This was where her remains had been interred. Composing her face, Vanna looked up at Abigail, who was looking down at her with a strangely hungry look.

"Thank you," Vanna said flatly. "I didn't know where she was."

Abigail nodded, smiling.

"Now where is my real mother? Where is Erica?"

"That's your real mother there," Abigail said, pointing at the marker. "Dead and worm-eaten."

"I want to see Erica. Where did you take her?"

"She's at my house."

"Will you take me there? I'll stay with you. You can let her go and I'll stay with you."

"You want to come to my house?"

"Yes. Will you take me there?"

Abigail just stood there, looking at Vanna. She was loving this. Her expression was smug as she looked at Vanna. As she made Vanna say what she wanted to hear. Vanna would say whatever Abigail wanted her to say if it meant that she could get to Erica. Abigail had put one mother in the ground already. Vanna couldn't let her do it again.

Abigail started to hobble through the grass back to the car again. Vanna walked beside her, not getting ahead or behind. Abigail had left the engine running, so there was no more playing with the screwdriver. Abigail pulled a black scarf out of her raincoat pocket and tossed it in Vanna's lap.

"Put that on. Over your eyes. No peeking."

Vanna obeyed.

"Can you see?"

"No."

"How many fingers am I holding up?" Did Abigail really think that Vanna would answer that, even if she could see through the makeshift blindfold?

"I don't know."

Something hit Vanna in the nose, making her yelp and jerk back, banging her head on the interior of the car. The blow made her nose start running or bleeding.

"Good." Abigail pronounced. "Give me your hands."

Vanna held them out to her, side by side, her hands in relaxed fists. Abigail bound them with some kind of zip-tie plastic handcuffs. Vanna let them fall into her lap.

"Okay now?" she asked.

"Sure."

Abigail pulled the car back out into the winding cemetery lanes. Vanna put her head back on her headrest, trying to stay relaxed and calm. Strangely, her heart was slowing down now, instead of speeding up as she drew to the end of her journey. She didn't know whether she would survive or not. But if she could, she had to help Erica.

Without turning her head, she watched out the bottom of the blindfold, out her side window. She couldn't see much other than pavement, which wasn't really helpful. But she wasn't really trying to cheat. She didn't want to do anything to upset Abigail.

There were lots of turns. Lots of times when Vanna was pretty sure they were going in circles or doubling back on their route. Of course Abigail would try to disorient her. She wouldn't want her to know where Abigail's 'home' was. It was an hour of dizzying circles before Abigail stopped the car again, in a crunchy gravel alley.

"Stay there," Abigail ordered. She got out of the car and Vanna listened to her footsteps come around the car, and her own door opened. Abigail pulled her out and Vanna followed the tugs and pushes to get her into the building. It had an echo and a musty smell. There were metal stairs going down below ground level. It was cold and damp and smelled strongly of mold. When they stopped, Vanna strained her ears for clues.

Abigail pulled the scarf away from Vanna's eyes. Vanna blinked and looked around the dark basement. It was obviously some kind of industrial building or warehouse. Not a house or apartment building. As Vanna's eyes got used to the dark, she made out a familiar pile of clothing a few feet away from her on the cold concrete floor. She stepped forward and knelt before Erica's prone body. Vanna's hands were tied in front of her, so she was able to grasp Erica's arms and turn her over.

"Mom! Mom, are you okay?"

Erica's face was bruised, one eye swollen. Relief flooded through Vanna as Erica opened her eyes. Vanna swallowed and sniffled and tears flowed down her cheeks. "Mom," she whispered.

Erica's eyes widened in horror. "Ivanna?" Her eyes slid past Vanna to Abigail. "No. No!"

"It's okay. It is going to be okay, Mom. I promise. You're going to be okay."

"How sweet," Abigail sneered.

Vanna turned and looked at her. "You said you would let her go. I came with you like you asked. So you'll let her go."

"I didn't say I would let her go," Abigail said. She smirked.

"Please. I'm here. You can do what you want. I will stay. But you have to let Erica go."

"I don't have to do anything. Say goodbye, because this is the last time you're going to see her."

Vanna leaned over Erica, pressing close against her. "Mom. It will be okay."

"I love you," Erica whispered. Her hands were also bound. She couldn't hug Vanna, but twisted her fingers together with Vanna's for a brief moment. "Please be safe."

Vanna stood back up, looking at Abigail. "Where are we going? Where are you taking me?"

"That doesn't matter right now."

Vanna shivered. But she stood firm. "You wanted me to be with you. So…"

Abigail looked at her for a long time. "Come on, then."

"Will you at least free her hands?"

Like Vanna, Erica's hands were tied with a zip-tie handcuffs. Abigail laughed. "Come with me."

"Okay," Vanna agreed.

Abigail looked suspicious, but Vanna followed, so she continued back up the stairs. No mask this time. Vanna tried to learn everything she could from her surroundings. If Plan A didn't work, she needed some way of finding her way back.

If Erica and Sweeny didn't do their parts, Vanna would have to come up with something else.

———

When they got into the car, they sat for several minutes in silence. Abigail seemed to be thinking things through. That was fine with Vanna. They could sit there all night if Abigail liked. She stared out into the darkness, thinking about Erica. The tightness in her chest was finally unclenching. Erica was alive. She was going to be okay.

"This isn't your house," she observed to Abigail.

Abigail turned her head a little to look at Vanna. "What?"

"You said you were taking me to your house. But this isn't where you've been staying is it?" She had seen no sign that Abigail was camping out in the old building.

"You think you know everything? I could live here. Just because you have never slept rough…"

Vanna would be surprised if Abigail weren't somewhere with a proper shower or bath and a full-length mirror. She certainly didn't look like she was sleeping on a concrete floor and washing in a sink. "Oh. Okay. I thought maybe you changed your mind or were trying to decide now whether to go home or not."

"You don't know anything."

"Obviously," Vanna agreed.

"Don't get sarcastic with me."

Vanna closed her mouth. When Abigail was in a mood, it didn't really matter what Vanna said, Abigail was just going to keep winding herself up more and more. And Vanna didn't want to be sitting right there next to her if Abigail blew up.

Vanna had seen how strong Abigail was, ripping things apart in Erica's room. She remembered the investigators in the murder case thinking that they were looking for man, not a teenage girl, because of the raw power required to throw around the furniture the way that she had and to force Julia over the balcony railing.

She remembered the single punch at the coffee shop. Vanna didn't want to be on the receiving end of that fist again.

"Good. You know when to keep your mouth shut," Abigail sneered.

She produced the blindfold again and threw it into Vanna's lap. Vanna picked it up with her bound hands. "I… don't think I can do this with the handcuffs on," she pointed out.

Abigail looked at her, considering. Then she yanked the scarf back away and wound it around Vanna's head herself. She tied a knot in the back. Tight. It pressed against a tender point on Vanna's skull, especially when she leaned back again. But Vanna didn't complain.

In another minute, they were on their way again. Vanna suspected that they wouldn't go far. Abigail's bed and her lair would not be far away from each other. She would want to keep a close eye on Erica and know if she was discovered.

The view when Abigail pulled the blindfold off of Vanna's face shocked her. She tried not to show it. Abigail stared into her eyes.

"You had no idea how close you were when you were nosing around here, did you?"

Vanna looked up at the apartment building. Julia's building. Vanna couldn't see the top of it now, up above the streetlights with only a few windows lit by weak lights. Abigail turned off the car and went around to Vanna's side to pull her out. She didn't cut the plastic ties, but walked boldly into the building with Vanna. Nobody looked at them except for the building manager that Vanna had talked to earlier in the day. He saw her face and looked a little surprised, but he didn't look down at her hands. Vanna had told him that Abigail was her friend, so why would he suspect anything? He ducked into a utility room as if he wanted to avoid her. Maybe he was afraid she wanted to question him further or ream him out for not telling her that Abigail was, in fact, a tenant. Either way, there was only a second of recognition and then he was gone.

There was no one else in the elevator. They rode up together to the ninth floor. Too high to survive a fall. Vanna would have to stay away from any windows or balconies. Abigail unlocked the door to one of the apartments. With a key, not a lock picker. She pushed Vanna in ahead of her and then turned on the light.

Vanna breathed out a sigh of relief. It was decorated. Lived in. Not just somewhere that Abigail was squatting or had dumped her things temporarily. That meant, Vanna hoped, that she wouldn't want to shove Vanna off of the balcony and then have to abandon her things. She would be attached to the place and the precious items in it after twenty years with nothing but a prison cell.

Vanna continued down the hall into the living room. She selected a seat on the couch. Abigail looked at her. Her expression had changed since they had been at the warehouse. She wasn't sneering and angry anymore. There was something else in her expression that Vanna couldn't identify. Vanna didn't say anything, trying to get a feel for Abigail's new mood.

"You look so much like her," Abigail said.

"Like… Julia?"

Abigail nodded. "You could be sisters."

She looked around and picked up a framed photo. She handed it to Vanna, ignoring her bound hands. Vanna could still take it and she did.

The newspaper articles had not done Julia justice. Black and white pixilated copies. Not the high-quality digital photographs that accompanied online news articles now. Abigail's photograph was starting to fade after twenty years, but it still showed a stunningly beautiful woman. She faced the camera casually, putting in or fixing an earring with both hands, her long hair swept back out of the way, a slight smile in the camera's direction. Her skin had a warm, dark honey tone that made her want to reach out and touch it. Vanna looked at her birth mother's sparkling eyes for a few more long seconds and then reached toward Abigail to hand it back.

"I'll never look that good," she observed. "She's gorgeous."

Abigail nodded, looking pleased. "She was the most beautiful woman I've ever known. Inside and out."

Vanna couldn't think of what to say to encourage her to keep speaking. She just sat there, nodding.

"I had a crush on her," Abigail was staring out the dark window instead of looking at Vanna. "I was only a kid. But I thought we could be a family. Julia, and me, and you. All together."

"But it didn't work out?"

Abigail's voice was far away. "I thought it would. We got along so well together. I liked to help with the baby. It was a safe place."

"Then what happened?"

As soon as the words left her mouth, she wished she could take them back. Abigail's eyes darkened. Her lips pressed together. When she spoke, her voice was low and threatening.

"It was that man." Her voice shook with barely-controlled

fury. "Smiling at him. Flirting with him. She was mine and she was looking at someone else. Slut! When I confronted her, she said she couldn't be with me. She didn't think of me that way. She wanted me to leave!"

Vanna breathed shallowly. "I'm sorry."

And she was. Sorry that she had asked. Sorry that Julia had crossed Abigail. Sorry that it had all turned out the way that it had.

"I could have been your mother," Abigail insisted. "I could have been."

"You… would have made a good mother. You're very loving. And devoted."

Abigail sniffled. She moved closer to the window and looked out. Vanna wondered what she could see from up there. But she wasn't about to get close to the window to find out.

"It's not my fault I had such a rotten life," Abigail said petulantly. "Why does everyone have to turn on me?"

"I don't think she meant it like that."

"She betrayed me. With that—that—stupid ape! What did she see in him?"

"Sometimes we can't really help who we're attracted to," Vanna said, thinking of Tino. She wondered how he was doing. Where he was. Not following her anymore. She had driven for hours and never seen him.

What she wouldn't do for a knight in shining armor now.

Abigail moved away from the window into the kitchen. Vanna couldn't see what she was doing. She measured the distance to the door. She could get out to the hallway before Abigail could stop her. She could scream, yell, make a fuss. But she wanted to give Erica more time. She had to keep Abigail away from the warehouse. And if Vanna escaped now, Abigail would go straight to the warehouse to head her off and Erica might not get away. The trouble was that there was no way for Sweeny to reach Vanna. They didn't know where she was and couldn't communicate with her.

She could hear Abigail start a coffee pot in the kitchen and realized that she could really use a cup. It had been a long time since having toast for breakfast and she'd had nothing else all day. It was a few minutes before Abigail returned. She handed Vanna a mug, which Vanna realized with a start was her own, the one that had disappeared from her apartment. She sat holding it between her bound hands, warming them and waiting for the coffee to cool to a more tolerable drinking temperature. Abigail put a plate of store-bought chocolate chip cookies on the coffee table. She stood looking out the window, sipping at her own steaming hot coffee.

"Thank you," Vanna said politely.

"You think I don't know about your plotting?" Abigail demanded. "Do you really think I'm that dumb?"

"I don't think you're dumb. Half the police force has been looking for you and they still don't have a clue where you are."

"Police," Abigail snorted. "You can't judge whether or not I'm smart by their bumbling around in the dark. It's like judging a prize bloodhound's sense of smell by comparing it to a human's."

Vanna laughed obligingly. "You're right. It's been very frustrating."

"You, though," Abigail tossed her flawless hair. "You knew exactly where to look, didn't you?"

"I didn't need to know where to look." Vanna shrugged. "It didn't matter where I went, I knew you would find me."

"That's right." Abigail took another swallow of the coffee. "I would. You can't get away from me. You can keep running, but I'm always going to be there. Always."

Vanna took a tentative sip of her own coffee. It was still too hot, but her body needed something and she took a few swallows even though it burned her mouth and throat. It wasn't the first time she'd burned herself, too impatient to wait for her coffee to cool. She hoped that the coffee would kick her brain into focus. So far it was whirling, trying to keep track of everything at once. Trying to sort out how long she should wait before making an attempt at escape. She could hear a television droning in the next apartment. That meant that the walls were thin enough to hear each other. If she made a fuss, people would know it. And there were bulletins out on Erica. People knew that a woman had been kidnapped. They would be on the alert. They wouldn't just ignore suspicious noises and behavior.

Abigail seemed to have slipped into a contemplative mood. She stood at the window drinking her coffee, no longer attempting conversation. Vanna continued to sip at her own coffee, but it wasn't helping her to get any sharper. She shifted and put it down on a coaster Abigail had left on the coffee table. Abigail turned to watch her. Vanna took a cookie and smiled.

"Can I use your bathroom?" she asked.

Abigail gestured at the door in the hallway they had come in by. Vanna considered making a dash for it, but she wasn't ready for that yet. She needed to splash some water on her face. The problem was that even if she escaped Abigail's apartment, that didn't mean that Abigail was out of her life. She had to find a way to ensure Abigail's capture and arrest, not just to get away.

In the bathroom, she sponged cold water on her face and neck, trying to counteract the heavy fatigue that was settling over her. It had been a very long and stressful day and her body and brain were grinding to a rapid halt.

She held onto the edge of the sink, vertigo sweeping through her. Making her nauseated. She tried to make it to the toilet to sit down or to throw up, but it was too far away and the floor rushed up way too fast.

Chapter Thirty

At first, Vanna thought she was back in her own apartment. She was on a bed rather than a couch or the floor and she wasn't in Mandy's nursery room. The powder blue walls matched those in her apartment. The pink satiny coverlet was her own. But as she became more aware of her surroundings, she found that it wasn't her room. It was a close approximation, but it wasn't her room. Vanna tried to remember what had happened.

Erica.

Vanna had been in Abigail's apartment, in the building where Julia had lived.

As she turned over, trying to sort everything out, her head spun. She felt like it was full of water and every time she moved, it sloshed around, echoed by a nauseated turn of her stomach. Vanna groaned aloud. She tried to suppress it, realizing that Abigail might still be somewhere close by. She needed time to think before she had to deal with Abigail again. Vanna closed her eyes briefly, trying to center and focus.

She opened her eyes again and looked around the room. There was a cell phone on the bedside table. Vanna knew that meant Abigail was long gone. It was a stretch to get the phone, which meant that she had to move, making her head and stomach slosh even worse. She pressed the button to wake up the phone and saw the wallpaper had been changed to a picture of herself sprawled drunkenly across the bed. Ignoring it, she dialed Sweeny's number from memory. He didn't answer it immediately like he usually did and she thought it was going to go through to voicemail. At the last minute, he picked it up.

"Sweeny."

She was so used to him greeting her by name when he saw her caller ID, that it startled her for a moment and she didn't respond.

"Who's there?" he snapped.

Vanna wet her lips and cleared her throat. "Vanna."

"Vanna! Where are you? Are you okay?"

"I'm okay. I'm at… Julia's old building. Where she died."

There was a surprised intake of breath and he started talking to someone else in the background.

"Ninth floor," Vanna told him. "Apartment nine-ten."

He relayed this information before speaking to Vanna. "Is Abigail there? Whose phone is this?"

"I think she's gone. I can't get up… but she left the phone here."

"Where the hell have you been? It's almost twenty-four hours since we got to Erica. She's been frantic."

"You got Mom." Vanna blew her breath out in relief. "I was so afraid that it wouldn't work."

"She turned your phone on as soon as Abigail was out of the building. She couldn't dial it because of the screen lock, but as soon as it started pinging, we were on it."

"Thank you."

"I'm not impressed," he growled. "Taking off on your own, cutting off all communications when we might have needed to reach you. Those were stupid moves. Lydia has been crying her eyes out."

Vanna just breathed. Her mom was safe and that was all

that she heard or cared about. Sweeny eventually took in her silence. "You said you can't get up. What's wrong? Are you injured?"

"I think she drugged me. My head's all wonky."

"Okay. You just stay put where you are. I'll get an ambulance there too."

"I'm not going to hospital again," Vanna protested instantly.

"You'll need to at least be checked out. Just lie still until they get to you. It won't be long before the Tactical team is there."

"There's a live-in building manager on the main floor. They can get the key from him."

Sweeny laughed. "You are your mother's daughter, you know that? Always concerned about doing things the right way."

Vanna was surprised. Erica was always concerned with impressions, about how people saw her or about doing things that would somehow affect her reputation. But Vanna wasn't like that. She didn't care about what people thought of her. But Sweeny was right that she cared about doing things the right way. About not hurting or offending others. It was such a small thing, getting the key instead of busting down the door. She couldn't see why the building's property should be damaged when it only took an extra minute to get the key.

"You still with me, Vanna?" Sweeny asked.

"Yeah. Just thinking. Mom is okay? She's not hurt?"

"Just banged up a little. No broken bones or internal injuries. I don't imagine she'll be making any public appearances for a couple of weeks."

"She just might. She can do miracles with concealer."

"Oh?"

"I had terrible acne as a kid. And... I tended to get into things. She was always trying to cover up one disaster or another."

"Did your father hit you?" he asked baldly.

Vanna drew in her breath. "No! Why would you ask that?"

"Abused families can get pretty good at covering up the signs. You've got the protective older sister. The social-climber mother. I know dad was a pretty powerful man politically when he was alive. That's not an unusual dynamic for domestic abuse. And from what I gather from what *hasn't* been said about your Mr. Peak, I suspect he's got a temper. Women who were abused by their fathers often hook up with abusive men."

"No. No, my father was a very kind, quiet man. Mom was the political force behind his career. And no, she didn't hit us either."

"And Valentine?"

"He *hates* it when people call him that! Umm… okay…" she felt herself blushing at having to admit it to Sweeny. "He did hit me. A few times. When he lost his temper. The rest of the time, he's a very sweet guy…"

"Sure. They always are."

"But in his case, it's really true. He's a nice guy. Loving, attentive. He just… he loses control."

"I believe that. But that doesn't make him less of an abuser."

Vanna sighed. It seemed like it was taking a very long time for the police to get there. But she knew it had only been a few minutes. She hadn't heard a sound from the rest of the apartment, outside the bedroom door. She was sure that Abigail would not have left the phone in her room if she was sticking around to get caught. She had probably left hours ago.

"Do you mind talking?" Sweeny asked. "Or is it bothering you?"

"I'm okay. It's nice to have someone to talk to. It's kind of creepy here, all by myself."

"Why don't you tell me what happened yesterday? How did you find Abigail and how did you manage to persuade her to let you see your mother? She ran a huge risk taking you there. And she obviously wasn't watching you that well, seeing as you managed to slip your phone to your mom."

"She didn't have a gun or anything. Not that I saw. I didn't want to do anything to aggravate her… make her decide to hurt Mom… I had to act like I was on her side. That we were friends… or family…"

"And she didn't see through it?"

"I think she knew what I was doing. She just didn't care, because it was what she wanted to pretend. And… I do feel sorry for her. I wish she'd had a better life."

"Uh-huh. So tell me what happened."

Vanna related the story. From driving around aimlessly hoping to spot her tail, to going to the apartment building and asking questions around the neighborhood and finally ending up at the mall where she'd been abandoned, where Abigail had found her.

"You were *trying* to make contact with her," Sweeny said, disapproval in his voice.

"I had to. She was the only one who knew where Erica was. She's gotten pretty good at staying away from police. You guys weren't going to be able to find her."

"You didn't really give us a chance. You just went out looking for trouble. You could at least have talked to me. We could have tracked you, kept in contact. What you did, going in without a net, was really stupid."

She couldn't help thinking that his tone was just a little admiring. "I know. But she wouldn't have come if there were cops around. She would have known what we were doing."

"She couldn't."

"She has up until now. I wasn't going to take that chance. Not with Mom tied up somewhere, bleeding. I couldn't let her kill another mother. And she would have."

There was loud knocking and a deep bass thundered: "Open up. Police!"

There wasn't a sound in the apartment. Sweeny was silent on the phone, obviously able to hear what was going on and waiting for the results. They must have done as Vanna suggested and gotten the key from the manager, because the crash of the splintering door that Vanna was waiting for never came. Instead, with no warning, there were heavy footsteps down the hall. The bedroom door was shoved open and Vanna turned her head queasily to look.

"Don't move! Stay where you are! Not a muscle!"

Vanna was so startled by the brusque command that she froze, not daring to even breathe. The black-uniformed cop swiftly searched the room, poking his long gun into the closet and even checking under the bed. There was an all clear call from outside the bedroom, and he nodded at her.

"Okay, ma'am. You want to get up slowly? Tell me your name and keep your hands where I can see them."

"Vanna. I'm Vanna Austin."

Vanna tried to lift her head or prop herself up on her elbow, but there was no point. She was way too dizzy to manage it. The cop secured his gun and walked up to her, reaching over to take her pulse at her wrist.

"Not feeling so good?"

"No."

Sweeny's voice sounded in Vanna's ear again. She had almost forgotten that she was still on the phone with him. "The EMTs shouldn't be too far behind the Tactical team. I'll be over shortly. I've got a couple of calls to make first."

———

She was too sick to be much good that evening, but after a fairly good rest on Lydia's couch, Vanna was feeling more herself the next day. Sweeny took her back to Abigail's apartment so that she could walk him through a re-enactment. Not that there was that much to see or do. It hadn't been complicated.

"This is where she was standing talking to you before she went to make the coffee?" Sweeny verified.

Vanna nodded. "Yeah. About there. She was moving around a bit, but she was watching out the window."

"Come stand beside me."

Vanna got up and went over to his side. She looked down through the window. She had an immediate sense of vertigo looking down at the street. Sweeny steadied her.

"Are you okay?"

"Yes. Just… a little dizzy."

"Look." He pointed.

Vanna focused on the building a few blocks away. She looked back at Sweeny. "Is that…?"

"It's the building she had Erica in."

"So she was standing here watching the police arrive the whole time."

He nodded. "She knew that Erica had been found. She drugged your coffee and left you here, knowing that she had to get out quickly without making anyone suspicious."

Vanna looked around. "Did you see the bedroom?"

"How sick is that? It's almost an exact copy of yours."

"More than that. It *was* mine."

Sweeny frowned. "What do you mean?"

"The stuff in there? The blankets on the bed, the pictures on the wall… the side table and the lamp… they *are* mine. From my storage locker."

He blinked, considering that. He didn't ask her how she knew. Of course she knew her own property when she saw it. "I'll look into it. Send some men over there to secure the rest."

"Yeah. The rest of the apartment… she's cleared out all of *her* personal stuff. Pictures. Little touches."

"And her clothes. The things that she's left behind are just incidentals that she bought since she got out of prison. Anything with a deeper connection, she took with her. It would have taken a few hours to clear things out, but with you drugged up, she had plenty of time."

Chapter Thirty-One

Vanna was in the kitchen helping Lydia prepare supper. Her thoughts were far away and they worked together in silence. They'd never had a problem connecting before. There was always something to talk about. But now everything seemed to stall. Vanna had to admit that it was probably her own fault. She didn't want to talk. She didn't want to go over the same ground again, to keep obsessing over her encounter with Abigail. Even though that is what Vanna was doing in her head.

John Paul came into the room and observed the two of them. "I came to see if you needed help with anything."

The boys were, for once, playing quietly in their room, focused on setting up some game that involved both toy cars and stuffed monsters.

Lydia wiped her forehead with her forearm. "I don't think we need anything."

John Paul approached and gave her a hug from behind, forcing her to stop cutting vegetables and lean against him for a brief cuddle. He kissed her on the temple. "It's awfully quiet in here. Everything okay between you two?"

Lydia looked over at Vanna. "We're just having some quiet time."

Vanna's face burned. When John Paul moved, releasing Lydia from the embrace, Vanna jumped, startled. She found herself shying away from him, even though he was several feet away.

He frowned. "You okay, Vanna?"

"I'm fine," she snapped, going back to shredding lettuce. There really wasn't any need to be terse with him. He hadn't done anything wrong and wasn't intruding by showing concern for her. But everything was irritating Vanna. Every look. Every word. Every movement. It seemed like the whole world was off-balance and it was all she could do just to keep from sliding off.

She didn't apologize for her tone and tried to focus on the task at hand, waiting for John Paul to leave. He should go watch television. Not get in the way of the work and demand answers to questions that couldn't be answered.

"If you need anything, just let me know," John Paul told Lydia, electing to ignore Vanna's behavior.

She'd always liked John Paul. He had been good for Lydia, even if she had seemed way too young to get married at the time. Vanna had decided that she wouldn't even think about getting married before thirty. She wanted time to figure out who she was and have time and space to herself before committing to someone else. But John Paul had been a rock for Lydia. He was stable, sturdy, and dependable. He didn't have a temper and fly off the handle at her. He was a good worker and a good father to the kids, like Donny had been to Lydia and Vanna. And, Lydia had hinted, he was good in other places and at other things. He'd always shown brotherly concern toward Vanna and had no problem including her in family activities. He always made her feel welcome. If he had any fault at all, it was that he was too good. Too stable and boring. A girl wanted some excitement now and then.

But lately, Vanna had not felt comfortable around him. It

felt like he was watching her all the time. His movements were too random and he asked too many questions. She knew she was being paranoid when she imagined John Paul being in cahoots with Abigail, but she couldn't stop her thoughts from running wildly off the tracks.

When he walked out of the room, Vanna tried to relax her body. But Lydia was looking at her, brows drawn down.

"What?" Vanna growled.

"I wish you'd tell me what was wrong. What's the deal with John Paul?"

"I didn't do anything. I just answered his question. If you don't want me to answer his questions, just let me know. I'll be happy to ignore them."

That was pushing it too far, she knew. Vanna put down the lettuce firmly and stared at it. Maybe it was just that they were in close quarters. Vanna wasn't used to being around people all the time. She was more comfortable in her own apartment, by herself. The constant noise and activity of the boys, not having any private space to withdraw to, that was all that was bothering her.

"I don't know what your deal is—" Lydia started.

Vanna pushed herself away from the counter and left the kitchen. She marched through the living room, where John Paul had, in fact, sat down to watch TV. He looked up at her but didn't say anything. Since she couldn't alight on her bed, which was the couch, Vanna kept going, upstairs to the bedroom, where Mandy was napping in her crib. Vanna shut the door quietly and sat down on the guest bed. She hadn't slept in there since the night that the baby monitor was hacked. But she wasn't going to sleep. She just needed to be by herself. She couldn't stand anyone else looking at her and asking her questions and she couldn't explain her own behavior.

She knew that Lydia had reached out a sisterly hand to her, inviting her to stay with them. She knew that Lydia was doing everything she could to support Vanna and had barely even censured her for shutting off her phone the day that Erica was kidnapped.

But it was like there were bugs crawling over Vanna's flesh. She couldn't sit still. It was like she was all buzzed on coffee or no-doze, even though caffeine didn't affect her like that.

No one followed her to get after her like a misbehaving child. They gave her space to sort things out herself. Lydia knocked on the door when dinner was prepared and poked her head into the room to make sure that Vanna was awake and had heard.

"I'm not really hungry," Vanna said.

"Well… it's up to you. But it's ready if you want to join us."

Vanna nodded and Lydia withdrew.

———

She should have known that the quiet would not last. It wasn't really quiet that she needed. The boys racing back to their room to continue their game didn't bother her. But when the house phone rang, Lydia answered it and brought the handset to Vanna.

"It's Mom. She said your phone is turned off."

Vanna took it reluctantly. Lydia waited for her to answer it and Vanna waited for Lydia to leave and give her privacy. Lydia shrugged and walked back out of the room, shaking her head. Vanna sighed.

"Hi, Mom."

"You need to leave your phone on so that people can reach you," Erica pointed out, without a greeting.

"I didn't want to talk to anyone. That's why I turned it off."

"It's not very considerate, especially when you have no voicemail."

"I don't want voicemails from her. What is it, Mom?"

"I wondered if you would come over for lunch tomorrow."

Vanna was taken aback. "Are you sure? You're still recovering…"

"Ivanna. You are in far worse shape than I am. I just have a few scrapes and bruises. It is you I am concerned about."

Vanna considered this. "I—I guess," she agreed. "But I'm okay."

"I'd like to see that for myself. Tomorrow at twelve-thirty, then?"

Vanna sighed again. "Sure. See you then."

Chapter Thirty-Two

As she expected, the lunch at Erica's wasn't a casual, relaxed affair. Vanna was happy to see that Erica's bruises were healing quickly or else were expertly covered by her makeup. There were only slight shadows under her eyes that gave away that she had been kidnapped and assaulted. There had been a number of headlines—one of the most prominent citizens of a small city being kidnapped was big news, even if she was returned within a day. But none of the papers had gotten pictures of her as she was when Vanna had seen her and when she had been rescued. Dark bruises, haunted and frail-looking. There had been some distance shots as she was taken from the building to an ambulance on a gurney, but no one had gotten a good shot of her face. That would have been devastating to her.

It meant that some of the details of Vanna's story had made it to the news as well. Reporters had called Erica's and Lydia's lines when they couldn't get a listing for Vanna. But Erica and Lydia hadn't helped them. So not too many details of Vanna's stalker and past had made it to the papers yet. But speculation was rampant.

Erica's eyes went over Vanna as they sat down at one end of

the big, dark dining table. Misty was on hand to serve them, setting dishes on the table with quiet clinks. Vanna looked at her.

"How are you, Misty? Are you okay?"

"I'm just fine. Thank you, Ivanna."

She didn't seem inclined to offer anything more, so Vanna left her alone. She looked reluctantly at her mother. Erica poured her some tea. "Lydia says that you have been on edge."

Lydia had been kind. "Yes," Vanna agreed. "Imagine that."

Erica smiled, thin-lipped. "I find myself jumping at nothing. A creak in the floorboards. A dog barking outside. The phone ringing jangles my nerves."

Vanna was surprised. Her mother did not admit to weakness. Vanna hadn't come expecting to find any solace. She had expected something more along the lines of being told to buck up and quit being such a baby. In a nice way, of course.

"It must have been awful for you," Vanna sympathized.

"No more so than for you. My abduction was over in a day. For you, this affair has been going on for months."

"It gets easier." Vanna shrugged.

"Does it?" Erica's brows arched up.

Vanna looked past Erica, out the window that looked out over the flat, green lawn. "Not really," she admitted.

"In fact, I think it has gotten harder for you the longer it has lasted."

"I suppose. I keep trying to get back on track, but…"

"You really should see a therapist. Get out and do something with your friends. Do some of your crafts."

Vanna didn't really disagree. But her old life seemed so distant now. Like a memory or a dream. It was hard to believe that she had once been so carefree. So free to come and go as she liked. That she could just go home at the end of the day and do her crafts and go to bed and sleep. Had she ever really lived like that and not known how lucky she was?

"It's not safe," she told Erica. "I can't go out with my friends or to their stores. It puts them in danger. Just like you."

"You came here today."

"I took a gamble that she wouldn't run me off the road and that your security would be… increased."

"I trust you found it adequate?" Erica said dryly.

Vanna smiled. Fort Knox might have been an understatement. There were guards both at the gate onto the property and at the door, inside and out. Not one of them had been inclined to allow Vanna in without scrutinizing her face and ID and comparing them to the pictures he had on hand. And they weren't just glorified valets with tasers. They had flak jackets and black helmets and all kinds of weapons in various holsters and body straps. Eventually, Vanna had run the gantlet and was allowed in.

"Is it legal for them to carry that kind of weaponry?"

Erica just smiled and took a sip of her tea. "Would you come and stay here with me?"

"Stay here," Vanna echoed. "Oh… I don't know."

"It is more secure than Lydia's and you would have more space. You can have your own bedroom and sitting room. If you want to take meals by yourself, you could have a fridge and microwave."

It was a tempting offer. She couldn't have her own place right now, not when she couldn't do her work. She hadn't wanted to rely on Erica for her support. But armed guards instead of an electronic security system that Abigail could hack might make her feel safe. Maybe she'd be able to sleep, in a bedroom all her own, knowing that Abigail couldn't get at her.

"I don't know," she repeated, still holding back. She had sworn when she left home that she would never go back. She wasn't one of those fledglings who returned to the empty nest, unwilling or unable to make it on her own.

Erica didn't try to talk her into it. She picked up a delicate sandwich and nibbled at a corner.

———

Vanna opened the door to the storage locker and looked over the contents. Sweeny had confirmed that it had been broken into, the lock cut with bolt cutters. So much for the on-grounds security that was supposed to be monitoring everyone who came and went. The pieces from Abigail's bedroom were still being held by the police for the case against Abigail for theft. But there was still plenty left in the locker. She could take the microwave and coffee-maker back to Erica's house. As Erica had suggested, she could have some semblance of her own independent life. Once she was up to preparing her own meals.

She pulled a couple of other homey touches from the locker. Her ergonomic work chair. Some artwork for the walls, if Erica would let her mount her own pictures. A few other bits and pieces.

She had been deep inside the locker, digging out a couple more small bits to take with her and she hadn't heard another vehicle drive up. But when she turned around and came out with her hands full, she was face-to-face with Abigail.

Again.

Of course, Abigail knew where her locker was. And of course, she knew that sooner or later, Vanna was going to come back for some of her things. Why weren't the police watching the locker? They knew it had been broken into once, and maybe they thought that meant that she wouldn't do it again. That whole thing about lightning not striking the same place twice. But what about criminals returning to the scene of the crime?

This time, Abigail had decided on a new approach. She wasn't the loving mother anymore. Nor was she the cocky kidnapper who knew she had leverage. This time, she had decided to enforce her approach a different way. There was a gun in her hand.

Vanna knew little about guns, but this one looked menacing.

It was all black, blocky in shape like a soldier's weapon rather than a collector's piece. She didn't know if it was automatic or semi-automatic or required some kind of safety release or priming to be fired. All she knew was that it was in her enemy's hand and it was pointed straight at her. It looked just about as lethal as anything Vanna could have imagined.

"Hello, Amelia," Abigail said. Her voice was cold and flat. The lack of expression, devoid even of anger, scared Vanna. She didn't know what to do with the things in her hand. She didn't know whether to put them down or drop them, or hold them in front of her as a shield. She didn't know if she should freeze, or try to run.

You couldn't outrun bullets.

"What do you want?" Vanna asked.

"Mealy Amelia. What a name. I always hated that name."

"Well, Abby, that's not what I go by anymore," Vanna sneered back. "You sort of took care of that, didn't you?" Being cooperative hadn't worked. Being polite and nice had never worked. And she was getting tired of the game. Weapon or no weapon, she was fighting back this time.

Abigail's eyes burned into her. "Don't call me Abby."

"What do you want me to call you? *Mommy?*"

Abigail took a threatening step forward. "You little—"

"Stay away from me," Vanna warned. She didn't retreat.

Abigail looked surprised. Vanna didn't have anything to threaten her with, but she stopped anyway. They faced each other, analyzing each other's positions.

"Get in the car," Abigail spat.

Vanna looked at them. "Which car? Mine or yours?"

"You think I'm going to get into a car with a GPS tracking device on it? Mine."

"You put *another* bug on my car?" Vanna heard the exasperation in her own voice. Well, let Abigail hear it too. Abigail shouldn't think that she could just push Vanna around all the time and not have to deal with Vanna's natural reactions.

"No, not me," Abigail wrinkled her nose. "Your boyfriend the cop. Just how stupid does he think I am? He thinks I would take you in your own car?"

Vanna wondered whether the bug was to track Abigail or to track Vanna. She had cut him out of the loop once before. Maybe the tracker was so he could keep track of what she was doing if she shut off her phone again. And it was off most of the time now. Didn't he need her permission to put a tracking device on her car? Or a court order?

"When did he do that?"

Abigail's mouth quirked up. "You didn't even know?"

Vanna shook her head. She went around to the passenger side of Abigail's car and got in, keeping a close eye on the gun. Abigail wasn't relaxing her guard at all. She got into the car on the other side, keeping the gun trained on Vanna.

"Put your seatbelt on."

Vanna obeyed.

Abigail tossed another set of zip-tie plastic handcuffs into Vanna's lap. "Put those on. Tighten them up good, I want to see them cutting into your skin."

Vanna slowly put them over her wrists. She realized that once the cuffs were on, she'd be trapped in the car, one hand on each side of the shoulder strap. But Abigail was watching her too closely for her to slip one of her hands around the strap. Vanna tightened the ties up tightly, as Abigail had instructed. They bit into her flesh. Abigail nodded, satisfied, and tucked the gun under her leg to drive. Vanna slid the handcuffs down her arms to make them more comfortable, but they were still too tight to consider trying to slip out of them. Abigail didn't look at her. Vanna didn't have a blindfold on and that worried her. She assumed that Abigail wasn't going to take her back to the apartment. She had something else in mind. Letting Vanna see where they were going meant that either it wasn't somewhere Abigail planned to ever go back to, or she wasn't going to let Vanna get back to Sweeny to report it. And she didn't like where that thought might lead.

"Where are we going?"

"Someplace special."

Vanna frowned, thinking about it. Someplace that was special to the two of them? There wasn't anywhere that came to mind. She really knew very little about Abigail's past. The girl had obviously grown up with some disadvantages. She had helped Julia out with child care and been taken under Julia's wing. And then they had fought and Abigail killed her. Abigail had a crush on Julia; that much Vanna understood. Had Julia ever seen Abigail as anything other than a helpful teenager? Had there been real feelings between them, or had Abigail mixed up the signals?

———

In twenty minutes, they were out of the city and cruising down the highway toward the mountains. Vanna had been unable to find a way to signal to passing motorists that she needed help. She had tried mouthing 'help me' through the window to cars that drove by them on Vanna's side. Abigail either didn't notice or didn't care. If she assumed that none of the motorists would be concerned enough to try to help, she was right. No one even looked at Vanna.

Now they were on the highway and Vanna was starting to panic. If Abigail was going to drive into the mountains, there were plenty of lonely roads to take. Plenty of places where a body wouldn't be discovered for a long time.

"You don't know what it was like," Abigail said abruptly, without introduction. "In prison. You don't know."

"How could I?" Vanna thought about it. "I wasn't the one who put you there, you know. If you're trying to get back at me for something that happened to you…"

Abigail looked at her for an instant, frowning. She turned

her eyes back to the road. "Prison is full of evil people. It's not a very nice place."

Vanna almost laughed at the statement. Not a very nice place? Full of evil people? What did Abigail *think* it was going to be like? She choked back the urge to laugh, but Abigail still sensed it and tried to bore holes through her with those burning, intense eyes.

"I don't just mean the prisoners," she said. "Some of them are actually okay. It's the staff. The guards and the administrators. They're the truly evil ones."

"What did they do?"

"You don't believe me?"

"No, I believe you. I just want you to tell me about it. What did they do? What was it like?"

"They would punish you by putting you in solitary. Not a dark hole in the ground, like you might see on TV. Observation cells. Glass all the way around so they could watch you around the clock. No privacy. No clothing or blankets in case you tried to hang yourself with them. Lights on all day and all night. Noise all the time, never any quiet. One meal a day." She looked at Vanna. "How would you like that?"

"I wouldn't. That sounds awful."

"For your own good, they said. For your own protection. That wasn't why they did it. They did it to hurt. To punish. If you didn't toe the line—even if you couldn't—you get put under observation."

"For how long?"

"Days, even weeks. Imagine that. Having someone watch you twenty-four hours a day for weeks."

Vanna refrained from making any reference to the way that Abigail had been watching and stalking her for months. Abigail wouldn't get the comparison. She wouldn't see the similarity.

"That would be awful," Vanna agreed instead. "Are they allowed to do that?"

"They said they have to. It's in the rules. If they are... it's a stupid law. You think it helps someone who is at the end of their rope to be watched all day? Nothing to do but sit there, being watched? Sleeping on the cold, hard floor with no blankets. Like sleeping on the street. Worse. At least on the street, it gets dark, and you can hide. In one of those cells, with the lights on all day and all night, you feel like a lab specimen. Keep waiting for the day they come to cut your head open with a knife to have a look inside your brain. Sometimes I ended up in hospital. It was the only way to get out."

"Didn't they let you out once they decided you weren't a danger to yourself anymore?"

"You think so? I told you, they do it to punish you. It's not because they want you to get better. The only way they want you to get better is by getting dead, but they won't give you anything to help you on the way."

"So…" Vanna was almost afraid to ask, but she knew she had to. She had to keep Abigail talking. To find a way to make some kind of connection. Or who knew what dense patch of trees she would end up buried in. "How did you get sent to hospital, then? How did you hurt yourself?"

"Bang your head on the floor. About the only way. And they wouldn't take you in until you had blood running down your face. Anything short of that and they wouldn't bother. One of the girls was good at choking herself. But most people, you can't really choke yourself, because when you pass out, your hands loosen. You have to have something. A ligature. To wrap around your neck."

Vanna swallowed. "That sounds… like a nightmare. But when you got back from the hospital? They would let you back out of isolation then?"

"Usually. Unless you did something else or they wanted to punish you more. Sometimes there was a problem on the bus or in your transfer… and you'd go straight back to the box."

"I can't imagine. I'm sorry that happened to you."

"Who said it happened to me?" Abigail snapped. "I said it happened. To people. I never said it happened to me."

"Oh… okay. Well, I would be sad… if it happened to you."

"Why?"

Vanna struggled to come up with an honest answer. "Because… I don't think they should do that. Not to anyone."

———

It wasn't a national park. If it were a national park, they would have had to pay a toll at the entrance and Vanna could have tried to get help. Surely a park officer leaning over to collect a toll and count the people in the car would see her handcuffed hands and get help. But there was no point in wondering about it because it was not a national park and there was no toll to be paid. They just drove into the mountains and into the trees.

It was green. A drizzly day. But the sun kept peeking out from behind the clouds and lighting up the trees in unexpected, spectacular vistas. Vanna wouldn't have thought that she could enjoy nature's light show on her way to possible death, but she couldn't help but be impressed. She was a city girl, but what she saw as they drove the smaller and smaller roadways winding through the trees was truly inspiring. Eventually, Abigail seemed to have reached her destination. She pulled her car into a parking stall in an empty lot below a hiking trail. There was no one else in sight. No sound but the rustling of the trees and the singing of birds when Abigail opened her door. Before getting out, Abigail brandished a large knife. When Vanna shrank back and held her arm protectively in front of her face, Abigail inserted the blade between Vanna's arm and the plastic bond and snapped it quickly away from Vanna, cutting off one of the handcuffs. Vanna held still while Abigail cut the other and then opened her eyes. She hadn't even realized that she had shut them. She was free. Her hands were a dusky blue and were numb, but the blood would flow back quickly enough.

"Get out," Abigail instructed. "Come on."

"Where are we?" Vanna asked. "Is there a public restroom? I could really use a break…"

"Come with me." Abigail was impatient. "No games."

"I'm not…"

Abigail grabbed her wrist and yanked her forward. Vanna didn't resist, but she stumbled, trying to keep up with Abigail's quick stride. After a minute, when Abigail could see that Vanna was keeping up and not fighting her, she let go. Then Vanna was able to use both arms for balance, which quickly became necessary as they hiked a meandering trail up the mountain.

"This is beautiful," Vanna observed. "Where are we going?"

"Just shut up."

But if these were Vanna's last moments on earth, she didn't want to waste them. She had lost enough of herself already, letting Abigail suck the life out of her. She had gone from being a happy, social, independent woman to being a paranoid, unpleasant recluse. She could see what she had become and even if she didn't like it, there was nothing that she could do about the backward slide. If she was leaving this world, she was doing it on her own terms.

"What's the name of this place?"

"I don't know. It's a place that Julia brought me once."

"Oh." Vanna thought about that for a while. She looked around. It wasn't exactly sacred ground, but she was walking where her mother had walked. She felt a little bit of something like kinship extend across the decades.

As they continued to climb, the feeling started to come back to Vanna's fingers. She opened and closed her hands, trying to hurry the process along. The stabbing pains were worse than the pins and needles she had experienced before. Much worse. At first they distracted her from the climb and from glancing back to see how steep the trail behind her was. She grabbed at a wooden railing over a small stream, suddenly dizzy. Abigail growled impatiently.

"What's the matter?"

"Nothing. I'm… not feeling so well. Just give me a second."

"What are you up to?"

"I'm not up to anything." Vanna lowered her swimming head.

"She had you in a backpack thing," Abigail said, looking back over the portion of the trail that they had already traveled. Vanna didn't dare look back again. "You were too little to make it up here by yourself, so she had you in a carrier. It made it harder for her to go up the trail, but she wanted to show it to me."

"It's very beautiful," Vanna puffed.

"What's wrong with you?"

"I'm just tired. I haven't been sleeping well."

"What, you don't have the right kind of satin sheets at your new mommy's house?"

Vanna pressed her lips together angrily. She hated Abigail even mentioning Erica. Abigail wasn't going to touch her again. Abigail shouldn't even mention her, but especially not in that snide tone. She took a deep breath and steeled herself to keep climbing.

"I'm good. Come on."

Abigail again took the lead, with Vanna just a step or two behind her. If Vanna slowed or considered making a break through the woods, Abigail was immediately beside her, chivvying her along.

"You want to see, don't you? See the place that Julia took me?"

"Yeah. Of course."

So they kept climbing. Vanna was sure it probably wouldn't have been any problem for an experienced hiker, but that was one thing she definitely was not. And whatever fitness level she had achieved before this whole thing had started was gone. She didn't eat, didn't sleep, didn't work out or even go out for walks. She just felt like a pile of jelly. The muscles in her legs were burning and fatigued. She was afraid that if she stopped again, she wouldn't be able to continue on. And she wasn't sure how she was going to get back down the trail again.

But maybe Abigail wasn't planning a return trip. Maybe this was it. As the last hike of her life, it wasn't too bad. But she wished they had brought some water.

There was a flight of stairs in the end. The trail was too steep to get up without one, but Vanna's fatigued legs did not take kindly to the steps. They were slightly too wide. Not close enough to take one step at a time and not space enough to take two steps. Just at the right spacing to force Vanna to take one and a half steps between stairs. She couldn't get the rhythm and kept shuffling and stumbling. Abigail was right at her side now, holding her by one arm, determined to drag her up those stairs if necessary.

When they finally reached the top, there was a lookout and Vanna just closed her eyes, happy that there wasn't any further to climb. For a few minutes, she just breathed heavily. Gradually, her heart and lungs slowed back to almost the usual pace. They were just slightly elevated with the burst of adrenaline that shot through Vanna as she realized that this was likely the end. The end of the trail for her.

Abigail was watching her. Close to her, but not quite in Vanna's personal space. Abigail motioned to the viewpoint and Vanna turned her eyes to the vista before them.

"Isn't it beautiful?" Abigail asked. "I remember the first time that I saw it…"

They were dizzyingly high above a riverbed. Exposed rocks jutted out below them. Trees that seemed to be anchored to nothing. Sprays of ferns clung to water-splashed ledges. There was a waterfall rushing downward, white with foam and deep green underneath. The blue sky was wide open up above them, immense.

Her stomach lurched.

Abigail grabbed at Vanna as her knees buckled. She held

tightly to Vanna's arm and levered her up to lean on the railing. "What are you doing?"

"Nothing. I'm…" Vanna swallowed and cleared her throat. It was difficult to talk when she felt like fainting and throwing up all at once. Not to mention that it was embarrassing and made her face and scalp burn like she was being scalded. "It's the height. I… have problems…"

"You're afraid of heights?" Abigail cackled with laughter. "Well, that's one thing you don't take after your mother in! She loved to climb."

Vanna ventured another glance down at the gorge, then closed her eyes, trying to breathe through the vertigo. She felt like she had left her stomach somewhere down the trail. Abigail's hands were on her shoulder and back. Vanna wasn't sure whether Abigail was stabilizing her or seeing how easy it would be to heft Vanna over the railing. Was that why Abigail had brought her up there? To send her toppling after her birth mother? Vanna's very existence was too aggravating. Just by living, she seemed to upset Abigail.

"Please, Abby…" she breathed.

Abigail's fingers hardened, digging into Vanna's soft flesh. "I said not to call me that."

Defiance probably wasn't the way to win any friends here, but Vanna was at the end of her rope. She had to be her own person, standing on her own feet, one more time.

"Why not? Is that what my birth mother called you? Abby?"

"When she brought me up here, it was so romantic. I thought she was going to ask me to move in with her permanently. I thought that she wanted a life together. But it was just… a picnic. It meant *nothing* to her. She was just toying with my feelings. *You* don't get to call me Abby."

Vanna heard voices. Down below them somewhere. Not down the trail that they had come up, but somewhere else. There was another trail on the other side of the lookout. Vanna had assumed that it went further up the mountain, but looking more carefully, she could see that it only rose slightly and then went down again. Where?

"Abby?" she repeated in a louder voice. "Crabby Abby? Did the boys at school used to make fun of your name? Did they used to make rhymes about you? Abby the shabby, flabby tabby? Is that it, Abby?"

"I said cut it out!" Abigail shouted, furious. She let go of Vanna and felt for her gun, which had been put away since they got out of the car. "You can't make fun of me!"

"Which one was it?" Vanna mocked "Crabby, flabby Abby?"

As Abigail managed to pull the gun free from her pocket, Vanna forced herself to move. She jumped from the lookout to the other trail in a single bound. Her feet got tangled up on her landing, but she managed to stay on her feet and get them both pointed in the right direction. She dashed over the hump and hit the downward slope much too fast. She heard a loud crack behind her. Gunshot. White-hot pain stabbed through her arm. Vanna yelped and stumbled. It was a steep downhill slope and she couldn't stop her fall. She tried to catch herself, scraping her hands and arms on the rocky trail.

Vanna scrambled to her feet and kept going but her legs were wobbly and slow to respond to her instructions. Gravity forced her to scramble faster than she was able and she again lost her feet, rolling and bouncing down the hill. She flew off the trail and crashed through the trees, falling down an even steeper slope.

She landed flat on her back on another rocky surface. She was stunned, the breath knocked out of her. There was pain everywhere. She knew she had to get up. Abigail would be right behind her. But convincing her body to move was another matter.

"Oh my! Oh my goodness! Are you all right?" There were hands on her, a woman's distressed voice.

"She's bleeding," a male voice observed calmly. "See if you can get a cell signal, Mary."

"What happened?" the woman's voice went on. "Did you slip and fall on the trail? From up there?"

Vanna tried to focus on them and to communicate the danger to her. Her breath was still strangled from having the wind knocked out of her. "Shot. A woman up there. With a gun."

The owner of the female voice was a woman perhaps in her late fifties or early sixties, tanned and weathered-looking. She was graying and had wrinkles, but had a healthy, outdoorsy vigor. She looked with concern at the man. He appeared to be her junior, with jet-black hair and fewer lines. She didn't voice her question, but he answered it with his actions.

"That did sound like a gunshot. We'd better get her off the trail if there's some mad gunman around. Try your phone."

Mary stared at him for a minute in silence, then pulled out her cell phone, a big old thing. Vanna was surprised that it was even functional. The man saw her look of dismay.

"It's a lot more powerful than any of those little flip or smartphones you're going to find today."

Mary pulled up an antenna and waited. After a minute, she gave a thumbs-up. "We've got a signal."

"I don't know if there's nine-one-one service out here," the man said. "But you can try."

Vanna forced her body to move. "Got to get away first." She was expecting to hear Abigail coming down the trail any second. Abby wouldn't be put off by witnesses, she had a gun and could just kill them all. "Please."

"Do you think you can get up?" The man bent down to assist her. "You took quite a fall."

"Please." Vanna took his hand and tried to pull herself up. Every bruise, scrape, and muscle protested, but she forced herself to keep moving. Her vision filled with bright sparkles, obliterating everything else. The man managed to get her arm up around his neck and wound his arm under hers and behind her back. That provided something sturdy to rest her weight on and keep her from falling down again. She tightened her grip on him the best that she could

"You'd better get on the other side," the man instructed his companion. "Help me get her moving. It's not going to be easy off the trail."

It didn't help that Vanna couldn't really see where they were going. She concentrated on finding stable ground for her feet and holding tight to her rescuers. Her head was wobbly and she struggled to keep from slipping into the darkness. They dragged her over and around obstacles and it wasn't long before both were breathing heavily.

"Stop here," the man said, after an indeterminate length of time.

Vanna panicked as they lowered her to the ground. "No, don't stop."

"Shh. Keep your voice down. Once we're down, we're well-hidden by the rocks. We're not going to be able to get you much further. Best to stop where there's a shelter."

Vanna couldn't see clearly enough to assess his choice of hideaway. They helped to lay her out. There were rocks and sticks poking into her body, but it was a relief to be able to lie still and rest. She could hear the two hikers taking off their packs and settling beside her. They spoke in low, urgent whispers.

"Call Sweeny," Vanna said. Her voice was weak and shaky. She didn't raise it for fear that Abigail would be close enough to hear her. "He'll send help."

"Sweeny? Who is that?"

"A cop."

"You have his direct number?"

Vanna tried to remember it. Her brain wasn't functioning properly. It was like fishing in a black hole. "My phone," she said. "It's on my phone."

One of them patted her body, pulling random items out of her pockets. Mary giggled, stress in her voice. "Which pocket?"

Vanna felt for it, her hands burning and throbbing from her fall. Mary slid her hand in and retrieved it.

"It's not on. Is it dead?"

"Turned off."

They waited for it to power up. There was noise nearby and everybody ducked, pressing themselves to the ground, even though they were hopefully already out of sight behind the rocks. They were silent, holding their breaths, listening intently to the lone footsteps crunching down the nearby trail. They stopped for a moment and Vanna waited for them to leave the trail where Mary and her friend had pulled her off. There was a long period of tense silence and then the footsteps continued down the trail. Vanna started to breathe again. The three of them stayed silent, not talking to each other, for what seemed like an eternity. Mary propped herself up on her elbows.

"You okay?" she whispered.

Vanna tried to nod but felt nauseated. "Yes."

"Okay, your phone is up. I'm looking for the phone number. Sweeny?"

"Yeah." Since Erica's kidnapping and rescue, Vanna had disabled her screen lock so that the phone was instantly accessible. She was glad she had, because just like with Sweeny's phone number, she could no longer remember the screen lock code.

Mary pressed the buttons on her huge phone. It sounded loud to Vanna's ears and she was afraid that it would draw Abigail back again.

"What's your name?" Mary asked.

"Vanna. Vanna Austin."

While Mary made the call, the man was quietly unzipping his backpack, moving the zipper very slowly. He knelt beside Vanna, examining her hands, head, and face. Vanna moved her hand creakily across her body to bare the place on the back of her shoulder that was throbbing and burning the worst. The man held her wet shirt back to take a closer look. He swore under his breath.

"You took a bullet. Is that the only one?"

"Yes."

"I'm going to clean and bandage it. It might hurt, but we want to slow the bleeding. I didn't even see it, with your dark shirt."

"Thanks," Vanna breathed.

She listened to Mary talking on the phone, explaining who she was and where they were. It was a little scattered, but Sweeny apparently got the main points. Mary moved in beside her partner.

"He wants to talk to her. Can I get in for a minute?"

"You'll have to wait. Let me get a bandage and some pressure on this."

"Oh…" Mary saw the bullet wound for the first time. "Oh, she's been shot!"

There was a burst of sound from Sweeny and more conversation and description by Mary. Vanna was drifting on the edge of consciousness. In spite of the increased pain from the man treating her wound, she could feel the heavy sleepiness seeping into her bones and her brain.

"Stay with me," he told her, giving her a little shake. "There, how's that?"

"I don't know," Vanna mumbled. She felt the edge of the bandage with the fingers on her other hand, but couldn't give him any feedback. If the bandage would keep her from bleeding too much, then it was good.

"Can I get in there now with the phone?" Mary prompted.

The man moved out of the way and Mary held the brick to Vanna's ear. "Here's your friend, Sweeny."

"Hi," Vanna croaked at him.

"What happened?" Sweeny asked. "I thought you were going to stay at your mom's."

"I went to the storage unit. I thought… you thought it would be okay."

"She breaks all of our theories. She *shouldn't* have gone back there."

"She knew that I would, sooner or later."

"Are you okay, Vanna? You sound pretty rough. I've got every cop and warden in the area headed to your location. Can you hang in there?"

"Mmm. Yeah."

"She had a gun this time?"

"I didn't know what to do. Guess I should have let her shoot me there. Closer to help."

"You cooperated with her. It should have been the right thing."

Vanna tried to readjust her position. There was a pointy rock jutting right into her spine. But when she moved, her shoulder flared and she was forced to be still, grunting in pain.

"Are you safe?" Sweeny asked. "Has she gone away?"

"Don't know. Can't hear or see her."

"What was she driving? Where did she park?"

Vanna tried to remember the details. "A white car… Mazda, maybe. Dirty. The parking lot was empty… I don't know where. There were no signs with a place name."

"A rest area? Historical site?"

"Rest area. Trailhead. I don't know. Down below here."

"Your good Samaritan says you're near the Blue Cascade waterfall."

"We climbed above here. A lookout for the waterfall. Up from the parking lot. Then over a hill and down… here."

"We can't get a signal on your phone. Not strong enough in the mountains. The one you're calling from doesn't have GPS tracking. But someone will be there to help you soon. They have an approximate location. You'll hear them once they get close."

"Yeah."

Vanna's head spun. She was starting to feel cold, even

though the sun wasn't going down yet. But maybe she was in the shade or a cloud had just passed in front of the sun.

The man was shaking her. "Vanna! Vanna, try to stay awake. Come on." He shook some more. "Wake up."

"I'm awake," Vanna mumbled.

The phone was no longer at her ear. Sweeny was gone. Vanna listened to the wind rustling the leaves of the trees above them.

"Where is she?"

"Where is who? The woman with the gun?" Mary asked.

"Yeah. Abby."

"She hasn't come back. We're safe here for now."

"What's your name?" Vanna tried to focus on something to keep herself awake. She didn't know why she had to stay awake. It would be so nice to just sleep.

"Mary."

"No. His."

"My name is Gerhard," the man said. "Most people just call me Gert."

"Gert." Vanna took a few shallow breaths. Anything deeper seemed to make her more dizzy and nauseated. "Thanks for bandaging. My shoulder. Thanks."

"Of course. I'm sure you would have done the same for me if I got shot by a madwoman and fell down at your feet." His voice was teasing. Vanna had to smile, even though it was an effort.

Time passed. Realizing Vanna was shivering, Gert dug a blanket out of his backpack and put it over her, tucking it close to her body. "I'm sorry I don't have anything better. I only brought my daypack."

"It's nice. Thanks."

She continued to shiver. The cold was seeping out of the ground right into her bones. Mary checked the bandage. She spoke to Gert in a whisper, but Vanna could still hear the words 'soaked through.'

There were noises on the trail, making Vanna jump. Gert and Mary ducked down, but then Gert slowly put his head up over the rocky ridge. "Our help has arrived," he announced. He stood up and called for help and in a few minutes Vanna was overrun with helpful offers. She closed her eyes, exhausted.

Chapter Thirty-Three

When Vanna woke up in hospital again, it was hard to put together the details in the right order and to remember what had happened. At first she thought she was there after the car crash, but the throbbing pain in her shoulder vaguely reminded her of something else. Her hands and arms were skinned, just as they had been after the car accident, when she had landed on the pavement with her hands stretched out. But this time there were a lot more gouges.

There was a guard outside the door, Vanna could hear voices whenever someone came to the door and wanted admittance. A few of them must have been turned away, because when Vanna waited for the door to open, it didn't. But Erica and Lydia were allowed in, as were a steady stream of doctors and nurses.

"You could have been killed," Erica said, not for the first time. "Somebody has to do something about this woman! She had a gun!"

"Nobody is going to do anything about her," Vanna said with a sigh. "She's too smart to let the police catch her. She switches cars whenever she feels like it. Who knows where she is staying now—in a new apartment, or a warehouse or street somewhere. You can bet she's not with a friend who could turn her in to the police. She's too smart for that."

"At least she hasn't come to the hospital this time."

"No… not that anybody has mentioned to me. But the guard turns people away. He never says who. I don't get to decide who I would want to see."

"It's for your own safety," Erica reminded her.

"I know that. But I wish things could be normal again."

"They will, someday. We'll get her somehow."

"I don't see how." Vanna stared out the window, but could see little other than the sky. "You would think it would be easy to track someone like that, someone who always kept going back to the same place, following the same person. But I'm starting to see how some of the women in the support group have been stalked for years. If you're patient, if it doesn't matter how long you have to wait, you can out-wait the police every time. Like Sweeny keeps saying… they just don't have the resources to guard someone twenty-four hours a day. Not for long. After you've been on the list for a few days, they decide that it's not worth it. But a stalker can wait for weeks or months. They don't have to attack until the police withdraw."

Erica shook her head.

"Well, what about a device of some kind? If they can put a GPS tracker on your car, why can't they put one on you? Why not track you, instead of your phone or car?"

"There are devices out there… maybe I'll try something… but you know if I get something, she'll know I got it and she won't let me use it. She knew Sweeny was tracking my car and I didn't even know that."

"How would she know? I could order something online, in my name. She'd never know."

Vanna raised her shoulders in a shrug that still hurt, despite all of the painkillers that she was on. Even if she couldn't find the flaw in Erica's argument, she knew it was there. She knew that Abigail would somehow know if Vanna had some kind of tracker on her.

"Besides. She doesn't have to take me anywhere. She's been escalating. She got a gun and took me away somewhere, shot me when I tried to escape. Next time she won't wait. She won't try to take me somewhere. She'll just shoot me."

"Don't say that!"

"She doesn't even have to get close to do it. Maybe this time… I won't be able to see it coming."

Erica's eyes were wide with horror. "Maybe she'll give up. She's seen that you're not going to give up without a fight. Maybe she'll decide that she's had enough. That they got too close to catching her this time. She'll decide that she can't get anything out of it and just let you go."

"Maybe," Vanna agreed listlessly. After a few minutes, she looked at Erica. "You're probably right."

"No, you don't really believe that. I can see."

"Mom…" Vanna swallowed. Her throat was tight and hot. "If something happens to me… I just want you to know… I love you. Okay?"

Erica grasped Vanna's hand just a little too tightly. It was still scraped and bruised up. "I love you too, Ivanna. I'm not going to let anything happen to you."

"I know. But just in case." Vanna nodded. "I really do. I'm sorry for all of the crap I've given you. All of that teenager stuff and even the last few years… acting like I know better about everything. I really do appreciate everything that you've done for me."

Erica stroked her hand softly. "Thank you, dear." Her eyes glistened, but she didn't shed any tears. "But I'm not giving up. This woman chose the wrong person's daughter to mess with."

———

After each escalation, there was a period of de-escalation and Vanna found that more disconcerting than the stalking. Sitting around waiting while nothing happened. No sign of Abigail. No notes or phone calls. No indication that she was watching Vanna at all. As Vanna had predicted, after a few days of a police guard, which was redundant with all of the guards at Erica's, the police force again backed off.

Sweeny apologized. Vanna could hear the frustration in his voice. "They think that she's run. That we scared her off after the last incident and she's given up." He made a growling noise in the back of his throat. "There's no proof that she is still stalking you, or even in the city, so we can't continue to spend our resources…"

"I know."

"I'm sorry. I would guard you twenty-four hours myself if I could and if I didn't have the rest of my cases. But I just can't."

"That's sweet of you. Really. I know you're trying."

"It's just so infuriating. You and I both know that she's still out there. She hasn't given up. She's just sitting pretty for a little while. Gone quiet. But she'll start to get wound up again, and…"

"There's nothing we can do. I know. I should have listened to the other women. I kept thinking that we could catch her and that this didn't have to go on. But I should have understood that there's actually nothing you can do. If someone wants to stalk you and they're smart enough to stay out of the way of the police…"

"Sooner or later, we're going to get her, Vanna."

"Or sooner or later, she's going to get me. My money's on her."

"Don't say that," he said fiercely. "Don't give up. You can't let her win."

"I'm not letting her… but I know she'll be back."

"I know."

"Can you do one thing for me, though?" Vanna asked.

"Sure. What do you need?"

———

Tino picked up the phone. His voice was surprised. "Vanna?"

"Yeah, it's me."

"I saw your mom's number on the Caller ID. But I didn't think…" he trailed off.

"It's me. I need to ask you for something. A favor."

"Yes! Anything, Van. You know I would do anything for you."

"This doesn't mean we're getting back together," Vanna warned. "And if the police catch you breaking the restraining order, there's nothing that I can do to stop them from charging you."

There was a silence as he thought that over. But when he spoke again, his voice was resolute. "No matter what could happen to me, I want to help you. What can I do?"

———

It was nice of Abigail to wait while Vanna went through all of the preparations. She kept thinking that Abigail would show up unexpectedly before Vanna got everything into place. She was counting on Abigail staying quiet for a while, yet she knew she couldn't count on it. Abigail could make her reappearance any time and there was no guarantee that it would be preceded by a letter or phone call this time.

And even though she was expecting it, Abigail's reappearance caught her by surprise.

Vanna couldn't just stay inside Erica's fortification for the rest of her life. She spent as much time recovering as she could, but she was going stir crazy having to stay at home in that quiet house all day long. Even with her television on in the background, it just seemed too empty and echoey. It had never felt like that as a kid. Not until after Lydia had left home. Now that it was just her and Erica and the staff, it was too much.

She had gone on several forays, carefully watching her rear-view mirror for any sign of Abigail. But so far, Abigail had failed to show up. While she couldn't really relax, Vanna found that she couldn't think about Abigail all the time. Eventually, she had to move on to other things. Erica insisted that Vanna had to start doing something with herself. Something to be a little more normal and a little bit less anxious and depressed about her lost life. So Vanna went on a few short trips to scout out crafting materials. She had Sweeny pick things up from the storage locker for her. That was one place that she couldn't go.

Vanna had just made a stop at the junkyard, where she had found a few fixtures and bottles to start a new pendant lamp. Most of her finds were on the seat beside her. She was stopped at a traffic light when she happened to glance in the rear-view mirror at the driver of a car who kept inching closer and closer to her. She saw Abigail's face. A shudder went through her, shaking her right down to her toes.

She couldn't face Abigail again. It was too hard.

Abigail's face was framed by dark hair instead of blond. One concession to the manhunt focused on her. Just one little detail to make her less visible. Vanna looked back out the windshield at the traffic light. She faked a big yawn, trying not to give away to Abigail the fact that she had been spotted. Not yet.

As the light changed and she pulled out, she reached forward to adjust the knobs on the radio. She faked singing along with a song that wasn't playing.

"Tino, come in. Are you there?"

She didn't know all of the intricacies of the radio that Tino had installed. The various bands and technicalities were beyond her, but Tino had left it tuned to the band that he would monitor. The hands-free mode meant that she didn't have to bring a mike to her face to give away to Abigail that she was talking to someone.

What if Abigail knew that she'd had the two-way radio installed and knew what channel it was tuned to? Vanna glanced anxiously at the rear-view mirror, but couldn't see any sign that Abigail was suspicious. Then again, Abigail was good at hiding what she knew. She knew that Sweeny had a tracking device installed in the car without Vanna's knowledge. But would she know that Tino had made modifications when Vanna had taken it to a small shop for an oil change? Had she suspected anything?

"Tino…"

"Vanny, I'm here. Are you okay?"

Vanna blew out her breath. "I'm okay," she confirmed. "She's on me, though. I don't think she knows I've spotted her. She's a couple of cars back, now."

"Where are you?"

"I'm at… McLaren and Alamo. Going south."

"Okay. Go to the White Spot. I'll park around back so she won't see the truck. I should be able to get there before you."

Vanna's heart was pounding hard. "I'm scared, Tino…"

"Don't be scared. I'm not going to let her hurt you."

"Don't let her hurt you, either. Remember she had a gun last time."

"I know."

"Should I call Sweeny?"

"She could be monitoring your phone. You can't take the chance. You know they'll just scare her off. She's got a scanner. She'll hear them coming."

"Please let this work…"

"Hang in there, Vanny. Stay cool."

"Are you okay?" she asked him.

"Me? Of course, I'm fine."

"I mean… you can keep it under control? You're not going to… lose it?"

He was silent.

"Tino?"

"I'm not making any promises." He sounded like he was gritting his teeth. "But I'm not going to hurt you."

Vanna felt a twinge of guilt. She felt awful about the whole plan and wanted to abort it right there. But she had to do what she did to get her life back. There was no other choice.

"Okay, I'm pulling in behind the Spot," Tino said quietly. "I'll be ready when you get here."

He was only a minute or two ahead of Vanna. She was glad that he had made it in time. When she looked in the mirror again, she didn't see the car and was afraid that she had lost Abigail. But she had to stick to the plan, so she turned into the restaurant parking lot and watched anxiously behind her for Abigail to turn in. She looked around tensely but couldn't see Tino either. Where was he?

Vanna sat there in the car, not getting out. Something was terribly wrong. She didn't know what had happened, but something had not gone according to plan. There was a screech of tires and Vanna looked up to see the tow truck pull out of the back lane onto the main road.

There were two figures in the truck. Tino was driving. Abigail was in the passenger seat. Vanna's thoughts whirled. Tino couldn't be in league with Abigail, but there she was, sitting in the truck with him. As if she had known all along what was going on. Had he been feeding her all along? Vanna pulled out of the parking lot to follow them. Not a logical move to become the pursuer instead of the target, but she didn't know what else to do. This wasn't in the script.

"Hello, Vanna," the radio crackled to life. Abigail's voice this time. "Surprised?"

"What's going on?" Vanna demanded. "I don't get it!"

"Your boyfriend and I have a little understanding. Don't we, Valentine?"

"Vanna, don't—" Tino's voice broke in.

Vanna could see them through the back window of the tow truck. Saw Abigail's arm fly up and connect with the side of

Tino's head or face. She heard the impact. The tow truck swerved into the left lane, then back again. Tino was swearing, his words slurred liked he'd just come home from the dentist, still frozen.

"What are you doing?" Vanna asked again. She stayed right behind them, gripping the steering wheel so tightly that her knuckles were pure white.

"It's always the men," Abigail snarled, "getting in the way where they aren't wanted. Stepping in and trying to seduce you. Why can't they just stay away?"

"Don't hurt him," Vanna begged. "It's not his fault. He didn't do anything."

"Didn't do anything? I know what he was doing. Don't try that on me."

"Where are we going?"

It was obvious that Abigail expected her to follow. Tino wasn't trying to lose her. Vanna was right behind them.

"Turn here."

Vanna followed the tow truck around the corner. She wished now that she'd called Sweeny. That they hadn't removed the tracker from the car. That somehow she could send out a distress signal. In a few more minutes, they were pulling into an empty lot. It was next to one of the junkyards that Vanna sometimes went to, but not the one she'd gone to today.

Vanna parked beside the tow truck. Abigail was getting out. The gun was pointed in Vanna's direction. She sat there with a billion thoughts running through her head, trying to sort out an appropriate plan of action. She was paralyzed with indecision. Abigail pulled her door open with a jerk. She grabbed Vanna's arm.

"Get out," she ordered, giving it a yank.

Vanna had her seatbelt buckled and Abigail had to let go while she unbuckled it. Tino made a sound or movement in the truck behind Abigail and she was momentarily distracted, her head turning toward him for a fraction of a second. Vanna grabbed one of the bottles from the seat beside her and as she got out of the car, she swung it as hard as she could.

She had expected it to shatter over Abigail's head and had felt a momentary twinge of regret, since it was the best bottle that she had found so far. But it landed with a heavy thunk and didn't break.

She heard the crack of Abigail's gun, a sound that squeezed her guts with terror in the instant before the blow hit her, like being kicked in the ribs by a horse. It blasted the breath out of her and she and Abigail were both falling together, grabbing onto each other to catch themselves or to restrain the other.

Vanna managed to hold onto the precious bottle and when they both hit the ground, again swung it over Abigail's head. The swing was not long enough, but connected solidly again. Abigail made a strangled noise and was still moving, trying to get up and get control over Vanna.

Vanna brought the bottle down a third time as hard as she could. She both felt and heard a crack and Abigail slumped over and stopped moving.

Vanna still couldn't breathe. She could barely move. But she forced herself to get to her knees.

She grabbed the gun and pulled it out of Abigail's lifeless hand.

Getting around the truck to Tino's side took longer. She could hear him screaming and swearing, yelling for her, unable to see what had happened.

He saw her as she came around the truck door, still on her hands and knees.

"Vanna! Van, are you all right? *Vanna!*"

Tears were rolling down Vanna's cheeks. She tried to climb to her feet, using the truck to pull herself up. Tino tried to help her up, but his hands were handcuffed through the steering wheel and he couldn't reach out more than a few inches. When she got close enough, he pulled her up.

"Are you okay?"

She tried to breathe, tried to speak. "I'm okay," she whispered.

"She shot you again. You're bleeding." His voice was panicked.

Vanna followed his eyes to look at the back of her shoulder, starting to bleed through her shirt. Not her ribs, where it was really hurting. She ignored Tino's look, trying to figure out what to do. Abigail had used the zip-tie handcuffs on him too. They looked at each other. Tino jerked on the handcuffs angrily, but couldn't break out of them. Vanna felt her pockets. She couldn't remember which one she had stashed the wire cutters in after using them at the junk yard, but after checking them one at a time with shaky fingers, she found the snips. After cutting free one hand for Tino, he took the cutters from Vanna and cut the other loop.

"Where is she?" he demanded, sliding out of the seat and making a movement to go around the truck.

Vanna grabbed at him for support. Tino stopped and put his arm around her. Together, they went around the truck to where Abigail was still lying motionless on the ground. Vanna tightened her grip on the gun, expecting Abigail to move and fight back again. She expected a renewed attack at any second.

"She should have more handcuffs," she whispered. "Check her pockets."

She leaned against the car for support. Tino stooped down and patted Vanna's pockets, then turned her carefully over. "Nothing."

Vanna looked at Abigail's closed eyes. "Is she still breathing?"

Tino leaned down. "Yes. We'd better call for the police. And an ambulance."

"How could she not have any handcuffs? She always has them. We need to find something to tie her with before she wakes up. I'm not letting her get away."

"Maybe her purse?" Tino grabbed it from the truck's

passenger seat. He poked through it so gingerly that Vanna almost laughed. Was he afraid of finding her feminine products? Tino shook his head. "Not here. Sorry."

"Do you have rope in your truck?"

He shook his head. Vanna looked at her car. "I have wire."

Tino leaned across the seat and looked at the jumble of junk. He pulled out a roll of wire. "This?"

"Tie her up, before she can wake up and get away."

Tino knelt down beside Abigail and pulled her hands together. He wound the wire around them several times and tried to knot it. When that proved impossible, he twisted the ends tightly, then wrapped them several times through the middle of her hands and twisted them again.

"That's the best I can do, for now."

Vanna slumped over and slid down the car to sit on the ground. She let out a long, painful breath. "Okay. Okay, we did it."

Tino was at her side in an instant. "Vanna." He touched her shoulder but didn't know what to do about it. "I'll get help. That policeman, what's his name?"

"Sweeny."

Vanna worked her phone out of her pocket and handed it to him. He swiped through the screens to find her phone app and contacts and dialed Sweeny. Vanna put her head back, closing her eyes. She was aware of Tino talking to Sweeny, trying to fill him in, as she floated in a sea of pain.

"Her shoulder," Tino insisted. "Her right shoulder."

She knew what Sweeny would tell Tino. That was where Abigail had shot her the first time. Not this time. The force of the gunshot had reopened the first wound. Tino touched Vanna tentatively.

"Van? Where did she hit? Did she hit your shoulder again? It's the same spot, right?"

Vanna shook her head. She tried to find the place in her ribs where the pain was focused. Tino pushed her hand out of the way. Pulled back her coat. Probed to find the wound. Without even opening her eyes, Vanna felt his eyes on her as his fingers stilled.

"You're wearing a bulletproof vest," he said with disbelief.

Vanna nodded, exhausted. "Sweeny got it for me."

Tino updated Sweeny. Vanna could hear sirens approaching.

Chapter Thirty-Four

V anna was working at an outside table in Erica's garden, taking advantage of a rare sunshiny day. She was working on a pendant light for Kelly to try selling at his booth at the market and was intent on her work.

"Vanna!"

Vanna startled· and just about dropped the glass bottle. A man's hand appeared at the bottom of the bottle, steadying it.

"I'm sorry. I didn't mean to startle you!" Sweeny apologized.

He was in her space, uncomfortably close, and Vanna shifted away from him slightly. She pulled the bottle away and set it down on the table.

"I'm still not used to people coming and going," she said. "I didn't see you coming."

"I should have let you know I was here."

"It's okay."

He looked at the bottles on the table. "They're nice. I should get you to make me one for my rec room, downstairs."

"Sure. I'd be happy to."

"I'd pay you. How much do they cost?"

"We'll see. Are you going to give me the other bottle back? I really loved that blue one."

Sweeny snorted. "Then maybe you should have picked one of the others to bash Abigail over the head with!"

"I can't believe I didn't break it. I was sure it was going to break."

"They must have made those old bottles with pretty thick glass. It was heavy."

"Yeah. Maybe lead in the glass, or something. I'll have to do some research."

She looked Sweeny over, wondering what he was doing there.

"I just wanted to check in with you," Sweeny said. "Make sure that you were okay. It's been a pretty rough few months."

"Mom finally talked me into seeing a therapist. I don't know how it's going to make any difference. I'm still really… anxious. I can't quite believe that it's over. Really over. I thought you might be here to tell me that they had to let Abigail go."

"No. We have enough evidence against her. She's not going to get out any time soon. You don't need to keep looking over your shoulder."

"The doctor says I have post-traumatic stress. He says there are things he can do to help. But… we'll see."

Sweeny nodded. "Stick with it," he agreed. "Give it some time."

———

Vanna was nervous meeting Tino for lunch. She had picked the location. A neutral spot where neither of them had been before. It was a cafe with a quiet atmosphere. Quiet, but not lonely. Lots of people still around, coming and going. A sort of a trendy place.

She faced the door so that she could see him come in and not be surprised. She had a script prepared, but it all flew from her head when he stepped in the door and looked around for her. He was good-looking. She'd always found him attractive. A big, protective teddy-bear of a man. And what more romantic name was there than Valentine?

Tino came over to her table and smiled down at her. He sat and motioned for a waitress. They both just ordered coffee to start with. Maybe there would be lunch later. And maybe not.

"You're looking a lot better," Tino observed.

"Being shot a couple times tends to cut the legs out from under you, a bit," she pointed out. "Even with a bulletproof vest, she still broke my ribs."

"Well, yeah. And even before that. You were always looking so tired and drawn. Hollow eyes." He touched the cheekbone under her right eye gently.

Vanna drew back. "Don't do that."

"What?"

"Just… don't touch me. Please."

"Don't touch you? I'm not doing anything to hurt you."

"I know. I'm just not comfortable with it."

"I thought… we were working together. I helped you. I thought you trusted me."

"I trusted you to help. I know you care. But I don't trust you enough to be in a relationship."

Tino's mouth was open. "What? What's this, then?" He gestured to their surroundings.

"I wanted to make sure you understood. That we couldn't. We can be friends, if it's okay with you. But not… we can't be together."

Tino sat back in his chair, folding his arms across his chest. "I've done everything you asked," he complained. "I've gone to the support group. I didn't contest the restraining order. I helped you with Abigail. *Why* can't we try again?"

"We've tried again too many times before. It doesn't work, Tino. I wish I could say it would, but I can't do it anymore. I can't keep trying and getting hurt."

"I'm not going to hurt you! I proved that to you."

"You haven't proven anything and I can't take the chance."

"Vanny…"

"No, Tino."

He gave her his saddest puppy-dog eyes, but Vanna was firm. She folded her arms and leaned on them and the table.

She wasn't going to be pushed around again.

———

There was a tap on her bedroom door and Vanna looked up. Erica hovered in the door of the sitting room.

"Come in, Mom. Sorry, I only have coffee." Vanna gestured to the service.

Erica inclined her head. She came and sat down with Vanna.

"You're looking remarkably comfortable," Erica observed, cocking her head slightly.

It was true. Vanna was feeling better than she had in months. Even after getting the news that Abigail was going to be in prison for a very long time, she hadn't felt comfortable and at peace. It had all been too unreal. She couldn't really believe it. Too much in her life had changed.

Erica poured herself half a cup of coffee and sat down. "What news did Officer Sweeny bring you?" she asked, her eyes twinkling.

Vanna held up her mug. Erica's brows drew down.

"Return of stolen property," Vanna explained.

"Isn't that the same as the mug you've been using?"

"Yes," Vanna admitted. "It's exactly the same. Part of the same set. But Abigail took this one. And now, Don brought it back."

"Don?" Erica repeated.

Vanna's face got warm. "Officer Sweeny."

Erica took a slow sip of her coffee. "I see."

Vanna squirmed under Erica's scrutiny.

Erica put down the mug, nodding. "I do like him better than Tino," she approved.

Vanna lowered her mug. If she'd had Lydia's complexion, she would be bright red right now. As it was, she was sure she was a little pink, and she couldn't restrain a wide smile.

"I do too."

Did you enjoy this book? Reviews and recommendations are vital to making a book successful.

Please leave a review at your favorite book store or review site and share it with your friends.

Don't miss the following bonus material:
Sign up for mailing list to get a free ebook
Read a sneak preview chapter
Other books by P.D. Workman
Learn more about the author

Sign up for my mailing list at pdworkman.com and get Gluten-Free Murder for free!

Preview of Gluten-Free Murder

Chapter One

Erin Price pulled up in front of the shop and shut off her loudly-knocking engine. She took a few deep breaths and stared at the street-side view. She hadn't seen it since her childhood, but it looked just the same as she remembered it. Maybe a little smaller and shabbier, like most of the things from her childhood that she re-encountered, but still the same shop.

Main Street of Bald Eagle Falls was lined with red brick buildings, pasted shoulder-to-shoulder to each other, in varying, incongruous styles. Each one had a roofed-in front sidewalk to protect shoppers and diners from the blazing Tennessee sun they would face in the coming summer. All different colors. Some of them lined with gingerbread edges or whimsical paint jobs. Or both. Some of the stores appeared to have residences on the second floor, white lacy curtains drawn in windows that looked down at the vehicles, mostly trucks, nose-in in the parking spaces. There was no residence above Clementine's shop. She had lived in a small house a few blocks away that Erin had no memory of. She had spent most of her time at the shop and did not remember sleeping over at her aunt's when her parents had brought her for a visit.

A US flag hung proudly on a flagpole in front of the stores, just fluttering slightly in the breeze. It was starting to get dark and she knew she'd have to find the house in the dark if she were going to stop and take the time to explore the shop.

With another calming breath, Erin unbuckled her seatbelt, unlocked the door, and levered herself out of the seat. She felt like she'd been pasted into the bucket seat of the Challenger for three days straight. She had been pasted into the bucket seat for three days straight, other than pit-stops and layovers. She wasn't tall, so she wasn't crammed into the small car, but she'd been in there long enough to want to get out and straighten her body and stretch her legs. And to go to bed, but bed was still a long way off.

Erin walked up to the shop and put her key into the lock. It ground a little, like it hadn't been used for a long time. Maybe it needed a little bit of lubrication to loosen it up.

The air inside the shop was too still and too warm. She remembered when the little shop had been filled with the smells of exotic teas and fresh-baked goods, but Clementine had retired and closed it years ago. It had been a long time since anything had been baked there. It just smelled like dust and stale air. Erin left the front door open to let some fresh air circulate while she took a look around. There wasn't much space to explore in front of the counter. She would need a couple little tables, with a limited number of chairs, for the few people who wanted to eat in. Most of her business would just be stopping in to pick up their orders. She walked behind the counter. Everything seemed to be in good shape. A good wipe-down and some fresh baked goods in the display case and she'd be ready to go. Maybe a fresh coat of paint on the wall and a chalk board listing the daily specials and prices.

She walked into the back. A kitchen with little storage and a microscopic office that might once have been a closet. The back stairs led to a larger storage area downstairs, she remembered. And what Clementine had always called the commode. There was a second set of stairs from the store front down to the commode for customers. Not exactly convenient, but it was a small, old building. The arrangement had worked okay for Clementine. As a girl, Erin had always been a little afraid of the basement. She would creep down the stairs to use the bathroom and then race back up again, always drawing a warning from Clementine to slow down or she would trip and catch her death on those stairs.

All the old appliances were still there in the kitchen. Even a decades-old industrial fridge stood unplugged and propped open. There was no microwave and Erin was going to need a fancier coffee machine, but everything else looked usable.

———

"What are you doing here?"

Erin turned around and saw a looming figure in the kitchen doorway at the same time as the clipped male voice interrupted her thoughts. She just about jumped out of her skin.

She put her hand on her thumping chest and breathed out a sigh of relief when she saw that it was a uniformed police officer. But he wasn't looking terribly welcoming, jaw tight and one hand on his sidearm. There was a German Shepherd at his side.

"Oh, you scared me. I'm Erin Price," she introduced herself, reaching out her hand and stepping toward him, "and I'm—"

"I asked you what you're doing here."

Erin stopped. He made no move to close the distance between them and shake her hand, but remained standing there in a closed, authoritative stance. His tone brooked no nonsense. Erin couldn't imagine that she looked anything like a burglar. A little rumpled from the car, maybe, but she hadn't been sleeping in it. Was a slim, white, young woman really the profile of a burglar in Bald Eagle Falls?

"I own this shop."

He raised an eyebrow in disbelief, but he did let his hand slide away from the weapon and adopted a more casual stance. Erin allowed herself just one instant to admire his fit physique and his face. He was roguish, with what was either heavy five o'clock shadow or three days' growth, but his face was also round, giving him an aura of boyishness and charm.

"You own the shop. And you are…?"

"Erin Price. Clementine's niece."

"If you're Clementine's niece, why haven't we ever seen you around here?"

"It's been years since I've seen her. My parents died and I lost all my family connections years ago, living in foster care. A private detective tracked me down."

He considered this and took a walk around the kitchen, looking things over. His eyes were dark and intense. "You'll be selling the place, then? Why didn't you just hire a real estate agent?"

"No, I'm not selling," Erin said firmly. "I'm reopening."

The eyebrows went up again. "This place has been sitting empty for ten years or more. You're reopening Clementine's Tea Room?"

"No, I'll be opening a specialty bakery, once I get everything whipped into shape." She folded her arms across her chest, looking at him challengingly. "I assume you don't have a problem with that?"

"No, ma'am."

But he didn't give any indication of leaving. Erin swept back a few tendrils of dark hair that had slipped from her braid, aware that she was probably looking travel-worn after several days in the car. She had put on mascara and dusty rose lipstick before getting on her way that morning, but she felt gritty and sweaty from travel and would have preferred a shower before having met anyone in her new hometown.

Erin strode toward the front of the store and the policeman

moved out of the doorway and then back around the counter toward the front door.

"You shouldn't leave the door wide open."

"I wanted some air in here. I've only been here five minutes. Do the police always show up that fast in Bald Eagle Falls?"

"I just happened by. Thought it was strange to see Clementine's door hanging open. Didn't recognize the car."

"Well, thank you for looking into it." Erin waited until he stepped out onto the sidewalk and then followed, pulling the door shut behind her. He watched as she locked it again. "You see? I have the keys."

"Where did this detective find you?"

"Maine."

"Is that where you're from?"

"I'm from a lot of places. Now I'm looking at settling back down here."

Erin looked at the German Shepherd, doing the doggie equivalent of standing at attention.

"I've never heard of a small town like this having a K9 unit."

"Well," he looked down at the dog, chewing on his words, "this is the extent of our K9 contingent."

"He looks… very well-trained. What's his name?"

"K9."

Erin cracked a smile. "Seriously?"

He kept a serious face, nodding once.

"Okay. Well, again, thank you for checking in on my store, Officer…?"

"Terry Piper."

"Erin Price." Erin offered her hand and this time Piper took it, giving her hand a brief squeeze as if he were afraid of crushing it.

"Pleased to meet you, Miss Price. Or is it missus?"

"It's Miss."

"Keep safe. Give us a call if you need anything." He produced a business card with a blue and yellow crest on it. "We don't exactly have 9-1-1 service but there's always someone on call."

Erin nodded her thanks. "I'll keep it handy. A lot of crime in Bald Eagle Falls?"

"No. It's a sleepy little town. Not too much excitement. Rowdy teenagers. Some of the drug trade trickling down from the city. The occasional domestic."

"Not a lot of break-and-enters?" she teased.

He didn't look amused. "You can't be too careful. Where are you headed now? There's a motel down the way…"

"No. I got the house too. I'll be staying there."

"You can't sleep there tonight. Won't be any water or power."

"They've been turned on. Thanks for your concern."

He looked for something else to say, then apparently couldn't find anything, so he nodded and walked down the sidewalk with his faithful companion.

———

Erin kept one eye on the GPS and the other on her rearview mirror to see if Officer Piper had any ideas about hopping into his car and following her home to make sure that she was properly situated. But apparently, he couldn't think of any laws she had broken and he never appeared behind her. Clementine's house was only a few blocks away. Erin parked on the street in front of it and took it in. It was a pretty little house with white siding and green shutters, roof peaks, and accents. The living room had big windows to let in the light and a window up at the top peak hinted at an attic bedroom or study. Beside and behind the house, beyond the fence line, were shimmering green, dense woods.

Erin got out of the car and grabbed her suitcase before walking up to the heavy paneled door and inserting her key in the lock. This one didn't stick, but turned smoothly like it was welcoming her home. Erin lugged her suitcase into the front entryway and closed and locked the door behind her. No point in inviting more visitors. She really didn't want to have to deal with anyone else until morning.

The AC was on, so the house wasn't stifling like the shop had been. Erin hadn't been sure what to expect. Burgener, the lawyer, had informed her that the house was furnished, but she hadn't known what kind of state it would be in. But it was neat and tidy. Furnished, but not cluttered. There were a couple of magazines on the coffee table in the living room that were months old, but other than that, Clementine might have just left it a few days before. Or still be in the other room just awaiting Erin's arrival.

She wasn't a believer in ghosts or restless spirits, but Clementine's smell and flavor still clung to the place.

Erin left her suitcase at the door and explored the house slowly. Living room, small dining room, kitchen, Clementine's bedroom, a guest room, and what Erin thought she might call a sewing room. There was fabric, rolls of wrapping paper, partially finished crafts, and post-bound books of genealogy, painstakingly written in longhand.

There were pull-down steps to the attic. If there had only been a ladder, Erin probably wouldn't have explored any further, but the stairs were well-made and modern and raised her hopes that the attic had been properly developed and wasn't just a storage space full of boxes, bags, cobwebs, and dust.

She mounted the stairs. At the top, there was enough light from below to find a light switch. Erin switched it on and had a look around.

It was a beautiful, bright room. Erin knew she was going to be spending a lot of her free time up there. White paneling and built-in cabinetry, soft, natural-looking lighting; it consisted of a reading nook, a writing desk, a comfy-looking couch, and various other touches that would make it a paradisiacal oasis at the end of a tiring day of baking.

Or driving.

After exploring the attic, Erin shut off the light, descended, and pushed the stairs up until the counterbalance took over and raised them to snick softly into place in the ceiling.

Erin returned to the kitchen for a glass of water, not looking forward to the fact that she was going to have to go out and pick up groceries if she wanted anything to eat. She found a sticky note on the fridge on notepaper preprinted with the lawyer's logo and phone number.

Welcome home. You'll find some basic supplies in the fridge. JRB

Erin opened the fridge door and sighed. Milk, juice, eggs, bagels, jam, and some precut fruit and vegetable packs. That and the coffee maker on the counter would do just fine. If James Burgener had been there, she would have hugged him.

A quick snack and then she would be off to the guest room for some shut-eye. Ghosts or not, she wasn't going to be sleeping in the master bedroom until she had made it her own.

———

Never one to let moss grow, Erin set to work immediately the next morning. She found a sort of a general store which carried both the small appliances she needed and painting supplies. With the back seats folded down, she filled the cargo area of the Challenger with as much as it would hold. She went back to the shop, opened the windows, and prepped the walls to start painting. Best to get a fresh coat of paint on before installing anything new.

"Knock, knock?"

Erin was startled out of her thoughts. She yanked the earbuds out of her ears and turned to face the woman who was trying to get her attention.

"I'm sorry," the woman said, giving her a tentative smile. She had a pleasant face; a middle-aged woman with ash blond hair. Either she had the perfect figure, or her clothes were hand-tailored. "I didn't want to startle you, but you were pretty engrossed…"

Erin wiped her forehead with the back of her hand. "Yeah. A little caught up in my music and my work."

"My name is Mary Lou Cox. I heard a rumor that you were here. So, I just had to come over and extend a good old Bald Eagle Falls welcome."

"Erin Price. I, uh… Clementine was my aunt."

"Well, if you're kin to Clementine, you're kin to half the mountain. Welcome home."

Erin nodded awkwardly. "Thank you. That's very kind of you."

"So…" Mary Lou took a look around the kitchen. "A fresh coat of paint and then I hear you're opening up Clementine's Tea Room again? I'll tell you, this town has surely missed the tea room."

"Uh. No. I'm not reopening the tea room." Erin enjoyed a cup of tea at the end of the day as much as anyone, but she was much more interested in baking. The groove she got into while painting was nothing compared with the nirvana she would achieve while baking. "I'm opening a specialty bakery."

Mary Lou patted her hair. "We already have a bakery in Bald Eagle Falls."

Erin ran the roller down the wall, watching carefully for seams or drips.

"I'm sure the town can support more than one bakery."

"But we already have The Bake Shoppe. We don't need another bakery."

Erin gave her a determined smile. "I'm opening a bakery."

"Angela Plaint owns The Bake Shoppe and does a really nice business, I'm not sure any of us would go to another bakery. It wouldn't be a very loyal thing to do."

"You could go to The Bake Shoppe for… whatever Angela Plaint is best at and then come to my bakery for gluten-free muffins."

"Gluten-free?" Mary Lou echoed.

"I assume you don't already have a gluten-free bakery."

"No, we do not. If you want that kind of baking, you have to drive into the city."

"Well, now you'll be able to get them in town."

"There aren't that many people that want that gluten-free stuff in Bald Eagle Falls. I don't see how you could make a living off it."

"We'll just have to see. I do other specialty baking as well. Dairy-free, allergy-free, vegan."

"We don't have a lot of *those* kind of people here. We like our meat. Whoever put meat in muffins anyway?"

Erin studied Mary Lou for a moment, trying to divine whether she was teasing or being sarcastic. "You might not put meat in a muffin, but you would probably put eggs and dairy."

"And you could make it without all those things? Who would eat such a thing? It would be like eating cardboard."

"Not when I make it."

"I guess we'll just have to see," Mary Lou said. "I sure don't cotton to the idea of you trying to take Angela's business."

"I guess we'll just have to see," Erin echoed.

———

Mary Lou was the first citizen of Bald Eagle Falls to express her opinion and welcome Erin to town, but she wasn't the last. Next came Melissa Lee, a woman with curly dark hair and a wide, even smile. And then Gema Reed, with her long, steel gray locks and a girlish complexion.

Erin did her best to explain to them that she wasn't there to horn in on Angela's business and take money out of her pocket, but to offer a new service that hadn't previously been available.

But it was like talking to the wall. Or yelling at an avalanche. It didn't stop them from dumping advice all over her, while smiling and telling her she was welcome in town.

She didn't feel welcome.

At least Terry Piper did not show up with his K9 to give his input on the matter.

It was a long day and Erin never did meet Angela, her competition. The end of the day, the walls were freshly painted. Everything looked fresh and new. Exhausted though she was, Erin spent a few more minutes in the tiny office, going through the papers and plans in the folders she had brought with her from Maine.

Then she locked everything up tight and headed back home.

Chapter Two

The day dawned bright and clear. Erin woke up earlier than she expected after her hard work of the day before. She was looking forward to each new day, rather than dreading another day of work.

Starting the day in her attic study, Erin wrote up lists of things she would need to get in the city. Not only did Bald Eagle Falls not have a specialty bakery, the general store did not carry any of the specialized flours or other ingredients that she would need. Erin had no intention of taking months getting outfitted. The store and the appliances were on hand and ready for use, so why wait?

It was late when Erin returned to the shop at the end of the day. Darkness was settling over Main Street and the streetlights were few and far between. As she juggled her first armload of goods while trying to unlock the front door, chiding herself for using the front door instead of the back—even though she would have had the same problem at the back—a voice spoke in her ear.

"Can I help you with those?"

The bag of flour she was pressing against the door with her

body in an effort to hang on to it while unlocking the bolt was removed from its position. Erin laughed a little and unlocked the door, turning to get the bag of flour back from him.

She froze, looking into the dirty, sweaty face of a man she had never met before. He was white, though the word white did nothing to convey the color of his skin, dirt ground into it as if he had been working in a coal mine or living on the street for weeks. He had a fringe of a mustache and a few bristles on his chin, looking more like he was careless with his shaving than that he had intentionally trimmed his facial hair in a particular style. He had a filthy, army-green cap pulled down low so she could just make out his dark eyes.

"I can take this in for you," he offered. His voice was gravelly and low, but polite. He didn't have the drawl that would indicate he was native to the area.

"Oh, no, let me take it back," Erin said, encircling the bag with her arm and taking its weight.

He looked at her with a sullen expression that told Erin he understood that she didn't want him in her store. She turned her back on him to take the supplies into the kitchen, mentally sorting out possible weapons and escape routes. She was sure he was going to follow her in. Would a scream bring Officer Terry Piper or whoever else might be on shift?

When she went back out to her car for the next load, the man was still hanging around, as she had expected. He took bags out of her car and handed them to her.

"Really," Erin told him politely, "I'm okay. I don't need any help."

He didn't react with anger or violence, but his dark eyes glittered under the bill of his cap. "Just trying to be neighborly."

"I appreciate it. You're very kind. But you're making me nervous."

She surprised herself by telling him that. Was she acting like a victim? Encouraging him to menace her further? She knew from self-defense classes that predators looked for shyness and low self-esteem. Did she sound weak saying he was making her nervous?

But the man immediately backed off, shaking his head. "Not trying to make anyone nervous, miss."

"Then please leave me alone."

He stood there looking at her for a minute, then turned without a word and walked away. Erin blew out her breath, relieved. Here she had thought that moving to a small town in the South, she would be safe from crime and unwanted attention, but obviously nowhere was completely safe. She needed to be realistic instead of idealizing small-town living as being something it wasn't. Next time, she would not be unloading her car after dark. She would plan ahead and be better prepared.

Erin took the rest of the supplies into the kitchen and put them away. She stopped in the office to pick up one of her folders, frowning. She had a strange feeling of vertigo, like everything was slightly out of place. She couldn't identify any one thing that would make her feel that way, but couldn't help feeling like her things had been touched and moved around. She found the folder she was looking for on signage and took it home with her, locking up carefully.

———

Traffic was even quieter than usual in the sleepy town when Erin got to the shop to finish organizing her ingredients and to make plans for what she would make to kick off her opening and really wow her customers.

She was sitting at her desk in the tiny office, scribbling away and flipping back and forth between recipes when she heard the bells over the front door jingle. She didn't want anyone sneaking up on her today.

Erin reluctantly stood up from her work and went out to the

front of the shop. It was Gema Reed, the beautiful gray-haired woman.

"I thought I saw your car outside," Gema declared. She couldn't very well have missed it. It wasn't exactly camouflaged. And it was one of the only vehicles parked on sleepy Main Street. "So, I thought I would drop in and make sure everything was okay?"

Erin tilted her head slightly, trying to figure out where Gema was going with the inquiry.

"Umm, yes. Everything is fine. Why wouldn't it be?"

"Well, being as it's the *Sabbath* and you're at work. I was worried maybe you had a water main break or vandals. Maybe even a fire. You never know what's going to happen."

"No, there's nothing wrong. I just wanted to get some work done. There's lots to do before I open."

They stood there looking at each other awkwardly for a few moments. Erin knew she was moving into the Bible belt, but she hadn't expected things to be that different from the way they had been in the North. Some people were religious and some people were not and everybody observed their beliefs as they wished. But apparently, things were not quite so straightforward in the South.

"Well, maybe no one invited you to Sunday morning services. You probably don't even know the schedule!" Gema proclaimed. "Now there are lots of churches to choose from, of course, but if you want to join us at First Baptist, just down at the end of Main Street and Garity, why, we'd *love* to have you!"

"I'm going to have to pass..." Erin said slowly, feeling her way through. "I'm not really the churchgoing type."

"Not the type? Why, bless your heart, dear, you don't have to be a type to join your fellow Christians at worship on Sunday! You... *are* a Christian, aren't you? Not one of these... other sects? I don't mean to put down Jews or Muslims or anyone else, but here in Bald Eagle Falls, we're Christian.

Baptists, Catholics, Protestants, it doesn't matter, as long as you're Christian!"

Erin cleared her throat. She wished she had brought a cloth with her out to the front, so she could occupy herself with polishing the glass and chrome display case and counter. Just to have something to do with her hands and somewhere to look other than Gema Reed's benevolent Christian face. "Actually, Mrs. Reed. I'm not."

"You're not… what? You don't look like a Jew or one of those… pagan people. Not everyone goes to church every Sunday, but…"

"I'm… not Christian. I'm atheist."

"Atheist!" Gema was aghast. She held her hand dramatically at her throat, halfway to covering her mouth in horror. She stared at Erin pleadingly, as if she thought it might just be a clumsy joke and Erin would change her tune. "You're not! Really?"

"Yes. I am. I'm sorry if that upsets you…"

"Well, Jesus loves every humble seeker of the truth. You are a seeker, aren't you? Not everyone can be converted, but as long as you're looking for the truth, you will find it in the end…"

Erin took a deep breath and let it back out again. As much as she wanted to smooth Gema's ruffled feathers, to just reassure her and send her on her way, she wanted to get it out in the open. Her real beliefs, not just rumors or half-baked explanations.

"Mrs. Reed—"

"Gema, sugar…"

"Gema. I am an atheist. Not an agnostic. Not an investigator or a seeker. An atheist. I'm not looking for something to believe in. I already have a belief system. And it doesn't include God."

Gema gasped audibly and this time she did cover up her mouth. "Oh, my dear…"

Erin forced a smile. "I'm not a witch or a devil-worshiper. And I won't try to talk you out of your beliefs. But I, myself, do not believe in God. Not a god of any sort. Not the universe, or Mother Nature, or a higher power, or Jesus. I'm sorry."

"Well." Gema looked for a moment as if she would flee without another word. Instead, she smoothed her waves of silver, took a calming breath and gave a polite nod. "Everybody is entitled to their own opinion, no matter how wrong. I'd better get on my way, or I'll be walking into service late. I just hope… that you won't be encouraging others to break the Sabbath by your blatant disregard for it. You won't have your bakery open on Sunday, will you?"

Erin gave a little shrug. "Didn't my Aunt Clementine have it open after services on Sunday?" she asked tentatively. Her memories of Clementine's Tea Room were startlingly clear in some respects and shrouded by fog in others. She was sure she remembered helping to serve the church ladies after Sunday services. They had all thought her such a cute, pretty young thing. She remembered her resentment over being treated like a puppy or a baby instead of a person with a mind of her own. She loved helping Clementine in the tea room, but she didn't like that part of it.

Gema made a noise of indecision, not wanting to admit that Erin was right and yet compelled by her Christian morals not to tell a lie. "Mmmmm… yes, it is true that she opened up for an hour or two after services on Sunday, so the ladies would have somewhere to go to discuss Christian services required in the upcoming week…"

"So, it would be okay, as long as I waited until after your worship services?"

"As an atheist, I'm not sure it would be the same…"

"I would be shunned for opening my restaurant, but a Christian would not? When it's against a Christian's beliefs, but not mine? Wouldn't it be worse for a Christian to do it?"

"I just don't know," Gema snapped, shaking her head in confusion. "I must get on now, but I'll… I'll think it over."

"Okay…" Erin gave her a little wave. "You be sure to let me know what you ladies decide. Someone mentioned that Clementine's Tea Room had been sorely missed and I thought that if I could provide a similar service…"

Gema Reed gulped. She shook her head and retreated. The bells tinkled behind her and Erin stood there, watching her get into her big red truck and pull out into the street. Then she was gone.

Erin went back to her office to continue working on her opening and marketing strategy. She added 'Sunday social tea' to her list with a wry smile and continued to look through her recipes.

After Erin finished her plans, she carefully filed her folders in the cabinet beside the desk. There was no reason to leave her lists scattered all over her desk and take the chance of losing something when she had a perfectly functional file drawer to put everything neatly away. She emptied the dregs of her cold coffee from her mug and washed it out, leaving it upside down on a towel to dry.

When she stepped out of the shop onto the sidewalk, she nearly collided with a woman coming the other direction. Sunday had been so quiet, she hadn't expected any foot traffic and hadn't even looked before stepping out the door.

"Oh, I'm sorry!" she apologized.

The other woman was ruddy, a redhead, on the plumpish side. Her hair fell in waves around her head, partially obscuring her face. She stepped back from Erin, folding her arms across her chest and staring at Erin as if she had just committed a mortal sin. Which, given Gema's reaction to Erin working on a Sunday, was probably the case.

"I didn't see you coming," Erin apologized. "That was my fault. I'm sorry."

The woman ignored the apology. "You're Clementine's niece."

"Yes, I am."

"You don't favor her, do you?"

"I don't remember her too clearly," Erin admitted. "And I don't really know what she looked like in later years."

"If you don't remember her, then what are you doing here? Why come to Bald Eagle Falls?"

Erin's mouth was dry. She tried to put together words that made sense, flummoxed by the woman's attack.

"I inherited the store and the house. I wanted to reopen the shop."

"Only you're not," the redhead hissed. "You're not reopening the tea room, you're opening a bakery."

"Well, yes. That's what I do, I bake. I'm still planning on serving tea after Sunday services each week, so the women can get together…"

"We don't need another bakery."

Erin sighed and shook her head. "It's a specialty bakery. It means people won't have to go into the city to get gluten-free or allergy-friendly baking. It doesn't directly compete with the other bakery."

"You are competing, little Miss Out-of-Towner. And you're not going to last a week!"

With that, the redhead marched on, shouldering past Erin with a force that staggered her and made her catch herself on the side of the building.

Looking across Main Street, she saw Officer Terry Piper watching her, K9 at his side. She considered calling him over to vent about the rude woman, but decided that would just be sour grapes. She didn't really want to charge the woman. There was no point in reporting the encounter to the police.

———

Erin yawned as she pushed open her door, sending the little bells tinkling in welcome. She was going to have to get used to getting up early if she were going to be running a bakery. She was going to have to get up while it was still dark and everyone else was sleeping in order to have freshly baked goods in the display cases when people started walking in for a little something to go with their coffees or office meetings.

Her day would start way before anyone else's and, if she were going to stay open past afternoon, she was going to need to find an assistant to split shifts with. It wouldn't have to be another baker, just someone who could answer questions about ingredients and work the cash register.

Taking into account the not-so-warm reaction she was getting from the women of the town, she might have to go to the city to find someone willing to work the bakery.

Erin juggled her keys and her bag of groceries to turn on the kitchen light and put her bag on the counter.

Her coffee mug lay on the floor, shattered. Erin frowned and looked around. A shiver ran down her spine. Had someone been there? Had her shop been broken into?

For a few moments, she just stood there, frozen, listening for any movement.

There was only silence. She considered the situation. Had she put the mug too close to the edge of the counter and it had fallen off by itself? Were there earthquakes in Tennessee?

The imprint of the mug was still in the towel she had left it sitting on. Close to the edge of the counter, but not over it.

She heard the bells on the front door ring and hurried out to see whether someone was leaving the shop. Had she actually walked right past an intruder? Maybe hiding behind the counter, below her eye level while she yawned and juggled her groceries in the morning dimness?

She stopped stock-still. Nobody had left the shop; wild-haired Melissa Lee had come in. She was all smiles and sweetness, launching into a long-winded description of some fundraiser that she and some of the other women were running. She cut herself off abruptly.

"My dear, you look like you've just seen a ghost. Are you okay?"

"I… I think someone has been in here."

"What do you mean, in here?" she asked doubtfully.

"I think someone broke in…"

"You have been burgled?" Melissa's voice rose, a mixture of disbelief and alarm. Such things were probably unheard of in sleepy little Bald Eagle Falls. "Honey, you stay right there while I get the police."

Melissa hurried back out the front door and, without a clue what else to do, Erin obeyed, standing there like a statue. It was only a few minutes before Melissa returned, Officer Terry Piper in tow with his K9. Melissa was babbling on about crime rates and burglaries. Piper ignored her and focused on Erin.

"The place was broken into?" he demanded.

"I don't know. I think someone has been here."

Feeling embarrassed that she might be overreacting, Erin took him into the kitchen and showed him the broken mug and where it had been sitting on the counter. Piper nodded and looked around, his brows drawn down.

"Anyone else have a key?" he asked.

K9 sniffed at the broken mug with interest, but didn't lead his master along a scent trail. He just sat back on his haunches and panted.

"No. I haven't given anyone else a key."

Piper looked into the small office. "Anything been touched in here? Anything missing?"

Erin hadn't yet had a chance to look. She gave a little laugh and slipped by him to see. The room looked untouched. Erin checked her file drawers.

"There was one other time… when I thought things had

been moved in here. I put everything away in my drawers, this time…"

"Do you have petty cash in here? A safe?"

"No. Nothing like that. And no cash in the register yet, either. I haven't opened for business yet." She knew she didn't really need to add that part. Terry Piper was undoubtedly aware that she hadn't yet opened to the public. If there had been any doubt, the fact that there were no baked goods in the display case or in the oven would pretty much be a giveaway.

"When are you opening?" he asked. "Assuming you still are?"

"Yes, of course. I'm just putting together my plans for a small opening celebration right now. A few days…"

He raised an eyebrow. "That quickly? I thought it would take longer to get things up and running."

"Everything is already in place. I've bought supplies. I am still waiting on signage and a few little things like that, but for the time being, I'll just put a handmade sign in the window."

He pursed his lips and nodded. He and K9 went to the back door and examined it to confirm it was still locked and had not been tampered with. He looked at the steep stairs to the basement.

"What have you got downstairs?"

"Storage and the commode. I haven't been down there yet this morning…"

K9's ears pointed down the stairs curiously.

"Does he hear something?" Erin asked.

"No… not yet. Come on, K9. Let's go investigate."

The dog eagerly led the way down the stairs. Erin realized she was holding herself tense and she tried to relax. There wasn't anything downstairs. She already knew it. There had been no sign of forced entry at either door. No open windows somebody might have crawled in through. She was going to have to accept that there had been a tremor or something else that had made the counter shake and caused her coffee mug to go crashing to the floor. The shops were all connected; perhaps someone had dropped a pallet of books with enough force in the bookstore next door that it had shaken the shared wall and sent her mug on its kamikaze journey.

There were no sounds of conflict downstairs. No sign that the officer had found anyone lurking below them. He was back up the stairs in a minute.

"All clear."

They went back out to the front, where Melissa was anxiously waiting. Piper examined the front door and frame.

"There aren't any signs of forced entry," he said with a shrug. "Is it possible you left it unlocked last night?"

"No, I'm sure I…" Erin remembered colliding with the woman on the sidewalk as she left. Had she locked the door afterward? Erin knew she had unlocked the door in the morning. And it could only be locked from the outside. If she'd had to unlock it in the morning, then she had locked it the night before. "Yes. I'm sure I locked it. It was locked when I came in this morning."

"Maybe you knocked the mug down without realizing it, last night or this morning. Or maybe a crosswind or the building shaking for some reason?" Piper shrugged.

"It's a mystery!" Melissa said in dramatic tones.

Piper gave her a tolerant smile. "Yes, Mrs. Lee. It surely is."

"Maybe it's a ghost! The tea shop is haunted."

"Bakery," Erin corrected, aware she was nitpicking, but irritated about the community's opposition to a second bakery opening.

"We haven't had a ghost here before," Melissa enthused. "I wonder who it could be. There are a lot of civil war ghosts in the area. We have a rich civil war history, you know. Why, the library is practically famous in these parts. There are so many legends of lost and buried treasure in the hills around here, a person can hardly go for a hike without tripping over one!" She laughed.

"If there hasn't been a ghost here before," Piper said gravely, "then the ghost must be of a more recent vintage, wouldn't you say?"

Melissa stopped and considered. "Well, yes, I suppose. Unless you've somehow awoken a restless spirit. You haven't been digging down there in your basement? Or in the back?"

"No," Erin assured her. "The basement floor is concrete and so is the parking lot in back."

"Then we need to think of who might have died recently that would have a reason to haunt the store." Melissa pondered the problem.

Erin exchanged looks with Piper. He appeared to be suppressing a smile.

"Maybe... the owner?" he suggested.

"Erin?" Melissa said blankly.

"The... previous owner...?" Piper prompted.

"Oh, Clementine! Why, of course it would be Clementine! Silly old me!" She put her hand on Erin's arm. Her dark curls quivered with her movement. "You are being haunted by your Aunt Clementine. Did you have any unfinished business with her? Something that she would be expecting from you?"

"Just opening the bakery. And why, if there was such a thing as ghosts, would my aunt's restless spirit want to break my coffee mug?"

"She's trying to reach you, dear. Ghosts are very limited in what they can do. Move things, appear to you, maybe make noises. It's not like on TV, where they can just walk up and talk to you and explain themselves in words. All she can do to reach you is to move things around."

Erin nodded. "I see. Well, I don't believe in ghosts, so I'm going to look for more earthly explanations. You can... believe what you like."

"Oh, I do," Melissa agreed. "I am going to talk to the others and we'll see if we can sort this out. After all, we all knew Clementine. I knew her my whole life. We'll figure out what it is that she wants to reach you for. Mary Lou's sister-in-law, she's very good with spirits. We'll see if she can come here and make contact with your poor dead auntie."

Erin glanced over at Piper, widening her eyes, sure she was being played. But Piper gave no sign that Melissa was joking. And Melissa continued to look earnest and excited about the whole ghost business.

"Isn't contacting ghosts considered sorcery in Christian circles?" Erin suggested.

"No, no! Mary Lou's sister-in-law won't be using a Ouija board or any other devil's tool. She just uses prayer. There's nothing wrong with that."

"Ah." Erin nodded. She looked at her watch as obviously as possible. Time was trickling by and she had work to do. "Did you want to leave me a flyer about your fundraiser, Melissa?" At Melissa's blank look, she indicated the woman's clipboard. "That was why you came in here, wasn't it?"

"Oh, yes!" Melissa pulled a fuchsia-colored page from her clipboard and handed it to Erin. "Of course, no one is required to donate or put time into it, but every little bit is appreciated! I'd better get on my way! If I stop to yap at every store, it's going to take me all day! I'm already busier than a one-armed paper hanger."

Erin nodded and gave a little wave, and Melissa went on her way. Erin sighed and looked at Officer Piper. He had a gorgeous smile, when he let it show.

"Miss Price, I'm sorry I couldn't be of more assistance. You feel free to call on me if you have any more troubles. Hopefully, your ghost won't cause any more trouble."

"Thanks," Erin said dryly. "Just tell me... everyone in town doesn't believe that, do they? In the existence of ghosts, I mean? And that they can just... be contacted?"

"Not everyone is quite as literal as Mrs. Lee, but... I do imagine most of them will agree that your shop might be haunted. They might not be willing to say that it is, but they won't say that it isn't…"

Erin shook her head. "I suppose it's harmless, as long as they aren't demanding to hold séances in here."

———

Gluten-Free Murder, Book #1 of the *Auntie Clem's Bakery series* by P.D. Workman can be purchased at pdworkman.com

About the Author

Award-winning and USA Today bestselling author P.D. (Pamela) Workman writes riveting mystery/suspense and young adult books dealing with mental illness, addiction, abuse, and other real-life issues. For as long as she can remember, the blank page has held an incredible allure and from a very young age she was trying to write her own books.

Workman wrote her first complete novel at the age of twelve and continued to write as a hobby for many years. She started publishing in 2013. She has won several literary awards from Library Services for Youth in Custody for her young adult fiction. She currently has over 50 published titles and can be found at pdworkman.com.

Born and raised in Alberta, Workman has been married for over 25 years and has one son.

———

Please visit P.D. Workman at pdworkman.com to see what else she is working on, to join her mailing list, and to link to her social networks.

———

If you enjoyed this book, please take the time to recommend it to other purchasers with a review or star rating and share it with your friends!

facebook.com/pdworkmanauthor

twitter.com/pdworkmanauthor

instagram.com/pdworkmanauthor

amazon.com/author/pdworkman

bookbub.com/authors/p-d-workman

goodreads.com/pdworkman

linkedin.com/in/pdworkman

pinterest.com/pdworkmanauthor

youtube.com/pdworkman